THE
GOLDEN
WOLF

ALSO BY LINNEA HARTSUYKER

The Half-Drowned King

The Sea Queen

THE
GOLDEN
WOLF

LINNEA HARTSUYKER

Little, Brown

LITTLE, BROWN

First published in the United States in 2019 by HarperCollins Publishers
First published in Great Britain in 2019 by Little, Brown

A CIP catalogue record for this book
is available from the British Library.

Designed by Fritz Metsch

Hardback ISBN 978-1-4087-0885-9
Trade paperback ISBN 978-1-4087-0886-6

Printed and bound in Great Britain by
Clays Ltd, Elcograf S.p.A.

Papers used by Little, Brown are from well-managed forests
and other responsible sources.

MIX
Paper from
responsible sources
FSC
www.fsc.org   FSC® C104740

Little, Brown
An imprint of
Little, Brown Book Group
Carmelite House
50 Victoria Embankment
London EC4Y 0DZ

An Hachette UK Company
www.hachette.co.uk

www.littlebrown.co.uk

The Golden Wolf

ICELAND
Reykjavik

Norwegian Sea

Arctic Circle

Trondheim Fjord
Smola
Geiranger Fjord
Naustdal
Sogn Fjord
Hardanger Fjord
Háfrsfjord

Faroe Islands

Shetland Islands
Orkney Islands
Hebrides

Atlantic Ocean

SCOTLAND

IRELAND
Dublin

North Sea

Nidaros
Trondelag
Yafjord
Maer
Sogn

Halogaland

NORWAY

SWEDEN

Modern day border

Vest-fold
Oslo Fjord
Skagerrak strait

Jutland

Scanie
Roskilde

Ribe

FRISIA

Kilometers
0 100 200 300 400
0 100 200 300
Miles

map © 2018 by
Laura Hartman Maestro

PLACES AND CHARACTERS

PLACES

NORWAY

Maer—a district in western Norway, where Ragnvald rules, formerly ruled by Solvi's line

  Tafjord—Ragnvald's seat of power, at the end of Geiranger Fjord

  Geiranger Fjord—the fjord in Maer

Sogn—a district in western Norway, south of Maer, claimed by Ragnvald, ruled by Aldi Atlisson

Trondelag—a district in northwest Norway

  Trondheim Fjord—the fjord in Trondelag

  Nidaros—King Harald's northwest capital, modern-day Trondheim

Halogaland—a district in northwest Norway, ruled by King Heming

  Yrjar—King Heming's seat of power in Halogaland

Vestfold—a district in southeastern Norway, ruled by King Harald

  Tonsberg—a market town in Vestfold

DENMARK

Jutland—Denmark's peninsula, ruled by King Erik

    Ribe—a market town and Jutland's capital

Roskilde—the seat of power for rulers of the rest of Denmark

SWEDEN

Skane—a lawless coastal area on the southern tip of what is now Sweden

VARIOUS ISLANDS

The Orkney Islands—islands north of Scotland, claimed by Thorstein the Red

    Grimbister—Orkney's main settlement

    Hoy—one of the other Orkney islands

The Faroe Islands—islands between Iceland and Norway

The Shetland Islands—islands north of the Orkneys

The Hebrides—Scottish islands populated by vikings

Iceland—a large island north and east of the Faroe Islands, populated by many who fled Harald's conquest

    Reykjavik—Iceland's primary settlement

CHARACTERS

Ragnvald Eysteinsson, king of Sogn

    Vigdis Audbjornsdatter, Ragnvald's stepmother and former concubine, now Guthorm's concubine

        Hallbjorn Olafsson, Vigdis's son with Olaf, who was Ragnvald's stepfather

        Einar Ragnvaldsson, Ragnvald's son with Vigdis

Ragnhilda (Hilda) Hrolfsdatter, Ragnvald's wife

> Ivar Ragnvaldsson, Ragnvald's son with Hilda
>
> Thorir Ragnvaldsson, Ragnvald's son with Hilda
>
> Hrolf (Rolli) Ragnvaldsson, Ragnvald's son with Hilda

Alfrith, Ragnvald's concubine

> Hallad Ragnvaldsson, Ragnvald's son with Alfrith
>
> Laugi Ragnvaldsson, Ragnvald's son with Alfrith

Sigurd Olafsson, Ragnvald's stepbrother

> Olaf Sigurdsson, Sigurd's son

Svanhild Eysteinsdatter, Ragnvald's sister

> Eystein Solvisson, Svanhild's son by Solvi, now deceased
>
> Freydis Solvisdatter, Svanhild's daughter by Solvi
>
> Bjorn Haraldsson, Svanhild's son by Harald
>
> Ragnar Haraldsson, Svanhild's son by Harald

Solvi Hunthiofsson, Svanhild's former husband

> Snorri, Solvi's man-at-arms
>
> Brusi, Solvi's man-at-arms
>
> Tova, Solvi's concubine

Harald Halfdansson, king of Norway

> Guthorm, Harald's uncle and adviser
>
>> Vigdis Hallbjornsdatter, Guthorm's concubine
>
> Asa Hakonsdatter, Harald's wife, King Hakon's daughter
>
>> Halfdan Haraldsson, Harald's son with Asa
>
> Snaefrid, Harald's Finnish wife
>
> Dagfinn Haraldsson, Harald's son by another wife

Gyda Eiriksdatter, Harald's betrothed, queen of Hordaland

    Gudrod Haraldsson, Gyda's nephew and adopted son

    Signy Haraldsdatter, Gyda's niece and adopted daughter

Aldulf (Aldi) Atlisson, steward of Sogn

    Kolbrand Aldulfsson, Aldi's son

    Dota Aldulfsdatter, Aldi's daughter

Erik, king of Jutland, Denmark

    Ragnhilda (Ranka) Eriksdatter, King Erik of Jutland's daughter

Thorstein the Red, a viking, formerly a companion of Solvi, now lives in the Orkney Islands

Melbrid Tooth, a viking from the Hebrides

Ketil Flatnose, a viking, formerly a companion of Solvi, now lives in the Hebrides

Unna, a woman in Iceland

    Donall, her man

Hakon Grjotgaardsson, former king of Halogaland, deceased

    Heming Hakonsson, Hakon's oldest son, king of Halogaland

    Asa Hakonsdatter, Hakon's daughter, married to King Harald

    Oddi Hakonsson, Hakon's baseborn son

    Geirbjorn Hakonsson, Hakon's son, outlawed

    Herlaug Hakonsson, Hakon's son, deceased

THE
GOLDEN
WOLF

I

FREYDIS SOLVISDATTER SAT ON A ROWING BENCH NEAR THE ship's stern, with the warp of her weaving tied to her belt, and the other end tied around a broken oar. She had chosen a simple pattern to work while sailing—the pitching of the ship and the yelling of the sailors were too distracting for anything more complicated.

Her companion distracted her too. Dota was the daughter of Aldi Atlisson, the steward of Sogn, close in age to Freydis's fourteen years, but far different in temperament.

"Is the pilot not handsome?" Dota asked Freydis, and when Freydis did not answer, she continued, "He is young to be a pilot—usually they are grizzled old men. But you must be used to far handsomer men in Tafjord. They say that King Ragnvald's sons are even better looking than Harald's sons, though I find that hard to believe. Gudrod Haraldsson visited Sogn last summer, and he is as pretty as a woman. What do you think? Which is the handsomest?"

Freydis saw a mistake in her weaving and had to take out a few lines of weft. "King Ragnvald's son Einar," she said quietly. He was the eldest of King Ragnvald's sons, a warrior and poet, with a severe kind of beauty that Freydis could hardly look upon without blushing. He was said to prefer boys and ignored most of Tafjord's girls, but he had always been kind to Freydis, and she often wished she could be more like him, strong and untouchable.

"What of Ivar?" Dota asked. "King Ragnvald promised that Ivar would marry me one day, so that my sons can be kings of Sogn."

"Ivar is handsome too," said Freydis.

"I've never seen him—does he look like King Ragnvald? Tall and grim-faced?"

"No," said Freydis. "He is much more handsome. Kind and friendly too. All who meet him admire him." And Freydis liked him too, for he treated her like a younger sister, teasing and protecting her, but he did not draw her gaze the way Einar did.

"Kind and friendly—he sounds dull," said Dota. "But at least he is wealthy. Are you not excited to go to Vestfold? I have never traveled so far."

Neither had Freydis. She had been born in Sogn but had lived her whole life in Tafjord's halls, until a year ago. She knew every stone, every living creature, and all the little spirits of Tafjord's glens and valleys. Then Hilda and Alfrith had sent her off to Sogn, saying she would be happy there, and now she was sent to Vestfold, like a sack of grain with no will of her own.

"Well?" Dota asked again. "Are you? There will be more young men in Vestfold. All of Harald's sons and Harald himself. And I've heard that Princess Gyda is the most beautiful woman in Norway, though she must be growing old now. Still, it is a wonderful story, is it not? Harald conquered all of Norway for her."

The wind fell off and the ship began to wallow in the troughs between swells. Freydis's stomach shifted uncomfortably. She untied her weaving, wrapped it around her hand, and focused her eyes on the horizon. Her cousin Rolli, one of King Ragnvald's younger sons, had taught her to avoid sea sickness that way. On the two days' journey that had taken her from Tafjord to Sogn last summer, she had spent the whole time vomiting, angering her mother, who wanted a daughter who loved the sea as she did.

"Who do you think you will wed, Freydis?" Dota asked. "You are pretty enough, and you're King Harald's stepdaughter. That should help."

"I don't know," said Freydis. She dreamed of becoming a priestess of Freya, a woman who looked into the future and ensured the fertility of the land. They were sometimes the mistresses of kings, and chose when to bear their children. But King Harald and King Ragnvald both had too many sons and too few daughters. Freydis would make a marriage to cement an alliance one day, and she must be resigned to it.

Freydis's cat, a gray and brown tabby named Torfa, crawled out from under the rowing bench and pounced on the strands of the warp dangling from Freydis's hand, then ran off with the weaving in her mouth. Freydis picked up her skirts and pursued her, but Torfa, dodging sailors' feet, grew more and more frightened and then wedged herself under a bench.

Freydis was crouched down, half under the bench herself, to coax Torfa out, when the ship made a hard turn and lost its wind. She stood up quickly, nearly hitting her head on the gunwale, and heard the pilot call out, "Raiders! From the north!"

Freydis turned and saw the ship that gained on them. It was small and narrow, almost too small for a dragon ship, though it had the shields arrayed upon its sides and the snarling figurehead affixed to its prow that meant attack. It cut through the waves, sending up spray, and quickly closing the gap between the two ships. Ahead, Aldi's other ship, the one that bore him and the bulk of his warriors, began to slow, preparing to turn and defend its weaker companion.

Aldi's son Kolbrand, standing next to Freydis, drew his sword. "Best pretend we have no women on board," he said to her and his sister, Dota. "Get under the benches." He grabbed Dota by the elbow, shoved her down, and threw a few empty sacks over them. Dota gripped Freydis's hand. It grew hot in their hiding place while they waited. Dota gulped breathlessly, and Freydis squeezed her eyes shut to keep from following Dota into her panic.

The attacking ship crashed against theirs and a voice called across, "Do not flee and we will be merciful."

Now that Freydis could not see the horizon, her sickness grew worse. She tried to view her discomfort from afar, the same way she did when sewing up a cut under the tutelage of her aunt Alfrith. The sight of blood and flesh churned her stomach, while her steady stitches pulled skin together and made it whole. She stroked Dota's clammy hand. One ship against two. The odds were with Aldi and his men, not the raiders.

Something heavy landed on the plank above Freydis's head. She turned her head and felt the point of a grappling hook that had come through the bench scrape across her scalp. The ship rocked as the attackers pulled the ships together so they could board. Dota began to whimper, but quieted when Freydis squeezed her hand again.

The ship rocked again as men's boots thudded on the deck. Freydis could see little from her hiding place; feet moved into her field of vision, then disappeared again. She heard a man's scream, and a body fell into the space between the benches, his dead eyes staring into hers, and a stream of blood flowed across the deck toward her.

"We are King Harald's men," the pilot cried. "You must not attack us."

"That's what raiders would say," responded a young man with a familiar, musical voice. "We are King Harald's men, and King Ragnvald's."

"That was Aldi's son Kolbrand your giant killed," the pilot replied, his voice high and panicked. "You will all die for that."

Freydis tried to swallow around a knot of fear in her throat. Dota began her frightened whimper again. Freydis took a deep breath and stroked her hand again, trying to quiet her, but what comfort could she offer? Her brother Kolbrand was dead. He never had much time for Freydis, but he had been affectionate to his sister, and had a cheerful spirit. Dota's quiet weeping was the only thing keeping Freydis from panic. Dota would need her to stay calm.

The sounds of battle quieted, and Freydis raised the flap of cloth that hid them. The flash of a man's ankle in bright wrappings made her draw back. She bit the inside of her cheek to try to stop her shaking. She must not give in to fear. She was the daughter of one of King Harald's most powerful wives, and niece to the most powerful man in Norway next to the king himself. Dota was the daughter of Aldi, whom King Ragnvald had chosen to watch over his southern kingdom. They could expect no worse from these raiders than to be held for ransom.

Freydis tried to compose herself, thinking over the words she would have to say: my mother, Svanhild, is King Harald's wife. I am a valuable hostage. Alfrith had always told her that women's words held the power to sway the fates, especially women trained in herbs and magic. She had been a simple wise-woman on the island of Smola before King Ragnvald saw her, and chose her to be his concubine and the mother of his younger sons. Perhaps Freydis would have to say no more. She hoped so; she always flushed and stammered when she had to speak with men.

A pair of feet walked back and forth a few times in front of her, and then Freydis's face grew cool as the sack that had been covering her and Dota was snatched away, pulling Freydis's head scarf with it. She shrieked and lunged for it without thinking. Someone grabbed her by her braid, dragging her from her hiding place and tearing her scalp, before flinging her down against a bench that hit her stomach hard and made her retch.

"I've found some women here—girls," said the raider in that same familiar, resonant voice. "Rich clothes."

One of the men towed Dota away as she screamed. Freydis curled up on the deck around her bruised stomach. She saw her head scarf on the ground nearby, and reached for it, but her captor grabbed her arm, wrenching it back. She felt something snap and her shoulder exploded in pain.

He let go of her hand and it fell at her side with a jolt. Broken or dislocated, she imagined Alfrith saying coolly, and gritted her teeth against the pain, cradling her arm with her other hand. Blood rushed in her ears, a tide of anger at her helplessness.

"Freydis, is that you?" the man asked.

She looked up and recognized Hallbjorn Olafsson, a half-brother to her cousin Einar, though the tangle of family lines meant that she shared no blood with him. He had the same red-gold hair as Einar, and the high cheekbones they had both inherited from their mother, Vigdis, though Hallbjorn was heavier in the face.

Hallbjorn had come to Tafjord last summer and been part of the reason Freydis was sent away to Sogn—her aunts had thought that he paid her too much attention. Freydis had also heard that he wanted King Ragnvald dead for killing his father, Olaf, but he would never carry out his revenge, not against such a mighty king.

"Freydis?" he said again.

Freydis nodded, and said, "Yes," in a voice that came out like a croak. She swallowed and then, looking at Hallbjorn's feet, began to recite: "Daughter of Svanhild, who is wife of King Harald. I am a valuable hostage if I am unharmed. If I am killed or spoiled there will be revenge. Dota is Aldi's daughter. The steward of Sogn, chosen and supported by King Ragnvald. She too is worth more as a hostage."

"Freydis, do not fear," said Hallbjorn. He touched her chin gently and raised it so she had to look at him. He had brown eyes where Einar's were blue, but the same sharp smile, and his touch embarrassed her. Freydis pulled free and cast her eyes down again.

"Stay here," he said, and she heard his footfalls receding from her.

A moment later, she saw a much larger pair of feet and looked up to see her cousin Rolli Ragnvaldsson, a happy giant of a young man. Her mother, Svanhild, had given Rolli his ship last year, and he had been playing at viking with his friends ever since. Of course he would be wherever Hallbjorn was. Rolli had always been friendly to her, though. He would treat her well. She sagged forward with relief and then flinched when the movement jarred her shoulder.

"Freydis, what are you doing with these raiders?" Rolli asked. He had a cheery, open face, and a broad forehead now furrowed with worry.

"Raiders?" Freydis asked. Rolli bent down to listen to her. "I am not with any raiders."

"This ship—whose is it?" Rolli asked.

"It is Aldi Atlisson's—steward of Sogn," said Freydis again.

"This is my father's ship—I would know it anywhere," said Rolli, "and it was not his pilot who sailed it. Where is my father? Where is King Ragnvald?"

"You should ask Aldi," Freydis said, wishing he would talk to one of the men on board rather than her. "He's on the other ship. We are sailing to Vestfold. What are you doing here, Rolli?"

"We—I thought you were raiders," he said. "I thought someone had captured my father's ship."

Now Freydis understood: Rolli had seen this vessel and believed he was protecting the Norse coast. Aldi's ships had been sailing far enough from shore to be suspicious, riding the strong winds outside the barrier islands in this fair weather.

"That was foolish," said Freydis, pain making her voice sharp. "Why didn't you ask? You have killed Aldi's son Kolbrand—it is a grave crime."

"Hallbjorn," Rolli said to his friend, with panic rising in his voice, "they are not raiders. What should we do now?"

"Take them to shore," said Hallbjorn. "Bring the ship. The other will follow, I think. Then we will sort all this out."

✠ ✠ ✠

DOTA AND FREYDIS huddled together as Hallbjorn steered Aldi's ship up onto the shore of a narrow dune island. It had no trees, only waves of yellow grass, and then sea again on the other side. The ship crunched on the sand and drifted to a stop. Rolli set up a ladder, and Hallbjorn beckoned for Freydis to climb down.

Dota rushed after her and sobbed as Hallbjorn shoved her back. "You stay on board," he said to Dota. "I've heard you'll make a good hostage."

Rolli had to help Freydis down the ladder, since she could only use one hand. Hallbjorn ordered some of his followers to bind the wrists of Aldi's men, and keep watch over them. Other young warriors from Rolli's ship laid out the four warriors who had fallen in the battle in a line along the beach, their feet pointed toward the surf. The faces of the dead men had already begun to turn gray, their wounds livid against the pallor of death. Kolbrand looked much like the others, death smoothing out the differences of rank and age among them. Rolli's mistake would not easily be fixed.

A strong wind blew offshore and kept Aldi's ship from making progress toward the island. Even oars could do little good against this fierce shore breeze. Freydis sat on a piece of driftwood while Rolli and Hallbjorn finished pulling up their ship out of the waves. One of their men made a fire, and Rolli and Hallbjorn sat and warmed their hands before it.

Freydis gathered her courage and sat down on a driftwood log near them. She ran her fingers over her swollen shoulder joint. Even a gentle touch made the pain bloom.

"Cousin," she said to Rolli, pitching her voice low to try to hide its quaver, "your friend dislocated my shoulder. I need to reset it quickly or it will . . ." She began crying too hard to tell them that if it healed crooked, she would be crippled and useless, a poorer marriage prospect, and a valueless hostage.

Hallbjorn rushed over to sit at her side. He put his arm around her, his touch making her scream. "Hush, hush," he said, still holding her injured shoulder. "We have no healers here. You will have to wait."

"Let her go," said Rolli. "You're hurting her."

Hallbjorn released her. The sudden lessening of pain made her cry all the harder. She tried to breathe through it until she could stop her sobbing.

"I . . . I am healer enough to reset my shoulder," she said. Her face itched from the tears drying upon it. "I know how, but I need help."

"You are a valuable creature then," said Hallbjorn. "Tell me what to do. I caused you pain and I want to set it right." He took Freydis's hand, and held it lightly, stroking her skin. His touch made her feel ill.

"No," she said. "Not you—my cousin Rolli. He is stronger." Hallbjorn's gentle smile ran away like water from a basket, but he let her go.

Freydis directed Rolli to hold her wrist, and moved herself against the tension he provided, gritting her teeth when the bones of her arm and shoulder ground against one another. Alfrith would tell her that pain was only a sensation, and she must move through it as though she were wading through a heavy surf. She could bear this. She let Rolli take more and more of her weight, and then jerked hard against him, feeling a pop and a rush of pain like someone had put a hot knife through her shoulder.

"Let me go," she said to Rolli. He let her wrist fall, and she knelt on the sand, cradling her arm. She waited, unmoving, until she heard Rolli and Hallbjorn sit again on the logs near the fire, and then stood up.

Moving her arm still hurt, but now it felt more sore than broken. When she felt she could bear it, she picked up a stick of driftwood and used it to tear a strip from her skirt, tied it into a loop, and placed it around her neck. Her arm would not obey her, so she had to use the other to place it in the sling, and then, finally, the pain receded.

Rolli's men had gathered at the fire with him while Freydis had been distracted. Rolli sat, chewing on a strip of dried meat, and ignoring them until one of his men spoke: "We're going to be in trouble," he said. "That was a king's son you killed."

"It was a mistake," said Rolli. "My father will pay the wergild." He sounded uncertain, and for good reason—Ivar was King Ragnvald's favorite son and his heir, while Rolli had often run off to play with the children of fishermen when he should have been learning king-craft. His father might not be willing to help a son who had so long rebelled. And if he did not, Rolli could be outlawed, cast out from his country and his family, for any man to murder at will, and no justice to be done for his death. Many did not survive even a short term of outlawry.

"Your mother will help you, at least," said Hallbjorn, and burst out laughing. Nobody joined him, though Freydis smiled tentatively. Rolli was his mother's favorite, her charming, giant son, and he doted upon her too. "Don't worry, boys," Hallbjorn continued. "As young Freydis has reminded me, we hold valuable hostages."

Near evening the wind changed and Aldi's ship finally drew near. Rolli arrayed his men along the shore, and they drew their swords when the ship's keel scraped along the beach. It tilted over as Aldi's men rushed to the gunwale and jumped over it into the shallow water. Rolli's men ran toward them, and pinned Aldi and his followers against the ship.

In the mass of warriors and weapons, Freydis could not see what was happening, but she heard Aldi's angry voice above the fray. "Rolli Ragnvaldsson, what have you done?" he asked. "Your father will be ashamed."

A few of Rolli's men backed away from his advance, but then Rolli lunged at him, and in a moment, his men had disarmed Aldi's, and herded them up onto the beach.

"Where is my son?" Aldi yelled. Two of Rolli's men held his arms. "Where is my daughter?"

Rolli opened his mouth, but stayed silent until Hallbjorn stepped forward. "Your son is dead," Hallbjorn told Aldi, "and your daughter is our hostage. You should think about what you will trade for her life."

The blood drained from Aldi's face, and he fell forward, letting his arms hang from his captors' hands. "What about the other captives?" Aldi asked, looking up at Rolli. "You had no right to take any of them. Does your father think so little of me he sends you to make sport of me?"

"My father didn't send me," Rolli protested. "I thought you were raiders—why do you sail in his ship, flying the wrong banner?"

"King Ragnvald loaned me his ship," Aldi replied. He stared hard at Rolli. "You will be outlawed for this."

"I could kill you now," said Rolli uncertainly.

"Yes, kill him—see, he kneels for the blow already," said Hallbjorn, "and we will sell the survivors south as slaves. Your father need never know about this."

"No," said Rolli. "You steered me wrong today, Hallbjorn."

Aldi scrambled to his feet and backed away. "Your friend is right—the best you can hope for is outlawry. You had better kill me now, or

I will take your life in payment for my son's. I should have killed your father when he caused the death of my father, Atli, but I was willing to trade my revenge for land. Not this time."

"I made a mistake," said Rolli, his voice breaking. "My father will understand that."

"If we are outlawed . . . ," said Hallbjorn.

"Stop saying that," said Rolli. "My father's steward can have his son's body and his daughter. The rest will be our hostages, to ensure that he leaves peacefully."

"Peacefully!" said Aldi. "There will be no peace after this."

"Go find his son," Rolli ordered Hallbjorn. Rolli sheathed his sword, and called his men away from Aldi's. "We will keep this ship, and you can return my father's ship to him."

"Your father will answer for this if you do not," said Aldi. He looked up at Rolli, his face white and drawn. Rolli's men retrieved the bodies from the shore, and Rolli helped Dota down from the ship.

Freydis waded out into the surf to give Dota a one-armed hug, and then walked with her over to where Aldi stood with his men. As they passed Hallbjorn, he grabbed Dota's arm and pulled her away from Freydis, and shoved her toward Rolli.

"We need more hostages," Hallbjorn said to Rolli, "or this man will kill you."

Rolli shoved her back. "Do you want to force Harald to outlaw me?" Rolli asked Hallbjorn. Then, to Aldi, "I am sorry for your son. I will make it right."

"Who is in command here?" Aldi asked. "Who is responsible for this crime?"

"I am," said Rolli.

Hallbjorn lunged suddenly, Dota shrieked, and Freydis whirled to see him holding Dota again, with a dagger to her throat. Dota's eyes were closed in fear, and Hallbjorn looked terrified too, darting his eyes from Aldi to Rolli. "I can't let you do this," Hallbjorn said. "We need hostages, or we will be outlawed."

Freydis stepped forward. Her mother often used words against men's swords. Freydis could do no less. "I am King Harald's stepdaughter," she said gently. "If you need a hostage, you already have me."

"Let her go," said Rolli.

Hallbjorn shoved Dota at her father, then grabbed Freydis's uninjured arm, and pulled her close so she could feel the heat of his skin and smell his sweat and the leather he wore. "That's true," Hallbjorn said to Aldi. "We have a much better hostage than your daughter. Now go before I change my mind."

2

GRAY CLOUDS COVERED THE SKY ON THE DAY RAGNVALD AND his party arrived on the coast of Jutland. Ribe, King Erik's capital, lay a short sail up the river to where it widened into a marsh. Ragnvald disembarked there with his son Thorir and Gudrod, Harald's son, and left his stepbrother Sigurd to see that the ship was tied up securely.

The week's journey south had taken them from winter into spring. Over the past months in Vestfold, Thorir had grown a patchy beard that marked him more clearly as a boy of only sixteen years than a clean-shaved face would have. He was almost as tall as Gudrod, though Gudrod was three years older. Ragnvald had to bless Hilda for that—his wife's height had made all of their sons tall.

Many of Ribe's houses were new, their logs still shedding bark—a far more pleasant smell than the marsh. King Erik's guards conducted Ragnvald and his party through the town, to where Erik held court. He sat on a roughly carved chair beside a young women who, from her pale, unbound hair, Ragnvald guessed was Erik's daughter, Ragnhilda, the object of his journey.

A young guard with a wide chest and a loud voice announced him: "Ragnvald Eysteinsson, Ragnvald the Mighty, King of Maer and Sogn. With him, Gudrod Haraldsson and Thorir Ragnvaldsson." Ragnvald bowed as he greeted King Erik. A breeze blew through the clearing, sending leaves from the previous fall skittering around their feet.

"Welcome, King Ragnvald of Norway," said Erik. He was a short, friendly-looking man, with round features, and light hair and eyes. Sun and wind had polished his cheeks bright and made him appear younger than his years—at least ten more than Ragnvald's, and most of them spent in battle against other Danish kings.

"I am only the king of a few districts," said Ragnvald carefully. "I come on behalf of King Harald of Norway."

"Oh?" said King Erik. "That is not what I heard."

Ragnvald swallowed down his uneasiness. "What have you heard?" he asked. He had come here to make a marriage for Harald's son Gudrod, and an alliance for Norway, but he had also heard rumors that Harald's eldest son, Halfdan, had come to Erik to stir up trouble against his father. If Ragnvald could return to Harald with proof of Halfdan's rebellion, then Harald would have to punish him—outlaw him, or at least send him far away.

Erik smiled. "I've heard that it is you who truly rules Norway, while King Harald lies abed with his new concubine," he said.

"Who did you hear that from?" Ragnvald asked.

"Everyone knows how Harald stole and wed his son Halfdan's Finnish concubine," said Erik. "That must have rankled you. When Norse merchants come here, they tell me that before then, Harald did nothing without your approval."

"Sometimes I wish that were so," said Ragnvald, with forced cheer. "But King Harald is his own man."

"Still, you are his eyes and ears, I am told," said Erik. "There is nothing that happens in Norway that King Ragnvald does not know."

Ragnvald nodded at the compliment. "I would serve my king better if I truly had eyes and ears everywhere," he said. Even though he and his sister, Svanhild, traveled the length of Norway every summer, meeting with local rulers and quelling rebellions, the fjord-cut, mountain-divided peninsula still harbored too many men whose aims Ragnvald did not know. "I have come with an offer of alliance from King Harald," he continued, "to be solemnized with a marriage—"

"Marriage to you?" Erik asked. "My daughter could hardly do better than the man who rules Norway in truth."

Ragnvald gritted his teeth. King Erik meant to irritate him. His accusation was the shadow side of Ragnvald's praise-names: Ragnvald the Mighty, whose might could eclipse Harald's; Ragnvald the Wise, whose wisdom could hide treachery. "Do you want to hear my offer, or insult me by questioning my loyalty to my king?" Ragnvald asked. Erik's courtiers whispered to one another.

"I have heard that you take offense easily," said King Erik, "but I did not know that even praise might offend." He smiled. "Tell me your offer."

"The Jutland and Vestfold kings are natural allies," Ragnvald replied. "Together we can control the entrance to the Baltic Sea, and tax our cousins in Skane and Roskilde. I have brought with me Harald's son Gudrod, to join with your daughter, Ragnhilda, in marriage. The wedding can take place in Vestfold at midsummer, when Harald weds Gyda of Hordaland, fulfills his vow to conquer all of Norway, and cuts his hair."

"I have heard you are eager for him to be shorn," said Erik, "for he will set down his sword and no more resist your rebellion."

Ragnvald reached for his sword. "Should I tell King Harald that all you have to offer him is insults?"

"Calm yourself," said Erik. "Of course, I do not believe such rumors." Ragnvald let his hand fall by his side. "I will consider this," Erik continued. "I would rather marry her to a king, though. You, or your Harald, if you prefer."

Ragnvald smiled slightly. "I am already wedded to a woman named Ragnhilda," he said. "Two wives of the same name is not a challenge any man would take on willingly." And in his youth, when he had little fame and no power, he had promised Hilda that he would never take another wife, a promise that had saved him from trouble before this.

"I think it would be easier!" said Erik. "My daughter goes by Ranka, though." Erik looked at her fondly, and she tossed her hair.

"I am curious," she said to Ragnvald, standing to show off a figure similar to her father's, round and short, "is there not another son I could have? King Harald has twenty or more." She smirked. "And taller ones."

Ragnvald glanced at Gudrod. "What are your objections to Gudrod Haraldsson?" he asked. Halfdan was taller than Gudrod—perhaps Ranka had already seen him and compared the two. "Gudrod was fostered with me for much of his youth, and I can vouch for his character."

Erik turned to his daughter. "He is young and comely," he said truthfully. Skalds called him Gudrod the Gleaming, for he had inherited Harald's shining gold hair, and more beauty than a man should possess.

Behind his back, he was called *ergi*, one who preferred the attentions of men as though he were a woman. But such accusations were often leveled against beautiful young men.

Ranka sneered. "Too young, and he is not tested in battle, or that would be his fame, not his beauty. Father—tell him I can do better." Ragnvald heard Halfdan's words in that too. Ranka continued, "King Harald is not too old yet, and he has many wives. He should take me as one of them. He is a proven warrior."

"Gudrod is as like Harald as any man," said Ragnvald. "He took a wound last year fighting the Scottish viking Melbrid Tooth who raided our shores. What more test would you like to see?"

"I cannot decide this immediately," said King Erik. "How long will you remain in Ribe?"

"A week," said Ragnvald. "We must return to Vestfold for Harald's midsummer wedding feast. I hope it will be your daughter's as well, but perhaps the king of Skane or Roskilde will want to make this alliance instead."

"You press me hard," said Erik. "Is the boy under a spell that he must wed immediately?"

"I seek to bring my king an alliance and a daughter-in-law as a wedding present," Ragnvald replied. "If a week is not enough time, send a messenger to Vestfold when you do decide. Perhaps the offer will still be open." Ragnvald bowed and retreated to join Sigurd in the crowd. Erik greeted other newcomers: some Frisian priests who wanted to set up a church to their Christ in Ribe, and after them a Spanish trader, with dark hair and heavy eyebrows.

Then Erik dismissed his court, and Ragnvald followed one of Erik's servants toward the hall where they would sleep. Thorir fell into step a pace behind him with Gudrod on the other side. "A week, Father?" Thorir said. "So soon?"

"Does the king of Skane truly have a daughter?" Gudrod asked. "I would be happy to escape this Ranka. She is pretty but ill-tempered."

Ragnvald wished Gudrod would pretend interest in the girl, at least for long enough to determine if Halfdan had been here. But he had not shared his suspicions with Gudrod, or anyone except his son Einar and his sister, Svanhild, the only two people he could trust to keep quiet.

"Erik is not very well informed," said Ragnvald. "There is no king of

Skane, at least not one that can be depended upon to keep his crown for more than a summer. Though with Harald's influence, a stronger man might emerge." Ragnvald had sent Svanhild to Skane to determine if Halfdan had been there too, making the same offer on his own behalf. "The tribes in Skane elect a new war-leader every few years. Harald will be happy to install one to his liking if Erik will not make a treaty."

"That is clever, Father," said Thorir. Ragnvald frowned at him. Thorir had emerged from a quiet childhood into a fawning adolescence, eager to praise anyone more powerful than him. Ragnvald wished he could have brought his older sons, Einar and Ivar, with him, but he had needed them to bring Harald's betrothed, Gyda, to her wedding.

"Gudrod, your father needs to make this alliance," said Ragnvald. "If you can make this Ranka warm to you, that will help. Her father seems to give her opinion some weight."

"She's too old for me," said Gudrod. "She must be more than twenty. Why is she not wed yet?"

"She is not so old," said Ragnvald, "and she is a princess. Listen to me. Women do not like to hear about their age, even less than young men like to hear about their youth. If you cannot charm her, I will find another of Harald's sons for the task. Then your father can find you a lesser wife, and you will not have to worry about ruling Denmark."

"Why do I need to rule Denmark if I am ruling Norway?" Gudrod asked, tossing his hair. He and Ranka would make lovely blond children, if they got the chance.

"Did all of your brothers die when I wasn't paying attention?" Ragnvald asked. "What makes you think you will rule Norway?"

"I will have a better chance if I'm not far away in Jutland," Gudrod insisted.

"A king must make alliances," said Ragnvald. "If you do not understand that, you will not be king."

✝ ✝ ✝

AS RAGNVALD HAD expected, the spring weather turned stormy in the evening. Erik feasted them, toasting Ragnvald's past successes, while Ranka kept glancing at Gudrod and Thorir. Comparing Gudrod to Halfdan, perhaps.

Halfdan's rebellion had begun when he brought his new concubine, the Finnish witch Snaefrid, to Harald's court in Vestfold. Harald had only to look upon her once to want her for himself; she had gone to his bed the very day she arrived. Ragnvald had been in Maer at the time, and had returned to Vestfold to find the deed done: Halfdan fled in anger, and Harald wed to a woman with nothing to offer but her beauty. He and Harald had argued, causing a rift between them that Ragnvald had not been able to heal, though he hoped that returning to Norway with a new alliance might help.

At first Ragnvald thought Halfdan had only fled his humiliation, but he began to hear rumors: a young king without a kingdom, consolidating his power, Norway on the brink of war again, and everything Ragnvald had built destroyed.

After Erik's women cleared away the serving dishes and poured sweet wine, Thorir stood to toast Ranka's beauty, his facility with praise well suited to this moment. Of all his sons, Thorir's looks resembled Ragnvald's the most—he had Ragnvald's dark hair and narrow face. Not pretty, like Gudrod, so he would never be mocked for it, nor did his leanness give him the wolfish look of Einar, Ragnvald's eldest son. Thorir spoke well, though, and Ranka nodded and blushed prettily at his words.

That night, Ragnvald dreamed again of the vision that had led him to follow Harald, nearly twenty years ago: a watery hall and a golden wolf with matted fur. Each of the men around the hall touched the wolf, cleaning a patch of its fur, and growing bright themselves. When Ragnvald touched it, flames consumed his hands, his shoulders, reaching up to burn the roof of the hall. As it crashed down on his head, he woke with his heart pounding.

✛ ✛ ✛

THE STORM CLEARED the next day, leaving the sky bright and cloudless. Ragnvald spent the morning in the Ribe marketplace, buying trinkets for Hilda and Alfrith, and seeing what the armorers had to sell. Frankish swords were far easier to acquire here than in Norway, since merchants did not have to cross the Skaggerak Strait and pay tax to raiders.

A Ribe smith told Ragnvald that he had recently sold a large number of swords to a rough man clad in homespun. Ragnvald pressed him for details and recognized the viking Melbrid Tooth from the description—a handsome man save for a deformed tooth that stuck out from his upper lip—not Halfdan, as Ragnvald had feared. Still, the news worried him. Raiders rarely bought so many swords at once, but a warlord arming newly trained warriors might.

Ragnvald returned to Erik's hall to look for Thorir, who had promised to spar with him in the afternoon. He found his son talking with Ranka outside the women's chamber, and smiled to see Thorir's dark head bent over Ranka's golden one.

Ranka looked up as Ragnvald approached. "Your son agrees with me, King Ragnvald," she said. She had a clear voice, low for a woman, a beauty that would remain to her even after age furrowed her face.

"I will leave you to such agreeable company then," said Ragnvald, moving to go.

Ranka called after him, "He agrees that I am a fit bride for King Harald, and too good for a son who may never sit on the throne."

Ragnvald turned back. Thorir gave him an uncertain smile. "Should I argue with a woman about her worth?" he asked.

Ranka's smile was more triumphant. Ragnvald tapped his fingers on the grip of his sword. "The weather has cleared enough for us to practice," he said to his son. "Come with me."

Thorir followed Ragnvald toward the practice ground, his footsteps landing heavily. Some of Erik's men were throwing axes at a target, but they left enough room for sword practice. Ragnvald massaged his hands, which, ever since his captivity and torture, near on fifteen years ago, grew stiff and painful when the weather changed. The broken bones had healed, but his knuckles remained swollen, and these past few years, he had lost the dexterity he needed to make the fine wood carvings that he had once used to pass long winter nights.

Thorir stood a little away from Ragnvald. He picked up a practice sword, and let the tip rest on the ground.

"Did she tell truly?" Ragnvald asked him in a low voice. "Did you agree that Ranka should marry Harald?"

Thorir twisted his sword point into the dirt. "I was only making conversation with her. I wanted her to like me."

"And now do you think that was the right decision?" Ragnvald asked.

"No," Thorir said questioningly. "I should have—"

"You should have tried to convince her of Gudrod's fitness as a husband, if you had to talk with her at all. Now, defend yourself."

Ragnvald could still best any of his sons in the practice yard, though he sometimes suspected Einar of holding back. Einar fought every encounter, even in practice, as if to the death—except with his father. Instead, he questioned Ragnvald politely about tactics, promised to improve himself next time, and left Ragnvald wondering if his son mocked him in losing to him and him alone.

Thorir, though, would give him little challenge. He already looked beaten, standing in the corner of the practice ground, his shoulders slumped, his eyes fixed on the ground. Ragnvald beckoned him toward the center of the practice ground so they would have more space, and then advanced. Thorir backed away.

"Forget anything else that has happened today," said Ragnvald. "There is only this." He advanced again, and again Thorir retreated. "Don't be frightened. I will do you no lasting harm. Not like a real enemy."

Ragnvald heard Gudrod laughing behind him. "I don't think it's a wound he's worried about, King Ragnvald," he said.

Ragnvald wanted to send him away—Thorir was at his best without an audience—but his son must learn to shut out distractions.

"You're next, Gudrod," said Ragnvald. Harald's son would give him a bit more of a challenge. "Come, attack," he said to Thorir.

Thorir lunged forward clumsily, and Ragnvald sidestepped the attack while bringing the wooden pommel of the practice sword down on Thorir's hand, disarming him. Thorir's unchecked momentum sent him crashing to the ground. He gave Ragnvald a sour look as Ragnvald extended an arm to help him up.

Thorir attacked the same way again, but as Ragnvald moved to disarm him, a bolt of pain shot through his fingers, and his sword fell to the ground a moment after Thorir's. Thorir scowled and rubbed at his wrist, too intent on his own pain to notice Ragnvald wincing as he retrieved his sword.

"What went wrong?" Ragnvald asked, pitching his voice low to hide his discomfort.

"You disarmed me," said Thorir.

"Twice!" Gudrod called out.

Ragnvald ignored him. "How should you have protected against that?" he asked Thorir.

"I wouldn't have attacked you," said Thorir sullenly, "then you couldn't disarm me."

Gudrod laughed, loud and mocking.

"Hold your sword more firmly," Ragnvald suggested. "Don't take your eyes off your opponent. But perhaps you should spar with Sigurd instead." He flexed his hand carefully. He had borne the constant, dull ache for years, and fought battles through it, but a sudden spasm like that could cost him his life.

"Do we have to stay the whole week, Father?" Thorir asked, still cradling his bruised hand. "King Harald's wedding is soon, and the crossing might not be as easy on the way back." His practice sword lay on the ground. Ragnvald looked at it pointedly until Thorir picked it up.

"We will leave soon," said Ragnvald. "And after your conversation with Ranka . . ." Thorir looked beaten enough that Ragnvald did not continue. "Soon. Be ready."

✢ ✢ ✢

RAGNVALD FEARED THAT the week he had given Erik to consider his offer would pass slowly with Thorir sulking and Gudrod refusing to woo Ranka. At least Thorir sparred with more skill against Sigurd and some of Erik's young warriors. He only lost his nerve against his father.

Ragnvald was glad to have an excuse to avoid holding a sword and the next morning went to find the bathhouse. Some heat might help his hands, and at least it would pass the time.

He found Erik outside, and moved to cede the wooden structure and its privacy, but the king invited him in. After they settled into the heat, and the servants had retreated, Erik leaned forward and said, "I would rather see my daughter wed to your son than any of Harald's. Your sons have land and prospects. Harald's are a pack of wolves who will tear one another apart for rulership of Norway."

"Have you met Harald's other sons?" Ragnvald asked.

"How could I tell?" said Erik. "There are so many of them!"

"Gudrod is one of Harald's most favored sons," said Ragnvald. The heat of the bath began to relax him and ease the ache in his hands.

"'One of,'" Erik quoted back to him. "Why should I give one of Harald's sons a throne?"

"You have no sons," said Ragnvald. "What do you propose should happen to Jutland when you can no longer protect it?"

"That is why I'd rather have one of your sons," said Erik. "If not young Thorir, then one of the others. I would trust a man raised by you."

It was the finest compliment Erik had paid him since he arrived. Could Einar be the son Erik sought? Ragnvald could give Einar a kingdom abroad, since he could not give him one in Norway.

Many times Ragnvald had wished Einar less gifted, so he did not always outshine his brothers. He was better with sword and ax than many men in the prime of their fighting years. He could compose a middling poem on demand, and a fine one given a little time. He had memorized all the laws of Norway from Hilda's father, finally endearing himself to Hilda in the years that they learned side by side. Ragnvald loved Ivar for his kindness and his cheer, but Einar would have made the better king.

Ragnvald sighed. If he married his baseborn son to King Erik's daughter, he would make the rumors about his treachery true. "You try to tempt me to betray my king again," he said. "I have come to offer Gudrod Haraldsson, and no other."

"I have another thought," Erik said. "Leave this Gudrod with me for a season—and your son too, if you like—so that I may better know what kind of man he is. If he pleases me, and my daughter comes to like him, we will have a wedding next summer."

Ragnvald frowned. "I don't think Harald would like me to leave a hostage against him in your hands."

"With as many sons as Harald has? You are the more valuable hostage, I think," said Erik.

"Am I?" Ragnvald asked, feeling chilly despite the heat of the bath. He took the ladle from the bucket by his side, and poured water on the coals, sending a cloud of steam into the air. "I thought we were your guests."

"Can I trust your discretion?" Erik asked.

"You mean, do I tell Harald everything?" Ragnvald replied. "I tell Harald what I think he needs to know."

Erik gave him a sideways smile, understanding from that what Ragnvald wanted him to. "Harald's son Halfdan is in rebellion. He claims that he can bring Harald down, and I think he may be right. Your allegiance is what could tip the balance. If you support him, he will succeed. If you do not it will be war—all of Norway's districts in disarray, and who will win then? Not you, not Harald, and not Halfdan, but Norway's enemies." His smile broadened. "Me."

Ragnvald had not known Halfdan had gone so far, nor gathered so many allies. Erik could be exaggerating, though, testing him. "If you come with me to Vestfold, and tell King Harald that, he will reward you, and you will have gained my friendship for life," Ragnvald offered.

"That would do neither of us any good," Erik replied. "Harald has too many sons. If Halfdan had not rebelled, another would have. Perhaps this too-pretty Gudrod."

"And for Halfdan to succeed he will have to kill all of his brothers," said Ragnvald carefully.

"You understand," said Erik. "But if you were king . . . you have a manageable number of sons, and you are the one who has forged most of Norway's alliances these past years. You and your sister, Svanhild."

"What do you suggest?" Ragnvald asked.

"Support Halfdan for now, but be ready to turn against him after he has defeated his brothers." He met Ragnvald's gaze. "To be sure, he will turn against you."

"Why should I not wait out this rebellion, and pick up the broken pieces?" Ragnvald asked. He needed to go outside soon before the heat muddled his head.

"I have watched you rise in Norway, while I have been rising here. You have built a strong kingdom and you will not want to see it broken." Erik stood. "I am done here."

Erik wrapped himself in a towel and walked outside. Ragnvald followed him into the anteroom where he splashed cold water on himself and toweled dry. Erik's words were strong flattery, pleasing and dangerous, but Erik had only told one side of the story. Harald was the one chosen by the gods. He was the golden wolf that Ragnvald had seen in his vision, and Ragnvald only one of the many he would make bright with his touch, and then burn and devour.

"I do not expect an answer now," said Erik. "But think about what I have said."

"And you will not wed Ranka to Gudrod?" Ragnvald asked. "Your mind is settled?"

"No, I will not," said Erik. "Would you, in my position?"

Ragnvald could not think of an answer that would both be true and keep him safe. Erik had hinted at taking him hostage—if he realized that Ragnvald would never betray Harald, he would not let him go.

Erik laughed at Ragnvald's silence. "Exactly. Give your king my best wishes for his wedding—for a fertile bride, even if she is old. He makes sons as though he thinks they are an army that will save him, but they are the wolves that will tear him apart."

3

EINAR RAGNVALDSSON RODE TOWARD THE HORDALAND FORT
on a shaggy, ill-tempered nag that he had named Krafla—Scratcher—
for her tendency to paw at the ground whenever she was impatient. His
brother Ivar's horse was the issue of one of King Harald's finest stallions,
bred with a sleek mare from their father's farms.

Next to Ivar rode Dagfinn, one of Harald's grown sons. He had his
mother's narrow face, his father's broad mouth, and was paler than either one of them. His horse did not seem to like him much, and when
it sidled into Ivar's, he laughed and kicked at Ivar, blaming him for the
collision. Einar glanced back at them to make sure it was all in fun.

"They're fine," said Bakur. He raised a dark eyebrow at Einar, and
Einar nodded and looked away. Bakur was the son of a Spanish explorer
and an Irish slave, raised in Harald's court, and far too handsome for
Einar's comfort.

A chill wind swept across the Hordaland plain, flowing down out of
the Keel Mountains. The day had been blustery and changeable, with
drenching cloudbursts broken by stabs of sunlight that made gold stripes
on the stubble of last year's hay. Einar had glimpsed the great fort in the
distance this morning, but though they had been riding toward it all day,
it seemed to grow no larger. He had hoped they would reach it by sunset.

Once they arrived, Einar would have too much work to do to worry
if Bakur's glances meant anything more than friendliness. If Gyda was in
rebellion, they might be attacked as soon as they arrived.

Ivar and Dagfinn had stopped kicking at each other and now dis-

cussed the women they would find at Gyda's hall. "Her nieces are all my
half-sisters," Dagfinn was complaining. "I can't wet my cock anywhere
in Norway without risking incest." Harald had fathered children on Gyda's sister after Gyda swore to keep herself a virgin until their marriage.

Einar allowed his horse to slow so he could ride next to them. "Go
overseas then," he suggested to Dagfinn. His father wanted Dagfinn left
behind to guard Hordaland, but he would be even happier if Dagfinn
quit Norway entirely.

Dagfinn grinned back at Einar. "You shouldn't mind incest, not with
your parents," he said, a familiar jest, for Ragnvald had gotten Einar
on his own stepmother, an act that Einar had trouble imagining of his
stern father, whose every choice seemed governed by a skald's litany of
proverbs. Einar clenched his jaw until he saw Ivar giving him a tolerant
smile. He should be used to these jokes by now.

Ivar kicked at Dagfinn playfully. "Your father marries so many
women, if you're not bedding your sister, you might be lying with your
future stepmother instead," he said to Dagfinn.

"Too true," Dagfinn replied. "You know, they say that the gods Frey
and Freya are siblings and sometimes lovers. If it is allowed for the
gods . . ."

"It will still not be allowed in Gyda's fort," Einar finished sharply.

Einar fell back, and Ivar slowed with him. "Why so grim this afternoon?" Ivar asked.

"Father has set us a difficult task," said Einar. "What if Princess Gyda
has heard of Harald's foolish marriage to that Finnish woman? What if
she will not come with us? What if she is in rebellion?"

"Have you not already answered these questions?" Ivar replied. "You
and Father both—you had so many answers my head was spinning."

"That was talk only. Now we must act, and who can know what will
happen?"

"Who indeed?" Ivar answered. "So why fret? You will make Father
proud, I am sure of it."

Einar was not—King Ragnvald found fault with him often—but
Ivar's confidence warmed him. Ivar rode ahead to catch up with Dagfinn and Einar fell in next to Bakur again, until the souring mood of
his horse told him they had ridden far enough, and should camp for the
night.

He found a flat spot and began clearing the rocks so he could set up his and Ivar's tent. Before he had finished, Bakur came running, followed quickly by scouts from the fort. The lead rider showed off his horsemanship by galloping into camp, coming to a quick stop, and leaping off before Einar's sword was fully out of its scabbard. Ivar and Dagfinn flanked him, their swords drawn as well.

"Do not fear, young princes," said the lead scout, a skinny, grizzled man of middle age. "My queen, Gyda of Hordaland, wanted to give you an escort for the rest of your journey. I am named Radulf. My companions and I are here to serve you."

"If you know who we are, then you also know why we are here," said Einar.

"Indeed we do, Harald's son," Radulf said, bowing to Einar.

Dagfinn stepped forward. "You do not know us as well as you think. I am Dagfinn Haraldsson. This is Ivar Ragnvaldsson, and his half-brother Einar."

"My mistake," said Radulf. "I had heard that King Ragnvald's sons were all dark-haired." He gave Einar a look that made him wonder if he had done it on purpose, to sow discord.

Radulf turned away to unpack his horse. He set up a large tent, finer than any Einar's party carried, and brought out flasks of wine and skins of ale. Einar added the last of his fresh meat to their stew. Radulf's fellow scouts passed around the skins of ale, and before the sun had moved much closer to the horizon, all of Einar's traveling party was drinking and making merry with the newcomers.

After finishing his supper, Ivar rose and raised his cup. "A toast to Princess Gyda of Hordaland—if she feasts us this well in the wilderness, how much better we will eat in her hall!"

The other men took up the toast, and Einar too—it was well judged. Radulf came and sat next to Einar. "I thought you were King Harald's son because you seem to be the leader here," he said. "I meant no insult by it."

"Who should you have insulted by your mistake? Me or him?" Einar asked.

"I also thought you were the leader because you were the suspicious one," said Radulf with a laugh. "Was I wrong about that?"

"Does your queen intend to marry King Harald, or is she in rebellion, as we have heard?" Einar asked. He waited through Radulf's silence. His father had taught him that the man who was willing to be quiet longer held power that a talkative man lacked.

"My queen is as loyal to King Harald as he is to her," said Radulf finally.

Einar laughed. "So she feels slighted that Harald has not yet married her. Tell me, has she already taken a new husband, or is she still looking for a suitable candidate?"

"Neither," said Radulf, and took a sip of his ale. A lie, then—Radulf had used his ale cup to hide his mouth, the body's apology for the tongue's insult. If she was already married, then Einar and his party rode toward a trap in Hordaland. Ivar and Dagfinn would make excellent hostages to keep her safe from Harald's vengeance. Einar must keep them out of her hands.

"That is well," said Einar. "Then we may make merry when we arrive, and celebrate all the way to Vestfold." He offered Radulf a piece of his last honey cake, baked by his stepmother, Hilda, and given to Einar as she extracted another promise from him to keep Ivar safe, as though Einar had not already sworn it before the gods. Radulf accepted the sweet, and chewed it slowly.

Twilight came, and Radulf lit a torch in a signal that was passed along the grasslands back to the fort. Einar walked restlessly around the tents and Bakur fell into step beside him. "I've watched you often on this journey, Einar Ragnvaldsson," he said.

Einar's face felt hot, his stomach pleasurably unsettled. "And what have you seen?" he asked.

"I've seen you watching me," said Bakur. His hand brushed against Einar's.

Einar stepped aside to put more distance between them. "I'm sure many do," he said. "You do not look like a Norseman."

Bakur shrugged. "Perhaps," he said. "But that is not why you look. I will sleep alone in my tent tonight. Come find me if you like."

Einar swallowed. He wished he could take Bakur's invitation, but while an ordinary man might sometimes take pleasure with a fellow warrior when no women were available and be thought no less for it, a son of King Ragnvald could not. And he had other plans for tonight.

Einar went to his own tent, while other men wrapped themselves in their cloaks to sleep on the ground. Talk quieted, and a few of the drunker men began to snore. Ivar bid good night to Radulf and his companions, and came to join Einar.

"Brother, I must go soon," he said when Ivar pushed aside the tent flap.

"I thought you were asleep," said Ivar, laughing and falling backward.

"Hush," he said to Ivar. Even in the dimness of a summer evening, he saw Ivar's cheeks were flushed with drink. "Princess Gyda means to take us captive and use us to gain concessions from our father and Harald. We cannot allow that. I will go to the fort with a few men. We will capture her if we can, but likely she will take us prisoner. Before dawn you must take Radulf and his men captive."

Ivar sat back on his heels. "You swore we would never do battle separately."

"I swore I would protect you," said Einar. "This is not a battle. It is . . . at worst, she will take me hostage. Our father does not care enough about me to go to war over it, so she will still have to negotiate."

"You know Father values you," said Ivar.

"He values you more," said Einar.

"I wish he did not," said Ivar quietly.

The old hurt tugged at Einar, but he could not indulge it now. "I will let Princess Gyda take me captive," he said, "and I will tell her that you have already sent a messenger to Harald with news of her betrayal. If she puts herself in your power, you will tell Harald that her betrayal was only a rumor. If she does not, Harald will bring the forces of all of his allies against Hordaland."

"Why do you need to be captured for this?" Ivar asked.

"Someone has to bring her the message—the fewer of us in danger the better. And if she has me, she will feel as though she has a bargaining chip, and she will be more likely to make a deal."

"Why do we not ride in as we planned?" Ivar asked.

"I do not trust her to welcome us and feast us in her hall. She might drug us, or have her men kill us in our sleep. Remember what our father asked us to do. If she is not married already, bring her to Vestfold for marriage. If she is . . ."

"Kill her and her husband if possible, and if not, at least return with

our lives," Ivar agreed. "I don't like it. We're not supposed to be separated."

"I swore to keep you safe, and I will." He gave his brother a quick
hug and a kiss on the forehead. Quietly, he woke Uffi, one of his father's
warriors, and then Bakur. They walked their horses until they had gone
far enough that the sounds of wind and rustling grass would keep the
camp from hearing them, and then mounted and rode across the plain.

✛   ✛   ✛

AT DAWN, EINAR and his men reached the walls of the fort, a steep
earthwork slope three times Einar's height. A boggy moat had been dug
around the perimeter, sure to foul the steps of horse or man. A pack of
Gyda's warriors loped down over the wall and laid planks across the
ditch so that Einar and his party could cross on foot, though the horses
had to stay outside.

Standing on the wall, silhouetted against the dawn sky, the princess
herself, a slim-hipped figure, with broad shoulders for her size. As Einar
walked toward her, details of her beauty emerged out of the shadows:
high cheekbones, a mouth like the bud of a flower, and tilted eyes, the
way Einar imagined an elvish maiden might look. She wore leather armor, shaped to curve over her waist, and a short sword hung at her hip.
Einar wondered if she knew how to use it. She stood warily, almost like
a warrior.

"My scouts said there were more of you," she said, when he stood an
arm's length below her—so that had been the message of Radulf's flash-
ing signals in the twilight. "Where are they?"

Einar bowed. "They and a few of my men went to do some hunting.
Your man Radulf said that the deer were fat and plentiful." He shrugged,
trying to show he did not care if she believed the lie.

"Did he?" Gyda asked.

Now Einar could see the lines around her eyes, and a hardness in
her hands and jaw, though somehow it did not detract from her beauty.
Einar more often found beauty in men than in women, but Gyda's cool-
ness and strength seemed as alluring as Bakur's warmer looks.

"Well," Gyda continued, "you and your men are welcome, and we
will feast the others when they arrive."

"They may not come, but you can feast me. I am Einar, son of King Ragnvald of Maer and Sogn, son of Eystein of Sogn, son of Ivar, king of Sogn," he said, puffing out his chest as though he were the self-important young man he pretended to be. "I have come to tell you that King Harald of all Norway, son of King Halfdan the Black of Vestfold, calls you to his side for a marriage long delayed. This is my message. We need wait on no others, only for you to make yourself ready to be his bride."

Gyda's lips quirked. "Do you think me a fool, Einar Ragnvaldsson? King Harald would not send so few. Not for me."

Einar relaxed his posture. "I am sent to find out if you are still King Harald's betrothed or if you have betrayed him. My fellows will not arrive until I ride out again to tell them it is safe for them to come."

Gyda's eyes looked clouded. "And my scouts?" she asked.

"Captive," said Einar. He held out his wrists toward her, thinking of the tales his father told of his own captivity and torture. Gyda would surely treat him more kindly than Solvi Sea King had his father. "As I am your prisoner, beautiful Princess Gyda. Do you want to bind me, or am I your guest, protected by hospitality and guest right?"

"My guest," said Gyda, hesitating slightly. She worried her lower lip with her teeth, a human gesture that made Einar's pulse jump. She feared something—something more than Einar's arrival. "As my guest," she said, "you may not do murder within my walls, no matter who you find here."

"Should I want to?" Einar asked quietly. "Perhaps you should make me prisoner, if there is someone here who needs killing."

Gyda gave him a measuring look. "Perhaps you are right," she said. She signaled to one of her men, who handed her a leather rope. She took Einar's hands in hers for a moment, and he felt the calluses on her palms, before she looped the rope around his wrists and tied them. She slipped a finger underneath to test the tightness of the bonds, and he shivered. "Come with me," she said.

He followed her down the slope and into the fort, fussing with the tie around his wrists until he found the place where Gyda had tucked an end under. She had not even bid her men take his or his companions' swords. He exchanged a glance with Bakur, who looked amused. He hoped Bakur's and Uffi's bonds were as loose.

The fort's walls kept out the wind from the plain, so it was much warmer once they descended the inside slope. The town, enclosed by an earthwork circle, reminded Einar of Harald's northern capital, Nidaros—a self-contained world, with artisans' buildings and sheds for animals ranged around a central hall.

Three warriors sat outside in the sun, away from the other groups of men. One was repairing leather armor, another sharpening his sword, and the third restringing a bow. They looked different from the men who had accompanied Gyda to the wall, more weathered, and with unkempt hair.

"You overstay your welcome, Ottar," Gyda said contemptuously. "When is my betrothed, Frode, returning?" Einar's stomach turned over. She was betrothed—he had indeed come into a trap and might now die with her when Harald came to take his revenge.

"A few days," said Ottar, who had been rubbing his sword with a cloth. Bakur touched his shoulder to Einar's. Einar glanced down at his hands and saw that the binding lay loosely upon them, and the only thing holding his wrists together was his own will.

"Who are they?" asked another one of the men, gesturing toward Einar and his men.

"Messengers from Harald Tanglehair," said Gyda. "He says he has fulfilled his oath and come to take me as his bride."

The three men laughed. "An insult only to send three messengers," said Ottar. "We can kill them easily, especially since they are bound."

"Is not a messenger sacred to the gods?" Gyda asked.

"My neck is sacred to me," said Ottar. He laid down his polishing cloth and advanced toward Einar, holding his sword. "They are young and handsome—the gods will like them."

Einar swallowed and flexed his hands. Had Gyda predicted Ottar's reaction and left Einar and his men free for this purpose? He would have to move swiftly and time his attack well. Bakur lunged first, before even drawing his sword, and rolled to earth as Ottar slashed at him. In the moment Bakur had given him, Einar let the rope fall from his hands and drew his sword, slashing into Ottar's neck before he had time to realize Einar was a threat.

The other two of Frode's men drew their weapons and advanced on Einar and his guards. For a moment, the five of them circled one another around the body on the ground, but then Uffi made a feint over it, and when his opponent lunged, Bakur stepped in to kill him.

When the third man realized that none of Gyda's warriors were going to save him, he took off running toward the wall. Einar caught up to him as he scrabbled up it and wrestled him to the ground. Bakur joined him and helped Einar pin him, then offered Einar the same length of rope that had been used to secure his hands. Einar bound him and brought him back to where his fellows lay slain.

"Traitorous woman," their captive spat at Gyda.

"Tie him well," said Gyda to her men. "Put him and his fellows in the empty barn, where he can think about his loyalties."

Einar felt shaky from the sudden fight, swiftly begun and swiftly finished. "What about your loyalties, my lady?" he asked. They had done as it seemed she wished, but she could easily add three more corpses to the pile.

"Come into my hall, eat, drink, and be my guests," she said.

"Where is this Frode, your betrothed?" Einar asked.

"He will be a few more days in the foothills, checking his traps," said Gyda. "Time enough to decide what is to be done. I am certain we can all come to an understanding."

"How, my queen?" Einar asked. "You have betrayed King Harald."

Gyda smiled at him. "Does your Harald Tanglehair want his most famous queen, the one for whom he swore to conquer Norway, to die a rebel, or live a legend, as his wife? You can choose, Einar Ragnvaldsson, and prosper or perish by your choice."

4

AS ALDI'S SHIP PUSHED OFF FROM THE SHORE, ROLLI KICKED at a tussock of sea grass until he uprooted it. Freydis's cat, Torfa, crawled behind her legs, and Freydis wished she could hide as easily.

"It was an honest mistake," Rolli cried. "I was trying to protect the coast, and keep thieves from my father's ships."

Hallbjorn paced next to him. "Aldi will find your father in Vestfold and then we will be outlawed—or worse," he said. He had begun to look less like Einar to Freydis; he had broader, sloping shoulders, compared with Einar's leanness, and she had never heard Einar speak in that querulous tone. Freydis wished more than ever that she had some of Einar's self-control. He would know what to do, other than fight back tears.

Rolli set his jaw. His face usually wore an eager, happy expression, and seriousness sat oddly upon it. "My father will see that I was only trying to help."

Hallbjorn rolled his eyes. "I'm sure that will make up for the death of Aldi's son," he said.

"My father is the most important man in Norway." Rolli kicked another tuft of grass.

"So perhaps he will spare you," said Hallbjorn bitterly, "and punish me in your stead."

Rolli looked confused. "But I killed Kolbrand. I will tell him the truth."

"Do you think that will matter to him?" Hallbjorn asked. "He's always wanted an excuse to be rid of me. I will be outlawed, and then?

How long do you think I will have before he sends someone after me to kill me? Perhaps he will give the task to Sigurd."

"Sigurd would never—he is your half-brother," Rolli protested.

"Arnfast then," said Hallbjorn, "or any of a hundred men who want your father's favor. I would not make it past the barrier islands."

Rolli stopped his destruction of the grasses and looked at Hallbjorn with concern.

"We can't go to him," Hallbjorn continued. "At least not now. We should sail south and sell off all the witnesses as slaves." Hallbjorn glanced at Freydis and gave her a conspiratorial smile that she hoped meant he did not plan to sell her. But he had dislocated her shoulder. That look might mean anything.

"We can sell off this ship too," said Hallbjorn. "Then none will know what we've done or where we've gone."

Freydis swallowed. Her throat was dry. If her mother were here, she would have found a solution already, something to make skalds sing of her. "I will speak for you," she said softly to Rolli. "I will tell Uncle Ragnvald that you were trying to save me."

"That might work," said Rolli. "Don't you think, Hallbjorn? I think it might work."

"You will still pay a great wergild for killing Aldi's son," said Hallbjorn. "If you return with gold, it will be better—and you can sell this ship and these people."

"Won't that make it worse?" Freydis cried.

"What do you know?" Rolli asked. "You're just a girl."

"She is the daughter of the great sea queen Svanhild," said Hallbjorn. "What should we do, Freydis? Freydis Svanhildsdatter?"

A child was only called by her mother's name if her father was unknown, and Freydis's father was Solvi Hunthiofsson, upon whom all raids of the Norse coast were blamed, so often that Freydis sometimes thought him more of a trickster spirit than a man.

"My father," she said hesitantly. She had never met him. She cleared her throat and spoke more firmly. Her words had saved Dota. They might have power now as well. "Let us go to my father, the great viking Solvi Hunthiofsson in Iceland. You can raid with him, and then go home rich."

"Iceland? How do you know he is there?" Hallbjorn asked her.

Freydis flushed—she did not know where Solvi was, but she had a better chance of being rescued on that journey than if they sailed south. "He is my father," she said.

"Solvi Klofe," said Hallbjorn. "Solvi Sea King. Yes, this could save us." He paced back and forth.

"Solvi is my father's enemy," Rolli protested. "He tortured him." He twisted his fingers together in an echo of a gesture his father often made. Freydis had heard the whispered stories—King Ragnvald had broken under Solvi's torture. It had made Freydis fear her father, since she knew of no man tougher than her uncle.

"So no one will think to look for us there," said Hallbjorn. "Solvi will help us for the sake of his daughter. And when you return wealthy, you can buy off Aldi and anyone else who troubles you."

"It is a thin chance," said Rolli.

"No, it is the best chance," said Hallbjorn. "Why did we set out if not for this? Do you really want to go back to Tafjord, or to Vestfold, and live in your brothers' shadows for the next ten years?"

Freydis almost smiled at that; Rolli was too large to live in anyone's shadow.

"How will we get there?" Rolli asked. "We have no sailors who know how to cross the open sea."

Freydis had not thought of that; she had only wanted to do what her mother would have done. "News will not travel too swiftly for us to go to Nidaros and find a captain bound for Iceland," she suggested, speaking before she could second-guess herself. "We should go there first."

"This girl knows a few things," said Hallbjorn approvingly.

"This girl wants to be rescued," said one of Rolli's men—a boy called Arn whom Freydis knew from Tafjord. "She thinks she's important."

"She is important," said Rolli. "None will harm her."

"Unless she means to testify against us," said Arn. "Women are treacherous." Freydis frowned at him, wondering what she had done to make him dislike her.

Rolli shrugged. "Aldi has sailed away with more than enough witnesses," he said.

"We can't go to Nidaros," said Hallbjorn. "We may be captured. But we can follow a ship bound for Iceland. That is a good thought. We will wait outside Trondheim Fjord until we find one."

✛ ✛ ✛

NEAR AN ISLAND in the entrance to Trondheim Fjord, a wide-bellied merchant ship wallowed through the waves, riding low in the water, its sail too small for the weight of the cargo it carried. Rolli's smaller ship caught up to it while Hallbjorn, piloting Aldi's stolen ship, followed behind. They chased the merchant onto the island, where he accepted a trade: his life and some of his goods for a larger sail and an escort to Iceland.

While the merchant replaced his sail and Rolli and Hallbjorn redistributed his goods, Freydis kept watch back toward the broad opening of Trondheim Fjord, hoping for a ship to turn and rescue her.

A few of Aldi's captured men tried to escape, but Rolli and Hallbjorn killed the two instigators, and then two more who complained about their deaths, after which the remaining ten resigned themselves to the journey. Hallbjorn left the four bodies rocking in the shallows during a dinner of spitted shorebird and hard rye bread softened in ale. Freydis could not make herself eat with the dead so close by.

She gave her food to Rolli and said, "Aldi's men must be buried, or they will follow us." She felt she had the fates' attention here, for Hallbjorn and Rolli had followed every suggestion she made. If only she could convince them to take her home, but she knew her power would not go that far.

Arn sneered at her. "Don't listen to this foolish girl. Slaves don't deserve a burial."

Rolli shifted uncomfortably. "She has been trained by my father's concubine, Alfrith, who is a great sorceress."

Hallbjorn gave Freydis a measuring look. "What should we do, young Freydis? Do you know the spells to keep them from following us?"

Freydis nodded. "I will need help," she said. She gave Hallbjorn her instructions, and he found four men to help move the bodies inland and dig graves for them. Freydis had known them a little in Sogn, but she could think of no words to say beyond the ritual prayers of peace and farewell. What rest could they find here, on this bare strip of sand?

Still, she touched their cold, wet eyelids to stop their sight. She tied strips of cloth torn from her under-dress around their heads to keep their mouths closed. She instructed the men to bury them with their feet facing inland, so if they did try to follow the ships, they would be confused.

The next day they set sail, and Freydis watched the four mounds recede into the distance behind them. Rolli's ship was lightly crewed, and Freydis feared it would be capsized by one of the gusts that kept trying to steal her head scarf, leaving her entirely in Hallbjorn's power.

She often caught Hallbjorn looking at her, and she looked away, blushing. She did not see why her eyes always landed upon him—he was taller and more handsome than the other men, and he did look a little like Einar, but she was no Dota, to think of nothing besides men and marriage. And he was cruel—her torn scalp and aching shoulder reminded her of that often.

On the second day she grew bored of watching open water go by and took out her weaving. Hallbjorn sat down next to her, sending her cat fleeing under the rowing benches.

"What are you making?" Hallbjorn asked.

"It was to be a ribbon for Princess Gyda," she said glumly.

"Come now, little Freydis, is this not better than a dull trip to Vestfold?" Hallbjorn asked. "To wait upon King Harald and praise him? How can Svanhild's daughter not crave adventure?"

"I am not my mother," said Freydis stiffly. If she had a daughter, she would keep her by her side, not abandon her to relatives who shuffled her from one farm to another like a piece of livestock.

"No, you are far prettier than she," said Hallbjorn, shifting closer to her.

He touched her hand as she twisted the cards for her weaving. "I regret hurting you. Tell me you forgive me."

"I forgive you," she said flatly. She did not see how she could say otherwise.

"You don't, not yet," he said, with certainty in his voice, "but this will be a long journey. You will like me by the end."

"Not so long," she countered. "We will see land soon." She kept her eyes on his feet, which were clad in shapeless boat shoes that made the bones of his ankles look oddly delicate.

"Why do you say that?" Hallbjorn asked.

"The birds," she said, pointing at the black shapes in the sky. "The merchant ship follows them toward land, and we follow it."

Hallbjorn put a hand to her chin and lifted her face so she had to look at him. "I thought you might be simple when I first came to Tafjord, for you spoke so little, but here I find you are a beauty who can heal broken bones, placate angry spirits, and knows something of sea navigation. What other surprises are you hiding?"

Freydis glanced around to see if any of Hallbjorn's men noticed them. When he had given her too much attention at Tafjord, she had only thought he meant to mock her. Was he so desperate for a woman, any woman, that he would pursue a girl child only just blooded, far too young for marriage?

"Please let me do my weaving," she said.

"Do I distract you?" Hallbjorn asked.

Freydis shook her head and refused to look at him until he left her alone.

+ + +

ANOTHER DAY OF strong winds brought the ships to the Orkney Islands. Since Harald's victory at Hafrsfjord, when Freydis was only a baby, the islands had become a haunt for the vikings and sea kings who could no longer make a home on the Norse coast. Perhaps she would find Solvi here instead of in Iceland.

The merchant approached through a gap between islands, sailing toward a rocky shore flanked by high hills and cliffs. Many Orkneymen stopped their work to look down at the ships as they beached, and Freydis's skin itched from having so many eyes upon her. Her mother would have counseled that they find another approach, and make landfall in a hidden cove. From there they could send scouts before exposing themselves.

Lush grass covered the island's upper hills, an even greenness broken by only a few scrubby trees and larger hummocks that were set in a regular pattern up the slope. Freydis could discern no buildings until she saw a small figure in homespun emerging from one of the hummocks.

Now the landscape resolved itself into an order she could understand. One of the larger turf houses could likely shelter fifty people, and was surrounded by smaller turf outbuildings. The narrow lines in the slopes were lichen- and bramble-covered rock walls. Sheep grazed among them. It was the scale that had confused Freydis, at once too large and too small, the cliffs rising as high as the fjord walls at home, but not set against the backdrop of mountain and forest. How could spirits live here with so little shelter?

More men sat on rocks near the shore, clad in armor and wearing swords. They did not appear threatening, but their posture showed a casual alertness that could turn to attack in a moment. One man grabbed the line that Rolli threw down, and pulled the ship up onto the shore as far as the strength of one man could take it. Rolli jumped down into the shallows. On seeing Rolli's size, the man took a few steps back, his hand at his sword. Rolli stepped forward to loom over him, Hallbjorn at his side.

"I am Rolli Ragnvaldsson, and this is Hallbjorn Olafsson," said Rolli. "Tell your master we have arrived."

"Will he care?" asked another man, who had come to join the first.

"He will," said Rolli. "I am the son of King Ragnvald of Maer."

"And I am Hallbjorn Olafsson," said Hallbjorn. "We come seeking hospitality, with no ill intentions, carrying slaves and trade goods to sell, and news from Norway."

The mood of the gathering crowd turned friendlier. More men came to help drag the ships farther up the beach and tie them up. Arn put down a ladder against the side, and the rest of the sailors disembarked. Hallbjorn stood at the bottom as Freydis descended, and when she reached the bottom, he picked her up around the waist and set her gently on the sand.

She followed the Orkneymen up to the long turf hall, where servants spread thick blankets over the seats to make them more comfortable. Women brought heated ale to warm them, and a big, redheaded man took the high seat.

"I am Thorstein the Red," he announced. "These are my islands. Now tell me who you are."

Rolli took a gulp of his ale. "I am Hrolf—Rolli—Ragnvaldsson, youngest true-born son of King Ragnvald of Maer."

A man of middle age stood up abruptly. Something about the shape of his face reminded Freydis of Rolli, though he was skinny to the point of emaciation. "I am Egil Hrolfsson," he said. "Your uncle—your mother's brother."

Rolli embraced him so heartily that Freydis worried he would break the man's back. "Uncle!" said Rolli. "I have more aunts than any man deserves, but few enough of those."

Egil smiled thinly in response. Freydis could not remember Hilda mentioning him.

Thorstein cleared his throat. "Your father is no friend to Orkneymen," he said to Rolli. "But you are under the protection of my hospitality now. And your handsome friend."

Hallbjorn smiled at the compliment. "My father was Olaf of Ardal, and my mother is Vigdis Hallbjornsdatter," he said. "She lives in Vestfold in the court of Harald and his uncle Guthorm. My half-brother is Sigurd Olafsson." Freydis sensed an uneasiness in Hallbjorn as he listed these connections. Rolli could name an unbroken line of ancestors back to Odin himself if he chose, while Hallbjorn's were more tenuous. Like Freydis: daughter of one of King Harald's wives, but not the king's daughter. Daughter of a legendary sea king she had never met, who might not be happy to see her.

Freydis was lost enough in her worry that she only heard the end of Thorstein's introduction. "I fought on the wrong side at Hafrsfjord," he was saying. "And in Orkney I am as close to being king as any man outside of Norway. I have women. I have timber now, and I will build a fine drinking hall with it. I plunder when I want. Harald has sent a few expeditions against me, but they usually attack Scotland instead, for the islands' tides and weather foul them. But what are you doing here? Why would the son of Ragnvald of Maer turn viking?"

"There are few enough lands to rule," said Rolli. "My father will have to divide his kingdoms among all of his sons and some of Harald's as well. And I would rather be a sea king anyway. Already I am too big to ride most horses." He laughed, but Thorstein did not join him.

"Would you?" Thorstein asked. "I do not think you know these waters well, or you would not have followed that wallowing merchant ship into the harbor."

"We are going to find Solvi Hunthiofsson and join with him," said Rolli. "My cousin Freydis is his daughter."

Thorstein gave Freydis a piercing look that made her wish she could shrink away into the ground, then turned back to Rolli. "Why would the son of Ragnvald the Mighty"—he said the byname with deep sarcasm—"want to join with an enemy of King Harald?" he asked.

Rolli told what had brought them to Orkney. "But if I make myself rich raiding, then perhaps I can buy my way back," he concluded brightly.

"You are a young fool," said Thorstein. "You should go home and beg for your father's mercy while you still have a chance. There is not so much gold to be had in viking as there once was, and I do not like to share."

Hallbjorn made a noise of protest. "The Great Danish Army still brings back great chests of hack-silver from England. And we go to Solvi Hunthiofsson, the greatest sea king that has ever lived."

"Ha!" said Thorstein. "Solvi Hunthiofsson has not left Iceland in over a decade. He is not what you think."

Freydis crossed her arms over her chest and hugged herself. She wanted to look at Hallbjorn, to see if he believed Thorstein, but feared what she would see.

"That cannot be," Rolli exclaimed. "Everyone knows that he attacks Norway every summer!"

Thorstein shrugged again. He seemed to like the way it drew attention to his massive shoulders. "As you say. But if I had a father as powerful as yours, I would return to my homeland and find an easier life than this."

✣ ✣ ✣

THAT NIGHT, FREYDIS shared a damp, mildewed mattress with one of Thorstein's serving girls. The next day, while Rolli and Hallbjorn tried to find buyers for their slaves and the merchants' wares, she made herself helpful in the kitchen.

She was tying up bundles of herbs, separating flavoring herbs from healing herbs, when she felt herself being watched. She turned and saw the girl who had shared her bed looking over her shoulder. In the daylight, she had a snub nose and freckles, and wore a sullen expression.

"Are you a wise-woman?" the girl asked. "You seem young for it."

"My aunt was teaching me," said Freydis.

The girl made a sign over her chest that Freydis had seen some of the Christian slaves in Tafjord make. "I don't hold with that—my mother says that Christ heals all. But one of the crones who lives up the hill helped me get rid of a child after one of Thorstein's men forced me."

Freydis nodded. "I have heard of such things."

"Can you?" the girl asked. "Do you know how to do that?"

Freydis looked at her sharply. "Are you pregnant?" she asked.

The girl shook her head. "No, but it could—it might happen again, and I don't want to go to the crones this time. If you give me the herbs, then I won't need them."

Freydis looked at the hall's collection tied in bundles at her feet, and did not see those that would loose a babe from its mother's womb before its time. "I don't have what you need," she said. "And it is dangerous—you should not take them without someone to tend you if it goes wrong."

"You're not much of a wise-woman then, are you?" said the girl.

Freydis shrugged, and the girl went back to her work.

When Freydis went to her pallet that night, it was empty except for her cat. She had lost the serving girl's companionship by refusing to help her. She sat down, pulled up her knees, and rested her head upon them, letting her tears dampen her torn under-dress. She had kept them at bay when she had people around her, watching her, but now she had no one. Thorstein had cast doubt on her father's power—he might no longer even be living.

She felt the mattress shift when someone sat down next to her, and turned to see Hallbjorn's silhouette.

"Why do you cry, my dear?" he asked. "Are you frightened?"

Freydis rubbed her tears away with her fists, and ran her hands over her hair to neaten it.

"Are you frightened of me?" Hallbjorn asked.

Again she did not answer. No words could do her any good now and silence did not help either, for it seemed to intrigue him. She did not like the way he made her feel: vulnerable, embarrassed, too aware of his nearness.

He brushed a finger across her cheek where a tear still lingered, gently removing it, and making her want to wipe away his touch. "I am sorry if you are frightened. I wish you were not so fearful of all of us. Of me."

He moved a little closer to her and put his arm around her shoulders. She held herself rigid, though a part of her wanted to relax against him. No one had comforted her since she left Sogn except him. His touch loosened something in her and she cried freely now, putting her head down on her knees again, and shaking with her sobs.

When she stopped, he gave her a bit of cloth to dry her face. She pressed her fingers to her flaming cheeks and her swollen eyes, and then tried to neaten her hair again. Hallbjorn caught one of her wrists in his fingers and pulled her hand into his. He brushed her hair back with his other hand, tugging apart the snarls so gently she wanted to cry again.

"You are a pretty girl," he said.

She turned away. Again he mocked her.

"I promise you, you are. Like ice and fire."

The fire was in her cheeks, the ice in her hands. He touched her chin, and then touched his lips to hers. The hairs of his beard, a soft, young man's beard, were gentle against her face. She held herself very still, neither reacting nor pulling away. Then he kissed her more forcefully, holding the back of her head and pressing his lips on hers, his tongue into her mouth. She pushed at his shoulders with her hands, kicked out until her feet made contact with his ribs, and he, laughing, let her go.

"You want me, little Freydis," he said. "And you will have me." She wiped her mouth with the back of her hand. He laughed again. "You are young."

She was meant for marriage someday, unless she became a priestess of Freya, and even then she would expect to welcome men into her bed—but she knew this was wrong. Hilda had sent her away from Tafjord to keep her away from Hallbjorn. She did not trust what he wanted from her, or trust herself.

5

SVANHILD SAILED HER SHIP EAST, WATCHING THE HORIZON where the thin dark line of the Skanian coast grew thicker as her ship approached, forming into stripes of shadowed forest, gray rock, and the churn of waves breaking on the shore below. Merchants who sailed these waters had warned her of the hidden rocks just below the surface. No tide was safe, they said, so Svanhild waited for the noon peak, hoping her ship's shallow draft would slip over any obstacles. Skane was a land upon which ships broke, and a refuge for broken men, outlaws, and escaped slaves.

On this clear day, she could see a curve in the land that hinted at a likely harbor. She ordered her pilot to turn, hoping to impress her men by making this landing on the first try. A male captain might rest upon past successes, and be forgiven for occasional mistakes, but a woman must always be perfect, or risk losing her men's confidence.

The cliff she had chosen rose higher than the rest of the coastline, shadowing the water below. Svanhild worried she had steered toward where sheer rock met water, but as she drew closer, she saw a strip of pebbles at the shore—a narrow beach. Perhaps the faint tracing that zigzagged over the cliff's face was a path.

"There," she said, pointing.

Falki passed the steering oar to his apprentice and stood next to her, close enough that she could feel the heat from his body in the cool air. "I see it," he said, excited. "An excellent spot." He turned toward the man at the steering oar. "Aban, can you make that turn?"

Aban al-Rashid, a young Arab explorer who had joined Svanhild the summer before, nodded and steered the ship through the wide arc that would bring it into the harbor. His name meant "rightly guided," a good name for a sailor. As news of Harald's rich court at Nidaros had spread through Norse trading networks, more explorers like Aban had come to see it for themselves. All of Svanhild's crew were men who did not fit well among Harald's warriors. Falki had been Harald's pilot, but preferred to sail with Svanhild.

"You are still the best at this, my lady," said Falki quietly. Svanhild wished she could lean back against him, as she had once done with her husband Solvi when they were at sea, to feel his lean, hard chest against her back. He too would have praised her sailing. Instead, she swallowed, and stepped forward to put a decent distance between them. She liked Falki, but he was not Solvi, and taking what he offered would not ease the ache she had felt since defeating her former husband in battle and sending him away from Norway.

She called out the orders to tighten and loosen ropes that would allow the sail to turn where she wanted it. The air grew cold when the ship passed under the shadow of the cliff. Rotten scraps of rope clung to one of the boulders.

She glanced back at Falki and met his eyes again for a moment too long. In her loneliness, she had become too friendly with him. A noise drew her attention—her servant Luta, the only other woman on board, had dropped her spindle between two of the rowing benches. She had probably done it on purpose, to remind Svanhild to keep Falki at arm's length. That was her task, beyond cooking and mending. Svanhild spent every night at Luta's side, so none might accuse her of licentiousness, of betraying Harald, no matter how little he still treated her as a wife.

"Where will we find these Skanians?" asked young Olaf.

"I think they'll come to us, Olaf," said Svanhild. He was her stepbrother Sigurd's son by a wife who had died in childbirth. Sigurd fostered him at Vestfold among Harald and Svanhild's sons, who counted him as an older brother. It had been strange, at first, to call a child by the name of her hated stepfather, though in time this friendly boy had come to replace him in her mind. Svanhild still wondered why Sigurd had entrusted his son to her care. The only one of her children she had tried to mother had died, ending her marriage to Solvi in a terrible fight, when they had each blamed the other for their son's death.

Her men jumped down into the surf and pulled the ship onshore. They set up a ladder and Svanhild climbed down onto the jut of stone that served as a dock. Long practice allowed her to walk as though she did not feel the earth shifting under her after spending a week at sea. Aside from some rotten ropes, she saw little sign that humans had made a mark upon this shore. The path she had seen from the water all but disappeared when viewed from below. Svanhild set some of her men to the task of unloading the supplies they would need to camp for a few days, while others stayed alert for attack.

The crew had just finished when Svanhild heard a man call out a greeting from the cliff above. "We have bowmen who can kill you where you stand," the voice said.

Svanhild tensed slightly, but she had dealt with unfriendly locals before. She called out, "I am the lady Svanhild Eysteinsdatter, Svanhild Sea Queen, wife of King Harald Halfdansson. I claim guest right and ask for your hospitality for me and my men."

"You ask guest right at a bare cliff?" the voice asked. "I cannot grant that, but my men will do you no harm if you sheath your weapons and make ready to turn them over to us."

A few of her guards had hidden themselves in the shadow of the cliff where the Skanians above could not see. She thought of mounting an attack, but she had come to negotiate, not do battle. A procession of warriors appeared on the path to help her decision—the Skanians were too many for her men to fight.

Their leader descended far enough that Svanhild could see him clearly. He was a short man with a beard that covered his face almost up to his eyes. His mustache was long and unkempt, half hiding his mouth. He looked at her for a moment, and then smiled, exposing a tooth that stuck out straight from his upper lip. This was Melbrid Tooth, a famous viking from the Hebrides, on the western coast of Scotland, who had recently attacked Norway's shores. He was a long way from home.

"A woman captain," he said, his smile turning to a leer. Svanhild glanced down at her tunic and trousers, no different from what any man wore. Often she was mistaken for a beardless boy at first, and Falki, or another of her crew, for the captain. "Are you lost, my lady?"

"Not at all," said Svanhild. "I come seeking the king of Skane."

Melbrid bowed to her. "We have no kings here, but the people of Skane have seen fit to elect me their leader."

"Will you give me the honor of your name?" Svanhild asked.

"You know who I am," he replied.

Svanhild smiled slightly and tilted her head. "Should I?"

"I am Melbrid Tooth," he announced, drawing himself up to his full height. He was not a tall man, but still a head taller than her. "Why have you come here?"

"I have come from my husband and king, Harald of Norway, to make an alliance with the Skanians," she said, though she did not know if Ragnvald would want her allying with one who had attacked Norway so often. They had both thought the king of Skane would be one of the wild men who lived there, elected for a few seasons, and then deposed by a younger warrior. "We come with gifts and offers of more treasure if you join with us."

Melbrid walked a little away from her, shaking his head. "Are you certain that is why you've come, my lady?"

"Do you mock me?" she asked.

"Do you not know? Truly?"

"What?" Svanhild asked. "I am here as an emissary for King Harald."

"I suppose it is well that you have come," he said, stroking his chin. "Or I would have to risk sending a messenger to Vestfold. I have something belonging to your king, and I think perhaps I should be paid for returning it."

"Something?"

"Someone," said Melbrid.

Svanhild smiled slightly. Ragnvald had guessed that Halfdan Haraldsson might come here, but he could have gone to any court in the Norse-speaking lands. Her luck had traveled with her to this wild shore. "How long have you had Halfdan the White and what do you want for his return?" she asked.

Melbrid grinned at her and nodded. "I should have guessed his absence would be noticed."

Svanhild found Halfdan to be an unpleasant, bullying version of his father—all of Harald's high-handedness without the charm that made it tolerable. "Only by some," she said. "I am not certain I want to bargain for him. It might be better if you kept him."

"He is not your son, then," said Melbrid. "I thought him too old for that, but you might have magicked yourself younger."

"He is not my son," said Svanhild, nodding to acknowledge the compliment.

"And if I keep him, is that less competition for your sons?" Melbrid asked. "Should I ask what you will pay me to keep him?"

She, Ragnvald, all of Norway, and even Harald, would be better off with Halfdan dead or kept away long enough for his name to be forgotten. She smiled more broadly at Melbrid. "We should discuss that as well. It does not change my purpose—Harald wishes to make alliance with you."

Melbrid laughed. "His son tells us that Harald wishes for nothing but to fall asleep between his new woman's thighs." He searched Svanhild's face, perhaps looking for anger at his words. Svanhild tried to reveal nothing. Long before Harald had married his son's concubine, he had ceased to invite Svanhild to his bed, leaving her no company at night but Solvi's memory. "Bring your gifts to our camp," said Melbrid. "We may be willing to give him up—or keep him, as you wish—for what you brought. We will feast you as best we can."

"Why should I put myself in your hands?" Svanhild asked.

Melbrid gestured up at the guards ringing the cliffs, and those that surrounded her men. "We will give you hospitality," he said. "No matter what you have heard, I am a man of honor. Still, you must give up your weapons and consent to be blindfolded while we take you to our dwelling place. When you leave, you may have your weapons back."

Svanhild looked up at Melbrid in a way she hoped he would find charming and untied the long dagger at her waist. She had a smaller one hidden beneath her trousers. "You must have heard of me," she said, "for it is true, I am as dangerous blindfolded as I am with my eyes open."

"I can well believe that, my lady," said Melbrid.

✣　✣　✣

MELBRID SHOWED HER a cave where she could hide her ship. It had an opening shrouded by overgrowth and the clever placement of a downed tree. His men and hers pulled the ship up onto the rocky shore, and then carried it a dozen paces to a cradle of leaves and pine needles within the cave. Her men gave up their weapons to the Skanians. She hated to see young Olaf have to give up his dagger too, a gift from his father, Sigurd, and beckoned him to walk close to her.

Melbrid handed bands of black fabric to Svanhild and her crew to cover their eyes. "I will lead you," he said. "Take hold of this rope."

A tug on the rope told her to start walking. After a few dozen paces the path grew steeper and Svanhild had to pick her feet up to avoid tripping. A breeze stole pieces of hair from under her scarf and the blindfold. Once they were under the trees' canopy, the breeze stilled and Svanhild became warm.

From beneath her blindfold she could see the rope and part of Olaf's hand where he gripped it—a child's hand still. He was the same age as her eldest living son, and a few years younger than Freydis. Svanhild often shied away from thinking of her daughter, a strange girl who had Solvi's face, but not his spirit—she was shy and humorless. The last time Svanhild visited her, a few years earlier, her likeness to Solvi had made it hard to look at her. Anyway, Freydis preferred Alfrith's company. She would not miss her mother.

Svanhild could not tell how far they had come when the rope stopped moving and her last step brought her almost into Melbrid's back. She lifted her blindfold. Dappled green light dazzled her eyes at first, and then she saw homespun tents of varying sizes standing in a clearing surrounded by short trees. A cave opened at the rear of the camp, its mouth twice the height of a man. A few women worked in front of their tents, dressed like thralls, in simple homespun tunics that ended at their knees.

"We are only starting to move out of our winter caves," Melbrid told her.

The settlement's impermanence made Svanhild feel uneasy, as though it could melt away into trees and nothingness, and take her with it. "Let me see Halfdan," she said.

Melbrid jerked his chin at one of his men, who walked over to a tent and said something in the entrance. Harald's eldest son, tall and pale as befit his name—Halfdan the White—lumbered out a few moments later, rubbing his eyes.

"Greetings, stepmother," he said, "or one of them, anyway." He stumbled next to Svanhild and sat down, but missed the log bench and fell to the ground instead, half onto Svanhild. He stank.

"What is wrong with him?" Svanhild asked, shoving Halfdan off her. He gave her a sheepish smile and settled on the ground next to her, leaning back against the log.

Melbrid frowned. "Someone must have brought him wine last night," he said.

"How long has he been here?" Svanhild asked.

"Since Yule," said Melbrid. "Are you sure you want him?"

"I am sure I do not," said Svanhild. "But what use is he to you if you don't ransom him?" She suspected she knew the answer. Halfdan had come here seeking allies in his rebellion against Harald. Melbrid wanted him to act the captive for Svanhild's benefit, but as soon as she left, he would become an ally again. What payment would Melbrid need to take him far away, to Scotland, or beyond, or better yet pitch him overboard in the middle of the North Sea?

"I'm sure he has some utility," said Melbrid. He gave Halfdan an amused and doubtful look that made Svanhild laugh. "We will discuss this later."

Dinner that night was simple, small fowl cooked over campfires, and an unfiltered drink of fermented berries that made Svanhild's throat burn. The blistered skin of the birds was delicious, but also crunched in places from the burned stubs of feathers that had not been fully removed.

"May we speak now?" Svanhild asked after she was done eating. She wiped off her hands, greasy from the fowl, on a rag that Melbrid handed her. "About King Harald's offer of alliance with Skane?"

"Ha," said Halfdan through a mouthful of food. "My father is not king—your brother is."

Svanhild had heard that said many times on her journey, and usually corrected it. Here she did not—she needed Melbrid to think her powerful. "King Harald can offer you better terms than his son can," she said. "Tell me what Halfdan has offered, so I may find something to better it. Anything I promise, Harald can make good on. Or"—she fixed her gaze on Halfdan—"my brother can. What does Halfdan offer?"

"Freedom and no punishment—for slaves and outlaws like ourselves, a precious thing," said Melbrid. "In return for our support against his enemies, he will leave us alone to rule ourselves—here and in Scotland."

"Who are your enemies, Halfdan Haraldsson?" Svanhild asked. "Do you plan to murder your brothers? Your father, whose only crime is satisfying that Finnish woman better than you did?"

Halfdan sprang to his feet, his hand going to where a sword should hang. But his belt was empty. Melbrid had taken some precautions with his new ally. "If you were a man, I would kill you for that," he said.

Svanhild rose as well. "Better men than you have fought Harald and failed."

Halfdan crossed the few steps that separated them. He towered over her, fully as tall as his father. Svanhild held her ground. "Do you always kill those who speak the truth?" she asked, refusing to crane her neck to look at his face. "A poor trait in a king."

"Speak up," said Halfdan. He shoved her shoulder, and she stumbled back. Immediately Melbrid interposed himself between them.

"You are all my guests and you will behave as guests," he said. "Tonight is for feasting and welcome. We will have time to talk about this tomorrow."

"I am honored to be your guest, King Melbrid," said Svanhild. "I feel certain we can come to an agreement."

"Don't be too certain of that," Halfdan said. "I have already sent messengers to my allies."

"Your allies?" Svanhild asked. "Skane could not field enough warriors to carve a single rock off of Norway."

"I have more allies than you can imagine," said Halfdan.

"Halfdan," said Melbrid sternly.

"No," said Halfdan, "I will make this unnatural woman respect me, since my father cannot."

"Who, Halfdan?" Svanhild asked. She felt no fear, only a brightness in her blood. Halfdan would tell her, and then she would tell Ragnvald. "Who are your allies?"

"King Erik of Jutland for one," said Halfdan, puffing out his chest. "More Scottish vikings like Melbrid than you could name—Ketil Flatnose, Geirbjorn Hakonsson, Gudmar Gudbrandsson are just a few—and the kings of Ireland and Sweden have both offered ships to me. My father will be defeated no matter what you offer."

6

BAKUR SAT NEXT TO EINAR, PICKING AT THE PORRIDGE THAT Gyda served them. She had shared a welcome cup with Einar, so now he and his men were her guests. Her respect for the gods should prevent her from harming them, but Einar did not trust her very far. He ate with a will, until he noticed Bakur's lack of appetite. "What troubles you?" he asked.

"My father taught me that corpses are unclean, and must be buried before the sun sets on the day of their death," he said. "I will not be easy until they are in their mounds."

Bakur's face was tinged with green, and his hands shook. He was hardly older than Einar, and had seen less battle. At least Einar had gone with Ivar and some of Harald's sons to clear out raiders in the barrier islands. In those small skirmishes, he had learned to trust his sword and his speed.

He put his hand over Bakur's and squeezed it. "You did well today," he said. He met Bakur's eyes for a moment, and then looked up to see Gyda standing over them.

"My servants have prepared the bathhouse for you," she said. The amusement on her lips irritated him.

Einar let Bakur and Uffi use the bath first. As the sun rose higher in the sky, he began to nod off where he sat, slipping into a dream in which his limbs entwined with Bakur's, dark and gold together. In the way of dreams, his father appeared, and though his mouth did not move, he still spoke words of reproach: Einar must put aside boyish things.

I will never have a wife, Einar told him wordlessly. Why do you deny me this?

The lash of his father's scolding lacked any words at all this time, and Einar screamed out his frustration, and woke with his throat hurting from unvoiced rage, and Gyda's cool fingers on his hand. He was still aroused and angry from his dream, and her touch made him think of her binding his wrists earlier.

"Your friends are done with the bath," she said.

He thanked her tersely and went to cleanse himself. Afterward, he found that Bakur and Uffi had already fallen asleep on pallets in the hall, and joined them in a deep slumber that lasted until the smell of hot food woke him again.

Einar rubbed his face and pushed aside the curtain to see a long table set up for a feast. He smoothed down his sleep-rumpled hair and joined his companions near the fire for some ale.

Gyda sat down next to Einar to share his cup, an honor to him. Younger women, with similar coloring to hers, joined Bakur and Uffi, laughing with them. These must be Gyda's nieces, Harald's daughters.

"What are your intentions, my lady?" Einar asked Gyda. "Your husband will return, and my brother and his forces will be here tomorrow."

"I am not wed," Gyda replied sharply, "and if your King Harald had protected me better, I would not have needed to—" She broke off and gave him a very false smile. "I am ready to go to Harald. Will you not trust me? Even after I helped you kill Frode's men?"

"Ride with me, alone, to my brother's camp, and then I will trust you," he said. As much as Einar enjoyed his brother's company, he enjoyed this as well, being on his own, relying on only his wits. His father had not spent his youth with an army behind him. He, too, had to win with cleverness and bravery.

"It will take some time to make ready to go to Vestfold. And who will guard my fort while I am gone?" she asked.

"You may leave your men behind—in fact, if you want Harald to trust you, you must."

"What if I simply keep you captive and never venture forth?" Gyda asked. "We have stores here to last—well, perhaps I should not tell you. You might grow to like it here."

Bakur was whispering something in the ear of the girl by his side.

A tide of foolish jealousy washed over Einar; Bakur should mean nothing to him beyond being a follower he must protect. He looked over at
Gyda, sitting by his side. She was as beautiful as a snowflake, as dangerous as a blizzard. Einar had rarely composed poetry about women, but
he thought she might merit it—except Harald would not want the truth
of this meeting to be shared. His skalds would tell the story of a loyal
bride who, if she needed to be killed, would die by mischance in an attempt to rescue her from her kidnappers. They would never tell the true
story of this Gyda, mistress of Hordaland and the fates of men.

"If you never let me go, what harm in telling me?" Einar asked, after
a long pause. If Gyda wanted a siege, she would get one. Ivar would go to
Harald, and though Gyda could escape while Ivar's force was gone, she
would have to live in the foothills and hide when they returned. "And it
does not matter how deep your stores are," he added. "Harald's armies
can last longer."

"Can they last through a winter in the mountains, though, with no
shelter?" Gyda asked. "I can send raiding parties over the wall during the
long nights, and I have allies in the mountains."

"My brother and I can kill your betrothed for you, as we have killed
his men," said Einar. "Then you may still be able to save face and marry
Harald."

"You will have to kill his family too," said Gyda. "Do you have the
stomach for that?" Her voice was light and teasing despite the grimness
of her words.

"Depends how big his family is, I suppose," Einar replied, imitating
her tone. "But you are right—we do not want a feud, so we must kill the
whole family. I trust there are no children to kill as well—no children
of yours?"

Her expression did not change, which Einar took as confirmation
that she did not have children with this man. No woman could think on
the deaths of her children without a flinch.

Gyda's servants brought dishes of food for the table on trays of wood
and in soapstone bowls. The seats filled with men of fighting age, more
than Einar had counted before, enough to match the warriors in Ivar's
party. Gyda introduced the older man who sat to her left as Omund, the
captain of her forces in Hordaland. He nodded and gave Einar a speculative look.

Gyda took up a drinking horn from the table, and let the servant behind her fill it to the brim. She gave a toast, saying, "A feast is pleasing in the eyes of the gods even when the guests are few."

She took a sip from the horn and handed it to Einar, her fingers brushing his. He knew he was expected to drain the whole horn to prove himself a man, but he was hungry and it would make him drunk, and perhaps foolish, when he needed his wits. He took a sip and then offered the horn to the captain Omund. "You do me so much honor I must share it. Your Omund is a hero of more renown than I, I am certain. Let him drink deeply, and if he cannot drain the horn, my men will help."

Omund took the horn and emptied it in one long draught.

"You are a strange boy," said Gyda, after they sat. "How old are you, truly?"

"I have seen nineteen summers," he said.

"So young," said Gyda. "But when I was your age I was betrothed, and queen of Hordaland in all but name."

Einar tried to remember his father's advice: do not be as other young men, do not be too protective of your pride. Easy to hear his father's lessons, harder to avoid rising to Gyda's baiting, protest that he had fought other battles, beyond what she had witnessed.

A skald took up a song about Gyda's father and kept Einar from having to respond. His eyes rested upon Bakur again.

Gyda spoke in his ear, "I see you watching my foster-daughter Signy and your man. Would you prefer a younger woman by your side?"

"Not unless you have one as beautiful as yourself," said Einar, a rote compliment.

"Or would you prefer to be sharing that young man's cup yourself?" Gyda asked.

Einar controlled his anger with more difficulty this time but still replied evenly, "Do you doubt your charms, my lady? I am honored to have you sit with me."

When Einar was done eating, he rose and recited a poem he had composed the previous year about Harald's oath to conquer Norway and then return for Gyda's hand. He improvised a verse about how Harald always fulfilled his oaths and expected others to do the same.

She smiled slightly when he was done and took a sip of her ale. Einar sat down again next to her. "I have seen you a few times before, I think," she said. "King Ragnvald's firstborn son, but not by his wife, passed over as his heir."

Einar wondered why she wanted so much to goad him to anger. Was it to give her warriors an excuse to kill him? "That is so," he said.

"Tell me, does it trouble your father that you are known as the most handsome and able of his sons?"

"I am not—" Einar began, hotly, half rising, ready to defend Ivar. He had seen Ivar and seen his own face in Hilda's silver mirror, and knew she lied. He stole a glance at her. The smile she gave him reminded him that he was facing an adversary as fierce as any warrior he had ever fought. "Did your father mind that you were born a girl?" he asked instead.

"Every day," said Gyda. "But don't you want King Ragnvald to make you his heir?"

Einar's mother was no thrall or peasant but a renowned beauty, mistress of kings and jarls. Many men would have made him heir, though not King Ragnvald, who had promised his wife that her sons would be his heirs and no others. Einar had heard this question whispered when he went to Nidaros or Vestfold, and heard it from men who would bait him in the practice ring. He had learned to ignore it.

He wondered if he should say yes, and hear what she would promise him to make that true—but he liked her, even with her baiting, and did not want to hear her offer him his brother's life. "My godfather, Oddi, tells me that no joy comes to kings, and recommends avoiding the notice of the gods," he answered.

"I think you will attract the notice of the gods wherever you go," said Gyda. She put a hand on his forearm and left it there, her cool fingertips on the skin of his wrist.

Einar had little experience of women—he had been with a thrallwoman once, and regretted it, not wishing to father a child who would grow up in bondage—and moments of pleasure with other boys had seemed safer. Gyda could not mean anything by her touch, except to make him nervous. She had been betrothed to Harald for many years. He wondered if she had taken a lover in all that time. Ragnvald had told Einar he thought not, thought Gyda too cold to want a man, but she did not seem cold to Einar.

"Why are you trying to anger me?" he asked. "You will not solve any of your problems by having your men kill me."

She looked at him thoughtfully for a moment, and then said, "My father was ill for a long time, so long I thought he might go on being ill forever. I wish he had." Her cheeks were flushed now from the ale she had drunk from the cup she shared with him. "His death has brought many wolves to my door, and the only way to keep them out has been to invite one in to protect me."

"So you are married then, my lady?" Einar asked.

"Not yet," said Gyda. "It has been my fate to have long engagements, and to set the men I betroth difficult tasks. I have asked Frode to bring me the heads of seven mountain bandits who have been troubling me. I gave him their names and distinguishing marks, so he could not come back with just any heads and try to fool me."

"He sounds like a farm cat, bringing songbirds to his mistress," said Einar. "How many has he brought you?"

"Six. You see, you have come just in time."

"This is too much like a tale, my lady. Seven bandits, six heads, the hero come just in time . . ."

"Are you a hero then, Einar Ragnvaldsson?" Gyda asked with a thin smile. "Will you make a song from this, golden poet and warrior? You and your brother are already like something from a poem."

"I have sworn by gods and by the fates, and by my love for my brother and respect for my father's wisdom that I will protect him and die for him if I must. Perhaps someone will one day make a song about it. That is all the inheritance I hope for." He rushed his words. He rarely spoke so plainly to anyone.

"You are a hero then," she said quietly.

"Yes," he said. "I am a hero from a tale, and you are a queen from a tale, and a bandit king goes off to kill seven bandit brothers—"

"I didn't say they were brothers."

"Yes, but it's better that way. I will make a song of it, and like all songs it will be mostly pretty lies, to distract from the uglier truth beneath. Unfortunately, I will have to change your name, and perhaps—yes, I will make you a giantess from a hundred generations ago, so no one will know that you even thought of betraying King Harald."

"Giantess?" Gyda asked, arching her eyebrow. "Do you wish to insult me?"

"Elf queen, then," he said.

"Do not sing it of me. I did not betray King Harald, but sent Frode out with a task he can never fulfill. He will only find a man matching the seventh bandit's description in a pool of water, for it is himself."

+ + +

EINAR WOKE IN the dimmest part of the night too restless to sleep, and went outside. The sun was only an orange glow on the southern horizon. He felt peaceful, even with so much hanging in the balance: Gyda's decision, Ivar and Dagfinn holding Gyda's men captive somewhere near the fort. Tomorrow they would arrive and show their strength. He could not tell what Gyda wanted, but she did not seem to want to kill him, at least.

The cool, motionless air felt good on Einar's sleep-warmed skin. He passed by a barn and heard the animals snoring within. Atop the fort's earthwork wall, he saw a silhouette of a slim woman. It could only be Gyda; no other woman in Hordaland, and few in all Norway, held themselves with that grace and strength. It seemed like fate that she had been woken by the same night spirit as he.

Einar crossed a plank bridge over the inner moat and climbed up to join her on the wall. She waited until he had reached her side before turning to look up at him. Then she turned back to the darkened plains before them. Einar could not discern where Ivar's camp might be in that midnight dimness. Perhaps they had hidden in one of the bands of forest that separated some of the Hordaland farms from one another. Perhaps they had learned something from Gyda's men that made them go back to Harald. In this mild night, Einar could not bring himself to worry.

"You could not sleep, my lady?" Einar asked quietly. He did not want to break the peace of the darkened plain.

"I am thinking of too many things," said Gyda. Her voice sounded like the wind sighing through the fields.

"There is not so much to worry about," said Einar. She seemed so different now; he wanted to put a hand on her shoulder to comfort her, as he would have his little cousin Freydis. "In the morning, my brother will come, and you can welcome them, and when this Frode comes, we will kill him."

She sighed. "I expected to be able to play this out a little longer. Every day until I marry Harald is another day I am queen." That was what she wanted, then, to keep her power.

"You will still be queen when you are married," said Einar. "Many of his wives live with their families, on their ancestral lands. Harald would not deprive Hordaland of its queen." Harald might not even notice his new wife, from what Einar had heard, but he would not reveal Harald's weakness and half-abdication to Gyda.

"He has sent his sons and armies," she said. "I expect you want to leave someone here to guard Hordaland while I am gone."

"To keep it safe," said Einar. And to occupy one of Harald's sons, to keep him from threatening Ivar's inheritance. Now he saw the price—Gyda's rulership.

Gyda turned to face him. "Harald will keep me by his side," she said. "He will want to show off his most famous bride. I will once again be queen in name only. I never wanted . . . I have escaped a woman's fate for so long and now—you are not the messenger I expected, Einar Ragnvaldsson. I think . . ." She put her hand on his arm as she broke off with a little sob. The tears on her cheek reflected the moonlight. Her loneliness pulled at something in him.

"I am sorry to bring you sadness, my lady."

She took a deep breath, which moved her hand slightly on Einar's arm. "You have seen me cry, which none of my subjects have ever done." She pinched the light fabric between thumb and forefinger. "You should call me Gyda."

"Gyda," he repeated.

"My last free night," she said. "Do not leave me." Einar stood still, uncertain. Was she offering what it seemed—and to him?

"I won't," he said. Gyda moved her hand from his arm to his chest, cool against his heated flesh.

"Or do you prefer the company of men entirely?" She smiled up at him, a little brokenly.

"No," said Einar gruffly. "You are beautiful to me." He wondered what his father would make of this—would a night spent in Gyda's arms make her more likely to surrender or less?

"Few men are indifferent to my beauty," she said, and it did not sound like vanity. "It has been one of my weapons, but I suppose it will fade one day, like the strength in your arm."

The sadness in those words did make him want to embrace her, but still he hesitated. "You were right—I know little of women."

"How different do you think it is?" she asked. "Touching a woman?" She moved her hand up to the open neck of his tunic.

"I think women want gentleness," he said.

"Do men not want gentleness sometimes?" Gyda asked.

Einar had shied away from gentleness when it was offered, fearing that it would unman him. He feared to accept it now. He touched her tears with the edge of his sleeve. She put her other hand to his jaw and ran her thumb along the hair there, close cropped to disguise its sparse coverage.

He touched her hand, and then took it from his face, holding it in his. "I think King Harald will want his queen untouched," he said.

"Are you rejecting me, Einar Ragnvaldsson?" Gyda asked, a hint of steel in her voice.

Einar swallowed. "I think there is nothing you might wish from me that you must buy like this," he said. "I cannot keep you free from both Frode and Harald. You must choose one."

"And I will, tomorrow," said Gyda. "Go back to your lonely bed, if you like. This was a foolish wish of mine."

He could, and tomorrow they would both pretend this had never happened. It was what his father would advise, but his father had not re-sisted his mother, and Einar did not want to go, to return to his celibate life at Ivar's side, and live with only the memory of her touch on his face. "Then it is a wish I share," said Einar.

She looked up at him, wonderingly, and then drew his face down to hers, touching his lips with her own, tantalizing him until he could not resist deepening the kiss. Yes, he wanted this, a far more dangerous pleasure than a stolen moment with Bakur. "Why me?" he asked when they broke apart.

She smiled slightly. "You are beautiful to me, like a new-forged sword. I want my own choice before . . . you remember the tale, I promised my-self to Harald when he and his forces besieged this fort."

"And made yourself the most famous woman in Norway," said Einar.

"And bought myself twenty years of freedom," she corrected. "I am as close to a virgin as my life has allowed. I have power, but I have never had a choice in that."

"Nor will you in the future," said Einar, understanding, a little. His choices too were limited.

"Yes," she said. "I will—I will surrender myself to your Ivar tomorrow, and with my men, you can destroy Frode and his followers. If my scout Radulf's signals were right, you will have enough men. And I will go to Harald."

"They say he is good at pleasing a woman," said Einar.

"And so I will be pleased and played upon, like all of his other wives, and forgotten as quickly." She turned back toward him, so he could see her eyes blazing in anger. He reached out to her.

"I could never forget you," he said. She caught his hand and pulled him to sit down in the tall grass of the slope next to her. She reached out to him and he kissed her again, feeling clumsy as he never did with a sword in his hand, and when they bumped noses, Einar broke off laughing.

"We are not very good at this, are we?" he asked. He moved his hands over her arms, her shoulders, her back. She had little softness to her, was instead a creature of lithe strength, like an animal of the forest.

"That was my sister's duty," said Gyda. "She bore Harald three daughters and a son." She laughed. "My sister bore the son I should have had. I have never taken a lover for pleasure. I feared what would happen if Harald should find out."

"And now?" Einar asked.

"You have already said you will hide the things I have done to keep my land safe. I believe you can hide this as well. But still, if you do not want . . ." She slid a hand up his thigh. He wanted her badly, foolishly. He tried to think of all the reasons he should not, that he could not have this—even if both of them kept it secret.

"What if you fall pregnant?" he asked.

He met her gaze for a moment. She looked up at him, and then her eyes traveled from his face down his body. "You are tall and comely and golden-haired. No one would ever know, not even you or me." She pulled her hand back. He rolled her on top of him, and pulled her down to kiss him again.

"What should I—how can I please you, my queen?" he asked.

"Gyda," she said, guiding his hand between her legs.

There was more clumsiness and laughter before they found their way together, with her still on top of him so her clothes would not be mussed by the ground. His homespun would show dirt less than her bright silks. Even when they had both had their pleasure, he did not want to leave off touching her. Her skin was as smooth as marble, and cool to his touch.

"I wish we did not have to hide this," he said while she was still astride him. "I have heard of Irish queens who took consorts, young men who fought for them while they ruled, and were replaced when they grew too old."

Gyda's speculative smile made Einar grow hard again. He should not have done this, but he had, and knowing she wanted him too made him feel giddier than a strong drink. He moved inside her, and she grinned with delight, rocking to meet him.

"I chose well," she said, her voice low and throaty. When he finished again, she rolled off him, running her hand over his side and then his hip as she went, stoking his hunger for her even as she slid away.

"Let us speak plainly, and not of tales and songs," she said. "I am not a fool—except perhaps in this moment. I know my only choice is to go with you and marry Harald."

"He will let you be queen again, and send an army with you to keep you safe." He had to clench his fists to keep from pulling her onto him again, to feel her skin again under his hands.

"With one of his grown sons to command it, and I will no longer be queen in truth. You know it is true."

"Is that not better than war and death? Do you see any other way through?" he asked.

She sat looking out at the field again, which was lightening as the sun rose. She looked over her shoulder at him. "Perhaps, if you were the one to command Harald's troops here. Would you be content to serve a queen?"

"I am sworn elsewhere," he said. "Where my brother goes, I go."

"I must meet this prince whom you esteem so highly. Anyone you think worth . . ." She shook her head. "But you command him."

"I do not," Einar protested. How quickly she went from woman to queen.

"You do. He may not know it but—you came here and left him behind. Is it not true that out there, on the plain, he obeys your instructions? You lead him and let him think he leads you. I have met your father a few times, and he does the same to everyone around him. He will never be led."

"But you want to lead me," said Einar. That troubled him less than her words about Ivar. His brother was to be king, not him. He had sworn before the gods and his father that the task of his life would be supporting him.

"I think we could lead together, if you can arrange to be sent to Hordaland with me. Your brother can come, if he must." She stole a fleeting kiss and began to arrange her clothes. "You should stay here until dawn. Then none will suspect."

"Will we . . . ?" Einar began. Would they have this again, even after Ivar came? It did not seem likely. He should not even ask.

"If we can," she said. "There may be a way."

7

THE WEATHER IN VESTFOLD WAS MILD IN THE DAYS LEADING up to the midsummer celebrations, so the morning after her arrival, Hilda joined the young women of Harald's court outside. After a long winter, and an uncomfortable journey from Tafjord, she longed to sit in the sun, to ease the aches in her body that had come from Rolli's difficult birth and never left her. The servants arranged a circle of chairs in a brightly lit clearing. The women gossiped of marriages and childbirth while Hilda listened with half an ear.

"And what do you think that Finnish woman does to keep the king so happy?" she heard one of them ask, a tiny blond girl with fine features marred by deep pockmarks from a childhood illness.

"I'd like to know that," said another, plain, tossing her dark braid over her shoulder. Hilda wondered if she thought she would need bed tricks to keep a husband happy.

"She must be a witch," said a third. "Someone should kill her before she enchants his manhood away."

"Perhaps she already has, and that's why he hasn't been with any of his other wives," said the first girl, giggling.

"Children, that's enough," said Hilda, though she too would have liked to know what hold Snaefrid had over King Harald. She knew it troubled her husband. Ragnvald wanted to admire Harald and found it difficult when Harald had not taken up a sword or held court to give justice in years.

The girls gave Hilda tolerant looks, and began talking of other things.

Some were daughters of rich Vestfold farms, sent to Harald's court to gain favor and husbands, while others were the wives of prominent warriors and jarls. Hilda recognized some of them from her visits to Nidaros.

She raised her head when she heard shouts from the harbor, and set down her spinning. A newly arrived ship might bear Ragnvald, or perhaps one of her sons. She had not seen Ragnvald in nearly a year, and she longed even more to see Rolli. Such a big, happy lad. No matter how stout she grew, he still picked her up and swung her around whenever he came home from his little sailing trips. Her other sons belonged to Ragnvald, his heirs and pupils, the boys he wanted to mold into men, but Rolli had resisted that molding, until his father let him choose his own way.

When Hilda came within view of the shore, she saw a man stumbling up the hill, carrying a body in his arms, his guards following uncertainly after him. Once he reached the soft, pine-needle-covered ground beyond the harbor's edge, he fell to his knees and set down his burden.

Hilda picked up her skirts and trotted toward him, gritting her teeth at the pain in her hip. She had grown nearsighted enough that she could not make out who it was until she was quite close, and then she saw that the man had the colorless hair and narrow face of Aldi, steward of Sogn. It was his own son whose body he brought to Vestfold's shores.

"Oh, Aldi," said Hilda, rushing to his side.

Aldi knelt beside his son's body, touching his face. The boy was the same age as Thorir. The wispy beard on his jawline was lighter than the skin that had gone a grayish blue since his death. The body's mouth was opened, and the lips purple. Hilda did not want to look, but her eyes were drawn back again and again, to check that it was indeed Aldi's son, not one of her own.

Aldi's shoulders shook silently. His men stood around him, shifting on their feet, looking anywhere but at Aldi's grief. Hilda bent down and touched Aldi's arm. A man could accept comfort from a woman that he would not from another man, and she had known him for a long time.

He looked up at her, his eyes red and cheeks streaked with tears. "Of course," he said bitterly, throwing off her hand with a shake of his shoulders, "Ragnvald's wife. I cannot escape your cursed family. You sow destruction wherever you go."

Hilda dropped her hand to her side. "What do you mean by this?" she asked.

"You—your son did this," he said.

"Which son?" Hilda whispered. "Who do you accuse?"

"Your giant of a son—Rolli," said Aldi.

Hilda's stomach clenched.

"He attacked my ship, and killed my Kolbrand," said Aldi.

"Where did he go from there?" Hilda asked.

"I do not know, nor do I care," said Aldi, "except to hope that justice finds him. I will accept no less than outlawry for this."

Outlawry—her boy to be outlawed, cast out from his family, cut off from his ancestors. Outlaws had no kin to rely upon or to intercede with the gods. Their only chance of surviving was to fight for foreign kings in foreign lands or become raiders. Hilda hated to think of her gentle boy killing men and stealing their goods.

She knew the law, though. "If you accuse him in error, it will be you who is outlawed," she said.

"It is no error," Aldi shouted. "Your son did this, just as your husband killed my father."

Hilda shivered from the breeze off the water. Ragnvald had set in motion the events that led to the death of Aldi's father, though he had found his end on the sword of King Hakon. Aldi had sworn not to take revenge on Ragnvald, his father having killed his murderer in the moment of his own death. Still, men always wanted more revenge. Ragnvald's guilt would make him feel pressured to give Aldi all he asked for and more.

"Old King Hakon did that," said Hilda. "I know you are grieving, but your accusations are dangerous."

"You know your husband caused it, just as he is behind this— depriving me of my heir so Sogn will go to his sons."

"You are steward of Sogn, Aldi Atlisson," said Hilda. "And it was always meant to pass back to my son Ivar, when he wed your daughter."

"Wed Dota to the brother of her brother's murderer?" Aldi laughed bitterly. "Never."

Hilda began to say something else, but stopped when she felt a hand on her shoulder. She turned to see Oddi standing by her side. He had brought some of Maer's guards with him. "How can I help?" he asked her in a low voice.

"This man's son needs to be buried," said Hilda. "Bring him to Ron-hild. Her women will wash and prepare him."

"Not you," said Aldi to Hilda, his voice poisonous. "If you touch him, he will bleed and you will keep him from his rest."

She looked down at Aldi's son again. A shaft of light through the trees gave his skin a golden glow, and Hilda saw the boy he had once been, one of many tearing around a Yuletide feast with her sons, now dead before even reaching manhood. Darkness gathered at the corners of her vision. One of the girls put her hand on Hilda's elbow and helped her walk toward the hall.

✣ ✣ ✣

HILDA LAY DOWN on the pallet in her dim chamber. It stank of the food that rotted among the rushes, of dogs and cats and mice, of damp wool and the mud that filled in chinks between the hall's boards and made up the floor beneath the planking. It smelled of sweat too, men's sweat, women's sweat, the sweat of rutting, of drunkenness, and of the livestock that spent the winter heating the hall with their bodies. Hall smells usually helped her escape into sleep, but this time, when she lay down, the dull weight of fear settled on her chest.

Rolli was in trouble, her boy who wielded a man's strength. Hilda remembered when he, no more than three, had come to her with a dead kitten in his hands, killed by too-rough play. He had learned to control his strength, but this seemed to her another boy's mistake. Ragnvald was harsh with his sons, often too harsh; he might not help Rolli. He had treated Einar as a man, and potential enemy, since the child learned to speak. He treated Thorir with contempt and Rolli with wariness. Only to Ivar had he given the gentle guidance that a child needed.

Hilda lay on her pallet until hunger forced her up. She took a piece of bread from the kitchen and returned to her bed while feasting contin-ued beyond the curtain. She listened to the clatter of dishes, the bark-ing and fighting of dogs over scraps, the cries of children. She was alone here, with neither sons nor husband, and now one of her sons had been accused of murder. Harald would outlaw Rolli when he emerged from his bower long enough to pass judgment.

Or worse, his uncle Guthorm would do it. Guthorm hated Ragnvald for supplanting him in Harald's affections, and would not hesitate to sentence Rolli harshly.

The songs of the poets were full of women who counseled their menfolk, brought about peace and good outcomes, but Hilda could bring herself to do nothing but lie in bed, only rising for a meal each evening before hiding again under her blankets.

On the morning of her third day in bed, Harald's mother, Ronhild, woke her, flinging the curtain aside and standing over her.

"Are you ill, Lady Hilda?" Ronhild asked. She was nearly as tall as Hilda, though not as stout, with broad shoulders and solid hips—a woman who could birth a man as big as Harald. Hilda felt a tide of helpless sadness tugging at her again—Ronhild had a giant son too, but hers was a king, not soon to be an outlaw.

"Did you hear about my son?" Hilda asked, her voice coming out like a croak.

"I did," said Ronhild. "I have also heard that your son told Aldi the death was by mischance, and further that Aldi brought no witnesses to the death."

Hilda sat up. She knew the law, but it seemed a thin thing, made merely of words, next to the certainty of Aldi's dead son. "The law says there must be witnesses," Hilda said. "Aldi has Kolbrand's body, and says that Rolli admitted to causing his death. But he has no witnesses. No very harsh sentence can be pronounced based on those facts."

Ronhild nodded. "I have heard that you know the law as well as any man. So what are you going to do?"

The question felt like a weight pressing Hilda back into bed. "Wait for my husband. He will know what to do," said Hilda.

"Will he?" Ronhild asked.

"Of course," Hilda snapped.

"At least get up," said Ronhild, wrinkling her nose. "Your absence has been noticed." She turned and let the curtain fall closed behind her.

✦ ✦ ✦

HILDA ROUSED HERSELF for dinner that night and sat next to Oddi— Oddbjorn Hakonsson—once Ragnvald's truest friend. Now he lived in Heming's court at Yrjar in Halogaland, far to the north. He had grown fatter over the years, as Hilda had herself, and no more handsome, but she still found him appealing, a man of cheer and appetite.

"My lady," said Oddi, his voice full of surprise and pleasure when he saw her. "You do me honor by sitting with me."

"Ragnvald has not arrived yet," she assured him as she filled his cup of ale and took her seat next to him. He seemed to relax on hearing it. Since the breaking of their friendship, he and Ragnvald gave each other a wide berth, and when they spoke publically it was with an elaborate deference that reminded her of nothing so much as how former lovers behaved with one another, which would have amused Hilda had it not given Ragnvald so much pain.

"But Aldi Atlisson has," said Oddi gravely. "I have heard."

Hilda settled into her seat and took a sip of the ale, sweet and nutty from the wheat used in its fermentation. "Yes," she said. "But let us not speak of that now. Tell me, are you married yet?"

"When you are already taken?" Oddi asked playfully. "How could I?"

Hilda enjoyed his flirtation. Few men had ever bothered to be gallant to her. "You would be an excellent father—I would still like to meet sons of yours one day," she said.

"Oh, I'm sure I've left some here and there," he answered. She gave him an exasperated look. "I do have a son in Yrjar—a good lad. Too good, I think, sometimes, for Harald's Norway. Or to have me for a father."

Hilda put a hand on his arm. "I'm sure that's not true. You have been a good uncle to my sons."

"That's easier," said Oddi.

They ate dinner and talked of inconsequential things. There seemed so many subjects she must avoid with him: Ragnvald, of course, but also Harald's long absence from Norway's affairs, the upcoming wedding with Gyda, and the thing Hilda's mind kept dwelling upon—the murder of Aldi's son.

"You are excellent company," said Oddi after he had finished his food and tossed his trencher to the dogs. "But you are unhappy. Tell me of your sons. I would hear your news. We can leave young Rolli for last, if you prefer."

"Ivar is a man now, with a full beard," said Hilda. She could not help but be happy to speak of him. "And of course he goes nowhere without

Einar. Like—" Hilda cut herself off. She had almost compared them with Ragnvald and Oddi, which would only sadden him. "As if they shared one soul," she said instead. "Though Ivar does not have Einar's head for poetry and the law. When my father lay dying these years past, he taught the law to me, and Einar stayed by my side."

"So you are a law-speaker now?" Oddi asked.

"I am no Svanhild Sea Queen," said Hilda. "Women cannot be law-speakers." She hated the thought of standing up before men like that, though she did like the way the law fit together, strands of words and ideas interlocking almost like poetry.

Oddi nodded. "What of your other sons?" he asked.

"Thorir is with his father, and Rolli—you are right. I fear for him."

"I wish I could reassure you," said Oddi, "but he has been party to a great crime. Aldi will demand justice."

Hilda had lain abed so long to avoid hearing anyone say that to her. If Oddi believed it, it must be true. "What is your advice?" Hilda asked. "Ragnvald—he will not—"

"I do not know what your husband will do," said Oddi, the warmth fled from his voice. "He protects those with little need, and abandons those who need him."

"Are you glad then? To see his son brought low?" Hilda asked, her voice choked.

Oddi shook her head. "No, never that. But I would advise you to look for aid elsewhere than your husband."

"Who?" Hilda asked. "Who would help me? Perhaps you are wrong about Ragnvald. He would listen to you, if you spoke for Rolli. Say you will try."

Oddi sighed. "I will—if I can. But if he truly listened to me, we would still be friends. Is there no woman who might help—Ronhild, perhaps?"

Ronhild had seemed contemptuous of Hilda when she roused her from her bed. No, not Ronhild. But Rolli sailed with Hallbjorn, Vigdis's son. Vigdis, who had borne Ragnvald a son before Hilda could. Vigdis, who had poisoned Ragnvald and Hilda's marriage before it had even begun. Hilda had hated Vigdis as long as she had known her, but their interests might be, for once, aligned.

Hilda bid good night to Oddi and went to her bed, where she slept poorly. The next day she forced herself to bathe and put on a fine dress, and then walked over to the hall that Vigdis presided over with Harald's uncle Guthorm. Vigdis always knew more than Hilda, and might be persuaded, or baited, into telling her.

Vigdis sat outside, for the day was fine, surrounded by young men, laughing with them. Some of them were Harald's sons, while others were merely handsome young warriors. She wore a dress of the fawn brown that had been her favorite color for years, over a blue under-dress, which made her skin and hair look even more like she had been dipped in honey.

"My lady Hilda Hrolfsdatter," said Vigdis as Hilda approached. She stood and bowed deeply. "You do us honor. Please take my seat."

Hilda felt awkward among the young men, and Vigdis knew it. "I came to speak with you about our sons," Hilda said. "Mine is still a boy, but yours is a man grown these past two years, is he not?" There, she had reminded Vigdis that her son Hallbjorn could face harsher penalties for the murder, and reminded these young warriors of Vigdis's age.

"Yes," said Vigdis, pressing her lips together. "He reached his majority recently. Come, it is a beautiful day. Let us walk."

The bright sun seemed to mock Hilda's black mood. She followed Vigdis behind the hall, ducking under the overhanging roof, and then along a narrow path that led by the river, covered with rough stones that pained Hilda's hip when she walked over them.

"I had not heard that . . . King Ragnvald was here yet," said Vigdis as they walked.

Hilda wondered if she imagined the yearning in Vigdis's voice. "I will not speak of him to you," she replied. She had hardly exchanged two words with Vigdis since they had both shared a roof, and Ragnvald's bed. "I have heard that there are no witnesses to the killing of Aldi's son. What have you heard?" Her face grew hot. She had not meant to ask so baldly.

"No more than you," said Vigdis. "Aldi and his men no more want to talk to me than they do to you. But . . ."

"What?" Hilda asked, stopping.

Vigdis turned to face her. "I know how you can save your son, but you must save mine as well."

"How?" Hilda asked.

"Promise me," said Vigdis.

"If you help me save my son, I will help you save yours," said Hilda.

Vigdis gave Hilda a smile, the honeyed one Hilda had always found infuriating. "Aldi would do almost anything to be able to pass Sogn down to his sons, as his father wanted."

"His son is dead," said Hilda, feeling slow.

"He has another, and he is not too old to get more," said Vigdis. "If he could pass Sogn to his son, he could be persuaded not to outlaw either of our sons. Convince your husband, and—"

"Impossible," said Hilda. "He might do it for Ivar, but not for Rolli. Everything my husband has done was for Sogn."

Vigdis cut her eyes to the side. "What if he does not have a choice?"

"What do you mean?"

"If everyone is in favor of this solution—Harald, Guthorm, Aldi— then he must. If you speak to Aldi, I will speak to Guthorm. That will be a start. By the time your . . . King Ragnvald arrives, it will already seem the most likely option, and be the harder for him to fight."

Hilda tried not to think of the enormity of what Vigdis suggested— altering the course of kingdoms for their sons. Ragnvald would never forgive her. Hilda shook her head slightly. "Why don't you speak to Aldi?" she asked.

"I was his father's concubine," Vigdis said. "He never warmed to me."

"Very well," said Hilda. "I will speak to Aldi. I do not think he will be much happier with me, though."

✢ ✢ ✢

ALDI HAD CAMPED with his men on one of the fallow fields near the Vestfold halls. He was playing knucklebones with his men, when Hilda found him. She had heard that the funeral for Aldi's son had been held while she lay abed feeling sorry for herself. She thought it better not to attend, for fear that she would offend him. The boy had been laid to rest among the noble line of Vestfold.

Hilda could never look on Aldi without seeing his father, Atli, in his face, narrow, with colorless hair and eyes. His father had been difficult, a clever trickster, a fierce raider, and an expert swordsman. He had been able to turn even his defects into advantages, and he had died storied and honorable. Aldi was a more stolid type. He seemed determined to be the opposite of his father in many ways, staying close to his home in Sogn.

"Greetings, Aldi Atlisson," said Hilda.

"You would do better not to talk to me," said Aldi. He sounded more weary than threatening.

"We should speak," said Hilda. "I want justice to be done." She spoke truth, of a sort; it could not be just to punish a boy like Rolli, far younger than the age of manhood, no matter how tall he stood. Aldi jerked his chin at his men, and they picked up their knucklebones and moved the game away, out of earshot.

"What justice can you offer?" Aldi asked.

"Should not Hallbjorn Olafsson be punished for this as well?" Hilda returned. Aldi had fixated on Rolli as the one at fault because of his long-buried anger at Ragnvald.

"They should all be punished," said Aldi. "They took my men as slaves and your niece, Freydis, as well. Such depraved young men do not deserve to live."

Hilda felt a chill. She had not thought of her niece, Freydis, who she assumed had been left behind in Sogn. "Who did they take as slaves?" she asked hollowly.

Aldi named some servants and a few warriors. "They would rather die than live as slaves, so you can probably add their lives to the cost of your son's misdeeds," he said.

"That is indeed a great crime," said Hilda. "But my son is not yet of age for a man's punishment. And what good can it do you to have him outlawed? It will not bring your son back."

"The gods demand justice. If I must lose my son, why should you keep yours? Be glad I cannot demand his death, though it will find him swiftly when he is outlawed and every man's hand turned against him."

Tears sprang to Hilda's eyes. "I do not understand men," she said. "You have suffered the pain of your son's death, and your wife will as well, so you want to add more pain to the world?"

"My pain will be less when you feel it too," said Aldi.

Hilda wiped her eyes. Her crying would not move him, only remind him of his greater loss. "Harald will not grant lifelong outlawry for the son of his most trusted friend. The most you can hope for is a few years and a wergild," she told him. "I do not want my son outlawed. He is destined for great things—a seeress has told me he will be the most famous of my sons."

Aldi flinched—it had been cruel to remind him that his son would never earn a great name. But he must understand how much Hilda would give to spare Rolli.

"Have you come here only to wound me?" Aldi asked.

"I want to negotiate," said Hilda. "What do you want to let my son go free, to bind yourself and your line against vengeance?"

"What do you think?" Aldi asked belligerently. "What should I be paid?"

"Sogn," said Hilda. Another woman might haggle, but Hilda only had one thing to offer. "Your father claimed to be its rightful ruler, and now you are only steward upon it, holding it in trust for my husband. Your sons will only ever serve my sons"—and die upon their swords, Aldi must also be thinking—"but one of them could be king in his own right."

"If one of your sons does not kill him first," said Aldi bitterly.

"If I can convince Ragnvald to give over Sogn to one of your sons, will you relinquish all claim against mine?" Hilda asked. "And Hallbjorn?" she added, belatedly. If she and Vigdis managed this, Hallbjorn would deserve his freedom.

"King Ragnvald would never do that," said Aldi, though he wore a curious expression. He had long desired Sogn, as his father had before him. "He would rather give up Maer than Sogn. It has always been thus, and he is not a man who changes his mind."

"There are ways," said Hilda. "Do I have your word?"

"Yes," said Aldi quickly. "Sogn is a fit wergild for my son. Shall I swear? Do we need a witness?"

"Not as long as I can trust your word," said Hilda. She felt dizzy. Ragnvald would hate her for this. He might even divorce her. But if she saved Rolli from the enormity of his crimes, it would be worth it.

8

THE KITCHEN IN THE ORKNEY TURF HALL WAS BLISTERINGLY hot on the morning that the servants baked bread for the week. Freydis felt foolish and dazed from the fire, as much as from Hallbjorn's kisses. An uncomfortable heat flooded her body when she looked at him or thought of him, very different from the pleasant warmth she felt when thinking of Einar, and too much to bear in the blast from the oven.

"What can I do to help?" Freydis asked the cook.

An old woman handed Freydis a quern for grinding grain; she took it, and sat next to the girl who had shared her pallet before. "Where were you last night?" she asked.

"It looked like your bed was full enough," said the girl.

"I didn't want him there," said Freydis.

"Didn't look that way," the girl replied.

"Please, come back tonight." Freydis blinked away the tears stinging her eyes.

"I've a man, and I don't want him jealous," said the girl. "I'm staying far away."

Freydis looked around the kitchen to see if anyone would help her, but their gazes seemed to slide off her as though she did not exist. When her tears began falling in the quern, someone took it away from her.

The girl put her arm around Freydis's shoulders. "What can you do? He's a handsome man. Better to give him what he wants than make him force you."

Freydis shook her off and ran outside. The cool air felt good on her face, and she took some long breaths that helped her stop crying. She saw Hallbjorn and Rolli walking together, and hid under the hall's eaves, where the grass from the roof nearly met the ground.

"She's only a child," Rolli was saying.

"You said she had seen nearly fifteen summers," Hallbjorn replied.

"Yes, a child," said Rolli.

"She could be married soon," said Hallbjorn.

"She's always been small," Rolli protested.

"Everyone is small to you. Don't you think her father will be more likely to help her husband than Ragnvald's son?" Hallbjorn asked.

Rolli laughed. "You think I should marry her? No, she is too young and skinny. One day I'll be a great sea king and marry a foreign princess."

"I meant me," said Hallbjorn. Freydis breathed shallowly, and squeezed her eyes shut. That explained Hallbjorn's interest: she had little value in herself, but she was a connection to Solvi Hunthiofsson, and even to the king of Norway through one of his queens.

"What if Thorstein is right?" Rolli asked. "What if Solvi Sea King has become a useless old man who can give us no help?"

"Thorstein doesn't want us to turn viking and compete with him," Hallbjorn replied.

"Perhaps he was right," said Rolli. "Perhaps my father—"

"You swore that we would share the blame. You agreed we should pursue the ship."

"It was your idea." Rolli sounded like a petulant boy.

"So this is your loyalty." Hallbjorn spoke in a harsh whisper. "You will go back to your father and tell him it was my fault."

Rolli was silent. Freydis strained to hear.

"Give me your permission," Hallbjorn said as he and Rolli walked farther away from her. "Then if you leave . . ."

Freydis edged out from underneath the hall's overhang. Hallbjorn was striding away from Rolli, who stood and watched the men cutting turf on the slope above.

Freydis gathered her courage and approached Rolli. "My lord cousin," she said, giving him the sort of curtsy that she had seen peasant women give King Ragnvald when they went to him for justice.

"You don't have to . . ." Rolli mimicked the motion. "We grew up together."

"Does that mean we're grown now?" Freydis asked, half to herself. Rolli looked impatient. "Cousin, I wanted to speak to you about him. Hallbjorn." She swallowed. She did not like saying his name; it felt like a transgression, like a spell that drew her closer to him even when she wanted to put distance between them. "I heard what Hallbjorn said. I think he will . . ." Her cheeks burned with shame. "Your father would not want me spoiled . . ."

Rolli looked at her appraisingly, making her feeling even more uncomfortable.

"As a marriage prospect," she clarified. Perhaps she did wrong to bring up King Ragnvald. She looked at Rolli's feet. She had found it far easier to speak on Dota's behalf, to offer herself as hostage instead. "I think you will be more easily forgiven . . . or rewarded—yes, rewarded—if you can help keep me safe."

"We are, none of us, safe here," said Rolli. She felt his eyes searching her face and kept hers down.

"I am not old enough for marriage," she whispered. "I have only seen fourteen summers."

"Have you begun your courses?" he asked.

Freydis felt as though her shame would choke her. "Only a few months ago," she mumbled.

"You are a woman, then," said Rolli decisively. "Old enough for marriage by law." He had learned some of the law from his grandfather, Freydis remembered, and was very proud of it.

"Most women have seventeen summers or more before marriage," she said quietly. "There is a proverb that goes: 'It is a danger to marry too young for—'"

Rolli interrupted her. "You sound like my father with your proverbs. Don't worry—Hallbjorn wants to marry you, not spoil you. You will not be shamed."

Freydis shook her head. "I just want him to leave me alone."

"Better him than some other man," said Rolli.

He sounded so much like the girl in the kitchen that Freydis grew hot with fury. "You should at least bring me to my father first, if you won't protect me," she said.

Rolli balled his hands up into fists. Freydis feared for a moment that he would hit her; but no, Rolli guarded his temper well, for his size and power meant that even a casual blow could kill.

"I am coming to you for help," Freydis pleaded, her voice thick with frustrated tears. "You are my eldest relative here—my only relative on this island—so you must be my guardian. Do you give me to him? Will you at least ask for a bride price so I am not shamed by marrying a man below my rank?"

"We are all free here," he said. "Do as you wish."

Freydis began to cry again. She felt as though she had done nothing else since her capture. She was Rolli's captive, and at Hallbjorn's mercy. She had less freedom here than when she was in Sogn, ignored by Aldi and his family. "You don't understand," she said thickly. "I need your protection."

"You will have Hallbjorn's protection instead," said Rolli.

✝   ✝   ✝

THAT EVENING FREYDIS dined in the kitchen with the other women, and then waited upon the men. Rolli and Hallbjorn sat with Thorstein and Rolli's uncle Egil at the head of the table. They all ate quickly and messily, seeming like animals in a burrow under the dirt ceiling of the turf hall. Hallbjorn, at least, had better manners, though perhaps he only ate neatly for Freydis's benefit. She felt his eyes on her often. If it had been Einar pursuing her this way, she would have been happy, and they did look very similar. But Einar would not have injured her, enslaved Aldi's men, or forced his kisses on her.

Freydis brought a heavy wooden platter back to the kitchen, and when she returned with more ale for the men's cups, they were arguing.

Egil sat close to Rolli, who was turned a quarter away from his uncle on the bench. "You should stay here, Rolli," Egil was saying. "There is no place for a man to be free in Norway, not with Harald as king."

Rolli turned back toward him slightly. "I heard you were outlawed when you fought against Harald at Hafrsfjord. That you broke your oath of loyalty to Harald, which you had given personally."

Egil jutted his chin forward. "There is no room for men of ambition in Harald's Norway. What land will be yours?"

"The sea," said Rolli, spreading his arms wide and half knocking Egil off the bench. He smiled and turned red, and then tucked his long arms back in.

Rolli's man Arn called out from lower down the table, "They say as many as a third of ships bound for Iceland are lost in storms."

"We could raid from here," said Rolli.

"No you couldn't," said Thorstein, speaking up for the first time. "These islands do not support many men, especially not men as big as you."

"He's right," Arn put in. "Harald means to clear the raiders out of the Orkney Islands, haven't you heard?"

Thorstein snorted. "But he doesn't come," he said. "Why do you think that is? Because no one can navigate these islands except the best sailors, who know them well, and even then the weather can turn against them in an instant."

"We are not the best sailors," said Arn. "All the more reason to go back."

"All the more reason to go on to Iceland," said Hallbjorn.

"Your father will protect you if you go home," said Arn to Rolli, sounding desperate. "What good is it to have such a famous father if he can't help you protect your friends?"

"I don't want him to protect me," said Rolli. "He has told me often— he did not have a father's help to make his fate."

✛ ✛ ✛

FREYDIS HID THAT night, sleeping in straw among the cows, and in the morning could not rid her nostrils of the dairy stink. The cook wrinkled her nose when she arrived to help, though the old woman in the kitchen gave Freydis a friendly smile.

As Freydis helped serve breakfast, Hallbjorn brushed by her, finding her waist with his fingers, a sensitive place that made her squirm and blush miserably.

Storms blanketed the island all day. When breakfast was over, Freydis took some mending to a small chamber full of wool where a few women servants gathered. A peat fire smoldered in one corner, giving off thick black smoke that made Freydis's eyes sting. When she stood up straight, her head brushed the ceiling.

She went outside in the afternoon and let the rain lash her skin.

The wind blew from the south today, and the rain was warmer than the wind that drove it. She closed her eyes and tilted her face toward the sky, letting the droplets wash over her, imagining she was home in Tafjord, standing by the spray of a waterfall. She had wanted a bath since even before Rolli attacked Aldi's ships, but the idea of disrobing made her feel too vulnerable. Perhaps if she reeked, it would keep Hallbjorn away.

The hiss of the rain kept her from hearing his approach until he was close enough for Freydis to feel his warmth as he blocked the rain from reaching her. She opened her eyes and saw him standing on the downhill slope below her.

"Are you a daughter of the sea goddess?" he asked. "Ran's daughters glory in wind and rain. I think you might be." He pulled on her head scarf and freed her hair so it started to gather rain as well.

Freydis turned to snatch it back from him. He retreated from her, and she chased him for a moment, and then stopped. She did not want to lose her dignity any more than she already had.

"Why are you doing this?" she asked, anger making her voice thick.

"I didn't mean to upset you, young Freydis," he said. "Here, you can have your scarf back." He placed it back on her head, and ran his hands over the sides of her hair, then tied it carefully on the nape of her neck. The heat of his touch on her cold neck made her shiver. Her eyes were level with the open neck of his shirt, a hand-spun of an indeterminate color, not rich, but clean at least, and he smelled clean too, like grass and fresh washed wool, and warm.

"Where are you going in this weather?" he asked.

She did not answer. She no longer wanted to bathe. The rain droplets made his skin shine. The feeling of freedom that the rain gave her had fled with his coming.

"Sweet Freydis, why do you torment me so?" he asked her. "Why are you frightened of me?"

So many reasons rose up in her that she felt as though if she gave any of them voice she would scream. "What do you want of me, Hallbjorn?" she asked.

"I want to be in your bed and to be your husband if you will have me. I have your cousin's blessing and we sail to your father now—will he object?"

"King Ragnvald would," she said.

"King Ragnvald killed my father and robbed me of my inheritance," said Hallbjorn. "And he is your father's enemy. We are, both of us, unwanted. We belong together."

"Why?" she cried. "I am too young, and I have—I can gain you nothing. I am worth nothing, except perhaps as a hostage." She looked up at him, and admitted, "My father does not know me."

He stepped in close to her and tipped her chin up to face him. His resemblance to Einar seemed like another aspect of his trickery. She felt as a hare must when a fox stalked it. If she ran he would pursue, and press her again. Better to give in to this, to meet him at least part of the way. He leaned down and kissed her softly, the way he had that first night. "I remember you do not like rougher kisses, Freydis. I will be gentle with you always."

"You hurt my shoulder," she said, laying her hands on his chest as if to push him away, but she put no strength into it, only rested them there. Would it be so bad to have this handsome, strong man protect her? She might aim higher, or she might fall to worse.

He reached out to touch it, and she flinched. "I am sorry for that," he said. "If I had—just know I am sorry for that."

He kissed her again, and a warmth spread through her that she mistrusted as much as she did him. "Sleep alone tonight and I will come to you and show you great pleasures. There is none to object."

When Freydis went back to the hall, the cook sent her to a stream where some of the women were bathing, enjoying the warm rain. Freydis stripped and washed herself, and resolved that she would not sleep where Hallbjorn could find her.

That night, though, she could find no servant willing to share her pallet, and after the rains that dampened the inside of the turf hall, even her cat, Torfa, had gone to sleep in the warmer confines of the kitchen and yowled when Freydis tried to move her. She waited in the kitchen until she thought the rest of the hall had fallen asleep, but as she made her way to the cow byre, Hallbjorn stepped out of the darkness to take her hand.

He was a black shape, outlined by the hall's only light from the embers in the fire. All smelled of peat and earth, as though she were underground. His closeness made Freydis's heart hammer with the fear of a trapped animal. She held still as he kissed her neck, put an arm around her and slid a thumb across her breast.

Perhaps it would be better to get it over with. Hallbjorn meant to have her, and to torment her until he did. He was gentle now, and he promised gentleness, but she had felt his blows and knew he had cruelty in him too.

He pressed his hand between her legs, and she felt pleasure from his touch. A part of her did want him, he was right about that. Perhaps this was why the women of Tafjord had warned her against being alone with a man, of listening to a man's praise.

Why should she fight him any further? She let him lead her to her empty pallet. He lay down next to her under the blankets, and put his hands where he wanted them. His fingers became more insistent, adding burning with their pleasure. He slowed when she murmured protests. She knew it would hurt eventually; she had listened to enough gossip to know that.

He made room for himself inside her, and pressed in, giving her some pain but also a pleasure that made her cling to him. She tightened her thighs on his waist, and he covered her mouth as he thrust into her and she made little cries against his fingers. Tears leaked from her eyes but still she rocked against him, and felt bereft when he stiffened, stopped moving, and slipped out of her.

He put his hand between her legs, touching the wetness there that they had made between them, and then he whispered in her ear again. "Perhaps I have made a son in you tonight, Freydis. If not, I will try again."

The words twisted in her stomach while her body betrayed her and she lifted her hips to press against his hand, wanting firmness rather than his too-soft touch. He kissed her forehead and left her to sleep alone.

✢ ✢ ✢

SHE WOKE THE next morning feeling sore between her legs, an uncomfortable sweetness and shame. It had not been a dream. As she walked toward the kitchen, her body reminded her of the reality of Hallbjorn's touch. Her clothes rubbing against her skin seemed like both too much sensation and not enough. When she saw Hallbjorn at breakfast, her face heated to a fever brightness, and she turned away.

She was walking back from the stream with a bucket of water for washing, when the old woman from the kitchen appeared. Her face was as wrinkled as an old apple, her eyes deep set, her eyebrows and eyelashes all gone.

"Freydis Solvisdatter," she said. Though Freydis had seen her before, she still wondered if this woman was one of the hidden folk, undying and inhuman, come out of the crumpled cliffs that resembled the wrinkles on her face.

"I am she," said Freydis.

"I am called Runa," said the woman. "You will be gone from here soon. Or you can stay, and hide on one of the outer islands. You can find a new home here, away from the foolish boys who have captured you."

The words woke a hunger in Freydis that she had buried under all her other miseries—a longing for her true home, Tafjord's cliffs, and Alfrith to guide and teach her. She had to take a deep breath before her voice would obey her. "You are too late," she said bitterly. "He has—I am already spoiled."

Runa laughed gently. "Is a ewe spoiled by a ram?" She shook her head. "No. You can be hidden here. Your captors can never search every island. They will dash their little boats apart first."

Even through Freydis's distress, she understood what Runa was offering. She was still a valuable hostage, and those who hid her would suffer for it. "No," she said, shaking her head sadly. "Rolli is my kin, and my best chance to go home."

"Kin, and not kin," said Runa. "You will never go back to your home. I have seen you returning here, but never there."

Her words seemed to have the force of prophecy, making Freydis feel rebellious. "You do not know me, old woman," said Freydis. "Now let me be."

Runa stood aside and let Freydis carry the water past her. She smelled of herbs and sweat, old woman smells, not like Freydis imagined a spirit would. She was still thinking of Runa's words that night, when Hallbjorn came to her again. She could hardly bear his touch, still stinging and burning from the night before, but he moved her and used her as though she were some possession of his, to do with as he wished. She had felt like someone else's property her whole life, moved from Tafjord to Sogn, then carried off to Vestfold, with no one asking her what she wished. At least Hallbjorn wanted her.

He and Rolli had continued to argue over the following days about whether they should stay or go on to Iceland, and came to blows one afternoon, nearly a week after they had arrived in Orkney. Freydis heard the commotion outside the kitchen door and went out with the rest of the servants to see what was happening.

Hallbjorn was shoving Rolli away from him. Rolli stumbled back a pace, clenching his fists. Hallbjorn looked like a child next to his huge-ness.

"Coward," Hallbjorn spat at him.

There had been something hesitant in Rolli's movements before; now that fell away, and he drew his sword in the space of a heartbeat. Freydis had forgotten how quickly he could move when he wanted to. His size made all of his movements look slow and deliberate, but he was a good fighter, better than many grown men, both fast and strong.

"You have been a friend, Hallbjorn, but I will kill you if you do not apologize," Rolli growled.

Freydis did not feel her usual fear as she ran between them crying, "Stop this. You are friends—sworn brothers. Why are you fighting?"

"I have learned something my father must know," said Rolli.

"What is it?" Freydis asked.

"Halfdan Haraldsson has made alliances among all of Harald's ene-mies. They are massing in Skane."

"You have only your oath-breaking uncle Egil's word for that," Hall-bjorn replied. "You want to hide behind your mother's skirts again."

Rolli advanced again. "Apologize, or I will make you," he said.

Hallbjorn pulled Freydis to him. "Careful, my dear," he said, holding her around the waist. To Rolli, he said, "I apologize. But think, Rolli, my brother, we go to Iceland and Solvi Hunthiofsson, the great sea king. We will be raiders. Great raiders. You will only be punished if you go crawling back to your father."

Rolli had begun to sheath his sword as Hallbjorn made his speech but withdrew it again as he finished. "You apologize and then insult me again in one breath. I should kill you and take my cousin back."

Hallbjorn moved Freydis in front of him and held her close to him so the whole of his body pressed along her back. Rolli started toward them, and Freydis felt something cold touching the skin of her neck. Hallbjorn's dagger. The cobwebs that had crowded her head over the past few days seemed to part, cut by Hallbjorn's knife. She deserved better than to be a pawn between these two. She should have run away when Runa gave her the chance.

"I do apologize," said Hallbjorn. "You are not . . . what I said."

"But now you threaten my cousin," said Rolli.

"She is my wife," Hallbjorn insisted. "Or next thing to it. I have had her maidenhead, and even now it is likely that she will bear my son. Go if you must, but I cannot let you take her."

"Is this true, Freydis?" Rolli asked.

"Don't let him hurt me," Freydis cried. "Rolli, please."

"Did he rape you?" Rolli asked.

She shied away from thinking of what they had done together, but no, she had feared him forcing her, and so she had allowed it, in the end. She began to cry, then stopped when Hallbjorn's knife scratched her neck. "Please don't leave me with him. You are a king's son. You owe me your protection."

"She had me willingly," said Hallbjorn, talking over her. "I will bring her to her father, and marry her in Iceland. I will be a good husband to her."

Rolli looked uncertain again. The onlookers' eyes seemed to burn into Freydis's skin. They knew her shame. Still more would know of it if she returned to Norway with Rolli.

Thorstein pushed through, his red hair a beacon in the crowd. "What is happening here?"

Both Hallbjorn and Rolli began yelling at the same time, Hallbjorn gripping Freydis tighter again in his anger.

"Stop, stop," said Thorstein. "I am ruler here. You will obey my laws while you are on my land."

"He wants to go back to Norway and beg his father's forgiveness," said Hallbjorn.

"As well he should," said Thorstein. "That is what I have been telling him."

"What about me?" Hallbjorn cried. "He may be forgiven, but I doubt I will find as warm a welcome. My friend who got me into this mess is leaving me."

"Rolli, if you would be a sea king, you must do right by your friends and followers," Thorstein said. "Hallbjorn, stop threatening this girl.

Rolli, put your sword away." He looked skyward. "Odin save me from foolish boys."

Rolli sheathed his sword, and Hallbjorn took the dagger from Freydis's neck. She wrenched free of his grasp, sobbing as the pain in her shoulder flared again.

"Girl, is this true? Has he taken your maidenhead?"

Freydis's face flamed. "Yes."

"Then he should have the chance to go to your father and ask for your hand. Both of you have spent too long here, eating my stores. Be gone on the next tide, and you may find welcome the next time you come here. Stay, and I promise your welcome will be short indeed."

9

EINAR DID NOT SLEEP AFTER HE RETURNED TO GYDA'S HALL but lay on his pallet, listening to the steady breathing of the other men, feeling weightless. In the morning Gyda, just as Einar had instructed, bid the great doors to the fort opened, and walked out at the head of all of her warriors to greet the force that Ivar and Dagfinn brought.

Einar signaled to his brother that he was safe. The sun was dazzling. The red-gold tendrils of Gyda's hair, tossed by the wind, kept catching his eye. He should have been tired from two nights with little sleep, but instead the brightness of the day and the broad expanse of grass before him matched his feeling of boundless potential. He wished to be in Gyda's arms again at this instant, and not for a moment of pleasure, but because he had not known a woman could be like her: as bold as his aunt Svanhild but far more beautiful, untouched by time except in the wisdom it gave her. A woman who seemed to have been waiting twenty years for him.

When Gyda and her followers came within earshot of Ivar and Dagfinn, Einar called out, "Princess Gyda is troubled by rebels in the hills and she needs our help." Belatedly, he remembered that Dagfinn and Ivar were supposed to be leading this endeavor. "If you agree, we can join forces with hers to root them out."

"Excellent," said Dagfinn. "We will do this and then bring my father's bride to him." His gaze fixed on Gyda in a way that Einar did not like, following the motion of her arm as she pulled her hair over one shoulder.

"Do not forget the feast that I will make for you in my hall," said Gyda.

"Of course not, my lady," said Ivar, ever gallant. "I will fight the harder knowing you will be our hostess after we win."

Gyda led the warriors into the fort. Once they were inside, Ivar pulled Einar into an embrace. "I thought you would be a hostage!" he said. "It is a blessing that she has agreed so easily."

"She is a woman," said Dagfinn scornfully. "You gave her far too much credit."

Einar smiled thinly. "That woman is perhaps the only person in Norway who has ever gotten the better of Harald."

"It's true," said Ivar. "Our father told us the story."

"He betrothed her!" Dagfinn protested.

"To save face," said Einar. Their father had told them how Gyda had said she would not marry Harald until he had conquered all of Norway, and thus spared her fort a battle, assured her place in the skalds' songs until the end of time, and bought twenty years of rulership for herself. Ragnvald did not want his sons to underestimate her. Had she only lain with Einar on the thin hope that he could give her back her district even after her marriage? Would she have tried seducing Ivar, or even Dagfinn had they come instead? Yes, Einar decided. Especially Dagfinn. She would pit father against son—throw another contender into Halfdan's rebellion to help herself. But she had wanted Einar too, she could not have counterfeited that so well.

"We must disperse ourselves among Gyda's troops to make sure they do not play us false," said Einar. "If you do not believe her capable of betrayal, believe it of her captains."

✣   ✣   ✣

GYDA'S WARRIORS AND those who had traveled with Einar made ready for battle the next morning in the shade of the fort's walls. Her captain, Omund, brought their captive out of the shed where he had been left with the bodies. His face was bloodied and puffy with swollen bruises even where it was whole.

"Bitch queen," he spat at Gyda. "False woman."

"Where is Frode?" Gyda asked, untroubled.

"My king is in the mountains, and you will never get him out." One of his eyes could hardly open and his lower lip was split.

Omund backhanded the man across the face, driving him to his knees. He made a choked-off noise that turned into a sob. Einar cast his eyes down and glimpsed Bakur doing the same. He did not like to see humiliation; it bothered him far more than blood and wounds. He could too easily imagine himself, broken and cowed, driven half mad from a night spent with the corpses of his friends. Ivar did not look bothered, not because he was cruel, Einar thought, but because he could never imagine himself brought so low.

"Where is the camp?" Omund asked. "How many men?"

The captive hung his head down. "The one in the northern foothills. Fifty men."

Gyda nodded at Omund. "No trouble for our combined forces."

Ivar raised his chin. "You know the place, my lady?"

"I do," said Omund. Einar controlled his expression. Of course Omund knew where it was; until yesterday Frode had been an ally. "Be ready to leave before the sun climbs above the southern foothills."

Einar retrieved his leather armor from Gyda's hall, and returned for help tying it on. Dagfinn had the finest armor, Ivar the newest, and Einar the oldest, bitten with strikes not just from his own skirmishes with raiders, but also his father's, who had worn it as a young man, before Harald had replaced it for him with steel.

"I am glad you are well," said Ivar again as Einar did up one of his straps. "Don't do that to me again! You should have at least told me what you had planned."

"I hardly knew myself," said Einar, warmed by Ivar's concern.

"You always run ahead of me," said Ivar fondly. "Let your slow brother catch up sometimes, and have some of the glory."

Einar heard an echo of his father's criticism in Ivar's words. Dagfinn smirked at Einar and Ivar helping one another. "Gold clad in dark, dark clad in bright," he said.

Einar pulled his helmet down over his hair's brightness. "It is not a bad line," he said. "You can make a song of this battle if it goes our way."

They marched toward the foothills, following Omund. He had told them the camp could be found in a flat grove halfway up the slope of one of the mountains, with enough trees to give cover, and room between their trunks to place tents. Paths led to the camp from three directions, which would make it difficult to pin any men there.

Before the party began their ascent to the camp from the Hordaland plain, Omund stopped to give his commands to the band of warriors. "Split forces here," he said. "Three kings' sons, three forces."

"I stay with Ivar," Einar countered. With so many of Gyda's warriors among theirs, he wanted to be sure he could protect Ivar at all times.

"I'll be fine," said Ivar.

"After your scolding? No, I'll stay by your side." Then, to Omund he said, "You take one of the parties. I have sworn an oath that my brother will never do battle without me."

"I don't need a nursemaid," Ivar protested. "I want to lead alone, as you did."

"I swore an oath." Einar reached out and gripped Ivar's arm. "You swore it too, I recall—neither of us will face battle without the other."

"Very well," said Ivar. "We may face queens separately, but bandit kings together. It would anger the gods if we do not."

Dagfinn gave Einar an exasperated look. "You will not be far distant," he said.

Ivar began to say something, but Omund cut him off. "No matter. The day I need boys to lead me into battle I will rush upon a bandit's sword. I will lead one party, Dagfinn Haraldsson the other, and the third to whichever of you is in charge, young princes."

"Ivar," said Einar quickly, before another argument could come up. "He leads."

Omund nodded. "Watch for sentries," he said. "They will have those too."

The slope was steeper than it looked. Ivar and Einar had the wind to climb it quickly, while some of Gyda's warriors who did more feasting than fighting became short of breath. When the trees pressed them too close for walking two abreast, one of Gyda's warriors went ahead to show the way. They followed a deer trail between pines, dry needles brushing off on each man who passed.

A crashing noise sounded some paces distant from Einar, followed by a yell. Two men struggled in the brush ahead: one of Gyda's warriors was killing one of Frode's sentries. Or trying to—the wounded man stumbled past, before getting caught in the branches of a tree. Einar took stock of him quickly; the sentry held his fist into his stomach and his hand was slick and red—he was gut-stabbed and would not live— but his screaming would bring all of his fellows down upon them. Einar grabbed a hank of the man's greasy hair, drew his dagger, pulled back the man's head, and cut his throat, gagging at the sound the man made. He looked around to make sure no one had seen his disgust.

One of Frode's men ran out from among the trees, past Einar, his hair as oily and lank as the man that Einar killed, and into the waiting swords of Gyda's warriors.

Einar threw a dagger at one of the attackers. It caught him just below the ribs and he collapsed against a small pine whose branches slowed his fall. When Einar drew close to retrieve his dagger, the man lunged out with a club that caught Einar on the side of the head, making his ears ring.

Einar scrambled back out of reach as the man rushed forward, tripped, and landed on his face. He crawled a body length after Einar, while Einar scrabbled backward, tree branches pulling at him like enemy fingers, but the man ran out of life before he could reach Einar. With his ragged cloak stuck through with pine needles, he looked as though the forest floor had already started to reclaim him.

Gyda's captive had exaggerated the enemy's numbers, though not their skill. All were hard men who fought fiercely. Einar rolled him over to retrieve his dagger, heard a yell, and ran toward it. He reached the camp a moment later, and saw that most of the fighting had stopped with Frode's men defeated, but his brother still sparred with a man wearing rich enough clothing he must be Frode himself.

"No, he is mine!" Ivar cried out as he saw Einar approaching.

Ivar looked like a hero from a skald's tale. He fought with pure strength and hardly any feints. He was hard to stand against, Einar knew, though he wished his brother had a little more cunning. Still, Ivar was younger and faster than his opponent, who took a cut whenever he tried to penetrate Ivar's guard.

Ivar fought Frode backward until he pinned Frode against one of his tents. Frode tripped over a tent stake and stumbled. Ivar held back, waiting for him to recover and regain his footing. In any other fight, Einar would have called it cruel, prolonging the man's death, but Ivar probably thought he was being fair—on the practice ground he would never attack an opponent who had tripped, especially not when he was the better fighter.

Frode stood, holding his sword lower than before, shaking with effort. Ivar would have him soon. Something caught Einar's attention out of the corner of his eye. He did not know what it was, but he moved without thinking, running at Ivar. He did not reach his brother in time, or the item was flung imprecisely, for it passed over the shoulders of Ivar and Frode, surprising both of them. Einar drew himself up short before he crashed into his brother.

"Get out of my way," Ivar yelled.

Einar retreated. He saw Dagfinn draw his sword again and go after whoever had thrown the missile. Frode had taken the moment of distraction to grab his dagger with his other hand, and he slashed at Ivar, drawing a thin line of red across his cheek. Ivar flinched.

Frode lunged again, this time making a cut with his sword that raked along Ivar's side, severing the leather straps that held his armor and touching the flesh beneath. Ivar grunted in pain.

Einar took a step toward him; he could stop this. But Ivar did not want his help, and these wounds would be more of an annoyance than a hindrance. Now Ivar fought more desperately and Frode attacked with renewed spirit, riding the duel's turning tide. Frode's energy did not last, though, and in his next advance, he stumbled over a root and crashed into Ivar's waiting sword. Not a killing wound, but Ivar's next one was, half severing Frode's neck. His blood sprayed Ivar, covering his face in a ruddy mask.

"Why didn't you help me?" Ivar cried as he wrenched his sword free. His voice and jerky movements showed his panic; Ivar had known mortal fear today, perhaps for the first time. "He was going to kill me."

Einar walked over to him, trying to see the wound in his side. "What did you think a battle was about?" he asked. He felt a strange brew of emotions: fear for Ivar's life, annoyance that Ivar had not trusted him, anger at Ivar for almost getting himself killed, for not being as fierce a fighter as he might be. But he felt, too, a sense of satisfaction and possessiveness; it would be a while before Ivar doubted him again, or tried to find a way to escape his protection. "You told me to go away. I was doing as you asked. Obeying the order of my lord, even."

"You—" Ivar began, then took a swaying step and sank to his knees.

Einar eased him down to sit on the ground. He could not read Ivar's expression with his face so covered in blood, and that bothered him more than anything else. "Come," he said. "Let us get you cleaned up, and see if you need a healer."

Ivar looked down at his armor, hanging off his flank. He pressed his hand to the cut and flinched when his fingers came away painted a brighter red than the drying blood on his face.

"You'll be fine," Einar told him. "Some pain when you move, until it heals, nothing more, I promise. You'll be fine." He looked around. A steep, rocky stream provided running water for the camp. Einar went to wet a rag from the pouch he wore at his waist, and returned to clean the blood from Ivar's face.

"I was doing well until that—someone threw a rock."

"Yes," said Einar. The blood was sticky and didn't want to come off. "That happens sometimes."

"And then—he wounded me. He could have killed me." Ivar twisted to touch the wound on his side again and hissed at the pain. Einar felt a ghost of Ivar's pain in his own side, as though the oath they had sworn had made them share this as well. He would have taken it from Ivar if he could.

"No," said Einar, "because you fought fiercely, knowing you could die. You should fight every fight that way. Your opponents surely will."

Ivar nodded, still touching his wound. Einar helped him take off his armor and tunic, to better see the wound, stark crimson on pale flesh. Not too deep, but not shallow either; a flash of white that might be a rib showed when he moved. Einar wondered what their father would say. At least Einar had a defense for this—his father could not want Ivar weak. This should have been a good lesson for him today.

"I need to find someone to sew it up," said Einar.

"Don't leave me," said Ivar.

"I'll be back soon," Einar promised.

Frode's camp was a pitiful thing, with battle over. Gyda's warriors pulled the dead to the side, so they could not foul the stream. A few of their own had fallen as well; Einar could tell who they were from their clean clothes and well-trimmed beards. The rest were Frode's.

Some of Frode's servants and thralls had been corralled against a thicket of brambles. Einar averted his eyes when he saw Dagfinn having his way with one of the captives, who was almost entirely hidden by his bulk.

An old hag was sitting by a fire on the outskirts of the camp, stirring a boiling pot. Einar approached her cautiously, with his sword drawn.

"Grandmother, do you know how to sew up a wound neatly?" he asked.

She turned and showed Einar the other side of her face, which was burned, seamed and rigid with scarring. Her hand too, the one that held the stick in the fire, was hardened with scarring into an immovable claw. She had no eye on that side, and no lips either, just a narrow slash of mouth, which stayed immobile while she chewed on a twig.

"Never mind," he muttered. This woman would be useless for anything but her current task.

"You do it, young Einar," he heard her say in a creaky voice. "You will not have many more chances to help him."

"What?" Einar asked. The woman could be a witch, to know his name. He should not be credulous, though, half scarred and half whole, she looked like the goddess Hel, queen of the dead.

"You heard me, Jarl Einar," she said, "and you know I speak the truth."

"I know nothing of the sort, hag," Einar replied.

"I speak the truth," she insisted. "You know that you fear and crave this future."

"What future is that? I am no jarl."

She laughed, a dry cackle, and poked her stick into the fire once more. "There is only one escape from this fate," she said, and turned toward him, faster than an old woman should, the stick raised up, its glowing tip coming toward his eye.

Einar thrust his sword into her without thinking, driving up under her ribs, and into her heart. She fell back, her hands clutching at the blade, and then went still. Einar pulled his sword free and saw that the unscarred side of her face wore a smile.

He stumbled and fell as a fierce wave of dizziness gripped him. Her burning stick lay smoldering on the leaves. Einar stomped it out.

Dagfinn walked over, still doing up his trousers. "What did that woman do to you?" he asked.

"She said things . . ." Nothing Einar could reveal.

Dagfinn gripped the woman's face to turn it toward Einar. Her open mouth showed within it broken teeth, and the stump of a tongue that had been cut off many years earlier. Dagfinn looked at Einar. "She couldn't have said anything at all."

10

RAGNVALD TIMED HIS ARRIVAL IN VESTFOLD FOR THE EARLY morning, when most of Harald's warriors would still be abed. They often feasted into the night, fell asleep late, and woke even later with aching heads. The proverbs might say that too much drunkenness was a shame to a man, but it was not a shame that many feared.

The sun was still hidden behind the hills around Oslo Fjord when Ragnvald sighted the Vestfold settlement from his ship. He woke Sigurd, who had been dozing on one of the rowing benches.

The breeze grew stronger and Ragnvald drew his cloak around his shoulders. It was made of a soft black wool that Hilda had spun and woven herself. They had been married for nearly twenty years, though for long stretches he had been far away from her. Their marriage had long, slow tides to it, the absences and meetings both sweet and bitter.

Among the small group that had gathered to watch the ship's approach, Ragnvald saw Hilda's solid figure. At times he had regretted his choice of wife, wishing for someone who could be a partner in keeping Norway's peace, but now Svanhild did that work, while Hilda made his home and raised his children. And during his recovery from Solvi's torture, when Alfrith had been the one to break and reset his fingers, he had sought Hilda's comfort and care, coming to value her more after the difficult beginning of their marriage.

The ship beached. Ragnvald climbed down and walked toward her on tottering sea legs. She gave him a worried smile that made him want to inquire further, but after accepting a kiss from him, she wanted to greet Thorir—almost a year had passed since she had seen him, and she exclaimed over how he was finally taller than her.

Ragnvald rubbed at his knuckles while she embraced Sigurd and noted Thorir's new beard. His hands always hurt from the damp of sea travel, and he had run out of the salve that Alfrith made for him, a mint rub that soothed the pain. Perhaps that was why he had lost his grip when sparring with Thorir in Jutland. No matter what, he had to face this: soon he must lay down his sword and let Ivar and Thorir take up kingship of Sogn and Maer. He would not risk their inheritances by trying to hold his throne beyond his fighting days.

"How lucky I am that you are not asleep," said Ragnvald to Hilda as Sigurd, Thorir, and Gudrod walked toward the hall in search of breakfast. "I'm sure the rest of Vestfold is."

She smiled and looked down. "Women rise early."

"You rise early, best of wives," he said.

She still looked troubled. Ragnvald called after his son, "Thorir, you and Gudrod make sure the ship is secured and emptied. When that is done, you can breakfast."

They obeyed with dragging feet while Ragnvald led Hilda out of earshot. He felt her anxiousness growing with every step. He stopped and touched her waist. "What is it?"

"I have news of Rolli," she said, in the flat tone she used when she was worried or angry. "And Hallbjorn. Aldi says that Rolli attacked his ships, killed his son, took away Freydis, and sold some of his men into slavery."

It was too much to understand at once. Ragnvald shook his head, trying and failing to imagine his happy son, only fifteen, doing these things. "And Rolli has not come to Vestfold?" he said.

"No," said Hilda.

"That makes it all the more likely this has some truth to it," said Ragnvald. "Are you sure?"

"Aldi arrived bearing his son's body. I wish he made the accusation in error, and could be prosecuted for it, but . . ." She spread her hands helplessly.

"I will learn more," Ragnvald promised.

"Aldi will ask for justice," said Hilda.

"And he must have it," said Ragnvald. "But I will know more first." Hilda's eyes swam with tears, and Ragnvald searched for some way to comfort her. "No matter what happens, I will care for him," he said. "No matter what Aldi demands, I will at least make sure he avoids a death sentence."

✛ ✛ ✛

AS RAGNVALD HAD feared, he heard no hint from Harald's warriors that Harald had emerged much over the winter. Servants brought food to his private hall and removed his dirty clothes for cleaning, but few had seen the man himself.

Ragnvald bribed a servant to let him into the outer room of Harald's hall. He heard soft breathing and low voices from the bed, which was separated from the main area by a curtain. At least it did not sound like he was making love to Snaefrid, though if he were, Ragnvald had re-solved to swallow his embarrassment and wait it out.

The servant said a few words to Harald from the edge of the cur-tain, and Harald appeared a moment later, wearing only short trousers. He shivered, picked up a sheepskin blanket, and threw it around his shoulders. Clad in a pelt, with his tangled hair spilling down, he looked like a wild giant come out of a legend. He greeted Ragnvald with a nod and sat down heavily in a chair. He was still a well-formed man, but Ragnvald noted a softness around his waist that had not been there a year ago.

"What is it?" Harald asked impatiently. "The last time we spoke, I did not think you would seek to speak with me again. Have you come to apologize to my wife?"

"I will," said Ragnvald. He had told Harald he should divorce Snae-frid and would apologize if it helped Harald to hear him.

"Is that why you have come to see me?" Harald asked. He took a sip of the ale that the hovering servant had poured. "I would not have al-lowed anyone else to disturb me."

Against his will, Ragnvald was cheered—Harald still valued him. "I have just returned from Jutland, where I was trying to make an alliance for you with King Erik," said Ragnvald.

"Did I want this alliance?" Harald asked. "Or did you seek to give me yet another task, without asking my leave?"

"If we do not make an alliance with someone across the strait, then we will lose revenues from ships passing through it," Ragnvald explained. He should have stayed home if Harald did not care. "It would not be another task, only more wealth. But I was not successful. Your son Halfdan got there before me. He has made alliances with many of your enemies, and I believe he is in rebellion against you."

"Or he is doing a better job making alliances than you are," said Harald, raising an eyebrow. "Does this mean Erik's daughter will wed Halfdan rather than Gudrod? It does not seem to matter which of my sons she weds. But you have never liked Halfdan much."

"Erik as much as told me that Halfdan has gone there seeking allies against you," said Ragnvald.

Harald waved that away. "He is sowing discontent. He would like nothing more than you, me, and all my sons to fight one another, while he gains all the spoils of the strait traffic."

"That much is true," Ragnvald allowed. If Harald would not discipline his son, Ragnvald must find some way to do it. Set him against someone equally dangerous, as he had done with Atli and Hakon? But the only person who came to mind, willing and able, was Einar, and that would mean his death or outlawry if he succeeded.

"Erik would admit to no firm decision," Ragnvald told Harald. "Ranka—his daughter—might have wed Halfdan in secret, but he also thinks of marrying her to you, or to me. He would not marry her to Gudrod."

Harald laughed. "You? You hardly know what to do with one wife."

Ragnvald smiled slightly, though Harald's words smarted. He had a wife, a concubine, and had fathered six sons, a more reasonable number than Harald's twenty or more.

"Now what is this I hear about your son Rolli?" Harald asked. "That boy was born to blunder into trouble."

Ragnvald repeated what he knew.

"It seems likely the fault is Hallbjorn's," said Harald. "But my uncle has come to see me about this as well. His mistress, Vigdis, will not like it if Hallbjorn has to take all the blame."

"I will pay the necessary wergild," said Ragnvald.

"You know that won't be enough. Aldi will ask for outlawry, and he should get it."

Ragnvald had mentioned outlawry to Hilda, but when Harald said it, casually weighing Rolli's fate, without even leaving this chamber to learn the truth himself, Ragnvald found it harder to stomach. "Then anyone could kill him," he said thickly.

"I have heard another suggestion from my uncle," said Harald. "Return Sogn to Aldi's family. Let his next son inherit. You and Aldi share a great-great-grandfather, if I remember rightly. I am sure Aldi would forgive anything to restore his line to the throne of Sogn."

"You promised Sogn to me," said Ragnvald. "You swore an oath, and restored my line." Harald put great store by oaths, and refused to let any men swear loyalty to him if they were sworn elsewhere. "My grandfather Ivar was king there until my father lost his lands. The work of my entire life has been to correct my father's mistakes and put my son on the throne of Sogn, as the gods intended."

"I thought the work of your life was to serve me," said Harald. "Yes, I swore. But you could give up Sogn for your son."

"Why do you want this?" Ragnvald asked angrily.

"There are those who say you have too much power, that you rival my own. I have heard the whispers."

Harald looked at Ragnvald in a way that made him feel as though all his rebellious thoughts had been laid bare. He bit down a reply about the other whispers, the ones Harald should give more weight, that he had abdicated his throne and been ensnared by a Finnish sorceress. "I am loyal to you," Ragnvald said. "I did not ask for Maer. It is not the land of my ancestors. You wished for me to guard it, and give up my own Sogn."

"And now Erik wants to marry his daughter to you," said Harald.

"Which I refused . . ." Ragnvald trailed off as Snaefrid emerged from behind the curtain, wearing only a silk robe that molded to her body like water slipping over it.

She gave Ragnvald a shy smile, then lowered her chin so her blond hair drifted over her face. It was so fine it moved around her like a cloud rather than hanging down. Ragnvald loved Hilda's long, thick hair, smooth and dark and strong as a stout rope, and Alfrith's too, that heavy curtain of black and white that reminded him of a snow-covered forest, but Snaefrid's hair suited her. She had long, half-lidded eyes, and an overbite so pronounced it was almost a deformity, though very alluring. Her voice was soft and childish, heavily accented by her native language, the Finns' magic tongue that only those born to it could speak.

She whispered something in Harald's ear, and he pulled her onto his lap. "Do you have anything else you need to tell me?" he asked Rag-nvald, while looking at Snaefrid.

"Svanhild has not returned from Skane yet," said Ragnvald. "I am worried."

"That woman can take care of herself," said Harald. "Too well." Snaefrid kissed his neck. "Though if she does not come back before the wedding, we should send a force to get her. What else?"

"Princess Gyda is coming soon in fulfillment of your oath to con-quer all of Norway," Ragnvald told him. Snaefrid took up a hank of Harald's snarled, golden hair and wound it around her narrow wrist. Harald had always said that Ragnvald would be the one to cut that hair, finally fulfilling his vision of his hands being the ones that turned mat-ted fur to the shining fur of his golden wolf.

"You should marry Gyda," said Harald. "I'd as soon bed your sword. That woman has no softness."

Ragnvald thought of Svanhild, another woman with no softness—another woman Harald had rejected for the pliant, melting Snaefrid. If Harald would not reward Svanhild—or Gyda—with tenderness, Rag-nvald would make sure he rewarded them with gold and power. "You swore it," he said.

"You are ever my conscience." Harald held up his cup for a toast, and Ragnvald returned the gesture. "Very well. I will leave this place, if my lady lets me."

"Not yet," said Snaefrid, and drew Harald back behind the curtains.

✠ ✠ ✠

MORE SHIPS ARRIVED all through the next day, many of them deep-bellied knarrs with sails weathered dun, containing supplies for the wedding feast. Guests' ships arrived too—even Vestfold's many halls and outbuildings would strain to house all of these visitors. Ragnvald looked at the tents covering every flat patch of ground and could not help but think of all the districts of Norway left without protectors. Arn-fast guarded Tafjord for him. He wondered who watched over Sogn, the land of his forefathers—but he could not ask Aldi.

Harald did not emerge when Einar and Ivar arrived with Gyda in the late afternoon, just in time for the evening's meal. In Harald's absence, Ragnvald went out to welcome them. Einar helped Gyda down from the ship in a careful way that made Ragnvald proud. His sons were growing into far better men than Harald's.

Ivar helped one of Gyda's nieces after her, a round armful of a girl, with Gyda's sharp features still beautiful on her plumper face.

"Father!" said Ivar, and greeted Ragnvald with a hug, though he winced when he let go.

"Son, what happened to you?" Ragnvald asked.

"I took a wound fighting some Hordaland bandits in the hills," Ivar said, looking proud of himself.

"Rebels," said Einar. "They are no more. Ivar killed Frode, who called himself king." The way he met Ragnvald's eyes told him there was more to the story.

"Well done, Ivar," said Ragnvald. "Songs will be sung of you."

"Einar did more than I," said Ivar as Ragnvald turned away to see Harald's mother, Ronhild, walking down to the shore, followed by servants who carried cups of ale to welcome the guests. She bid them follow her to the feast in Vestfold's largest hall, and the men followed her.

In the warming weather, Ronhild served mostly cool food: stewed fruit, yogurt porridges, and cold roast fowl so tender and fatty a toothless man could eat it. Oddi sat by Einar, and the two of them conversed in low voices during much of the feast. At least Ragnvald's rift with Oddi had not spoiled that friendship. Einar would benefit from Oddi's example—a man who had renounced ambition for service to others, once Ragnvald, now his brother Heming.

Ivar sat next to his brother, joking with Harald's sons, and joining in the young man's game of catching at the wrists and waists of passing serving women. They called for ale, and ate more than their share of the food, in a carefree way that made Ragnvald feel a warm affection for all of them, even as he worried about their future enmity.

Ivar pulled Gyda's niece Signy into his lap. She laughed and played with his hair. Dagfinn tried to tickle her and Ivar pulled her away. Oddi was still speaking with Einar, who nodded at Oddi's words, though his gaze rested on the high table where Ronhild sat with Gyda and Asa, Harald's first wife. Gyda's face was as unreadable as Ragnvald remembered, and she seemed distracted, smiling slightly at whatever was said to her half a beat too late. She had always liked being Harald's betrothed better than the idea of becoming his wife. At least she had come more or less willingly to Vestfold—one fewer district from which Ragnvald need fear rebellion.

After several courses, Ivar banged his cup on the table, and said, "Come on, brother, tell us a tale! You are better than any skald!" Ragnvald smiled, though nothing would allay his fears that one day the two brothers would come to blows. No matter how many oaths and promises of friendship and brotherhood lay between them, how could a young man like Einar not want every reward that his abilities should give him?

Einar stood. He appeared to enjoy himself when he spoke publicly, without the diffidence that Ragnvald always felt when he had to address a crowd. Einar did not fear praise, and he liked telling a story, finding as much joy in the crafting of it as a master wood carver in drawing interlaced shapes of animals out of the lumber's grain.

"Tafjord had a skald visit from Dublin this past winter," said Einar, "and he told us the tale of the ancient Irish king Finn MacCool and of his wife Grainne and his warrior Diarmuid. It is a sad tale—would you hear it?"

Many cheered that they would. A woman sitting near Ragnvald sighed and said she would listen to any tale from such a handsome young man. Even Hilda smiled at that. Before the death of Hilda's father, Hrolf, she and Einar had both learned the laws from him, and Hilda had become much friendlier to her stepson. Sometimes Ragnvald heard them repeating the law to one another to test their memories.

"Of course we do!" Ivar called out. Einar looked down at Ivar affectionately, and put his hand on Ivar's shoulder to steady himself as he stepped out over the bench.

"Very well," said Einar. "Here is the tale as best I remember it. In days long past lived Finn MacCool, a great Irish warrior, the leader of a band of Ireland's best fighters. He had been married in his youth to a fairy woman who died, and he mourned her for many years—but that is a tale for another day. When Finn grew older, he decided he should take a wife again, and his favor fell upon the beautiful Grainne, which is also the name that the Irish give to the goddess Freya. She was as beautiful as Freya, this Grainne, with"—he glanced up at the high table, where Gyda sat, looking back at him—"golden hair whose curls could ensnare a man's heart, and eyes as blue as one of our fjords—"

"They don't have fjords in Ireland!" someone called out.

"Still, they were that blue," said Einar smoothly. How politic of him to flatter Gyda before her wedding, without Harald there to do it. She was no longer young, and must fear for her fading looks. Ragnvald looked over at her and saw her watching Einar as raptly as all the other women.

"Finn MacCool was entranced by her, and she was pleased to have the attention of so great a warrior. But at their wedding, her eye fell upon one of Finn's young warriors, Diarmuid MacAengus, and his beauty captured her, for Diarmuid was young and unscarred, with raven hair and red lips as vivid as blood upon snow, and Grainne knew she would have no other man.

"When the guests grew sleepy with drink, she went to Diarmuid's chair and told him she would wed no man but him. Diarmuid did not want to betray his king, but in truth, he did not resist very much, for Grainne was very beautiful, and the adventure of it appealed to him.

"He took her into the woods that night, where they became husband and wife in the eyes of the gods. When Finn MacCool woke, and learned what happened, he vowed he would not rest until he had captured the pair and killed them both. But Diarmuid was a popular warrior, and Finn's vow divided his force between those who would hide Diarmuid, and those who smarted at the insult to their leader.

"For years Finn pursued them. Diarmuid and Grainne never had a moment's peace. It is said that if they breakfasted in one place, they supped in a second, and slept in a third.

"Still, the gods of Ireland favored them. Rain rarely fell upon where they made their bed. Every hand was open to them, and every mouth silent when Finn came asking who had seen his runaway wife.

"Finn was an expert hunter, who, it was said, could track a deer across dry rock in summer. Eventually, in the waning of his fifth year of pursuit, he caught up to the lovers and found them sleeping in a bower of dried branches. The full moon shone down as Finn pushed aside their covering, and the light fell upon Diarmuid and Grainne, on the silver that had come into Diarmuid's raven hair, and the lines that now etched Grainne's face, for living on the run had been hard on them. Finn meant to slay them both, then and there, when something stayed his hand, perhaps the ghost of his dead wife, or perhaps his own spirit's greatness, for he knew he would not have still loved Grainne when her beauty faded, and Diarmuid had.

"Diarmuid had left his badge of membership to Finn's warrior band behind when he fled with Grainne. This Finn placed upon Diarmuid's breast as he slept, and that night, he swore to the gods that his pursuit of the couple was done."

Einar took a drink and made as if to sit down, leaving the story with an ending that felt abrupt to Ragnvald. What had happened to Diarmuid and Grainne? Did this Finn allow the traitorous couple to live in his land without seeking revenge for the rest of their lives? The clamor around him echoed Ragnvald's thoughts. Einar took another drink of his ale and set his cup down slowly, then smoothed his tunic down over his waist, still holding all attention.

"What happened to Diarmuid and Grainne?" Einar asked the crowd. "I do not know. Some say they were given land on the outskirts of the kingdom, and some say Finn thought better of his mercy later and slew them both, and then was slain in his turn, for he had outlived his skill at arms and it was time for him to die. All I know is that Diarmuid and Grainne betrayed their war-leader, but were loyal to each other, and the gods' mercy grew from that."

He bowed his head again and would not be persuaded to speak more. Ragnvald joined the throng of people who wished to give him congratulations, to beg one more scrap of the tale off him. The tale had left Ragnvald unsettled. The betrayal of an old king—did Einar mean Harald or himself?

All of his sons suddenly seemed grown beyond him: Einar with motives he could not plumb, Ivar who had taken a wound and killed a bandit king, and Rolli, his foolish giant of a son, who had committed a grave crime. Ragnvald made alliances between kings, but his own sons could not be managed.

He clasped Einar's forearm and congratulated him, then leaned in, close enough to speak in his ear. "What do you mean by telling a tale like that on the eve of Harald's wedding?" he asked.

Einar's smile disappeared and his throat worked. "Did it insult him?" he asked quietly. "He does not marry a woman far too young for him. It should be a compliment to his good sense. And anyway, he is not here, is he?"

"It is good he is not," said Ragnvald. "Though his betrothed was. Perhaps she will think you intend to carry her off." Einar shrugged and darted his eyes toward her. "It was well told, my son, though a strange choice. You must tell me what happened in Hordaland. Is there anything I should know?"

Einar pressed his lips together. "It was well we came when we did," he said. He glanced at the men and women standing around them. "There is not very much to tell, but what there is I can relate tomorrow."

Dismissed by his own son, Ragnvald returned to his seat, next to Hilda. "He is a fine boy," she said. "You can be proud of the raising of him."

Ragnvald put his arm around her waist. "I had little to do with it. He was born to be a success."

"Do you think Rolli truly killed Aldi's son?" she asked.

Ragnvald pulled her closer. "I do not know," he said. "I will do my best for him. And even—"

"What?" Hilda asked sharply.

"I will do my best for him," said Ragnvald. "You must believe that." He squeezed Hilda's hand under the table. Rolli could only be outlawed for his crime—Hilda would have to face that. If he acted as a man, he must face punishment as a man as well.

II

THORSTEIN LET HALLBJORN STAY ANOTHER FEW DAYS AT GRIM-
bister while the merchant they had followed from Norway finished his
trading. Freydis asked the cook if she knew where she could find the
crone Runa, and was told that she came and went as she willed, but she
had a house high on the hill above the settlement. Freydis abandoned
her duties in the kitchen to visit the house the next morning, found it
empty, and returned to the kitchen, both disappointed and relieved that
she need not choose. Hallbjorn might use her body, but he would also
carry her to Iceland, where Thorstein had said she would find her father.

Thorstein himself came to bid them farewell. Hallbjorn had not let
Freydis stir far from his side after her attempt to find Runa, and he shared
her bed each night. He had his hand on her still-tender shoulder when
they stood on the beach waiting for the tide to turn.

"Carry my greetings to Solvi," said Thorstein. "Tell him we finally
have a chance to defeat Harald if he comes here after midsummer."

"How?" Hallbjorn asked.

"Harald's own son Halfdan is gathering allies against him. King Erik
of Jutland has joined with him, and I hear that even King Ragnvald is
considering rebellion," said Thorstein.

Hallbjorn snorted, his hand tightening on Freydis. The touch was not
yet painful, but she felt his potential for violence in the pressure of his
fingers. "Not likely," he said. "Halfdan hates him, and I would not join
any rebellion with my father's killer."

Thorstein shrugged. "I do not think your sword will turn the tide."

"I would help defeat Harald if I had the chance," Hallbjorn protested.

"Come, and bring Solvi if you can," said Thorstein. "He's not much of a fighter anymore, but if his mind is still sharp, I would follow him."

These Orkneymen were so isolated—could they bring a war that would destroy King Harald? He and King Ragnvald seemed to Freydis as though they were part of Norway's very stones—they could not be brought down by tattered island raiders. Though she had never expected her own life would be thrown into such disarray, as it had these past few weeks. Nothing was as permanent as it seemed.

Thorstein looked over Hallbjorn's shoulder. "You had better catch the tide," he said.

They pushed off, following the merchant who had led them to the Orkneys as he continued his journey. It was strange to be back on a ship, to feel it move under her feet when she scrambled from one side to the other to avoid the sailors raising and lowering the yard. Somewhere beyond the horizon, Rolli sailed back to Norway, bringing news of what had happened. She wondered what her mother would think on hearing of her—would she care, or would she only worry about whether Freydis's fate diminished her own legend?

The wind was steadier on this leg of the journey, so Freydis was able to work her more complicated ribbon-weaving—a weaving that she would never gift to Harald's new bride now. Perhaps she could buy some goodwill in Iceland with it. Torfa batted at the strings that hung down, making Freydis smile through her worry.

They sailed north from the Orkney mainland, stopped in the Shetlands for a night, and then continued to the Faroe Islands. It took the better part of a month to sail around these small northern isles, to stop and pass news, to trade goods. On nights when they slept on land, Hallbjorn often joined her, and on nights when he did not, she stayed awake, wondering if the previous time had been the last. She still avoided him during the day, and now that he had her, he no longer tried to charm her or even talk to her. When she looked at him during the day, she did not know how she had ever thought him handsome like Einar. The differences between them made him ugly to her now.

Sometimes Freydis saw other men looking at her, and wondered if they saw her, or only her shame. When Hallbjorn came to her at night, though, her body still responded to his, turning as traitorous as everyone else who had abandoned her: Rolli to Hallbjorn, Aldi to her fate, Hilda and Alfrith sending her to Sogn, and her mother leaving her when she was just a baby.

The evening before they were to set off from the Faroes, Hallbjorn asked, "It has been a month since I first took you. Are you pregnant yet?"

"I don't know," she said. She knew she was supposed to have her courses every month, but it had only happened once, before she departed Sogn.

"Then I shall have to keep at you, my Freydis, and believe me, it is no hardship."

She ducked her head. She had not become any more comfortable talking with him, even though he had such freedom with her body. He had encouraged her to become familiar with his, placing her hands where he wanted them, but she still rarely touched him of her own volition.

She had heard that pregnancy felt strange, but her body felt strange all the time, as though it belonged to Hallbjorn more than herself. Perhaps it had never been her own. Her body had felt alien too when her courses arrived, bloodying her thighs and reminding her that she would be a woman whether she willed it or not. That was the loneliest she had ever felt until now, away from Alfrith, and the rites and wisdom that Alfrith had promised her when she became a woman.

Now her stomach twisted as the ship moved under her, and she knew her body was not her own in a new way, belonging to a new life within her, a hook placed there by Hallbjorn, an argument that said she should marry him.

As time passed without sight of land, Hallbjorn's men grew more ill at ease and whispered charms against the spirits of the deep, but Freydis felt calm, suspended out of time during the long crossing. Hallbjorn would not take her during a night that never came, on board a ship, among so many other men.

She was almost disappointed when they caught sight of Iceland. This was her father's place, the place from which he sent his raiders, the place where he had retreated. She might find a legendary warrior or an old and useless man, a father who valued her or merely another owner.

The black rocks of Iceland rose against a charcoal sky. The ship passed a bay choked with ice of purest blue, so blue it seemed as though the eye of a god looked back at her when she peered into it. Eddies of different colored water washed out from streams, this one clear as crystal, the next a cloudy white. Freydis watched these with interest, even as the swirls in the water made her stomach twist. The men behind her still spoke in superstitious whispers. Freydis murmured the prayers that Alfrith had taught her. The spirits of this land might be strange, but they could not be more alien than the spirits of the open sea.

The first night they camped on a black and empty beach. The green hills looked close, but the merchant Torveig said they were more than a day's walk from the water's edge. Hallbjorn set up a tent and pulled Freydis into it after she had washed her hands from dinner in the chilly surf. He put a hand over her taut, skinny stomach, still sunken below too-prominent ribs. She had not eaten well on this journey. She had tried to hide her pregnancy, new as it was, from Hallbjorn, but he had told her he would know, having made thralls pregnant before.

"It is my son," he said. "You are pregnant."

"It is too early," said Freydis. "I have not yet missed my courses." If she was truly pregnant, he would insist on marrying her.

"I know women," he said with a laugh. "And I know girls like you. It is a son. My son. Your father will have to accept me." He laughed again, made bold in his plans by this triumph.

"It might be a daughter," said Freydis, pulling away from him.

"Then we should make sure," he said.

She did not answer, nor did he seem to want her to. He slept next to her that night, as he sometimes did. She stayed awake until he loosed her from his arms and rolled away. Then she dreamed of the fire she had heard of that roared from Iceland's mountains, a liquid fire that burned everything in its path. She dreamed that it swept down the black slope above their campsite, burning away her and Hallbjorn, picking up their ship and settling around it, like metal around a gem.

She woke feeling as though she herself were that molten fire grown hard, metal around the gem growing inside of her. Hallbjorn called it a son, but Freydis, wrapping her hand over her abdomen, prayed for a daughter. If any of Alfrith's magic had passed to her, let it be this, the power to transmute the seed within her to a girl child, to anger Hallbjorn and set her free.

✜   ✜   ✜

ANOTHER DAY OF sailing brought them to Iceland's main settlement, a small trading town set within a wide bay. Hallbjorn asked a grizzled fisherman who sat on one of the shore rocks where he could find Solvi. Freydis stood carefully still, trying to keep her pregnancy sickness from making her vomit amid the strange smell of sulfur and more usual smells of rotting seaweed, refuse from the town, manure that ran off of fields and from byres in brown rivulets toward the water.

"The dwarf farmer!" said the fisherman. "He lives up yonder, next to Unna's farm."

"Who is Unna?" Hallbjorn asked.

"Who is Unna?" the man repeated incredulously. "Everyone knows Unna. You will be better asking for her than for Solvi. He keeps mostly to himself."

One winter when Svanhild stayed in Tafjord with her sons, Freydis had asked about her father. Her mother told her of adventures in foreign lands, and of her farmland in Iceland, which she had claimed in a ritual sacred to the gods. She had left that land behind in the care of a woman named Unna, her friend and mentor, a hard woman who bowed to no man. Unna had advised Svanhild to disobey Solvi and claim the farm in Iceland, where she and her son could live while Solvi went away to war. "I wonder if he has gone to my farm," Svanhild had mused to Freydis, "the one he did not want me to claim. It would be justice indeed if he is trapped there by a vow while I can still sail and make war."

Freydis followed Hallbjorn along a path that wound between juts of hard, broken rock twisting up out of the earth, before reaching soft green fields that looked closer to those Freydis had left behind in Norway. The settlers had carved out patches of home in this alien place.

Solvi lived on a piece of land far enough from the sea that Freydis could see only the masts of the ships onshore, and the gray horizon where sea met sky in the distance. Some thralls worked the fields, identifiable by their close-cropped hair, clothes of rags, and clean-shaved faces. Another man drove an ox that pulled a plow behind it, a simple spike that split the earth. When he turned at the end of a row, Freydis saw the ruin of his face, lips split above and below his mouth. A skilled healer could have sewn it back together better than whoever had done the work. Alfrith could probably still fix it even many years later, closing tattered lips over a cleaved-in jaw. This man was old, though, and he must have grown used to it.

"We come seeking the great Solvi Hunthiofsson," said Hallbjorn. "This is his daughter."

If those words gave the disfigured man any surprise, he did not show it, only jerked his head toward the house. The clouds lowered as the afternoon wore on. A breeze on Freydis's face made her think rain would come soon.

Hallbjorn took her arm and pulled her so she had to trot after him. She was out of breath from their brisk walk; she had not had to walk more than the length of a ship in almost a month.

When they reached the house he let go of her, and she rubbed at her shoulder. Solvi's dwelling was a small structure made of wood, one of the few Freydis had seen on Iceland where most houses were made of turf. A goat grazing on the roof climbed down and made a noise of curiosity at them.

A man who could only be Solvi emerged from under the eaves. He was as short as Freydis's mother had told her, but his smallness was still a shock to Freydis. He walked impatiently, with a stick to support him. His gait had a quickness to it that put Freydis in mind of a crab, as if his way of walking, though not the way a man usually walked, was entirely natural to him. He was older than Freydis had imagined, and had piercing eyes with wrinkles at the corners that only came from many years at sea. His features had a pleasing symmetry to them, and his hair was silver with only a hint of the red-gold Svanhild had described.

Freydis had wondered what she would feel when looking on her father for the first time. A shock of recognition, or perhaps revulsion, for songs sung at King Ragnvald's feasts made much of his deformity, though also of his skill in battle, for it was better to defeat a strong enemy than a weak. Instead she only felt helpless.

"My lord Solvi Hunthiofsson," said Hallbjorn with a bow. "I bring to you your daughter, my intended, Freydis. Freydis Solvisdatter."

Freydis searched his face for some feeling on his part, and thought she saw the lines on his face deepen.

"I have never acknowledged a daughter," he said gruffly.

A rushing filled Freydis's ears, as though she had foundered in deep water. She had not thought that she hoped for anything from Solvi, but she did; she wanted him to make her feel less adrift than she did in Hall-bjorn's power. She hugged herself, her eyes burning, and let her hand creep up to her shoulder again, which ached from Hallbjorn's tugging on it.

"Why is this girl crying?" Solvi asked him.

"He dislocated my shoulder when he took my guardian's ship," said Freydis, surprising herself by speaking. Her voice sounded sullen to her ears and she kept her eyes on Solvi's feet, which were shod in thick-soled boots. Threadbare wool wrappings covered his legs. "And then he made me pregnant. He says he will marry me but I do not want him to."

Hallbjorn whirled toward her, and hit her across the jaw so suddenly that she was on the ground before she realized what had happened. Her head spun when she raised it, so she remained sitting where she fell, holding her hand to her face. Solvi's man from the field took hold of Hallbjorn, wrenching his arms back. Freydis hoped it hurt.

Solvi had another young guard, who came from behind the house, advancing toward Hallbjorn with his dagger out. Freydis looked at Solvi. She saw an expression she recognized pass over his face—a deep and par-alyzing fear—and then quickly disappear. She had only seen a man look that frightened once before, a man who had come to Alfrith to have his infected foot amputated. She had done a good job, but still he died of fright and shock under her knife.

Solvi took a few steps toward Hallbjorn. "You bring my daughter here and then abuse her before me?" he asked, in a forced whisper. If Freydis had not seen the fear on his face, she would have found it men-acing. Hallbjorn looked frightened.

"You said she wasn't your daughter," said Hallbjorn. He struggled against his captor.

"I said that I had never acknowledged a daughter. I do so now. This is my daughter, Freydis Solvisdatter, and her mother is Svanhild Eysteins-datter. She is my true-born daughter and my heir." Solvi took a deep breath. "You say you are her intended? Based on what she said, I tell you that you are not. I say that the child she bears is not yours."

Hallbjorn spat. "Ask her—it is mine. She has spread her legs for me every night for a month. Who else's could it be?"

Solvi turned toward where Freydis still sat on the grass, tipped over where she had landed on the side of a tussock. "Tell me, daughter, what you would have me know of this business. Do you want him to be the father of your child?"

The words were so exactly what she wanted to hear that her tears spilled over again.

Hallbjorn struggled in his captor's grip. "What does it matter what she wants?" he asked. "The child is mine."

Solvi advanced toward Hallbjorn, staying well out of sword range, though Hallbjorn's arms were still pinned. "I am certain someone else can be found to acknowledge it," he said. "Or if she would rather expose it or get rid of it, that can be done. She is over-young to bear a child or to marry if I reckon the years right."

Freydis had wondered if she would be able to find the necessary herbs in Iceland, even if she could get away from Hallbjorn and take them. The herbs were dangerous and did not always work. And Freydis did not think she could bring herself to expose a healthy child, even if it came to her unwanted.

She shook her head slightly. There would be time to think more on that later. If Solvi acknowledged her as his daughter, then by law, he had to give his permission for the marriage.

Solvi gave her a look that seemed scornful, and Freydis wiped her eyes. She must answer him, if she could gather herself enough to speak. He nodded at his men, who took Hallbjorn's sword and dagger from him and flung them away on the grass. The younger one forced Hallbjorn to his knees and pulled his head up.

"You are frightened," the disfigured man said to Freydis, speaking slowly to make sure she could understand him. "But if I can speak, so can you."

His words gave her courage. "I cannot escape that he is the child's father," she said. "But if I can escape marriage with him, I would do that."

"You will have to repudiate him as the father then," said Solvi. "They are very particular about the law here in Iceland." This he added with some scorn.

The disfigured man spoke again. "I will acknowledge her child, if someone is needed."

Hallbjorn, still held captive, laughed sharply. "No one would believe that."

"So much the better," said Solvi. "It matters not what is believed, but what she is willing to claim and all of us to witness. Now, get out of my sight before my man Brusi cuts your throat."

Hallbjorn snarled. He lunged at Solvi's man, who stepped aside so Hallbjorn stumbled, flailing his arms.

"I will return for her," Hallbjorn promised. "You had better set a double guard and sleep with a dagger under your pillow. I will not let you keep me from my son."

"Should I kill him now?" Brusi asked, grabbing Hallbjorn with surprising swiftness. He wrenched Hallbjorn's head back again and held a dagger to his throat.

"Who is his family?" Solvi asked Freydis. "Would anyone avenge him?"

Hallbjorn's eyes moved wildly. He gave Freydis a pleading look, then focused on Solvi, who walked toward him with his sword out, his teeth gritted. Freydis allowed Solvi's other man to pull her to her feet.

She brushed off her dress from the ground and touched her face where it was tender from Hallbjorn's blow. She liked the fear in his eyes. If only he could be made to feel as powerless as she had in his bed.

"His father was Olaf Ottarson, who was killed by King Ragnvald long ago," she said. "And his mother is Vigdis Hallbjornsdatter, who is now the mistress of Lord Guthorm, King Harald's uncle." Hallbjorn looked at her with that wild hope again. She smiled slightly. "I don't know how much they care about him, though." He flinched.

"An enemy of Ragnvald Eysteinsson, then," said Solvi. "Pity. Had you come here under different circumstances, we might have been allies. Still, I will not kill you. Perhaps one day you will take the revenge on him that I cannot."

Solvi looked at Freydis. Her shyness returned, and she looked at his feet again, nodding. She did not truly wish to see Hallbjorn killed.

"What about my sword?" Hallbjorn asked.

"Brusi, escort him to the edge of my property and give it back to him," Solvi commanded. Brusi picked up Hallbjorn's sword and used it to prod him away, down the hill.

"Come here, to me," said Solvi. Freydis picked up her satchel, which she had dropped when Hallbjorn hit her, and walked over to him, her eyes still downcast. He put his hand under her chin and turned her face one way, and then the other. "You are not what I thought a daughter of myself and Harald's queen would look like, but I see both of us in you, and I cannot doubt it." He sighed. "I have not expected either of my children to be as they were; it should not surprise me that you are strange to me. And both my children have been timid."

Anger lit up Freydis's blood again. She had been timid sometimes, but she did not want to be. She raised her eyes to his. "I did what I must to survive," she said. "It was I who suggested we come here, rather than sell the captives south."

"Oh?" Solvi asked. "I shall have that story from you, then." He looked at her again. "Later, though. Come with me. I have a woman here who can care for you."

12

EINAR SAT IN HIS TENT, WONDERING IF GYDA WOULD FIND her way to him. Likely she could not steal away from the chambers where Vestfold's women slept. That tale had been a foolish risk, enough to make his father scold him, though not guess the reason for it. If his father should discover this—Einar imagined justifying his actions by saying that it had helped Gyda leave her fort without violence, but that had not been the true reason. He enjoyed having this secret, the love of a queen.

He saw a woman's silhouette in the door of the tent, and felt her cool touch on his ankle, then followed her out into the dimness. He knew where the Vestfold scouts patrolled, and how to pass between them. He led her down on a path that bordered the fjord and ended in a pine grove where the ground was covered with the soft needles of seasons past.

She seemed to want him ever more urgently each time they met, as the day approached that might be their last. They had no need to speak, though Einar wanted to ask her many things: what she thought of his tale, what plans she had for the two of them, a reassurance that she still wanted him. Only the moment of his release made his mind stop turning. When she rolled off of him and lay next to him on the ground, she sighed.

"I thought . . . ," she said.

"You thought what?" he asked, rolling over to face her. She still looked up at the sky, a deep midsummer blue with only a few stars visible. She sighed again.

"I thought he would at least greet me," she said. "Harald."

"Well," he said, curtly. "It is good you have me for a poor substitute." Gyda curled next to him and put her arms around his shoulders, her breasts pressing against his side, at first a cool touch that then warmed as she leaned against him.

"That is not what I meant. I only—" She broke off to kiss his neck, her hair brushing against his skin making him shiver with pleasure.

"Can this truly last, Gyda?" Her name tasted sweet to him. He wanted to say it again.

"I don't know," she said.

"And so you think to spend your last days of freedom tormenting me, trying to make me into an enemy of my king and your husband?"

"You could refuse me," she said.

"I can't," he said. "I will do whatever you want."

"Ivar has been with my niece Signy every night of these past weeks," she said. "I could insist on a marriage, especially if she becomes pregnant— she is Harald's daughter. Then you can both return with me to Horda-land, and you can be my champion."

Einar did not answer. Now that he had seen his father, and how suspicious Einar's tale had made him, it seemed far less likely.

"This will be difficult," said Gyda, leaning against him. "We cannot afford to mistrust one another. We should have no secrets."

Einar had already told her of his secret ambitions, his wish that he and his brother might both find success, that neither need eclipse the other. But he had also held back—he had not shared the witch's words, which haunted his dreams every night, or his father's plans. He was sure Gyda hid as many secrets from him.

"My brother already has a kingdom to inherit," said Einar. How far could the sons of Ragnvald's ambitions extend?

"He can rule there until it is time for him to inherit," Gyda offered. "And then . . ."

Einar felt a chill. Gyda seemed to speak with the witch's words. Ivar would inherit when their father died, something Einar could not imagine, and she herself would be old then. "I am yours to command, my queen," he said. "In anything that does not violate my oath to my brother."

She rested her cheek against his shoulder. "I command you to satisfy me again. Give me treasure against the lean times to come."

Was this how his father had felt about his mother, Vigdis, knowing the danger but unable to resist a desire that built again as soon as it was slaked? Gyda kissed his ear, his shoulders, the sword calluses on his hand, and drew him down next to her again.

They lay face-to-face this time, her leg over him, fitting them together so he could move in her slowly, feeling as though this could last forever, until he could stand to wait no longer and rolled her onto her back. He thought he saw a man's shape in the woods and froze, but Gyda raised her hips to meet his again, and his pleasure overtook him. Whoever had seen them, it was too late to change anything now.

✛ ✛ ✛

EINAR SENT GYDA from the bower first and waited until he judged she had returned to her bed before he walked back to his tent. He could not stop thinking about the figure he had seen, though no evidence of the person remained near his and Gyda's pine-needle bower. But it had not been a trick of the light, or a vision based on his fear. They had been seen. The thought made him feel sick.

He tried to put himself back in that moment, Gyda's legs tightening around him, the pure smoothness of her skin under his hands, and someone standing among the thick trunks of the old pines—a man with a light beard. One of Harald's sons? Harald himself? Einar stared up at the shadowed ceiling of his tent, trying to call up the man's face in his memory, but the more he chased it, the more it faded, until all he could remember was dark spots suggestive of eyes and a mouth. Perhaps the interloper had not recognized them either. But he could not rely on that. He would have to tell Gyda, and make sure any future meetings were better hidden.

He dozed eventually, until someone shook him awake in the early morning when the camp was still quiet, with a rougher touch on his ankle than Gyda's had been. Einar had his hand on his dagger before he fully opened his eyes and sprang toward this intruder, with a mind to make him regret waking him, but drew back when he saw his uncle Sigurd's face, his eyes shadowed by sleeplessness.

"Is your brother here?" Sigurd asked, his voice hardly above a whisper. The rest of the camp must still be asleep.

"He's found someone else's bed to share," said Einar. He replaced his dagger in its sheath.

"Come, let us talk," said Sigurd. He looked at Einar until Einar grew discomfited and lowered his eyes.

Einar pulled on his trousers. "Why are you up so early?" he asked Sigurd. Hilda had always teased Sigurd that he slept like a boy whenever he could, late into morning, no matter how much noise went on around him.

"I think you know," said Sigurd. Einar swallowed. Sigurd had been the one to see him last night. It could have been worse—one of Harald's sons—but Sigurd was loyal to Ragnvald above all others.

Einar followed him up the hill behind Vestfold's halls. Sigurd was taller than him, and set a pace that Einar had trouble matching, even though he had kept up his stamina over the long winter in Tafjord, putting on snowshoes to race his brothers up the steep slopes to the cliff tops whenever the weather allowed.

"I saw you," Sigurd said when they reached the crest of the hill. "You and Harald's queen. She is a beautiful woman, but this cannot continue."

"I love her," said Einar. "She has a plan for us."

"What can come of it?" Sigurd asked. "She is too old for you, and far too dangerous. I have asked your father to meet us here—"

"No!" Einar cried.

"I am not as clever as you or my brother Ragnvald," said Sigurd. "But think—how can this possibly end well? If anyone else finds out, both of you will die."

"So don't tell anyone," said Einar sullenly.

"If I saw you, anyone could."

"Harald will send Gyda back to Hordaland," said Einar. "My brother Ivar will marry Signy, her niece, and I will go to Hordaland with both of them."

"And live as husband to Hordaland's queen?" Sigurd asked. "You will only delay Harald's vengeance."

"We would keep it secret," Einar protested. "Harald doesn't care for any of his wives except his new Finnish witch. He will ignore us."

"He may ignore his wives, but he will not ignore a slight to his honor. Einar, please." The tone of Sigurd's voice made Einar's eyes sting with sudden tears. "I only have one son, and I fear for him every day—he is with Svanhild in Skane. If I can do something to save you, I will, even if you hate me for it."

Once, in his seventh year, he and Ivar let the hall's chickens loose, and a fox killed half of them. Their father had punished them, giving Einar five switches for every one he gave Ivar. The law punished the baseborn more severely than nobility, but Einar had not thought his own father would apply it to him. Sigurd had told him that Ragnvald was a hard man, but a fair one, and how, when he was a boy, urged on by his father, Olaf, Sigurd had once tried to kill Ragnvald. When Ragnvald killed Olaf, he might have killed Sigurd as well, but instead he called him brother, and Sigurd had been loyal since then.

Einar took a deep breath to steady his voice. "My brother spent the night last night with Gyda's niece. This plan is already in motion. If Gyda makes Ivar her heir, what is to stand in our way?"

"You are determined to do this?" Sigurd asked.

"What better future do you see for me?" Einar cried. "I will never—" He cut himself off. He could not reveal to Sigurd that he imagined a greater future for himself than always protecting his brother.

"I will tell your father unless you promise to end it. See, here he comes."

Sigurd raised his hand in greeting and Einar turned to see his father climbing the slope behind him. "I promise," Einar said desperately. "I promise."

"What do you promise?" Ragnvald asked. "Why did you call me up here, Sigurd?"

"I . . . ," Einar began. He could mislead his father more easily than Sigurd could. "Ivar was with Gyda's niece Signy last night. I thought he might like to rule Hordaland, since Aldi will refuse Ivar his daughter now. Sigurd thinks it's a bad idea."

Ragnvald rubbed his forehead. "Sigurd is right. That is the last thing we need," he said. "Already Harald thinks I have control over too many districts."

"I promise to make an end to it," said Einar.

"Well, we should discuss this," said Ragnvald. "Your ambition for your brother is admirable, but misplaced. I have news from Jutland— Halfdan's rebellion is certain, King Erik admitted it to me. And now

your aunt Svanhild has not returned from Skane. If she has been captured, we will need to take war there as well."

Einar's heartbeat began to slow back to normal. His father had not
seen through his half-truths. He was not Odin, seeing all from his high
seat.

"There was almost rebellion in Hordaland as well," Einar said. He
told his father how cleverly Gyda had played the rebels against one another, using her betrothal to Frode to do it, and how he and his brother
had defeated the last of them.

Ever since the witch's words, he had been wondering what would
happen if Ivar died, testing the thought like a sore tooth, where every
touch gave more pain than letting it alone. He thought of asking his father about her prophecy, how she had spoken to him without a tongue.
His father had experiences with prophecies—his vision of Harald had
long guided him—and might have wisdom for Einar, but her words
would awaken every fear his father had of him.

"With so much rebellion, how can Harald cut his hair, and marry
Gyda, and fulfill his oath?" Einar asked instead.

His father looked at him sharply, and Einar tried to maintain a neu-
tral expression. No, his father was not Odin, but he did see clearly—too
clearly.

"Because this is not a song," Ragnvald said. "Because the sooner Harald weds a new woman and fights some battles, the sooner . . . He must
wed her, it is foolish to suggest otherwise." He rubbed his forehead. "I
saw that Dagfinn Haraldsson returned with you."

"I tried to leave him in Hordaland, but Princess Gyda is a strong-
willed woman," Einar replied. He braced for a scolding, but his father
only shrugged.

"We have bigger problems now. You have heard of what your brother
Rolli is accused of, I am sure. People said I should have killed Hallbjorn
when he was a boy rather than foster him. But if I killed the kin of every
man I killed . . ."

Sigurd laughed. "If you did that, Norway would have only women
living in it," he said.

"And women more vengeful than men," said Ragnvald. He shook
his head. Einar glanced at Sigurd. Hallbjorn was half-brother to both

of them. "Find out what you can," Ragnvald said to Einar, "from Aldi's men, from your mother—anything that will help me save your brother."

"My brother Rolli?" Einar asked sharply.

Ragnvald looked back at him, and Einar regretted his words. He did not need to give his father reason to doubt his loyalty, not now. "Both of them, of course," he said flatly.

✣   ✣   ✣

EINAR WANDERED BACK down the hill, leaving his father and Sigurd, toward where Aldi's men camped. Before he could decide what to say to them, he saw his mother approaching, looking handsome in her blue and gold. She waved him over and he followed her to the small grove that separated Guthorm's hall and Harald's outbuildings. She pulled him into an embrace that smelled of honey and amber, then held him at arm's length for a moment before letting him go. Stray pieces of hair escaped her head scarf and softly framed her face.

"You should have come to see me sooner," she said.

Einar sighed. "Hello, Mother."

She touched his cheek lightly. "You went away a boy and you return to me a man," she added. "The years pass too quickly."

"Perhaps they do," said Einar. "How is Lord Guthorm?"

Vigdis waved her hand at the hall behind her, a jewel box with even the roof tiles painted. Valhalla itself could not have looked richer. "A storm must be coming," she said. "His joints pain him. How is your father?"

She asked casually, but Einar stiffened. She never spoke to him without trying to find out about his father and his enemies. Einar pulled out of her grasp. "It is of my brothers that I come to speak," said Einar. "What do you know of Rolli and Hallbjorn killing Aldi's son?"

Vigdis pressed her lips together. "So you are here after some business of your father's, rather than coming to see me for myself. It is always that way."

"How should it be any different?" Einar asked.

"You could stay with me in Guthorm's hall, because you love me and owe me duty."

"I have always heard it said that you are subtler with men than this," Einar said.

Her smile faded entirely, making her look far older than she had when she approached him. "Is that what your father told you?" she asked.

"You mean him ill," he said. He supposed he should prefer this naked trading of advantage to her earlier charm, but he missed her smile now that it was gone.

"A time may come when you mean him ill as well," said Vigdis.

"Then I will know where to go," said Einar.

"Yes," said Vigdis. "There are things brewing, things your father cannot prevent. If you would trust me, I could tell you how to stay ahead of them."

"Because you know so much?" Einar asked sarcastically. For a moment, Einar thought she would slap him, and he would deserve it.

"Not one of Harald's sons wants your father to keep his districts," said Vigdis. "I don't think even Harald does."

Yes, and his father had said that Halfdan was in rebellion already. Perhaps he should let Vigdis bring him in closer, in case it gave him the opportunity to kill Halfdan. He had a different mission today, though. "I will think about it," he said, more gravely. "For now—my brothers Rolli and Hallbjorn are guilty of a great crime. Is there anything you can tell me to help save them?"

"I know how this will go," said Vigdis, her voice rising. "If Hallbjorn can be blamed and Rolli Ragnvaldsson spared, it will be so. You know your father."

"He is my brother," said Einar. "They are both my brothers."

"Then you should be the one to decide between them. Ask Harald to give you the decision. He will like that solution. I will ask for that."

He should have run away when he saw her waving. He had often heard the story of how his father had almost lost Harald's friendship when he was forced to act as judge for him. "If you love me as you claim, please do not ask for that," he said.

"Why?" Vigdis asked. "Wouldn't you be fair?"

"You know it would put me in an impossible position."

"You would judge fairly. You are too much your father's son not to."

"You trust me that much?" Einar asked, discomfited by her praise.

"Yes," she said with a sigh. "You are too much like him. You would never risk your reputation by being publicly unjust."

"And my father would never ask me to."

"So you say. So you will do this? Decide their sentences?"

Even his father would like this, but he could not. He would only make enemies. "I have another idea," he said. "Harald has said he will give justice before his wedding. But I think I can prevent that—give Rolli and Hallbjorn some time to appear and plead their own cases. If I do that, will you keep this foolish idea of my judging them to yourself?"

"How will you make that happen?" Vigdis narrowed her eyes. Einar tried to look as bland as possible. He feared his affair with Gyda was stamped on his face for all to see, especially someone as skilled in manipulation as his mother.

"I will come and tell you it is done later today," said Einar. He bent to kiss her on the cheek.

Vigdis took his hand and held him. "You should not tie yourself so tightly to your father."

"You've said your piece," said Einar. "Unless you can tell me more, something concrete."

She looked down. "I hear rumors, that is all."

Einar pulled his hand from her grasp. "You start rumors, I think. Now let me be."

✢ ✢ ✢

VESTFOLD'S WOMEN SAT outside in the late spring sunshine near one of the halls. The light made Gyda's hair look like sparks of fire. It was a risk to approach her now, but he did not want Vigdis's foolish plan hanging over him like Sigurd's threat to tell his father.

He could not wish any of his moments with Gyda undone. Today she worked with a small spindle that she flicked in a bowl rather than letting it fall and rise. She drafted out a thread so thin it looked like spiderweb in the afternoon sun. Einar remembered hearing his aunt Svanhild call her more elf than human, and she did look otherworldly next to the solidness of the other women. She pressed her lips together when she saw him, warning him off, but her eyes softened.

"I have a message from my father for Princess Gyda," he said. "My lady, will you speak with me?"

Gyda set down her work and joined Einar. They walked together toward the water.

When they had gone far enough, she stopped and crossed her arms. "What does your father want to tell me?"

"Nothing," said Einar. She turned, and Einar reached out to stop her. She shook off his touch.

"This is dangerous," she said.

"I need to ask you something," he said. Quickly, he sketched out what he knew of Rolli and Hallbjorn's crime. "If I am forced to act as judge between my brothers, it will not go well for me. I cannot help but angering some, perhaps all. If you care for me, help me delay Harald's justice, and take this task from me."

"Why should I?" Gyda asked. Einar thought of his mother, her desire to trade advantage for advantage. During the day, at least, Gyda was no different. The possibility of a future with her seemed very remote.

"If you still want me to come with you back to Hordaland, you will not want my father and Aldi both angry at me. Aldi might kill me, and my father could . . ." He could not say what his father might do—his disapproval seemed far more frightening than simple violence from Aldi.

"Very well," she said. "Ivar will need Hordaland, even more than you thought, since your mother is set to give away Sogn."

"What?" Einar cried.

"Your stepmother, I mean. Hilda—she has arranged to trade Sogn for your brother Rolli."

Einar was certain his father did not know of this. "My father will never give up Sogn," he said.

"Very well," Gyda replied. "I will ask Harald to move up our wedding, to hold it on midsummer's day itself, to spare you, and delay Harald giving justice for your brothers' crime." Her throat moved as she swallowed. "I would not think you in a hurry to put me in his bed."

A picture formed in Einar's mind, so clear to him that he saw it instead of Gyda's angry frown: Harald's golden head bending to hers, the long tangle of his hair hiding her face, his wide back hiding her body, her thighs, which had wrapped around him only last night, parting for Harald this time.

"I am not glad of that," he said, low and angry. "What would you have me do?"

Her face softened slightly. "I would have us gone from here quickly."

"I am doing what I can," he said. "I will return you to the women now."

"I can find my own way," said Gyda. She walked back, holding herself stiffly upright. Einar wanted to try to salve her anger, but it might be better if this was the end of things between them. She would do what he asked and then go to Harald's bed.

13

FREYDIS HAD EXPECTED SOLVI'S HOUSE TO BE A GRIMY, MALE space, but inside it was neat and well organized. A woman sat combing wool by the kitchen hearth, while a cat lounged near her feet, idly licking itself.

"Tova," said Solvi, in a tone that mixed diffidence and uncertainty. "This is my daughter, Freydis. By"—he swallowed noisily—"Svanhild. She has suffered at the hands of a young fool, and needs Unna's care."

The woman turned, and Freydis caught her breath at the woman's beauty, her large dark eyes, and vivid mouth, open in surprise, a stunning contrast to bright hair that looked like molten metal in the firelight. Freydis's mother would look quite plain next to Tova.

"I have a few questions," she said, with a dry humor in her voice.

"I know as little as you," Solvi snapped. "Take her to Unna's, or I'll have Snorri do it, but I think she'd prefer a woman's company."

Freydis already liked the kind, disfigured Snorri, but she felt so uncertain she could not speak, at least not unless someone asked her a question. Tova flung a shawl over Freydis's shoulders and led her back out of the house. She walked a half step behind Tova over the broken ground of Iceland's scrubland, which looked like stew that had frozen in the midst of a hard boil and then shattered.

Tova told her of Unna as they walked: she was a healer and a witch, she half ruled the Reykjavik settlement, dispensing wisdom, healing, and even sometimes justice, and she had used her magic to enthrall her lover, Donall, who was far too handsome for her, but would not look at any other woman. She said that Unna had been the one to care for Solvi and Svanhild's son, who had died before Freydis was born, and that Unna did not make friends easily, but Tova thought she and Svanhild had been close.

"She's a hard woman," Tova said. "But fair and kind as well. She would treat you well no matter what, and will even better, because of your mother."

Unna's house nestled between two hummocks nearly as tall as the walls, and was made of stacked turf. Its overhanging grass roof brushed the tops of the hummocks that sheltered it. Unna came out to greet them. She was a tall, imposing women who looked as strong as an iron bar. Her man was younger than her, with a friendlier face, though he frowned when he saw Freydis. She wished she could hide the bruise on her cheek. It felt tight and hot, still swelling from Hallbjorn's blow.

"This is Solvi's daughter," said Tova. "Svanhild is her mother."

Unna stepped close to Freydis and gripped her chin with fingers as hard as wood. She turned Freydis's face this way and that, much as Solvi had. "Yes, she has the look of both of them," she said. "Who has been mistreating her?"

"A young man," said Tova.

Unna snorted, her contempt embracing Hallbjorn and all men like him.

"And she is pregnant, or so she thinks," Tova explained. "She is over-young to have the child. Perhaps you can help her be rid of it."

"Don't I get a say?" Freydis muttered.

"What?" Unna asked sharply. "I am hard of hearing."

Freydis shook her head and looked down. Unna picked up her chin again, and Freydis pulled herself out of her grasp. "I asked if I get a say," she said loudly, her voice thick with angry tears. "In whether I bear this child, in whether I am left here or with my father or—or—sacrificed to one of the dragons in the mountains!"

"You do get a say," said Unna. "It is entirely your choice. Your mother was dear to me. Solvi farms her land with the understanding that if she or any of her offspring appear, the land will be theirs. You are heir to that land, not Solvi Hunthiofsson. Your child will be heir to it as well."

"Unless I get rid of it," said Freydis. She hugged her arms around herself. "Does rue grow here?"

Unna raised an eyebrow. "You have some knowledge. I have had better luck with a mixture of rue, a particular spruce, and a certain mint that is hard to find here in Iceland—but I have some dry bundles of it."

Freydis nodded again.

"How far along are you?" Unna asked.

"Not long," said Freydis. "It has not yet quickened."

"And you are a child yourself," said Unna. "A child who is going to have another child."

"It cannot be more than a month gone. Before then I was a virgin," said Freydis, trying to ignore her heating face.

"Then herbs will loosen your womb," Unna told her, "and you will have your courses. It can be dangerous, though. Do you want to risk it?"

"I should ask," said Freydis turning to Tova. "What do you think my father wants?"

Tova shrugged, her serene face revealing nothing.

"What he wants does not matter now," said Unna. "Perhaps he would tell you to rid yourself of it because he does not want competition for his land. Or because he does not want a new life to force him out of the path he has chosen to walk, through fear and bitterness. You must decide for yourself."

"I thought he was a great sea king and explorer," Freydis protested. "That is what my mother always said."

"He was, once, but he now is much diminished," said Unna.

"But you let him live here," said Freydis.

Unna's face hardly shifted, but Freydis could tell she was pleased—perhaps because Freydis had acknowledged her power. "At first it was for your mother's sake, but he is a good enough neighbor. I understand his choices, even if I could wish them different. You will inherit . . . well, let us speak of that later. I have much affection for your mother and long to see her again, but seeing you is almost as good."

Freydis looked evenly at Unna. "You should know that I am nothing like my mother," she said carefully.

"You look very like her, though I think you will be prettier—and whatever your father's failings, ugliness is not among them. He would have been a fine-looking man if he grew to his natural height."

Freydis looked down again. She could fight against the force of Unna's will, but compliments confused and weakened her. She stole a look at Unna's man, who was comely, though Unna was no beauty. Freydis had succumbed to Hallbjorn's beauty, his resemblance to Einar. If he had been ugly, would she have fought him more? If she could truly imagine another choice, she would never forgive herself.

"Of course," said Unna, bringing Freydis back to herself, "most of your mother's beauty is in her boldness, and you have little of that."

Freydis pulled her shoulders back. She did not know who she would be here in Iceland, but she wanted to be more than her mother's daughter. She longed for Alfrith's advice—Alfrith would know what the gods wanted for her. If Freydis had time, she would speak the prayers Alfrith had taught her, and see if they gave her an answer. Unna looked at her expectantly.

"I want to be rid of the pregnancy," said Freydis. "I will be grateful for your help."

Unna nodded. "I will care for you, as I would have cared for your brother, given a chance. You will stay with me until we have gotten rid of this belly of yours, and then—we will see what is to be done."

✝ ✝ ✝

FREYDIS'S WOMB SEIZED and released, only to clench again as soon as she took a deep breath. She curled on her side, waiting for one wave of pain to pass and another to start. She had chosen this, she reminded herself. If only she could purge the memory of Hallbjorn so easily.

"You are barely a woman," Unna had said when she examined Freydis. "You hardly have any hair between your legs, your breasts are scarcely more than budded. But you have had your courses?"

Freydis had only been able to nod, wracked with embarrassment. Now two people had touched her intimately, both with a kind of invasive certainty that they knew her body and her needs better than she did. At least Unna did it with the intention of helping her.

"How many times?" Unna asked.

"Only once. Then we traveled and it didn't happen again. And then there was Hallbjorn."

"And you are certain you are with child?" Unna asked again.

Freydis had nodded, for when Hallbjorn's seed took hold, her body shifted in some way that she could hardly describe. Her food tasted different. Her body responded to his differently, craving different things from his touch.

"I believe you, child," she said finally. "And I suppose if you are wrong, the worst that will happen is these herbs will bring your courses out of time, and you will have some cramping." And the next day she gave Freydis the herbs.

The pain knotted her womb as though a hard fist squeezed it. She remembered what Alfrith had said about bearing pain, that it was best to go into the sensation, feel its waves, and rest in the times when it was less, but Freydis could not detach from her fear.

She heard a commotion outside, but did not fully register it until she heard a man shouting, "Where is she—where is my bride?"

Freydis curled tighter around the wad of blanket she had clutched in her arms. It was Hallbjorn, coming for her.

"You are not welcome here." Unna's voice, calm and implacable.

Freydis struggled to sit up. Black spots ate at her vision. Solvi had returned Hallbjorn's weapons to him. He might murder Unna and Donall—he was strong, and they were old.

Freydis wrapped a cloak around her shoulders and stumbled out into the sunlight. Her hair was unbound, for Unna said she should have nothing knotted about her when she was trying to loosen her womb. It blew across her face, soft and fragrant from the washing Unna had given it this morning. She had combed it out with her own hands, something Freydis could never remember her own mother doing.

Hallbjorn had his sword out, while Donall, Unna, and some of their male servants stood in a circle around him.

"Hallbjorn Olafsson," Freydis said, her voice high and loud. Maybe she could scream out her pain at him and purge it that way. "I do not wish to go with you. I do not wish to marry you. I do not wish to bear your son. Go away from here."

"You heard the girl," said Donall in his heavy accent. "Go away."

"What can you do about it, old man?" Hallbjorn asked. His sneer made him ugly.

Freydis tried to run toward them, to put herself between Donall and Hallbjorn, but her cramps doubled her over. Unna put her arms around Freydis's shoulders and tried to draw her back.

"No," Freydis cried. "Let me."

"I came here to get help from your father," said Hallbjorn. "Make him give it to me and I will go away."

"He will never help you," Freydis cried. "He hates you as I do." She was in too much pain to fear her boldness, and now the pain was more than cramps; this must be what it felt like to be stabbed, only she did not bleed, but fell to the earth in a swoon.

Dimly she heard some kind of scuffle, but no shouts, and it was Unna's cool hands that touched her shoulder gently, until she woke enough that Donall could help her back into the house.

"What happened?" Freydis cried, struggling in Donall's arms.

"Hush, he's gone now," said Unna. "Rest and let your body do its work."

She lay on a pallet for another two days, waiting for the cramps to subside. Sometimes Unna stroked her back as she curled around her pain. Sometimes she bade Freydis stand and walk about, leaning on her, as though she were a woman in childbirth.

Finally the pain retreated, leaving only weakness behind. Freydis felt between her legs, hoping for the slick wetness of blood, the tide that would carry Hallbjorn's seed away, but her hand came up dry. Without the pain her body felt wrung out. She fell into a deep sleep, passing a full day and night in unconsciousness. When she woke and went outside, she saw it was afternoon, with the morning's sun giving way to clouds. Before dinner it would storm.

Unna was in the garden, digging at onions with a sharpened spike. She pulled up one of the plants, and the scent rose to Freydis's nose, a sharp and sour smell like a man's sweat. Hallbjorn was still here on this island, Freydis felt sure of it. And his child was still rooted in her womb.

Unna separated the onion bulbs with her hands, and put them into holes she had dug, making more plants from where there had once been one. Freydis's gut twisted in a way that was not a cramp this time, but the same pregnancy sickness she had felt on Iceland's shore.

"I am still . . . ," said Freydis, passing her hand over her womb. She was; her body knew it as well as the prickling in her skin could tell her that rain approached.

"So I feared," said Unna. "The child has taken strong root. If I give you more medicine, you might die along with the babe."

Freydis took a step backward. No, she could not bear to die like that, trapped in her pain. If she could not rid herself of the child, there were other ways to die, Alfrith had told her. From time to time, the task of a healer was to ease the dying out of the pain of this world and into the peace of the grave. Freydis pressed her fist into her abdomen, as though she could press the child out by hand. She tried to imagine it growing, ridging her skin with stretch marks, swaying her back forward with its weight. Then the pain and risk of childbirth, a babe splitting her narrow hips.

"Perhaps it is as the gods have willed it," said Unna. "Your mother might like a grandchild."

"My mother!" cried Freydis. "If she was any kind of mother I would not be here. She would not have let him . . . she would have taken over the ship and sailed it to Vestfold or some such thing. She would have a song made of it. Instead I let him . . . and now I am here, and you and my father wish I were her."

She ran into the house and collapsed back on the bed. Her pillow smelled of her sick sweat from the last few days of pain. In the corner of the room, lit by the open doorway, she saw Unna's collection of herbs hanging to dry. Some she recognized even from here. She rubbed her eyes and walked over. Tansy, pennyroyal, and rue—the herbs she had taken. Mint and willow bark. Chamomile, feverfew, and lavender— good for mild ailments. A line of small leather pouches stood on a shelf. Freydis opened one and found a brown powder she could not recognize. The next held tiny dried mushrooms—these gave visions and illness, and a painful death in large enough doses. In another were the mush- rooms she sought, the ones that brought only death, and quickly. They had been Alfrith's final medicine.

She shook a few out into her hand and swallowed them dry before she could think better of it. She walked over to her pallet. Did she feel the effects already, or was this floating sensation only the result of too little food over the past few days?

Through her thin shoes she felt every bump on the floor. A breeze from the open door made her shiver. She lay down and smelled the hay in her mattress, warm and sweet. She would miss these things in her barrow, but she had made her choice.

14

RAGNVALD WALKED TOWARD IVAR WHERE HE SAT WITH GYDA'S
niece Signy under one of the trees on the hill that overlooked the harbor.
They seemed well matched, smiling and laughing together, hands entwined. She might be a good wife for him, were the marriage not certain
to anger Harald.

All Vestfold hummed with the news that Harald had become impatient to marry Gyda, and would do it on the day of midsummer and
no later. Many hoped that he had finally thrown over the Finnish witch
Snaefrid, or at least that her hold on him had loosened.

Ragnvald had heard other rumors, though: that Gyda had been the
one to ask, and it was her eagerness, not his, that had moved up the
wedding. Neither seemed likely; Gyda had waited twenty years and had
needed Einar to pry her out of Hordaland.

The change suited Ragnvald well enough. Svanhild should have been
here by now, and if she did not return from Skane after the wedding,
Ragnvald planned to go there himself. Likely she was delaying so she
could miss the wedding of her husband to another new bride. She pretended not to care what Harald did, but Ragnvald saw through her pride
to the loneliness underneath. Harald was not the husband to her that
Solvi had been, at least until the death of their son.

Ivar looked willing enough to be interrupted, even by his father, and
he whispered something in Signy's ear before sending her away. "What
is it, Father?" he asked.

"Your brother told me that you put yourself in Signy's way so you could wed her, and rule Hordaland," said Ragnvald.

"It's hard to stay out of the way of a girl like that," said Ivar, his dark eyes merry. Sometimes he reminded Ragnvald of Oddi at his happiest, when he had been Ragnvald's friend and cheered him out of his black moods. "She knows what she wants," Ivar added. "Anyway, it was Einar's idea—he said that Gyda would pass Hordaland to me if I wed Signy. But Signy says that as long as Gyda is alive she will rule it herself."

At least Ivar was not protesting his love of Signy. "Was it difficult to convince Gyda to leave Hordaland?" Ragnvald asked. "I'm not sure your brother told me all of it."

"He would never lie to you, Father," said Ivar. "I don't know why you mistrust him."

"I do trust him," Ragnvald protested. In some ways, it was true. He shared more of his worries and doubts with Einar and Svanhild than anyone else, but Einar was Vigdis's son too. He had betrayal in his blood. "Tell me, then, how did he convince Gyda to come here?"

"I hardly know," said Ivar. "He did it all. He left camp one night, and when we reached the fort he had the doors flung open and stood there with its queen. He should be the one to wed Signy and inherit Hordaland, I think—then I would have my best friend as my brother king."

Ragnvald frowned. Hilda had told him that Einar had pulled Gyda away from the women's circle yesterday with some story of a request from him, and after that the wedding day had changed. She had blushed like a girl when Einar told the story of Diarmuid and Grainne.

Only one conclusion fit all of those facts, and it justified Ragnvald's mistrust. Gyda was not the sort of woman to make herself foolish for a young man, even one as brilliant as Einar. Before today, Ragnvald would have sworn that Einar was immune to women's charms—he had suspected his son was one of those who preferred men as bed partners, and half hoped it was true. A man like that would be less likely to produce heirs to challenge Ivar's sons.

But no, his cool, secretive son had taken Princess Gyda to bed, risking his life and hers, and any who kept it from Harald. Ivar was still waiting for him to speak. "Harald already thinks our family has too much power," Ragnvald said. "We must not overreach. Find another girl to keep you warm."

✛ ✛ ✛

RAGNVALD HAD BEEN avoiding all of the jarls and lesser nobles who wanted favors from him, but now he walked into a crowd of them to find Sigurd, who was playing at dice, losing cheerfully to a group of warriors that included Oddi.

The men made room for Ragnvald, keeping from jostling him as they did one another. He waited until Sigurd finished his turn and lost a handful of hack-silver with a rueful laugh, before saying, "Sigurd, I need to speak with you."

Sigurd shrugged and pulled himself to his feet. Ragnvald always forgot his stepbrother was taller than him until they stood next to one another— usually because of the way Sigurd moved, a little hesitantly, ducking his head, like the runt of a dog pack, expecting a swat from a bigger dog.

The crowd dispersed, except for a few servants who waited to see if Ragnvald needed anything. He waved them off. "What were you and Einar speaking about the other morning?" he asked Sigurd. "It was Einar's choice of women, wasn't it? Not Ivar's?"

Sigurd's smile faded quickly. "I said I wouldn't tell you if he promised to end it," he said.

That was all the admission Ragnvald needed. He rubbed the scar on the side of his mouth, Solvi's first mark on him. He hardly had time to decide what to do about Rolli's misbehavior—and now this. Sons gave a man greater heartache than a woman ever could. "You did not tell me. I guessed," said Ragnvald. "And did he? End it?"

"He promised, so he must have," said Sigurd. He scuffed his foot against the ground.

"That stupid boy," said Ragnvald. "After everything, I should have known he would do something like this."

"He is not stupid." Sigurd tried to meet Ragnvald's eyes. "He is very like you."

Ragnvald heard that often and never liked the comparison. "I have never known what to do with a son like him," he replied. "He burns too bright. I wanted him to be content as Ivar's companion."

"Would you have been content to serve someone else your whole life?" Sigurd asked, sounding truly curious.

"Haven't I?" Ragnvald asked, stung. "I have served Harald."

Sigurd smiled, somehow both innocent and knowing. "You are still Ragnvald the Mighty," he said. He saw Ragnvald too clearly sometimes. "He will no more be Einar the Mighty than I will be Sigurd the Mighty. I am content, but I am a simpler man than either of you."

Ragnvald laughed ruefully. "You give yourself too little credit. You will be long remembered, and you are more clever than you realize. Tell me what I should do, about Einar—or about any of my sons. They all seem bound for different kinds of trouble."

"By the gods, I do not know. Why did you think I let Svanhild raise my son, Olaf?" Sigurd furrowed his brow. "Do you think they will be coming to Vestfold soon?"

"I hope so," said Ragnvald. "The Skanians are more trouble we don't need."

✤ ✤ ✤

RAGNVALD TRIED NOT to see his son's face the next morning, as Gyda and Harald approached the wedding canopy, which was decorated with garlands of spring flowers and banners of silk, set in a grove near the water's edge. If Gyda had done Einar a favor by changing the wedding day and delaying justice for Rolli, then he could not have ended their liaison as he promised.

The wedding witnesses gathered in the natural bowl formed by the hills of Vestfold. The weather was perfect, cool with a hint of warmth on the breeze, the promise of summer and a rich warring season. The gods had smiled upon the day, as they did on all of Harald's deeds.

Guthorm acted as priest for the ceremony. Gyda wore a dress in a silvery green that made her hair look like tangles of copper wire, and her skin as pale as snow. Even in bright sunlight, she looked more beautiful than she had at fifteen, when she had outwitted Harald and kept her fort and her virginity. He could see what had attracted his son—Einar could not help but reach for the most difficult challenge, and what greater challenge than Harald's most famous conquest?

Harald wore a blue tunic that made his shoulders look as broad as the sky and his tangled hair as brilliant as the sun that lit its strands. Ragnvald had missed seeing him these past years, watching him walk among his followers, drawing all eyes. Without him Vestfold, and indeed Norway, felt like a cold and empty hall.

Einar wore a rich new tunic, richer than Ragnvald had ever seen him dress, and knew its source when he saw Vigdis touching Einar's shoulder and elbow. A part of him wanted to offer comfort too: he knew what it was like to be parted from a woman he craved, though now when he looked upon Vigdis, he saw all barbs and no lure. Perhaps Einar would see Gyda that way one day.

When the wedding ceremony was done, guests made the ritual toast and drained their cups of ale. Harald stepped forward, leaving Gyda behind him.

"I have conquered all of Norway," said Harald, his voice ringing out to reach even the common folk who had come to see this day. The sun made Harald's tangled and matted hair shine like gold. "I ask my uncle, King Guthorm of Vestfold, who set me on this path, and my most loyal friend, King Ragnvald of Maer, to cut my hair for me. I have married Princess Gyda of Hordaland, as I swore. I trust no one as much as I do these men—and I must, for they are putting blades very near my neck!"

Servants brought a seat for Harald to sit upon. Ragnvald drew his dagger, honed to such a sharpness that it could cut flesh without pain. He had known this moment was coming, dreamed of it for years, the fulfillment of his vision, but after he looped a lock of Harald's matted hair around his blade, he stopped without cutting.

"My king," he said, in the resonant voice that he used when he wanted everyone to hear him, "I fear I cannot do this thing. Your wife, my sister, Svanhild, has not returned from Skane. Norway is conquered, but what of the threats on our borders?"

Harald's face did not alter but somehow changed from warm to cold. Ragnvald wanted to look up, to see if a cloud had blocked the sun, but no, that was Harald's power. He could hide for years, leaving other men to rule his kingdom, only to emerge and take up kingship as another man might pick up a stone from the ground.

"And I still have not defeated Solvi Hunthiofsson, as I once swore," said Harald, after a moment. "You are right to remind me of this, my war crow. You will cut my hair, but only after I have retrieved your sister from Skane, and routed out these raiders who send their ships against us. When do we leave?"

"Tomorrow?" Ragnvald suggested. If they moved quickly enough, it might further delay Rolli's justice, until Ragnvald could be sure Harald would not require Sogn as the price for his son's crime.

"I will go with you, Father," Ivar called out.

"And I," echoed Einar.

"Harald's sons will fight Harald's wars," said Dagfinn, striding forward, with Gudrod following. Ragnvald fell back as younger men crowded toward Harald.

Einar stepped forward to stand almost next to Ragnvald. He held himself taut as a bowstring. Would he be foolish enough to say something, to object to the wedding if Harald did not cut his hair in recognition of his old oath?

"Today is still a wedding," Ragnvald said loudly, putting his arm over Einar's shoulder. "Today we feast, tonight we put the couple to bed, and tomorrow we fight."

The assembled guests took up the cry for feasting, and Harald and Gyda led the bright-clad crowd toward the feasting hall. Ragnvald still held Einar's shoulder as he watched them pass. When even the lowliest had left the wedding area, Ragnvald let go, and said, "Come with me."

He set a brisk pace toward the path that climbed the hill above the grove. Einar followed, and when they reached the crest of the hill, they looked down upon the buildings of Vestfold between the sparse trees, to the harbor choked with ships and the fjord beyond.

"I don't know what to say," said Ragnvald sadly. "I thought you had better judgment. I thought you were wiser."

"Sigurd said he wouldn't tell you," Einar mumbled.

"You left signs for anyone with wits to read," said Ragnvald. He took a deep breath to try to calm his anger, remembering Sigurd's words. "I have long thought that you were my cleverest son, but this is the choice of a foolish boy."

Einar brought his head up, and Ragnvald saw a look of fury on his face that he had not seen since Einar was a rebellious child, complaining of a punishment.

"Anyone else would use this as a hold over you," said Ragnvald. "Or me. Do you hate life as my son so much that you would prefer exile or death? Because that is what you are courting. What did the princess promise you?"

Einar remained silent.

"In your ambition you had your brother Ivar wooing young Signy. Do you think silence will protect you? Or Gyda?" Ragnvald asked.

"She wanted me to return with her to Hordaland. Let Ivar be king as Signy's husband and—"

"You as the true ruler, I see," said Ragnvald. "So you would betray your oath to your brother, while pretending to fulfill it. It cannot be. Gyda cannot go back to Hordaland. One of Harald's sons must rule."

"Why?" Einar cried. "Harald has abandoned Norway, and his sons rebel against him. Why should one of them get Hordaland instead of Ivar?"

"Enough. You have used this dalliance for one good thing—delaying Rolli's justice. Now you must end it. And I need something else from you. Harald will sail for Skane with many warriors, but I need you to remain behind and defend Vestfold. I do not know what Erik of Jutland is planning."

"And Ivar?" Einar asked.

"He is coming with me to Skane."

"Is this punishment, Father?"

"For what would I be punishing you?" Ragnvald replied.

Einar stumbled slightly on the slippery, pine-needle-covered ground. "It was you who asked me to swear—swear that my brother Ivar would never go into battle without me, nor me him. And now you want me to break that oath." His voice quivered and he swallowed. "Guthorm will stay here—you do not need me."

"You speak of your oath, but you have already betrayed it," said Ragnvald.

Einar looked at the ground. "At most I thought Ivar and I could be Gyda's champions in Hordaland while—" he said.

"While I still live? Are you so eager for my death?"

Einar shook his head angrily, and Ragnvald continued, "I need you here. And I need your cleverness. Stay here, and when Rolli comes, persuade him to leave Norway, go to Iceland or the Orkneys or wherever he can hide himself. Go with him if you have to. And tell him"—Ragnvald faltered for a moment, then pressed on—"tell him that the only way he can win my forgiveness is to rid Norway of Halfdan."

Einar looked up at Ragnvald in shock. "Then you mean for him never to return," he said.

"He will be outlawed either way," said Ragnvald. "At least this way . . ."

"He will be useful," said Einar bitterly. "But I heard the lady Hilda meant to trade Sogn for Rolli's forgiveness."

Ragnvald would never have thought that suggestion had come from Hilda. "No," he said. He would not question Einar about the doings of his stepmother. "If you will not do this because I ask, do it because of this: you have a secret, and that gives those who know it power over you."

Einar raised his eyes, and Ragnvald felt suddenly that he was in the presence of a wolf, barely controlled, who looked through him to see the bones under his skin. "You mean it gives you power over me. Because you want me to break my oath to my brother."

"Doesn't it?" Ragnvald asked.

"Yes," said Einar. "But it will only work for so long."

Ragnvald frowned. "Why?"

Einar gave him a strange smile. "Because, soon, anyone who finds out will blame you as much as me, for keeping our secret." He walked away, down the hill toward Harald's drinking hall, and did not look to see if Ragnvald followed.

15

DONALL ARRIVED AT SOLVI'S HOUSE EARLY ONE MORNING AS he lay in bed, dreading the moment when he would have to put weight on his legs. He kept the smallest farm on Svanhild's land that could support Snorri, Tova, his guard Brusi, and a half-dozen servants, but it still required work from dawn until dusk, work that became harder every year.

Donall accepted a bowl of porridge from Tova as Solvi sat up and swung his legs down over the edge of his bed. He quickly pushed his feet, mangled and missing toes, into his shoes. Tova handed him a bowl.

"How is my daughter?" Solvi asked.

"She has said she wants to be rid of the child, and Unna tries but the child's roots are deep," Donall answered slowly.

A pain seized Solvi's chest. He imagined Freydis, carrying a smaller version of herself in her womb, its eyes closed, clinging to life. He squeezed his own eyes shut.

Tova set down her spoon with a clatter. "She is too young to bear a child, both in body and in spirit," she said. Her face showed sorrow, but her voice sounded dull. Whatever Freydis had been through, Tova had suffered far worse. She had told Solvi she was the daughter of a concubine and passed from one man to another as soon as she was old enough to attract their attention. Solvi had taken her from his warrior Ulfarr, and given her to another man to gain him as an ally. In payment for her services, he offered her the reward of her choice: any husband she wished, or wealth of her own and no companion at all.

She had followed him here, and asked nothing more than to keep his house and her continued freedom to choose the life she wanted. Other men in Iceland, wealthier men, had offered for her over the years, but she said she preferred the simplicity of life with Solvi. They shared a bed most nights, for she slept lightly and would wake him from his nightmares, and he did the same for her. He had tried to lie with her again many years ago, but after the battle where he had failed, he had found it easier to bury his desire along with much of his former self.

Donall continued, "I come to tell you also that the boy tried to take her away. You must get rid of him, or he will try again."

Solvi stood quickly and regretted it, gripped by a fear so strong it made him feel faint. His worst nightmares began like this, with a call to a battle he could not win, like the one in which he had lost Tryggulf, and his nerve. His legs had failed him, and Tryggulf had taken his death for him. Solvi saw his friend lung-stabbed, dying on a rowing bench, for a moment, instead of Donall's face.

He glanced at Snorri, whose eyes, soft and understanding, threatened to unman him. "If I must, I must," he said, in a strained whisper.

"Good," Donall replied, pretending not to notice Solvi's fear. He finished his porridge, thanked Tova, and stood to leave.

Solvi glanced at Snorri. His mangled face could be hard to read, but Solvi saw hesitation in the set of his shoulders. "What is it?" Solvi asked testily.

"She is your daughter," said Snorri.

"Just because he says little doesn't mean it's profound when he speaks," Solvi said to Tova. It was his frequent joke, and Tova usually smiled. But Snorri wanted Solvi to know that he had to do this, for her. He could not deny his daughter, or the duty he owed her, even if he had learned of her only a few days earlier.

He had heard of Svanhild's sons by Harald, born in quick succession, one year after another following their wedding. When she left him, with their son's body still smoldering, on the shore of Trondheim Fjord, she had told him she was pregnant. Solvi had assumed the child died, like all his seed. He was not destined to have a living son, and he had not imagined a daughter—and rumor had not told of one. Daughters were only mentioned when they wed, or if their rape or murder provoked revenge.

But here she was. Their daughter. Pregnant, beaten, and cowed. He had hated Svanhild all these years, nearly as much as he missed her—for giving him a son whose only fate was death, for leaving him so easily, and for choosing Harald. He hated her when he heard of her new sons, and longed for her when he heard of her triumphs, the way one might hate and love the gods, far away, and unlikely to interfere. He watched Tova working in the kitchen, silhouetted by the kitchen fire, and imagined her smaller, narrower, turning to show him Svanhild's sharp little face instead of her own. Now he hated her in a new, more intimate way for letting their daughter come to this pass.

And now he owed Freydis the protection that Svanhild had denied her, he who was gripped by phantoms of fear every night, who could barely protect himself. He could send Snorri—let him be the one to drive Hallbjorn out of Iceland. Snorri had always tried to stand between Solvi and harm, even now that he was Solvi's last remaining friend.

"Yes," said Solvi. "She is my daughter. Snorri, bring Hallbjorn back here, alone. Tell him I have changed my mind. I will help him." That should keep Snorri safe, and help Solvi avoid confrontation. But it would also bring Hallbjorn too close to Freydis again. "No—go after Donall and borrow Unna's horse, the one that's big enough for both of us."

He watched Donall and Snorri walk off, their long strides swallowing up ground that Solvi would have had to totter over, and when they disappeared behind a hummock he went into the house. He packed a small sack with items he might need in town, a handful of hack-silver, a golden coin stamped with the curls of the Arabs' writing, a cloak clasp of hounds with the legs interlaced. He buckled his sword to his belt.

Snorri returned with the horse, a big plodding beast with a back that seemed as wide as a feasting table. Solvi hated to ride; though he could cover more distance, he found it as uncomfortable as walking, and he needed so much help to get into and out of a saddle that he was rarely willing to bear the indignity.

He visited Ingolfur first, Iceland's original settler and most important resident. Ingolfur sat on the usual bench outside his hall, drinking a cup of ale and watching the business of Reykjavik's harbor.

"Solvi Hunthiofsson!" Ingolfur called out, pulling himself to his feet with some difficulty. He was a large man, and grew ever more stout with the passing years. "It has been a long time for you to come a short way. But then you don't walk very well, do you? I will give you a pony if you wish, then you can go anywhere. I had some likely foals last year and now they are eating every blade of grass in my fields."

Ingolfur had said this sort of thing to him before, but free men did not ride ponies—those were for slaves and children and women. "Thank you for your offer," Solvi replied, "but I must refuse."

"Yes," said Ingolfur, "you are proud. Too proud. You are old, like me. Why fight it? What brings you here, within view of the sea you left behind?"

Words like that never failed to sting him, especially when the breeze off the ocean smelled cool and fresh. He missed those days, but a man who could no longer fight, turn a steering oar, climb a mast, or lay down cargo, had no business sailing.

"There is a young man recently come," said Solvi. "Hallbjorn Olafsson. I need to speak with him."

"That one." Ingolfur shook his head. "He has not been here long, but he has already worn out his welcome. He has been trying to persuade some of my young men to attack Unna the Wise."

Unna, not him. That was an insult in itself. "Has he had any luck?" Solvi asked.

"Some young men from the families of those she could not heal have heard him out, though none will commit to an attack. Sometimes they grumble, but many of those families have others who owe their lives to Unna. If she is a witch, she is the kind of witch that we need here."

"Where can I find him?" Solvi asked.

"I don't keep track of all the foolish men of Iceland. If I did, I'd do nothing else!" Ingolfur laughed.

Keeping track of himself, one foolish man, was certainly enough for his aging wits, Solvi thought. "Do the young warriors still gather on the gaming ground near your hall?" he asked.

Ingolfur said they did, and Solvi limped around to the other side of the hall. He found a mostly flat area with targets for arrows, knives, and axes on the far end. Some wooden practice swords stood against the side of the hall. A half-finished wall of narrow staves sheltered the area from the gusts that came down the hills. The young men who had gathered there were dicing, though, not sparring. Good—Solvi did not want to face anyone with even a practice sword in his hand.

Enough of Solvi's old reputation still clung to him that the young men parted for him, looking at him curiously. The murmur that passed among them gave him a measure of courage, along with some control over the reasonless fear that gripped him whenever he had to face armed men.

Hallbjorn sat in a smaller group of players. He watched Solvi's approach, making Solvi even more conscious of his limp, and the horrible, yawning terror that made him want to squeeze his eyes shut.

"Hallbjorn Olafsson," said Solvi. His voice had a shrill note in it, fear bleeding through. He took a deep breath, and said Hallbjorn's name again, this time trying to put into it the power that could once command sailors in the midst of a sea gale. "Come, speak with me. There may be a way to give you what you want."

Hallbjorn's expression turned to one of hope, and he became, again, a very handsome young man. Still, Solvi understood why Freydis did not want him. Solvi would have trouble trusting a man who smiled like that, even if he had not beaten and impregnated his daughter. His daughter who truly was too young for a man—she was even younger than Svanhild had been when he first set eyes on her, and far less certain of her desires than Svanhild had been.

"Go away," Hallbjorn said to his friends. "I wouldn't want to make my son's grandfather walk any farther than he has to." They grumbled but dispersed, and Solvi eased himself down on one of the vacated benches.

"What will you do for me now?" Hallbjorn asked. "You humiliated me and forbade me your daughter."

"Things have changed," said Solvi. He smiled back at Hallbjorn, a sharp smile that he had not worn in a long time. He could do this, gather pieces of his old self and tack them over his weakness, at least long enough to fool Hallbjorn.

"What has changed?" Hallbjorn asked. "She doesn't want to call that hideous old man of yours—Snorri—my son's father after all? Did she refuse him? Does she want me back?"

Solvi kept smiling. Hallbjorn was a belligerent young man who talked too much—even as diminished as he was, Solvi would have to be dead before he could be bested by one of those.

"Why do you think she doesn't want to wed you?" Solvi asked.

"Because I hit her," said Hallbjorn truculently. "She was hot enough in my bed, but cold outside it."

"She's young," said Solvi acidly. Let Hallbjorn see his anger—he meant to bait him. "I won't have you hitting my daughter. And what can you do for her other than that?"

"I have a ship," said Hallbjorn.

"Ragnvald the Mighty's ship," said Solvi. "He may want it back, and even if not, how does that help my daughter? Will you break it down for a cradle for your child? A house to shelter her?"

Hallbjorn scowled and shook his head. "But I can get wealth with it," he said.

"Can you?" Solvi asked. "My daughter will need a husband, that much is true, and I want to give her one who can provide for her. Come back and drape her in gold, and I may change my mind. So may she. Carry her off, and I will turn every viking in the North Sea against you."

"You!" said Hallbjorn. "I see what you've become—you are nothing more than a farmer now, too old and weak to hold a sword."

"You did not come to me, bringing my daughter, because I am a farmer. I can help you or hurt you." He pulled the gold coin with the curves of Arabic writing upon it from his hip pouch. "Go to Scotland," he said. Solvi's friends would remember that he had gone to Spain, and been given gold by its rulers, in return for the slaves and ermine pelts he brought, along with tales of northern wonders.

He described the islands of the Hebrides, the rocks and hidden harbors, where Ketil Flatnose made his home. "Tell Ketil I said you were a likely raider, and he should share his attacks and his spoils with you. Come back when you have something to offer my daughter more than your blows."

"I've heard this tale," said Hallbjorn. "I give him this coin, tell him you sent me there, and he sees it and kills me. How do I know you do not mean me harm?"

Solvi sighed. Hallbjorn was a little more clever than Solvi had credited him, but only a little. "She can inherit my farm, that is the best I can do for her—but I want more for her, and away from Norway, which is a place that has only brought me pain." He gestured at his legs. Better Hallbjorn should think his weakness was physical, not of the spirit. "I want her to have a husband who cares for her and stays by her side. She is not her mother; she will be a good wife to any man who is kind to her. And she already welcomed you to her bed and thought you handsome."

Hallbjorn preened at the compliment.

"That was a girl's desire," Solvi continued, "but she bears your son now, and she will have a woman's needs. As her father, at least I can make sure you will satisfy them."

The truth of his words made Solvi's throat feel tight, and his eyes burn. He had spent only an hour in his daughter's presence and already he wanted a good life for her, though not with this cruel boy. Hallbjorn looked moved by Solvi's words as well.

"Do you want that?" Solvi asked Hallbjorn. "Do you want the best for her? If not, do as you will. If so, take this coin and earn her hand as she deserves."

"I promise," he said, taking the coin from Solvi. "I will return more worthy."

He could hardly return less worthy. Solvi wished he did have a signal for Ketil to make him kill this young man. Perhaps Hallbjorn would dash himself to death on Scottish rocks, and Ragnvald's fine ship with him. Or perhaps he would, against all odds, return worthy of Freydis. Marriages had been made on worse. His and Svanhild's had hardly started much better.

"Go then," said Solvi. "If you do not, I will hear of it."

Hallbjorn bowed, and Solvi walked away, slow enough that he could minimize his limp. He and Snorri rode back toward his house, but when he passed by the path that led to Unna's house, Donall came running out to greet him.

"Freydis is near death," he said. "Come quickly."

Solvi had no time to feel anything, as Snorri tugged on the horse's head to turn it. He had heard that trying to get rid of a pregnancy was risky. He should have invited her to stay with him, not sent her to Unna, who had already tried and failed to save his son.

"If you have killed another one of my children . . . ," said Solvi to Unna, who looked stricken even before his words.

"She took my death-cap mushrooms," said Unna. "The child would not loose itself, and after Hallbjorn came, I think she decided she did not want to live." Solvi had never heard that tone in Unna's voice before, even when she sat by the beds of the dead and dying. It was the dullness of despair, an echo of the heavy stone lying on Solvi's own spirit. "She still clings to life, though, as does the child."

So there was still hope, which seemed another kind of cruelty. A seeress had once told Solvi that he would only have one son, and that son had died. His first wife had exposed their daughters. The gods did not shower their gifts on those who rejected them. He did not deserve for Freydis to live.

"You must see her," said Unna. "Perhaps you can convince her not to die."

"How?" Solvi asked bitterly. "Life is bitter enough to me that I cannot convince someone else of its sweetness."

"Yes," said Unna, "I know it is bitter for you, but she is young and beautiful. And strong—otherwise the mushrooms would have already killed her. She can live if she wills it."

Solvi went inside, full of trepidation. At first his eyes refused to adjust to the dimness, to see the small, flat form of his daughter lying in her pallet, her skin gray, as though she were already dead. Her eyelids fluttered when he limped across the floor to sit on the stool next to her.

"Daughter," he said, his voice thick. "Unna tells me you have tried to flee from life."

Tears leaked between her eyes and she turned her face toward the wall.

"I have sent that young man away," Solvi said. "He will not trouble you again. I want you to live. I have had little joy since your mother and I parted. I too have not thought much of life." In the songs warriors who had outlived their abilities often sought death rather than die of old age. Solvi had clung to his life, though—he had fought too hard for it as a child to throw it away now. He took a ragged breath. "With your coming it has begun to look sweet to me again. Do not take that from me."

He hated that Unna must see him like this, tears spilling from his eyes that he did not trouble to wipe away. He reached under the covers for Freydis's hand and held it in his own. It was light and cool. "Unna tells me your child wants to live also. Whatever you want for your child, I will help both of you. But please live. If not for me, then for her."

"Her?" Freydis asked weakly. She turned back toward him, her lips curving into the slightest of smiles. "Do you think it will be a girl?"

He had spoken to Hallbjorn as if she bore a son, but looking at her, he hoped for a daughter, a girl like her. If a line of such women could be his legacy, he would be well pleased. Solvi looked at Unna, who shrugged. "It is hard to know," she said.

"Do you, Father?" Freydis asked. "Do you think it will be a girl?"

"Yes," said Solvi. "I do."

16

EINAR SPENT THE NIGHT OF HARALD'S WEDDING WANDERING the path that led to where his bower with Gyda had been, near the wooded shore of Oslo Fjord. He had gone briefly to the wedding feast but found he had stomach for neither food nor drink. He tried to imagine himself as the legendary Diarmuid, torn between love and duty, but by morning he felt dull and grubby, daylight stealing the beauty from his tragedy. If their father had discovered Ivar having an affair with Gyda, would he too have been ordered away from battle?

The tides meant that Harald's force could not leave Vestfold until midafternoon the following day. Einar looked for Ivar to bid him good-bye and found him outside the bathhouse, where a servant was trimming his dark beard close to his chin. Nearby, other warriors waited their turn—no one wanted a long beard in a battle.

Einar waited until he was done, and then told him the part of their father's edict that was no secret: he must remain to protect Vestfold. Ivar's eyes went wide with concern. "He must have a good reason for it," he said.

"Yes," said Einar. "I suppose he must." The betrayal of Rolli to a life of outlawry. Einar's habit of protecting his father's secrets was too strong to share that even with Ivar.

"You might come in one of the other ships," Ivar suggested. "He cannot have his eyes everywhere."

"But should I disobey him? Or disobey my oath to you?" Einar asked. "We have never fought separately."

Ivar looked troubled for a moment longer, and then smiled slightly. "Perhaps Father doesn't mean for me to fight."

"Perhaps," said Einar.

"Perhaps—it was foolish to hope that we would always fight side by side like something out of a song," said Ivar gently. "Who can do that, in truth?"

Einar shook his head. "Our father and Oddi did for six years," he said.

"That is longer than we have had," said Ivar. "I will ask him."

Later, when Einar went to find some porridge—he might be able to stomach that—Ivar met him again outside the kitchen, looking unhappy. "He told me he wants to give you your own command, that I should not stand in the way of your elevation."

Einar almost laughed at his father's cleverness. Ivar would do nothing to prevent his brother's rise, any more than Einar would. "I don't want to be elevated if it means separation from you," said Einar. "I swore to be your retainer and remain by your side for the whole of my life."

Ivar clasped his arm. "I think our father wants more for you than that." He smiled. "And you should too. You think I don't see how capable you are? Perhaps there is a kingdom in your future."

The words were so like the witch's words that Einar's skin went cold. At his look, Ivar said, "What do you want, truly?"

Einar never let himself think of that for very long, to imagine glory for himself. "What do *you* want?" Einar asked, trying to distract him.

"My name remembered by my sons and their line, forever," said Ivar. "I want sons—the sooner the better. I wish Father hadn't made me give up Signy."

"Don't you want to be king?" Einar asked.

"It's better than not being king," said Ivar. "I will be king—I know that. But if I were not born to it . . . I would not have given what our father did for a throne." He looked at Einar shrewdly. "And I think you would."

Einar shook his head vehemently. If the witch spoke true, that way lay Ivar's death. "I only want to come with you," he said. "I never want us to be separated."

"Don't you want your own kingdom, and sons to pass it to?" Ivar asked. At Einar's troubled expression, he added, "It's what any man would want."

"I am not—" Einar began.

"You are not allowed to," said Ivar.

Einar looked at him, surprised.

"You think I don't see?" Ivar asked. He put his hand on Einar's shoulder. "When I have my own sons, I will make no difference between them, no matter who their mothers are. And I would not make any difference between our sons either."

"Perhaps Father is right to keep me here," said Einar, embarrassed by Ivar's generosity. "But I still don't want you to fight without me."

"I'll be back soon, brother. Don't you trust my sword arm?" With this Ivar made a ridiculous whirl and parry, thrusting at Einar with a phantom sword. Einar responded halfheartedly, until Ivar tripped him and Einar had to yield, laughing.

Still, as soon as he left Ivar's company, his fear returned. His father was right: Einar had betrayed his brother by going to Gyda's bed, and then keeping it secret. He must accept his punishment.

✣ ✣ ✣

WHEN THE SUN reached its zenith, Harald made his blessings over the assembled forces and asked the gods for an easy crossing and an easy victory. He called for all of the women of Vestfold to bless the departing men, and a wave of women stepped forward. This pomp and ceremony made Einar feel easier about the upcoming battle, though seeing Harald bid Gyda good-bye with a kiss that she returned warmly turned his stomach.

Einar watched Harald's vessels sail down the fjord, growing smaller in the distance, set apart even in the crowd of watchers. He found himself avoiding Gyda's eyes when she tried to catch his attention. That night and every one that followed, he slept in Harald's hall, surrounded by warriors, so she could not come and draw him away. The coward's way of ending it, his conscience reminded him while the snores of men around him kept him from sleep.

A few days later, scouts reported that they had seen a small vessel, too far away for them to identify, rowing slowly toward Vestfold. It did not have many oars out and the morning breeze was against it.

At breakfast Hilda served Einar a bowl of porridge glistening with butter. "I know this ship," she said. "It is Rolli. It is my son."

Einar was not sure—the ship did look like Rolli's, but it could be anyone's. It could have even been Svanhild's. If it was her then Einar could send a messenger to Skane and recall that force, and his brother to his side again. But as it drew closer, he saw the huge frame of his half-brother standing in the prow. His face was serious in repose, but when he saw Einar he laughed and waved, calling out, "Greetings, brother!" and transforming into the charming, good-natured giant that Einar had left behind in Tafjord earlier in the year.

"Welcome," Einar yelled in return, though with less enthusiasm. It seemed impossible that he must convince Rolli to accept a life of outlawry and murder.

Rolli's smile faltered when he saw the grim faces of his mother and brother. "I suppose you heard," he said.

"Indeed," Einar replied. "Did you bring—is Hallbjorn with you? Is Svanhild's daughter?"

Hilda went to embrace her son, laying her head against his shoulder. Rolli patted her, in no hurry to let go, and answered Einar over her head. "No, they—Hallbjorn judged it better to press on to Iceland."

"Iceland!" Hilda exclaimed. "How far have you gone?"

"It has been"—Rolli counted on his fingers—"six weeks since we left Tafjord. And we had good sailing to the Orkney Islands and back here, although it was harder with less crew. Some of them went with Hallbjorn."

"Why did you want to leave Norway, my son?" Hilda asked, as though that were his biggest crime.

"What happened, brother?" Einar asked. "Or, wait." He glanced at Vigdis, who had come running as well, and drew up short when she saw that her older son was not among Rolli's crew. He spoke in a low voice to Rolli. "Tell me in private. We can decide best how to proceed."

Rolli ducked his head. "Yes. But I'm hungry. Can I eat first?"

Hilda took his arm and tucked herself next to him as the three of them moved toward the hall. She bustled about, preparing a huge trencher piled with leftover food from dinner the night before, as well as a bowl of porridge. Einar watched, oddly fascinated, as Rolli ate it all, methodically, without speaking. Hilda sat by his side, gazing at him and spooning more food onto his trencher whenever it started to empty. Not until Rolli finished eating did the worry lines between her eyebrows reappear.

"Tell us," said Einar. "Our father has left me in charge while he is gone. Harald is gone too, and Aldi, whose son you killed. There is none here to give justice now, so we have time to plan."

Rolli picked something out of his teeth, stalling for time, while Einar tried to be patient. "We saw Father's ship, with another in pursuit, and thought it was raiders," Rolli said finally. "So we attacked, and Aldi's son was killed in the fighting."

"How could you mistake our father's ships for raiders?" Einar asked.

"It was an honest mistake," said Rolli. He jutted his chin forward. "They should have identified themselves."

"Was it a mistake, or did you see what you wanted to see—you were looking for adventure and hadn't found it yet?" Einar asked.

Hilda gave Einar an injured look. "Death by mischance is a cheaper wergild, as I recall," she said. She looked to Einar for confirmation. He nodded. "What did you do next, my son?"

"We took some of his men as slaves to buy our way if we needed to," said Rolli.

"Why did you return, then?" Einar asked. He did not think there was a penalty for selling someone's free men into slavery. Once a man consented to be a slave, he lost his honor, and it was as if he had always been a slave.

"He should exile himself for a mistake?" Hilda asked.

Rolli looked concerned. "Thorstein the Red, in the Orkneys, thought I should come back and make peace," he said. He explained that they had first planned to go raiding and earn enough to pay for the damage they caused, but when Rolli had learned of the threat to Harald, he returned.

Hilda laid a hand on his forearm. "It is good you did," she said. "I have a plan to prevent your outlawry."

"Giving away Sogn?" Einar asked. At Hilda's surprise, he added, "It is not as secret as you think, my lady. You would trade Ivar's inheritance for Rolli here."

"What if I would?" Hilda asked. "Ivar will have Maer. And Rolli will be safe."

Rolli looked uncomfortable, and he put his hand over his mother's. "My father would not want that. Nor I. I want to be a great sea king—a sea king can face a few years' outlawry."

"Father and Harald have gone to Skane with our brothers, Harald's sons, and many warriors," Einar told him.

"Without you?" Rolli asked.

"I disobeyed our father in Hordaland," Einar said, turning truth into a lie. "I left Ivar alone while I went to negotiate with the princess. He said I had broken my oath."

"That is bad," said Rolli, wonderingly. "You are never apart."

"I thought he would be in danger if he came with me in Hordaland," said Einar. The pain he let into his voice was no lie. "Now we are separated in truth."

"Skane—I heard tell of Skane in Orkney," said Rolli excitedly. "We have to go there." He told them what Thorstein had said, that there was an alliance among the Scottish vikings with Halfdan Haraldsson and Erik of Jutland. "We have to tell them this force is coming, and they must flee."

"You should stay here, son," said Hilda. "Aldi is in Skane too and he will be tempted to take his revenge in that lawless land."

"Let him try," said Rolli. "I'm a match for him."

"Father wanted me to convince you to leave Norway," said Einar, "go back to Iceland or wherever you wish. In time, you can earn his forgiveness."

"His forgiveness!" said Hilda. "He should pray for *my* forgiveness, if that is his plan."

"I thought—everyone told me Father would help me," said Rolli. "He is the most important man in Norway." His face crumpled, and Einar wished he could say something to comfort him.

"No," said Einar. "He serves the most important man in Norway. He knows the difference, and you should too."

"I can't see why Father doesn't just make it right," said Rolli. "Harald owes him many favors. Everyone says so."

"He won't," said Einar. "He wants you to leave Norway."

"Harald will, for Sogn," Hilda insisted. "Vigdis said Guthorm talked to him."

"Hallbjorn told me the only way to make it right would be to do King Harald a great service," said Rolli.

Einar needed to speak with Rolli in private, immediately. Rolli could do a great service, but only if he left.

"I'll go to him—in Skane," Rolli was saying. "I'll tell him about the alliance against him. He'll want to know that."

"Father knows more about alliances than you can possibly understand," said Einar. "I can go with you—back to Iceland. Father said that if it would help you accept your exile, I should go too."

"You would do that, brother?" Rolli asked.

Better that than face his father's anger if he failed. "Yes, I would. Neither of us can inherit now. Staying we can only make trouble for our brothers."

"No!" said Hilda. To Einar she said, "Your father does not want your exile." Then to Rolli, "And I do not want yours. Stay and Ivar will still have Maer. It is a bigger and richer district, and Aldi does have a claim to Sogn. Stay here and wait for Harald's decision."

"No," said Rolli. "I am going to Skane. Harald values boldness. He will reward me."

Einar and Hilda both argued with him for a while longer, but Rolli would not change his mind, and eventually Hilda stood up to fetch more food. Einar drew Rolli away, behind one of the horse barns, where they could talk privately.

"Father wants you to leave," Einar told him. "He has kept this secret for fear it would make Harald look weak to have his son Halfdan in rebellion. Harald will not punish Halfdan, so our family must. Father said that the only way he would forgive you is if you go away, accept outlawry, and are ready to kill Halfdan when the time comes."

Rolli's face showed a welter of emotions, from disbelief to sorrow, settling into stubbornness when Einar had finished speaking. "I don't believe it," he said. "If I kill Halfdan, I will be outlawed for life, not a few years. I won't do it. I would be a murderer. Of the king's eldest son."

Einar had always envied Rolli's ability to shrug off their father's wishes, when they lay like chains upon him. "Perhaps you are right," he said in a low voice. "Perhaps I should be the one to kill Halfdan."

"No," said Rolli. "You shouldn't do it either. It will get you killed, and then Ivar will get himself killed avenging you. Father is wrong."

"He's not," said Einar. "Who else can do this?"

Rolli threw his hands up. "I don't know—maybe one of Harald's other sons, or maybe Father should do it himself if he thinks it's such a good plan. All I know is I won't, and you shouldn't either. I'm going to Skane—Harald will be glad to learn my news, and he will forgive me. And Father can go suck corpses."

✣ ✣ ✣

SINCE RAGNVALD AND Harald left, Einar had been avoiding Vigdis, but now he had no one else he could ask for advice. He found her in Guthorm's hall sitting with him near the fire. Einar remembered him as an imposing and vigorous man who could best warriors half his age on the Nidaros practice grounds, but he looked very old now, far too old for the still-beautiful Vigdis, who rose to greet him when he entered.

Einar related most of what Rolli had said, and what he planned. "What should I do?" he asked her. "Should I imprison Rolli to keep him from disobeying my father?"

"How many did he bring with him?" Guthorm asked.

"Ten," said Einar. "I can't imprison all of them. I should—what—set guards? And would my father forgive me that? And who would do it? Sogn and Maer men who imagine they might one day call Rolli their king?"

"Let him go to Skane," said Vigdis. "What care do you have for any of it? If he is disgraced, it can only be good for you."

"Not when my father wanted me to send him away from Norway," said Einar.

"And what power do you have to do that?" Vigdis asked. "King Hakon once wanted your father to make Heming Hakonsson and Harald into friends, but no man can change the thoughts of another if he wills against it."

Einar had heard of that, though his father was loath to admit failing at anything. Heming and Harald were allies now, so perhaps he had not heard the whole story.

"So I should let him go?" Einar asked.

"Think of what will serve you best," said Vigdis.

"If that was all I cared for, I would go raiding in Scotland too and claim land in Iceland," Einar cried. "There is nothing for me here, not even my brother Ivar anymore."

"Calm yourself," said Vigdis. "You do not need to leave Norway. There is a future for you here, if you make it."

"That shows how little you know," said Einar, and he stormed from the hall.

✣ ✣ ✣

EINAR DID NOT know where to look at dinner that night. Gyda had seated herself by his side. Hilda and Rolli sat together again, speaking quietly.

"My lord Einar," said Gyda, after the meal was over, and a round of toasts had been celebrated. "You are as fine a storyteller as I have ever heard. Will you not entertain us with a tale?"

He wanted desperately to beg off. He wanted to touch her. He wanted never to see her or think of her again.

"Must I?" he asked Gyda in a low voice, leaning in toward her. He smelled her scent, like frost and metal.

"You are lord here," said Gyda lightly.

"Hardly," said Einar. Her fingers lay upon the arm of her chair, less than a hand's breadth from his wrist. If he had to disobey his father in the matter of Rolli, why should he not lie with Gyda again?

"Please," she said.

"As it pleases you, Princess Gyda," he said, standing and bowing to her. "Here is my tale. Once there was a beautiful giantess. Her father had died, and she held her mountain fortress against seven giants, all of whom tried to claim her hand." He continued, as he had once promised Gyda, telling the story of how she had outwitted all of her suitors by pitting them against one another, until she had to agree to the terms of the last one. He invented more details as they came to him, feeling as though he stood outside himself.

Finally he neared the finish: "'One more task I shall set you,' she said. 'Go forth and slay the giant with brows as white as frost, and mouth as wide and red as the setting sun. Bring me back his head and I will be your bride.' The giant went out, and though he searched far and wide, he did not find his target, for the only place he would have seen that face was in a pool of still water."

Einar stopped, waiting for inspiration that would tell him what would happen next, but it did not come. Gyda's story was unfinished.

"So did the giantess rule alone?" Gyda asked.

"There is another story that many of you know," said Einar. "Gerta, the giant's daughter who was courted by the god Frey. Perhaps that is the end to her story."

"Perhaps?" Gyda asked.

"Follow any story too long and it ends in death," said Einar. He had not been speaking loudly enough for all to hear, and small, grumbling conversations began around the room. Einar sat down, feeling bereft of the applause and cheers that usually accompanied his tales.

Gyda leaned toward him. "I thought you were going to make me an elf-woman," she said.

"Giantess is better," said Einar. "No one would think it was you."

Gyda smiled slightly and inclined her head in response. With Harald's warriors gone, few wanted to feast late into the night, so after the tables were cleared men began making their beds in their accustomed places. Einar went outside, walking slowly in case Gyda followed him. She caught up with him outside the hall.

"You have been avoiding me," she said, her voice low and flirtatious. Einar felt a flush of anger, that she seemed so unchanged toward him, even after wedding Harald, and that he still wanted her. He should have kept his attentions to young men—to Bakur, who he had still not touched, who had noticed his lack of interest and folded himself back into Harald's mass of warriors when they reached Vestfold.

In the shadow under the hall's eaves, they were hidden. He grabbed her arm and squeezed hard enough that a look of pain crossed her features. "That is what you do to me," he said harshly. He had never touched her other than gently before, and this rougher touch made him feel a harsher sort of urgency for her. Maybe that would disgust her and she would stay away.

"I am expected to share my mother-in-law's bed while Harald is gone," she said to him in a whisper that curled into his ears, more intimate than a touch.

"Then you had better do that," said Einar.

"Are you angry with me?" Gyda asked.

"More angry with myself," he said. "Everything I want, everything I must do, conflicts with every other."

"So I have gathered," she said. "And forgive me, I would give you one more choice: bring your brother Rolli to Hordaland. He will be safe from justice, and you will have fulfilled your father's command."

So tempting—he could serve himself, and anger his father while still obeying him. "No," he said. "Think that through. You would strain every division in Norway, and they are strained already. Harald would view it as rebellion."

"Would he?" Gyda asked. "Would he even care? I only want my independence—that is all I have ever wanted. I thought you wanted to help me. We were planning this together."

"My father knows," Einar blurted out. "He found out. We were seen. We cannot—it was a foolish dream." Gyda looked steadily at him. Einar rested his gaze on her mouth rather than her eyes. It was shaped like a rosebud, perfect even in her anger.

"We are, both of us, too cold for a romance out of a song, I think," she said, softly, drawing closer to him. He raised a hand to reach out, if only to touch her shoulder, but then pulled it back. She smiled and tucked a strand of stray hair behind her ear. "I enjoyed you, young Einar," she said. "Never think I did not."

"Gyda," he whispered.

"You can still come to me in Hordaland, but I may not be able to hold your place. I will rule there, whatever it takes."

Einar had nothing more to say, and so he watched her walk away into the twilight.

✣ ✣ ✣

EINAR FOUND ROLLI awake early the next morning by the shore, talking with his men about how to load his ship. Hilda sat, moving grain from one sack to another. He would not be able to catch Rolli alone now. Einar had tried to shape events—perhaps now he should only ride on the currents of fate.

"So you will allow this?" Einar asked Hilda. "Would Rolli not be safer staying in Vestfold?"

"Perhaps he would," said Hilda. "But if he is going to Skane, I will go with him."

Einar rubbed his forehead. He could not hold his brother prisoner, nor force him to Iceland or Hordaland. But he could not let Hilda face the dangers of travel without his protection. His father would not forgive him that either.

"And I too, I suppose," said Einar. "Though I wish you would not."

"You should come with me!" said Rolli. "We sail to glory."

After they boarded, Einar made a place for himself on one of the rowing benches, next to Bakur. Rolli's ship was the smallest Einar had ever ridden. He could hardly believe it had crossed the vast sea between Norway and the Orkney Islands. He had grown up hearing tales of waves ten times the height of a man, sent by Ran, the greedy sea goddess, that pulled ships down to her cold hall. His father, Ragnvald, had even seen that hall once in a vision, and always believed that Ran waited for him still, at the end of his life.

"What do you think we sail toward?" Bakur asked.

Einar glanced at him, wondering how much of his agitation Bakur could see. "Perhaps war, perhaps nothing," he said. "I know no more than I told you before."

Hilda sat at the base of the mast with some sewing in her lap, her dress pooling around her. She, who never liked to venture from her hall at Tafjord, seemed serene in the care of her young son.

The weather favored their journey, cool and cloudy, but with a steady breeze that never pushed the small vessel past its capabilities, and in five days, they saw the dunes and low cliffs of the Skanian coast.

IN FAIR WEATHER IT TOOK ONLY A FEW DAYS TO SAIL FROM Vestfold to Skane, where Ragnvald hoped to find Svanhild safe, and probably annoyed that he had come to her rescue. His ship had a good pilot, and the sailing was easy, so he had ample time to think over his decisions of the past week and regret many of them. He had left Einar with Gyda—a risk, and another test: Would the boy stay away from her, as he had ordered?

From Einar's birth, Ragnvald had sensed something hungry about him. He had felt that way too at Einar's age, jostling for the scraps that men like King Hakon and Harald let fall. Now Ragnvald all but ruled Norway at Harald's side. But Norway did not have the opportunities it had then, empty thrones and districts in chaos. Instead Harald's sons strained its seams, would-be kings who needed kingdoms.

Harald rode in Ragnvald's ship, seeming uncertain as he never had before, not even as a boy king. On the first day of the journey, he remained silent and spent his time watching the passing shoreline. Ivar too seemed subdued. He had never been away from Einar for longer than a day, and Ragnvald had once hoped he never would.

Neither of them could sustain a quiet mood for long, though. Even with two of Harald's sons present, Ivar quickly became the leader of the flock of young men. They ran about the ship, climbing as far up the mast as they could with hands and feet only, playing some half-formed game of tag as though they were still boys.

"Remember when we were that young?" Harald asked after Gudrod nearly knocked him over. Ragnvald smiled—he had fostered Gudrod for a few years, and liked to see him acting like a boy, rather than the haughty young man he had taken to Jutland, who thought himself too good for King Erik's daughter. Even Thorir had joined in the play, shedding his self-consciousness for once.

"I don't remember being that carefree," Ragnvald admitted.

Harald raised an eyebrow. "And you were acclaimed king far younger than these, and had no brothers."

"I remember," said Ragnvald, with a slight smile.

"Ha," said Harald. "What happened to my self-effacing friend, the one man in Norway who never boasts?"

"Was he not tiresome?" Ragnvald asked. "At your side, I have gained so much power and wealth—it would be churlish not to boast of it."

Harald shook his head. "You have an answer for everything—that has not changed."

Clouds drew in as they approached the Skanian coast. Even when sunlight touched them, the cliffs looked gray and forbidding.

Harald pushed the mass of his tangled hair back behind his shoulder. "I miss her," he said. "Her touch . . ."

No need to ask of whom he spoke—Snaefrid, the Finnish witch. "Women are like that," said Ragnvald. He missed Hilda and Alfrith when he was away from them and felt more balanced when they were near.

"But I think I should put her away," Harald added. "For the sake of my kingdom."

"I would not be the one to suggest it," said Ragnvald.

"You think so loud I can hear it!" Harald exclaimed. "These past years, whenever I was with her, I heard your voice telling me to end it."

"That must have put a damper on your lovemaking," said Ragnvald.

"I persevered," said Harald, echoing Ragnvald's dry tone. "Gyda was eager enough in my bed—women are not so different, really. And now that I am away from Snaefrid I can see how ensnared I was. But if I see her again, I will be entranced. Promise me you'll get rid of her when we return to Vestfold. Any other man, and I'd fear he'd be ensnared himself. But you'll manage, won't you?"

"Yes," said Ragnvald, though he would be cautious and enlist Harald's mother to help him, sorceress against sorceress, woman against woman.

"If you are in a listening mood," he continued carefully, "perhaps we should speak of Halfdan's rebellion. I fear we may find him in Skane, behind all of this."

"I am tired of this song," said Harald. "He is my son."

"And sons have never turned against fathers?" Ragnvald asked.

"Not as often as powerful district kings do," said Harald, his voice suddenly chilly.

"Yes," said Ragnvald. "Halfdan has made allies of a few of them." He glanced around at those who might overhear them, but they had as much privacy as they could get on board a ship. The boys played on, heedless, jostling one another off the capstan pedestal.

"But not you," said Harald. "You call him my enemy, though you have brought me no evidence. From what you say, he has been traveling, and gathering allies—nothing different from what you have been doing these past years."

"Would you have preferred I stay home?" Ragnvald asked with some bitterness. "I would have. I wanted to preserve your kingdom, the one we fought for, the peace that allowed my sons to grow up safe and my district to prosper. Should I have stopped? Ignored the growing rebellions? I want to make your kingdom strong enough that I can cut your hair and return to my kingdom and grow old there."

Harald looked out at the passing shore. The dark shapes of rocks made shadows under the glittering surface of the water. "It will never stop," he said. "As long as there is power, there will be men who want that power. Now it is you, or it is my son. If both of you were gone, it would be someone else, and will be, until the end of the world."

Ragnvald looked at him closely—it seemed like some other power spoke through him. "Then will you never cut your hair?" he asked.

"I have to, don't I?" Harald replied. "If only as a symbol. Then those who oppose me will be traitors, not merely kings who do not want to join me. When we have routed the raiders out of the Scottish isles, I will do it, but do not make the mistake of thinking it means our work is over. Can you blame me for taking a year or two of pleasure, amid all this? Have you never taken a year away from my wars?"

"You know I have," said Ragnvald. He had taken time to build his kingdom and raise his sons, but Harald had always called him to battle again.

"If my son is in rebellion, I will do what I must to bring him back to me," said Harald with a sigh. "You think because I have so many sons, I do not care for them as you do yours, but I do. Do not forget that."

"How?" Ragnvald asked. "How will you keep them from each other's throats? And mine?"

"They will need tasks and districts. It was my plan that each of them would be heir to their mother's districts, with the most able to succeed me," said Harald.

Could he not see the danger in that? Setting them against the sons of district kings? Two of Harald's sons now rested on the rowing benches, sprawling across them, long-legged and fearless. Harald then intended Gudrod to be heir to Hordaland. Halfdan would never be satisfied with cold, remote Halogaland, even if Heming let him inherit. Each one of these strong young men carried dangerous ambitions in his breast.

✦ ✦ ✦

THE CONVOY MADE for a beach at the southern tip of Skane. From there they would be able to see any approaching ships. Ragnvald had heard that this part of Skane had once been as populous as Vestfold, until a great sickness killed all of its inhabitants. Now it seemed as wild and unsettled a land as Norway must have been before the gods made men to populate it. The only sign that humans had once lived here was a series of burial mounds. The shorebirds did not even know enough to be scared of humans and were easily caught, plucked, and spitted for dinners.

The wind blew through the grasses that spread over the low dunes, a constant moan that made the land seem even emptier. Ivar and Harald's sons were still in good spirits at least, eager for an adventure and a little battle, though Ragnvald could not help but see Ivar as half of himself without his brother.

He had turned soft as he neared middle age, and Einar had taken advantage of it. He had been so certain as a young man, willing to make harsh decisions that led to hurt and anger—he had known that his defeat of King Hakon might cost him his friendship with Oddi, and done it anyway. The man he was today would have begged for Oddi's forgiveness, promised anything, wished it undone. He looked down at his gnarled hands, the swollen knuckles, and fingers that could not straighten. Solvi had broken something in him; he could no longer cause pain without feeling it too.

They spent a few days on the beach, waiting to see if Skanians would come to offer terms for Svanhild's release, but the scouts who patrolled the edge of the forest saw no one. Harald authorized a party to go farther into the woods.

Ragnvald kept watch while many of the warriors around him fell asleep. As the sun lowered behind the clouds on the southern horizon, lighting the sky with fingers of pink and orange, Ivar sat down next to him.

"What if they do not return?" Ivar asked.

"At least then we will know there are people here," Ragnvald answered.

"But what then?" Ivar asked.

"What do you think?" Ragnvald asked. This reminded him of times he had conversed with Einar, training him to think through possibilities, make plans, turn all ends to himself. He had not trained Ivar the same way.

"Then we must send more parties," said Ivar.

"So they can be captured?" Ragnvald asked.

"Then all of us should go," said Ivar, picking impatiently at the grass growing next to him.

"That is a better idea," Ragnvald allowed, "though some should stay and guard the ships. Still, we wouldn't know what we were marching into."

"What would you do, Father?" Ivar asked.

"They will likely return," said Ragnvald. "They cannot walk very far in the time they were given. But I suppose I would take out some ships and try to capture one of theirs for information. That is less risky than a march into enemy territory."

"It is all so uncertain," said Ivar.

"Yes," said Ragnvald. "Only death is certain, and even then *draugrs* walk."

Ivar bid him good night, and Ragnvald continued to watch the sunset. Many of the warriors had fallen asleep by the time the sun finally dipped below the horizon, leaving a stain of orange behind. Ragnvald watched as it faded, and then grew again, red into orange into yellow.

He dozed on a dune, and woke with the sun high in a faded sky, his ankles itchy from the sand fleas that had bitten him during the night. The advance party had not returned.

By breakfast the following day, the mood in the camp had turned very quiet. At dinner, Harald sat next to Ragnvald, methodically sucking the meat off the bones of the shorebirds, then throwing them over his shoulder for gulls to squabble over. Dagfinn sat with them, making his own pile of bones, while the rest of the young men played on the shore with a leather ball.

Harald smiled and joked with his warriors until he finished his meal and turned toward Ragnvald, his eyes haunted. Ragnvald felt it too, the vast emptiness, with the sky wide and watchful overhead.

"Do you think they will return?" Harald asked.

"No," said Ragnvald. "They are captive or dead."

"What should we do, then?" Harald asked.

"If the Skanians could defeat us in open combat they would have come by now. They want us to divide our forces for them," said Ragnvald.

"Then we should all go," said Harald.

Ragnvald smiled. He sounded just like Ivar. "Or we wait them out. There must be a reason they do not want to meet in the open."

"What do we do if no one comes?" Harald asked. "We will run out of provisions before they do." His hair, which had grown darker with so much time indoors, was bleached gold again from the sunlight. His face had burned red and peeled across his nose, showing tan underneath, as though the young king Ragnvald had once followed was hidden under his skin.

Ragnvald made his suggestion about taking to the sea. "Or failing that," he added, "the kings of Roskilde have always desired control of Skane—we could make a common cause with them and see if, with their aid, we can do better than we can alone."

Some argument between the young men ended the play at the shore, and they tramped over to Harald's fire. Ivar picked through discarded bird carcasses for scraps, while Gudrod slaked his thirst with a skin of ale, and Thorir sat down next to Ragnvald.

"You don't think we have enough warriors to take battle to them?" Harald asked.

"I do not like to go blind into a trap," said Ragnvald.

"We should not wait," said Gudrod. "We should send a larger party into the woods and try to find them."

"I see you do not know your history," said Dagfinn. Ragnvald could not help but smile. Dagfinn liked nothing better than to show off his memory for Norway's laws and legends. He continued, "When my father and King Ragnvald fought in Naustdal, King Vemund's much smaller force still caused great losses because they knew the land better. There is a song, would you like to hear it?"

"No," said Ivar and Gudrod, practically in unison. Dagfinn did not look offended—his suggestions were usually greeted that way.

"We can't just sit here," said Ivar. "Father, give me leave to take a bigger scouting party. If we go inland for a few days, we are certain to find something."

"And give the Skanians more hostages?" Ragnvald asked, frowning at him. "No, I forbid it."

"You think they will come to us?" Ivar asked. "How would they know we are here? We have seen no one."

"They know," said Ragnvald.

"What if another force is coming to trap us here?" Dagfinn asked. "That's what happened at the battle of Hafrsfjord, where Solvi Sea King and all of his forces—"

"Yes, yes," said Ivar impatiently, cutting off another tale.

Gudrod cleared his throat. "We should take a larger party into the woods, capture one of their scouts, and torture him for information," he said to Ivar. "Your father is too cautious."

Ivar looked at Ragnvald, who shrugged. He had been hearing such complaints his whole life and they had ceased to trouble him much. "It is Harald's decision," said Ragnvald.

Harald looked at him and shook his head slightly. "I will decide tomorrow," he said.

✢ ✢ ✢

THORIR PRODDED RAGNVALD awake early the next morning. "Father, Ivar and Harald's sons have left without your permission. They've gone to find the Skanians!" Thorir told him.

Ragnvald rubbed his eyes and listened, but it took a couple repetitions before he woke enough to grasp that they had taken a party of thirty warriors on this mission, against his orders. "And you did not wake me until now," said Ragnvald.

"I only woke to see them leaving, and I ran after them," said Thorir defensively. "They said they would not turn back. And . . ." He seemed loath to continue.

"And?" Ragnvald prompted.

"And they said that they would all be kings one day and I should remember that. And I said I would not follow them in this foolishness."

"But you knew of it?" Ragnvald asked. He had fallen asleep listening to the young men boasting idly of what they would do if they had a Skanian scout in their power. They had not seemed motivated to do more.

"Is this so terrible, Father?" Thorir asked. "They will bring back information."

"Or they will be captured," said Ragnvald.

Thorir wore a self-satisfied expression, and Ragnvald wondered if he liked that idea, realizing he would benefit from the loss of his brother, or simply liked that he had behaved better than Ivar. Harald's sons might not be the only brothers destined for conflict.

"Does Harald know yet?" Ragnvald asked. He pulled on his shoes and stood. He should have foreseen this and kept watch.

Harald had discovered what happened at the same time as Ragnvald, and met him at the breakfast cook-fire. "I suppose they are too old to be beaten when they return," he said, looking more bemused than annoyed.

"Gudrod is with them, and he is a good tracker," said Thorir.

Harald shrugged. "I suppose he probably is. He spent his early years in Princess Gyda's upland fort. There is good hunting on those plains." He turned toward Thorir. "How many did they take?" he asked.

"Thirty," Thorir answered. "Enough to scout, and defend themselves if attacked, don't you think?"

Ragnvald had fought King Vemund on his own territory many years before, and did not think ten times as many men would be enough against a force used to fighting by stealth, on land they knew. Skanian warriors might be watching them even now.

"This decides it," said Harald. "Our full force must follow them—my men, as well as Aldi's and Oddi's, while you wait here. If you do not hear word in a week, you must go to muster all of Norway on my behalf."

"You should not risk yourself," said Ragnvald.

"They have three of my sons and only one of yours. I should go."

"Three?" Ragnvald asked.

"You said that Halfdan is likely here, and he is still my son," Harald reminded him.

Ragnvald shook his head. "I should go," he said.

"No, you are the one who should not risk himself. I know your *wyrd* is to die for me one day, but I would not have it be today. My luck will protect me. The men of Norway respect you as much as they do me." He smiled ruefully. "If not more, these days. You will have as much luck mustering them as I will."

Ragnvald argued with him a little longer, but Harald would not be swayed. His party marched out that morning, flattening the grass of the dunes with their passing. Soon Ragnvald lost sight even of Harald's shining head among the trees in the distance, he too swallowed up by this hungry land.

18

THE SYMPTOMS OF THE MUSHROOM FREYDIS HAD TAKEN WERE strange, not what Alfrith had led her to expect. She drifted in dreams and did not know when she slept and when she woke. In one, her mother had come to stroke her hair, while Freydis watched her brother, still a small boy, as he had been at his death. He played in a carpet of flowers that grew next to her bed. In another, Solvi came to her and promised her that Hallbjorn's child, her child, would be a girl.

She thought of that, resting her hand over her womb, and smiled a little. Perhaps she was not going to die. She became aware of Unna watching her and turned away.

"Freydis, look at me," said Unna.

Freydis stared up at the ceiling instead. "I dreamed my father said it would be a girl. My aunt Alfrith said that dreams are true sometimes. Do you think that one is?"

"That was not a dream. He did say that," said Unna, her usual dry tone tinged with worry.

So that had been real. Tears wet Freydis's cheeks before she realized she was crying.

"Is it so very bad?" Unna asked. "Would you rather die than bear your rapist's child?"

"It was not rape," Freydis protested. "I let him do this." Her throat hurt as she made herself say it. "I let it happen, and now I am trapped. More than I ever was before." She wiped her face angrily. "If it had been rape, then I could bear it, but this is mine. This is my shame. And now I may die in childbirth. Better to die now."

"You may," said Unna. "Though I will use all my magic to prevent it."

"Why should I not die now? My only value was in marriage, and now that is spoiled."

"Well," said Unna, "if marriage is what you want, that handsome young man has offered it."

Freydis cried harder. "No, I will not go to him! And I will not—I cannot bear this. I cannot." Even through her misery she heard uneven footsteps, someone coming toward her. She opened her eyes and saw Solvi standing over her, his eyes grave. He sat down by her and took her hand, a bit awkwardly.

"You are not trapped," said Unna. "I will care for you as long as you need, and the babe. I owe that much to your mother."

"My mother," said Freydis. She drew her hand away. Both of them wanted Svanhild, not her.

"I will too," said Solvi. "You can stay with me or with Unna. I would not have sent you away from me if I thought it would drive you to this."

Unna cleared her throat. "She can stay with you, Solvi Hunthiofsson, but not until this recent danger is past, and I am sure she will not try to take her life again."

Solvi frowned. "Will you, Freydis? Do you truly want to die?"

"I don't want to die in childbirth," she said. "I don't want it to hurt." Her face reddened—she sounded like a child herself.

Solvi sighed. "I wish I could promise you it won't." He looked up at Unna. "Life brings pain, and so does death. But stay for me, if you will not stay for yourself."

Freydis could not bring herself to speak, but she did nod, and Solvi stood, looking relieved. "I must return to my farm," he said. "Please come when you are well. You are my daughter."

✣　✣　✣

UNNA BUSTLED AROUND the house, fixing dinner, sorting herbs, keeping within view of Freydis as she dozed. The other servants came and went, speaking quietly to Unna. Eventually the light from the doorway turned into the blue glow of twilight, and Freydis pulled herself up to sitting. She took a sip of water from the cup by her side.

"Are you hungry?" Unna asked. "If you eat, it will help clear the poison."

She had a sudden memory of Unna feeding her milk after she ate the mushrooms, and something else to make her vomit. Of Unna cleaning her face with a cloth, and even changing her soiled bedclothes. She thought she might cry again, and hated herself for it. If she was not going to die, she must make herself useful, so Unna would not regret saving her.

She touched her stomach. She was not hungry, but she thought she could eat, and that doing so would make Unna glad. She nodded, and Unna brought over a bowl of stewed rye berries. She sat with Freydis as she ate it, and then took the bowl from her hands.

"Lie down again, child," she said. "You will need a great deal more rest before you are well."

Freydis lay down again, placing her cheek upon Unna's thigh. Unna made a startled noise, but then began to stroke Freydis's hair. When she found a snarl, she eased it out between her fingers. Freydis had almost fallen asleep again under her soothing hands when Unna said, "I had a daughter once. When I was very young in Scotland."

"Tell me," Freydis said. Unna's leg made a comfortable pillow, made of warm flesh, not the iron Freydis expected.

"I was born on a Scottish island," said Unna. "My mother was a Scottish thrall and my father was a Norse raider. I wed one of my father's men as soon as I was old enough to bleed, for women were scarce there. I was not much older than you the first time I fell pregnant."

Freydis tried to picture her as a young woman, with the pure black hair Unna must have had before she went gray. Still tall and strong, or had that come later? Did she once feel as young and trapped as Freydis did now?

"What was he like, your husband?" Freydis asked.

"A mighty warrior, I was told. Now I would reckon him a young man, but he seemed old to me then, when I was a child. He was not gentle, but he was not so cruel either. My first child was a boy, and after his birth, my husband treated me better. It took some time, but I think we grew to care for each other over the years. I bore him four sons before I bore my daughter, whom I loved more than all the others. She was gentle and fierce, and I promised myself I would give her the girlhood I never had."

She stroked Freydis's hair for a time without speaking. Freydis wiped her face on her sleeve. Her eyes and throat felt raw from all her crying.

"What happened?" Freydis asked.

"She died in the same sickness that took my husband, my sons, and all of the servants save Donall." Unwillingly, Freydis pictured it, the dead and dying, and Unna unable to save her family, even with her healing magic. A black-haired woman and a red-haired servant finding pleasure and comfort together when everyone else had become corpses. Donall would have been very young then, just come to manhood.

"How did you end up here?" Freydis asked. Unna continued to stroke Freydis's hair. The calluses on her palms caught and pulled at loose strands.

"I ran away," said Unna. "I sold the farm, and bought passage for myself and Donall on a ship bound for Iceland. I wanted a new place, where my children had never been. I had enough silver left over to hire servants to clear the land. I did not know what I wanted besides that. I never fell pregnant again, so I will have no one to pass this land on to. Perhaps, after I die, Donall will take a wife and make an heir for this place."

"Why are you telling me this?" Freydis asked.

"Because I survived the death of my family, and you can survive this. In Scotland I was only the wife of a warrior, but here I have power and freedom."

"Was it worth it?" Freydis whispered. "Surviving?"

Unna sighed heavily. "If the gods accepted such trades, I would have my family back," she said. "I would see my daughter's face again." Freydis turned over onto her back so she could look up at Unna. She heard tears in Unna's stony voice, but her face was as stern and hard as ever. "They do not, though. Now, swear to me that you will not seek your death. Swear it, child, or I will make the choice for you, and tie you up if need be. I will not let you choose death."

"I want this child to be a daughter," said Freydis. "Will you help me? Help me give her what I did not have?" She would give her child a mother who would comb out her hair, teach her about being a woman, and protect her from men who would despoil her.

"Yes, child. And until then, I will keep you strong."

✛ ✛ ✛

UNNA INSISTED THAT Freydis spend a few more days in bed. She checked on her frequently, made sure she ate and did not again try to rid herself of the child, or her life. Freydis floated between those moments, looking up at the turf ceiling of Unna's house, which pressed through the woven cane that supported it.

The smell of her stale, sick sweat rose up to her nostrils. Her vision blurred when she swung around to put her feet on the floor. The rushes and pebbles, and other detritus were painful beneath them. She was nearly too dizzy to walk. When she went outside, the gray light from the cloudy sky hurt her eyes. Unna was working nearby in the garden. In the furrow between her rows of vegetables, a late lamb toddled on unsteady legs. It must have been rejected by its mother and no other lambing sheep would take it. At Tafjord such a lamb would be slaughtered and eaten immediately—better not to waste the effort.

As Freydis watched from the door, the lamb nosed at Unna's thigh. It grew more and more insistent and then started to cry before Unna brushed off her hands and scooped it up in her arms. Freydis had seen a pitcher of milk in the kitchen and went to get it, along with a small rag, though she had to brace herself on the doorframe again to avoid fainting.

"Freydis," said Unna. "You are feeling better?"

Freydis winced at the sound of the lamb's crying. "I thought I was," she said with a frown. "Can I feed him?"

"Her," said Unna, inclining her head toward the creature. Of course, Unna would not have saved a runt of a ram that would never give milk or birth more lambs.

Freydis picked it up, gently and firmly, and balanced it on her hip until she found a stone where she could sit and drip milk into its mouth. At first it would not take the fabric and would only suckle from her finger, crying again when it only drank one drop, but eventually she convinced it to take the rag and was surprised when she found she had emptied the bowl of milk.

"She was hungry," said Freydis.

"You can have the feeding of her, if you want," Unna replied. "I don't have time to give her the attention she needs."

And, Freydis was sure, Unna thought this task would reconcile her to the necessity of bearing and then caring for her own child. She could expose her baby after it was born—the other way to deal with unwanted children—but she did not think that if she survived birth she would have the stomach to let her child go. The little lamb in her arms, satisfied, seemed to smile up at her as it fell asleep.

Why should she let Hallbjorn punish her so much, not only with exile, nine months of pregnancy, and the pain of childbirth, but also with the pain of losing the child she bore? No, she would not punish herself and her child out of anger at him.

She named the lamb Torfa, after her cat, who sailed with Hallbjorn now. She hoped Torfa scratched him every chance she got.

She made the lamb into her pet, even letting it sleep next to her at night in her pallet, until it fouled her bed and she had to make a nest of straw for it in the corner of Unna's house. As she grew stronger, she took on more work, milking Unna's goats, sheep, and cows, learning which ones were docile and which ones kicked.

From time to time, she accompanied Unna to other farms, to care for the sick and injured, and learned the stories of other Icelanders. Many had come here because they had nowhere else to go, and Freydis felt at home among them.

19

SVANHILD WALKED THE PERIMETER OF MELBRID'S CAMP, COUNT-
ing sentries while she picked berries for tomorrow's breakfast. A mist in
the treetops coalesced into drips of water that made the fires steam and
her clothes grow heavy and itchy. A pair of warriors followed her, one of
Halfdan's and one of Melbrid's. She hoped to find one who would come
with her to Vestfold and tell Harald what they knew of Halfdan's plans,
but had no luck so far.

A squirrel darted out from the underbrush, its black eyes shining, and
for a moment Svanhild was back in Iceland with her son Eystein, who
loved to coax small animals to eat grain from his hands. If he had lived,
he would be a young man now, perhaps with the same gentle spirit he
had as a boy. A blur of tears made her wander closer than she intended to
a sentry. He held her there until her guards caught up with her, and then
they escorted her back to the smoldering fire that Luta kept lit near her
tent. She sat down and poked at it with a stick, sending up a few sparks
into the damp air.

Falki came to sit next to her, carefully allowing a small gap between
them, though his closeness still warmed her.

"My lady," he said, "I know how to get back to the ship, if you wish it."

"Thank you," said Svanhild. "I will, and soon, but my work is not yet
done here. Do you know what they have planned?"

"More or less," he said. "Halfdan has sent a messenger to Erik of Jutland to bring his force here, since it is only a few days' sail from Vestfold."

"Or Tonsberg," said Svanhild heavily. The trading town was only a little farther west, and largely undefended. Harald's reputation had kept it safe until now, but that was fading. His son in rebellion would erase it entirely. Halfdan might make himself king, or he might only plunge Norway into chaos, breaking it back into the warring kingdoms that Harald had united, leaving it ripe for conquest from Denmark and Sweden.

She went to take a bath in the chilly stream favored by the camp's women, on the inland side. Afterward, Luta combed her hair out slowly, with patient, gentle strokes.

"You shouldn't worry I would tell," said Luta as she worked.

"Tell what?" Svanhild asked. The movement of Luta's fingers through her hair was hypnotizing.

"If you take that Falki for your lover. I have heard—the king is no husband to you." Svanhild stiffened, and Luta stroked her forehead until she relaxed again. "I wouldn't tell," Luta repeated. She cackled suddenly. "But I would want payment."

Svanhild swatted at her. "You grasping old witch," she said, laughing. "And I'd pay you too, but it would still get out. I made an oath."

"Seems to me, so did he," said Luta.

Svanhild did not answer, and Luta said no more, only finished braiding Svanhild's hair into plaits that would keep it out of her way for the next week.

If she could trust Luta—no, better not to think of it. She could trust Falki with that secret, and with her life, but though Svanhild liked Luta, she might be under the pay of one of Harald's other wives, trying to elevate herself at Svanhild's expense. Better to laugh about it and keep Falki at arm's length.

Halfdan came to sit next to Svanhild while they ate dinner—deer killed the day before by one of Halfdan's men, and stewed over the day with foraged root vegetables. Though he had been here for a while, some uneasiness existed between his men, Melbrid's, and the Skanians whom Melbrid had come to rule.

"I shouldn't have spoken to you that way, before," Halfdan said to her.

"How?" Svanhild asked coolly. She usually tried not to think of how small she was compared with the men who surrounded her. If she conducted herself like a goddess, untouchable by mortal weapons, men usually treated her that way as well, but Halfdan had pierced that illusion.

"I am apologizing to you," he said.

Svanhild gave him a thin smile. "I thank you, and I accept your apology," she said. "Tell me, how did you come to be here?"

"After my father—" He looked away. "Well, you probably heard—but I don't know why he had to marry her! Bad enough to take his own son's woman. He always said that I had to marry well, and here he is, scorning his other wives for a commoner."

"It was ill done," Svanhild agreed. She had often thought Halfdan a bully, and he was sometimes, but she enjoyed his unguarded speech now.

"Yes," said Halfdan. He kicked at a vole that ran between his feet and the fire. "My mother deserves better. You deserve better." His mother was Asa Hakonsdatter, who lived in Halogaland with her brother King Heming. Halfdan might claim Heming's loyalty through that kin relationship.

"So you left after that," said Svanhild.

"Of course." He ran a hand through his hair. It was too short for braids but would make an appealing frame for his face if he trimmed it evenly. "You cannot be happy with what Harald did to you, to all his wives. Why not support me and Melbrid against him?"

Svanhild smiled more fully. No other woman in Norway wielded as much power as she did. "And be your first Norse ally?" she asked.

"King Erik of Jutland says he won't ally with me unless Ragnvald does too," said Halfdan, sidestepping her question, if he had even noticed it. "But you'd be almost as good."

"How flattering," said Svanhild dryly.

"I think he's wrong," said Halfdan. "I suppose a king must have all the allies he can find. But I cannot believe Ragnvald would betray my father."

"Men call him Norway's true king up and down the Norse coast," she said. "Where his loyalty goes so does all of Norway's. Even, I suspect, your uncle Heming's." She watched Halfdan's face to see what he would reveal, but he remained impassive. "What do I get if I bring Ragnvald to your side?" she asked. Some perverse spirit prompted her to continue. "If you were king, would you allow me to bring back Solvi Hunthiofsson?"

"Ha! Your brother would never let you," said Halfdan. "Better to join me without him, and then we'll see. If Ragnvald joins my rebellion, I'll be only a figurehead king, just as my father is."

"Perhaps you are right," said Svanhild. No need to argue with him. If he defeated Harald—she could hardly imagine that, but if he did, she truly could set off in her ship to find Solvi. She had promised to come to him if her marriage with Harald failed, and it had, long ago. He had been her true husband, her partner as Harald never had.

✛ ✛ ✛

KING ERIK OF Jutland arrived a few days later, bringing chaos along with his men and baggage. Svanhild had been able to learn no more about Halfdan's alliances and plans. Falki had been pressing her to leave, but she thought that with the coming of Erik she might learn where they would attack. She joined in his welcome, standing side by side with Melbrid, Halfdan, and a few of the comelier women from the camp.

"My lady," Erik said to her, after kissing her hand, "rumors of your beauty have not been exaggerated."

She thanked him, though she had seen a mirror recently enough to know that her beauty would no longer be noted if she had not married a king. She had learned to be charming, while sun and wind stole her beauty, roughening it and carving lines that would not mar the faces of housebound women until their next decade.

"Melbrid tells me your brother may join our cause," said Erik. "That would be a windfall."

That must have been one of the things Halfdan and Melbrid had been arguing about yesterday. "And if he does," said Svanhild, tossing her hair, "should my loyalty lie with my husband or my brother?"

"I like this not at all," said Halfdan in a deep growl. "King Ragnvald's power has grown far too great. It is one of the reasons I have rebelled. And why this lady makes a good hostage."

"Hostage?" Svanhild asked lightly. "I am Melbrid's guest, as are you, and he is not a man to dishonor the gods."

"Neither am I," said Erik, touching the amulet he wore at his neck. "And why should we threaten one who can deliver Ragnvald the Mighty to our side?"

"She cannot, nor should we want her to," said Halfdan angrily, "but you will see that soon enough."

This rift would be useful—the promise of Ragnvald's aid worth more than Halfdan's threats. Halfdan was a figurehead already, whether

he knew it or not. Perhaps Svanhild should leave now and lay the problem at Ragnvald's feet. He could dangle himself as an ally, and play these
men off against one another.

That afternoon she found Falki sitting on a log and feeding one of
the camp's semi-tame chickens from a small cache of seeds in his hand.
Svanhild did the same, so their activity would cover their talking.

"What do you think of our chances if we leave tonight?" she asked him.

He grinned at her. "I know where they post their sentries, and with
the chaos that Erik has brought, we will be easy to overlook."

"I do not mean to stay and be used as a weapon against my brother,"
she said. "Tell me your plan."

"There will be a signal," said Falki, "and when you hear it, follow the
path east of camp back to the sea. That will lead near enough where the
ship was."

As the day wore on, Svanhild saw the suspicion between Halfdan's
and Erik's warriors break out into small squabbles. Erik and Melbrid
spent long hours talking together and seemed not to include Halfdan in
their discussions, so he had to barge in.

Twilight came as Svanhild finished eating a late dinner. Luta sat next
to her, chewing on a flavorful twig. She broke it in half and gave part to
Svanhild to clean her teeth.

"You can come with me if you wish," said Svanhild, "or you can stay
here. It may be safer."

Luta looked offended. "We have sailed through storms far worse
than this," she said.

✤   ✤   ✤

SVANHILD LAY DOWN and breathed deeply, hoping her guards would
think her sleeping. Before long, she heard the guard change and had
her sailor Mani take his place, and then the signal she awaited. She
put her head out of the opening of her tent. She wore a dark wimple
over her hair, and in the dimness of a midsummer night, her clothes
would fade into the blue as well. She already had her small dagger tied
around her waist under her dress. She would have to leave her larger
dagger behind in the care of Melbrid's guards.

Behind her, in the Skanian camp, a few torches still burned. She followed Falki, watching his heels tread the pine needles, placing her feet

where his had fallen. Soon pine-needle paths gave way to bare rock, and she felt a damp breeze on her face that could only come from the sea. She saw it a moment later, broad and flat, her only true home since she was a child.

They reached the edge of the cliff as the sun began to rise, though long before the camp would wake. It spent very little time below the horizon at this time of year. This was not where she had put ashore before, but as the sun rose higher and painted the cliffs red, and then gold, she recognized the point of land to the north that sheltered the bay where she had landed. When she reached the hollow where her ship was hidden, she found twelve of her men already there, moving the ship by slow degrees down the slope toward the water. Olaf, Sigurd's son, helped direct them. Luta sat on a rock nearby, stabbing at a piece of cloth with her needle.

A false birdcall made Svanhild look up. Men on the cliffs above began their descent.

"Keep shifting the ship," she commanded. Moving, they would be harder for arrows to find, and the ship hid most of them. The rocks at the shoreline, when they reached it, would hide them still better. "Put it in the water immediately. We can put the lines right once we're at sea."

Her men worked quickly, but not quickly enough, and by the time they had brought the ship down to the shore and were readying to push it off, Halfdan's men had encircled them. Halfdan approached Svanhild, his hand resting on his sword.

"Your escape was well planned," he said. "I would like to know how you did it, but we will have time enough to discuss it back at camp."

Two of his men came and took hold of Svanhild's arms. More of them approached Svanhild's men with their swords drawn. Her men were unarmed.

"Your Melbrid took my men's weapons and now you will kill them?" Svanhild asked. "There is a word for men like that."

Halfdan smiled unpleasantly. "You think my men fear being called murderers?" he asked.

"Do they fear being called cowards?" Svanhild asked, loudly enough for all of them to hear.

"Who is going to call them that?"

"I will—unless you intend to kill me too, and I am far more use to you as a hostage. You should let my men leave. You do not need them to hold me ransom."

"If I let them go, that is a dozen more fighting on my father's side," said Halfdan. He tightened his grip on his sword as Svanhild struggled ineffectually against her captors.

One of his men yelled something out from his perch and pointed. Svanhild turned and saw another ship approaching with its shields out. A small ship, and one she recognized immediately—she had designed it and ordered it to be built for her nephew Rolli. She waved.

"I have help now," she said to Halfdan. "That ship you see is mine as well, and is crewed by the best of my men, expert archers all."

"One ship," said Halfdan scornfully.

Svanhild smiled, as if she had planned for this. "You did not bring your new allies," she said, looking around slowly. "Why is that? Could it be that you wanted some advantage over them, to keep me as your hostage alone?"

Halfdan looked uncertain, so Svanhild continued, "Not all my men are with me here. Some remained in Melbrid's camp, to make sure that I was not pursued—or did you not count the number of my followers?" By Halfdan's panicked look, she knew he had not. "Have your men seen those who track them through the Skanian brush, as silent as death? Leave me be, and they will let your men live when you go back into the forest."

"You're a lying woman," said Halfdan.

"Would you risk it?" Svanhild asked. "Risk the few men who actually follow you, and not your allies?"

Rolli's ship reached the shore before Halfdan made up his mind. He made an abrupt gesture, and his men retreated away from Svanhild's. As soon as they were free, they pushed her ship into the shallows and climbed up into it. Only Falki remained on land, ready to help Svanhild climb up.

"If you mistrust your allies now, how much worse when there is really something at stake?" she asked. "Come with me and ask your father's forgiveness. He will grant it, even if he shouldn't." Halfdan did not answer. "Or stay here and die," she added. "Less competition for my sons."

He shook his head, and in that moment, Svanhild ran away from him, jumping lightly over the slippery rocks toward her ship, before Halfdan could move to stop her. Falki helped her up just as a wave rocked the ship, and then Rolli's flung rope helped pull it out of the breakers. Once they had gone a few boat lengths, Svanhild brought her ship up along Rolli's and climbed aboard.

She recognized Rolli's companions from among the young men at Tafjord. She greeted Einar, whose narrow, handsome face looked troubled, but then, it often did. Behind Einar, sitting at the base of the sail, she saw the brown bulk of Ragnvald's wife, Hilda. Svanhild blinked in shock.

"Hilda, sister," she said. "What in heavens are you doing here?"

Hilda tilted her head toward Rolli. "He needed me," she said. Then more warily, "I suppose you have not heard."

Svanhild laughed. She was free and safe now, skipping away from danger once again. "I have been a somewhat unwilling guest in Skane. I have missed some of the gossip."

Hilda told her of Rolli's deeds. Svanhild felt colder with every word, and when she heard Hilda say her daughter's name, she sat down heavily on a rowing bench.

"So you think this was all Hallbjorn's fault?" Svanhild asked, her voice going high with anger.

"Rolli says they both thought that Aldi's ship was a raiding vessel," Hilda admitted.

"And now my daughter, my Freydis, is wed to this Hallbjorn?" she asked.

"I do not know if they are wed yet," said Hilda. "Rolli said that Hallbjorn intended it."

Svanhild gripped the bench hard enough that the rough wood hurt her hands. Freydis kidnapped, taken far from home, with a young man who intended her ill. "I should take Rolli's ship away from him," she said, half to herself. "It was built for me."

"It is not a bad match," said Hilda. "Hallbjorn's mother, Vigdis, is now Guthorm's mistress. She can do much for him."

"He is the *nithing* son of a coward and a whore," Svanhild replied, rising to her feet.

"You wed Solvi Hunthiofsson," said Hilda.

"The son of a king," said Svanhild, angrily. "I will not have my daughter wed against her will. Where is she now?"

"He took her to Iceland," she said. "To . . . to Solvi Sea King, is what Rolli said."

Svanhild sat back down, heavily.

"What will you do?" Hilda asked.

"Get her back, whatever it takes," said Svanhild. "I will go myself or"—she laughed, high and mirthless—"Harald has always wanted to take war to Solvi and now he will get his chance."

20

THE TWENTY WARRIORS LEFT BEHIND WITH RAGNVALD ATE around only one campfire. Sigurd did most of the cooking, a skill he had acquired sailing with Ragnvald these many years. By now the shorebirds had learned to fear them, so tonight's meal was dried fish stewed and pounded into edibility, made even saltier by the brackish water, which was all they could find near the shore. Ragnvald slaked his thirst with more ale than he ought to drink, taking the king's share, now that Harald was gone.

"The Skanians have my son also," Sigurd said. He had been a constant presence at Ragnvald's side since the battle of Hafrsfjord. And if he was less of a comfort than Oddi had been, at least Ragnvald need not fear that Sigurd would grow to hate him. If killing Sigurd's father had not done that, nothing would.

"I'm sure Svanhild will not forget him in the negotiations, don't worry," said Ragnvald, feeling guilty he had not remembered the boy himself.

"Why did Harald bring a force against them if he only means to negotiate?" Sigurd asked.

"He needs to show that if the Skanians harm their hostages, we can destroy them," said Ragnvald. "It is a stronger negotiating position, and he can protect himself from being made hostage."

"Of course," said Sigurd happily, and Ragnvald wished he could be so easily comforted.

If Harald did not return in a week, then he would need to muster all of Norway's warriors for a battle in Skane. But would Harald's jarls and kings come, or would districts that had governed themselves for centuries without Harald's rulership become separate again? Denmark's districts had given fealty to old King Gorm only to fall apart again under his sons.

Every day dawned the same, with low clouds on the horizon and a mist over the sea. At midday high cirri formed overhead, driven by strong winds, good for sailing, but wasted with Ragnvald stranded here. In the evening, the clouds blew away, leaving a broad, open sky that faded from pale blue to orange, and then back to deeper blue in the evening.

Ragnvald could not believe that Harald would not return—his own vision and Ronhild's said that Harald would live a long, charmed life, and never lose a single battle. Ronhild had also prophesied that Ragnvald would give his life for Harald. Perhaps here was where he would fulfill that *wyrd*, marching into this trackless land after Harald. Perhaps a monster lurked there, a relic from the time of the gods that killed all who entered the wood. It would explain this strange and empty land.

As the week neared its end, Ragnvald felt too shadowed by doom to sleep. He was trying to plan his journey gathering forces from Norway's districts when Thorir, with his sharp eyesight, saw a figure walking toward the shore across the waving field of grass. Sigurd led a small band of warriors out to capture him, and returned escorting a young man with a patchy mustache and a self-important air.

"King Ragnvald of Norway," he said, with a bow of greeting, "King Erik of Jutland begs that you, the true king of Norway, come to negotiate for the exchange of hostages and the end of hostilities."

"Erik!" said Ragnvald. That explained much. The Skanians on their own might capture a small band of warriors, but not the bulk of Harald's forces. "What is your name?"

"Sverri," said the young man.

"Did King Erik make sure that King Harald heard him give you that message?" Ragnvald asked.

Sverri nodded, looking scared. His fingers flew to his sparse mustache.

"And who are you? Who is your father?" Ragnvald asked.

"I have no father," Sverri said quietly.

Disposable then, not worth using as a hostage.

"King Erik told me to tell you whatever you wanted to know," said Sverri. When he dropped his hand away from his face, his upper lip quivered. Ragnvald smiled slightly. This boy could not be older than Thorir. And no matter what, Ragnvald had no stomach for torture, nor did he trust what was learned from it. A man would say anything, as he knew too well. His fingers grew tight at the memory. He flexed them as he began to question the boy.

He learned that Harald's force had marched into the Skanian camp, taken captives, and surrounded the Skanians, trapping them in their winter cave. They were, as Ragnvald suspected, fewer than Harald's forces, but had enough men, with Erik's infusion of warriors, to hold their hostages and keep Harald's forces at bay.

"Tell me who the hostages are," said Ragnvald. Perhaps they did not know that Sigurd's son, Olaf, would be worth anything in ransom or trade. That might help the boy survive if things went badly.

"Ivar Ragnvaldsson, Dagfinn Haraldsson, Gudrod Haraldsson, and assorted warriors who look useful—that's what King Erik said."

"What about Svanhild Eysteinsdatter?" Ragnvald asked, feeling cold.

"King Erik told me to make sure you knew that she had gone."

Ragnvald sighed, relieved and annoyed. They need not have come at all. If Ragnvald truly had designs on Norway's throne, as Erik had insisted, Erik might think he was offering Ragnvald the chance to begin his rebellion. He queried Sverri further to learn the exact layout of Harald's forces, and this too the messenger told him, sketching out their positions in the wet sand of the beach. Ragnvald gathered fifteen of his warriors to him, leaving Sigurd behind with Thorir and three other men on the beach. The Skanians had done what Ragnvald feared, dividing their force down to nothing. Skane was like porous sandstone; it could absorb all of them and leave no sign.

Ragnvald's party followed Sverri on a track through the woods. After walking for the better part of a day, they emerged into what had once been a clearing. Saplings, clothed in the bright leaves of summer, filled the space with dappled green light.

Ragnvald had just put his hand to his sword when Aldi and some of his men came crashing out of the underbrush, with their swords drawn, and Oddi following behind. Ragnvald drew his, while his men arrayed themselves around him.

"We're more than you," Aldi growled.

"Yes," said Ragnvald.

"Yes," Oddi echoed him. "And I told you Ragnvald would not attack King Harald. If he had wanted to usurp Harald's place, he could have done it much more easily, anytime in the past few years."

Ragnvald frowned and sheathed his sword. "I came because I was asked to come," he said.

"You may mean Harald no ill, but what about me?" Aldi asked, his sword still out.

Ragnvald sighed. "If I meant you ill, would I have given you my land, and let you grow rich there for all these years?" he asked wearily. "If I could have kept my son's ship from attacking yours, I would have."

"But you won't admit he killed my son?" Aldi cried.

"That is a matter for trial," said Harald in a booming voice. He had come to stand on the outside of the crowd of men, towering over them. "And we have more pressing concerns." He gave Ragnvald a measuring look. "My friend, let us speak in private."

Ragnvald looked behind Harald, to see how Harald and his men had surrounded the Skanians in their camp. A ring of his warriors stood ready to attack should any of the Skanians try to escape. Harald looked tired, as did his men. They must be sleeping little to maintain this vigilance.

Harald walked a short way into the woods to a point where they could see the border between the two factions, but were out of earshot.

"How many more are inside the cave?" Ragnvald asked.

"Who can say?" Harald replied. "Not enough to resist us, but they have my sons, so what does it matter?"

"My son too," said Ragnvald. "But not Svanhild, I hear."

"No, she was too crafty for them, it seems," said Harald. He frowned at Ragnvald. "Tell me, why will this Erik deal only with you? Why will he not negotiate with me?"

"He means to stir discontent between us," said Ragnvald. "And I see it is working."

"He has been telling me that you are king of Norway in truth and I am a mere figurehead. Is that what you told him too, when you went to arrange a marriage?"

"No," said Ragnvald. "It was the excuse he used to refuse the marriage. I wanted your Gudrod married to his daughter."

"And you agree? That I have been a mere figurehead?" Harald asked.

"A figurehead needs to be seen," Ragnvald muttered.

"So I have been less than a figurehead?" Harald's voice rose.

Ragnvald cursed his exhaustion—usually he guarded his words better than that. Harald had valued his honesty in the past, but it was always a difficult tack, to give a king honesty without offense. "My king, you have been absent," he said. "You said so yourself. In your absence I have tried to strengthen your kingdom. There have been times when some have assumed . . . what King Erik claims. There have been times when I have not corrected them, since it seemed to serve your interests more for kings and jarls to think me powerful. There have been times, as with King Erik, that I have spoken the truth, and denied such claims—why would he marry Gudrod to his daughter if he is the son of a powerless king? This is the argument he made to me, and that I tried in vain to refute."

"That is many words for Ragnvald the Wise to speak at once," said Harald. "They do not entirely have the ring of truth. I know the sound of a man trying to justify himself."

"Then believe what Oddi said," said Ragnvald. He rubbed at the old scar on his cheek, a habit he had never been entirely able to break.

"What was that?" Harald asked.

"That if I had ambitions like that, I would have found a better time to realize them than now."

Harald laughed shortly. "I suppose you must negotiate with Erik, since he will only speak with you. But hear this: if this negotiation benefits you too much I will have reason to believe my suspicions, and he will have another hostage."

Ragnvald swallowed down his unease. He could not predict what Erik wanted. Perhaps if Erik understood that Harald's warriors would not back Ragnvald in any rebellion, he would cease this willful misunderstanding.

✢   ✢   ✢

RAGNVALD NEGOTIATED AN exchange of hostages to put himself in Erik's hands: himself for Harald's son Dagfinn, who had been annoying the Skanians with his never-ending stories. The Skanians' camp was full of dirty men, and a few cowed-looking women. Ragnvald insisted on seeing the hostages first. He walked toward the group of men, who sat in a circle on fallen logs, wearing only shirtsleeves, cloaks cast off in the warmth of the day.

There was Gudrod, slim and handsome, and Halfdan, big and blond. And next to them, dark-haired and laughing louder than any of them, sat Ivar. He leaned forward, putting his elbows on his knees, and shook some dice in his hand. He blew on them, cast his eyes up to the gods, murmured a prayer for luck, and then threw them on the ground.

Another cheer followed by some groans sounded. Ivar cupped his hand, and the other men put bits of hack-silver and, in one case, a short jeweled dagger into them.

"Son, you live," said Ragnvald.

Ivar stood and laughed. "Of course, Father. We are only hostages. I'm glad you've come."

For a moment, Ragnvald could not tell what caused the heat in his face and pain in his stomach, until he realized it was shame, shame on Ivar's behalf, shame that Ivar had failed to feel for himself. Had it been Einar trapped here, he would have found a way to escape already, as Svanhild had. He would not have been so foolish as to get himself captured in the first place.

Finally Ragnvald swallowed and nodded. "Good, you are all well," he said. "I will negotiate your release."

He followed King Erik back into the fresher air outside the cave. Halfdan rose and followed them, looming over Ragnvald, blocking the light from the camp's torches. Melbrid joined them as well, his famous tooth making it look as though he had a growth on his upper lip.

Ragnvald spoke first. "King Erik of Jutland, you are making trouble for me with my king. Let us negotiate and put an end to this."

Erik shook his head. "It was a grave mistake to allow your son to fall into our hands," he said with mock sympathy. "Had he not, you could have let me take care of Harald and a few of his sons, leaving Norway for yourself."

"What can I do to convince you that usurping Harald was never my aim?" Ragnvald asked.

"Nothing," said Erik. "No man who has risen as far or as fast as you could be willing to put a limit on his ambition. In the old days, the strongest, ablest man was voted king, and you would win that vote."

"Those days are not past," said Melbrid, his voice dangerous. Erik smiled again, and Ragnvald curled his hands into fists. He had been too flattered by Erik's words in Jutland. He should have allied with the Roskilde Danes against Erik as soon as he refused alliance with Harald.

"No they are not," Ragnvald said. "The Norse kings and jarls acclaim Harald their king, and I would not gainsay them, nor plunge Norway into war by trying to change what the gods have decreed. Harald has promised my death if this negotiation favors me more than him."

Erik shrugged. "I have enough men to join with your Harald, and defeat Melbrid and Halfdan," he said. "Most of the warriors you see here are mine. Some are Melbrid's and very few are Halfdan's. They all wait for my command."

Melbrid and Halfdan both wore twin expressions of disbelief and anger, but before their hands could find their swords, Erik's warriors descended upon them and disarmed them.

"So I see," said Ragnvald, trying not to show his own fear. There was nothing to stop Erik from holding him hostage or killing him.

"You will agree then, that I have the advantage," said Erik. "I have your son and Harald's. I have a big enough force to do yours some damage, even if you were willing to give up your son's life. And I have an agreement with King Bjorn of Sweden to control the Skaggerak Strait. Your Harald claims Vermaland, which has always been Sweden's, and Bjorn would love nothing more than to take it back. I don't see why I should not wait here for my allies to come and crush you between us."

Ragnvald did not see either, but if this was Erik's final offer, he would not have made his move against Halfdan and Melbrid now. "Harald's offer of marrying his son Gudrod to your daughter, Ranka, still stands," he said. "Norway is far more powerful than Sweden. They can only tax the Baltic vikings and merchants, while together we can control all of the traffic through the strait."

"Gudrod," Erik scoffed. "I have spent long enough with him to know he is nothing more than a spoiled boy. What if, instead, I give you your son, and with my forces, we kill Harald and anyone who follows him, and make you king of Norway?"

What indeed? Would he trade his son's life for Harald's? Was the true meaning of Ronhild's prophecy that he would die a traitor? Ragnvald squeezed his eyes tight against the horror of that thought.

He heard Erik laughing and opened his eyes. "No, I don't think I will offer that. You would be too strong a king, and I do not think our alliance would last for long. Try again—offer me something I want."

Ragnvald's voice did not feel like it would work. He saw Halfdan struggling against his captors between the trees. "Have your daughter wed Halfdan," he said. "His father will forgive him, give him land in Norway, and he will give you strong grandsons who can sit on the thrones of Jutland and Norway."

Erik stroked his beard. "I do want my grandsons to be kings, but Harald has so many sons. How can I be sure that the son I marry my daughter to will be the one who wins their coming battles? They will be at one another's throats like hungry wolves."

"Harald could swear to it," said Ragnvald.

"No, I think it would be better if I marry my Ranka to Harald himself," said Erik.

Ragnvald nodded, feeling desperate. "Yes, I believe I can convince Harald of the rightness of that. For that you will accept an alliance and give up your hostages?"

Erik paced back and forth before Ragnvald. "The problem remains—I want my grandsons to be kings, and your Harald has spread his seed all over Norway. Here is my offer: Harald will divorce all of his other wives before marrying with my daughter. Her sons will be his first heirs. Then we will make good on your plan to control the Skaggerak Strait. This will make us two kings rich and powerful."

Ragnvald's stomach sank. This was the very limit of what Harald might accept. The only bright spot was that if Harald divorced Svanhild, he would never accuse Ragnvald of engineering this for his own benefit.

"What of Melbrid and Halfdan?" Ragnvald asked to buy time.

"Melbrid claims to be king of the Skanians—perhaps an alliance with him will be of use," said Erik. "As for Halfdan, his ambitions are limitless. Norway will never be safe until he is dead. I will kill him for you, to sweeten the deal."

If only it were that easy—but Ragnvald knew he would be blamed if harm came to Halfdan. "I must think on this," he said. "It is a bitter mouthful to swallow."

"Do you have another offer?" Erik asked.

What could he offer? Erik held all the counters. If Harald attacked, many would die, including both of their sons. If Ragnvald rebelled in truth—no, he could not trace that through, not when he still reeled from Erik's earlier suggestion. "If Harald divorces all of his other wives, he will throw Norway into chaos. It will be an insult that Norway's district kings will not easily forgive. You forget, most of his wives are the sisters or daughters of the district kings."

Erik grinned again. "I have not forgotten that," he said.

"Do you not want a strong ally?" Ragnvald asked.

"Not too strong," said Erik. "I feel certain that with all his wealth, and more to come from taxing the strait, your Harald can buy the goodwill of the districts."

"I must speak with Harald," said Ragnvald. "I cannot agree to this on his behalf."

"Of course not," said Erik, giving him a too-understanding nod.

"This will even weaken you," said Ragnvald.

"I think not," Erik replied. "Speak to your king."

Ragnvald returned to Harald and told him what Erik had proposed. Harald sat down heavily on the stump that served as his chair. "I just wed Gyda," he said. "In fulfillment of my oath."

"And that wedding was completed and you were bedded," said Ragnvald. "She may even bear you a son. But you would have to make Ranka's sons your heirs."

"For now," said Harald grimly.

"Yes, for now." Ragnvald tread back and forth before Harald's makeshift throne. "Same with the divorces. Pay your wives and their families handsomely to take away the sting of divorce. Once Ranka has borne you a son, remarry your wives. Erik will not be in a position to cause you harm at that point. I will make sure of it."

"Do you think my wives will accept it?" Harald asked.

"We will make them accept it," said Ragnvald. "Each of them will have a price. Princess Gyda wants nothing more than to be queen of Hordaland again, so let her have that. We will have to speak with the others. And you already wanted me to put Snaefrid aside for you."

"What of Svanhild?" Harald replied. "What will she ask?"

Ragnvald did not want to think of that. Like Asa and some of Harald's earlier wives, Svanhild was now wife to Harald in name only, and she kept her bed empty of all but her ugly old chaperone. She took far more joy of her ship and her duties as one of Harald's captains than as a wife. Still, she was not a woman who swallowed insults easily.

When Ragnvald did not answer, Harald stood and began pacing the same track that Ragnvald had worn. "Or perhaps my question should be, what will you ask?"

This was his chance. "Three things," said Ragnvald quickly. "Sogn for Ivar, Maer for Thorir, and . . ." He hesitated for a moment. "And for you to believe me when I tell you Halfdan rebelled against you. He, Melbrid, and Erik had an understanding until Erik had his men take the other two prisoner."

Harald looked pained. "Then Halfdan is now one of Erik's captives. He is another son to ransom."

"Just—if you will not punish him, send him away for a time. Make him an envoy to the Great Danish Army—or Constantinople, perhaps. But do not doubt me. I have always acted in your interests. You are my sworn king, and always will be."

"What of young Rolli's crime?" Harald asked.

"Must we discuss this now?" said Ragnvald.

"Yes. Your wife wanted me to trade Sogn for his forgiveness, and I have been advised that it is the best decision for Norway."

Advised by whom? Ragnvald wanted to ask. Probably Guthorm, urged by Vigdis, trying, as always, to cut Ragnvald off at the knees. It did not matter, though, all that mattered was saving Sogn for his line.

"Rolli deserves outlawry," Ragnvald said, "but he is young. Make it a short term and let me help him leave Norway safely." And Harald would send Halfdan overseas, directly into Rolli's waiting sword.

"Rolli murdered Aldi's son, and took others as slaves," Harald reminded him. "I cannot see a sentence of less than seven years being just."

"Seven years, then," Ragnvald said. "Sogn for Ivar, Maer for Thorir, and your forgiveness."

"You fight my wars for me, and make my alliances for me. As I have your loyalty—and your sister's—so do you have mine." He gripped Ragnvald's forearms. "Everyone will be assured of this when I hold Rolli's trial."

He sent Ragnvald to tell Erik that they had agreed. It was not until Ragnvald was falling asleep that night that he thought over Harald's words again, and heard the warning in them. He could never stop fighting Harald's wars, whatever they might be, never stop making his alliances for him. Ragnvald would defend against threats to Harald's kingdom until he died, just as Ronhild prophesied.

21

THORIR AND SIGURD HELPED HILDA DOWN FROM ROLLI'S SHIP
onto the Skanian beach. She hugged Thorir fiercely, though she had seen
him only a few weeks earlier in Vestfold.

"You are so skinny," she said, when his shoulders dug into hers. Thorir
rolled his eyes, the way boys always did.

Sigurd greeted his son, Olaf, while Thorir told his mother what had
happened here, of the parties that had gone off and disappeared, one after the other. Hilda looked toward the gray forest that had captured her
husband and eldest son and shivered.

Svanhild's laugh drew her attention as she joked with Sigurd as though
she were his brother, not his sister, kicking his shin when she thought he
took too long to tell his tale. On board Rolli's ship, Hilda had watched
Svanhild order her men around with an ease that did not seem natural.

At least she had Rolli with her. Hilda cooked for Svanhild's and Rolli's
crews and the few men that Ragnvald had left behind on the shore, and
when that did not take up enough of her time, she washed some of the
men's soiled garments in seawater.

Three days later, Harald, Ragnvald, and their warriors returned,
marching out of the woods in waves. Ragnvald looked fierce and tired,
like a graying old wolf, with more threads of silver in his hair than Hilda
remembered from even a few weeks ago. He did not even look happy to
see Svanhild, and his frown deepened when Rolli greeted him.

"Wife, what are you doing here?" he asked, giving her a perfunctory
embrace. "This is the last place—"

"You!" Hilda heard Aldi shout. She turned to see Aldi advancing on Rolli, with his sword drawn. "You have the gall to come here? You should have fled. You should have stayed away forever."

"Aldi!" said Hilda, interposing herself between them. That brought Aldi up short, even as Ragnvald gripped her arm painfully to pull her back.

"Mother, get out of the way," said Rolli, drawing his own sword. He advanced on Aldi, pressing him back toward the shore until waves lapped at his ankles. "Let us duel now, Aldulf Atlisson, and end this."

Harald waded into the surf behind Aldi. He was still a finger's breadth taller than Rolli, and together they looked like envoys from a race of giants.

"Stop," Harald roared. "I have forbidden unsanctioned dueling. Even here, you are my subjects and you will accept my justice."

"I want to duel," said Rolli. "Give us permission."

Hilda had a memory of her father reciting the law that was so strong it felt more real than the scene taking place in front of her. "First blood," she cried out. "Rolli, take three years' outlawry if Aldi wins, and if Rolli wins, Aldi will take the standard wergild for a jarl's son."

"Yes," said Rolli, "I accept this. Aldi?"

Harald looked from Rolli to Aldi and back again, and finally at Hilda, seeming to notice her for the first time. "Aldi, do you accept this?"

Aldi glanced at Hilda and shook his head slightly. "No," he said. "I want your justice. My king's justice." He sheathed his sword.

"Very well," said Harald. "You shall have it."

☩   ☩   ☩

HILDA FOUND SIGURD working by her side during her tasks that night, a pleasure she had not had in a long time. His son, Olaf, too, worked shyly next to him, pounding fish with his skinny arms. For a few moments Hilda forgot about the trial that was coming, happy with her simple tasks and the pleasure of seeing her family together in one place, Einar and Ivar sitting side by side again, as though Ragnvald had never parted them.

It had been a rare occurrence these past few years, with Ragnvald always away. And then Rolli had his ship, and Ivar and Einar their errands, taking them away from her side. This was her family as it was meant to be, even on a foreign beach, with tension running high around the various campfires.

During dinner, though, Ragnvald would barely look at any of his sons. Vigdis had been right: he would rather let them be punished for what he saw as their failures than use his power to help them.

Rolli ate a small dinner even for a normal-size man, much less a giant who was still growing. When he had finished, he tucked his hands under his thighs, and leaned forward. "Father, I know you are angry with me—"

"My anger does not matter," said Ragnvald, his voice harsh. "Your crime does."

"But I came to tell you something important," Rolli cried. "Halfdan is going to betray King Harald, and he has lots of allies. All the Scottish vikings! Thorstein the Red said so!"

"Thorstein," said Ragnvald, more thoughtfully. "I remember him as a young man." He rubbed his knuckles on hearing the name. Thorstein had been one of Solvi's captains in the battle of Hafrsfjord, and before then one of Ragnvald's captors, present when Ragnvald's hands were broken under torture.

"He's a big man with a big red beard now," said Rolli. "Not as big as me though."

"He could hardly grow a beard before," said Ragnvald, half to himself.

"Halfdan has allied with King Erik of Jutland. Also Ketil Flatnose, Melbrid Tooth. We saw him—Halfdan—when we rescued Svanhild." Rolli sat back, looking pleased.

"King Harald has allied with King Erik now, and his son's rebellion is broken," said Ragnvald. "You come bearing old news."

Rolli slumped forward. He had put so much hope into the intelligence he carried. "What can I do, then, Father?" he asked.

Ragnvald stood and brushed the crumbs off his trousers. "Hope that Harald is feeling merciful," he said, and went off to visit one of the other cook-fires.

While Sigurd banked the fire to keep the coals burning through the night, Hilda stood and pulled her stepson Einar aside. "You know the law," she said. "You must help me."

"You did well enough on the beach," he said, with an ironic twist to his lips. Ragnvald looked like that because of his scar, but Einar had let his own spirit do this to him.

"Please," said Hilda.

"I cannot do anything against Father's wishes again," said Einar. He looked very like Ragnvald in the twilight that faded his golden hair to dark. "Do not ask me."

Hilda twisted her hands together. "You would not be working against him if you helped me remember some law that would help Rolli. Please. He is not even of age yet."

Einar's mouth was a thin line. "If he is not tried as a man, then Father will be held responsible for his actions and pay the wergild."

"Aldi will ask for Sogn," said Hilda.

"But Rolli commands a ship and wields a sword," Einar continued, as if he had not heard her. "He acts as a man, and can be tried as one. Do you think Father will take responsibility for this?"

Hilda shook her head. "But leave your father aside," she said. "Help me with the law. What can I do? I cannot lose him."

"Beg for him," said Einar. "Harald will decide what he will decide. He is king, and kings do not care very much for the law."

"You are a poet—give me the words," said Hilda.

"Tell me what you would say," said Einar.

Hilda took a deep breath and spoke before she could think too much and grow nervous. "I would say . . . ," she began. "I would tell him that I am a mother whose joy is my sons. My two eldest are heirs to Norway's finest districts, but my youngest is my own comfort. In outlawry any may slay him, and he is only a boy. There is nothing I would not give to keep him by my side. Please do not take away the son of my heart."

"That is well said," said Einar, with a deep sadness in his voice. "I can think of no way to better phrase it."

✛ ✛ ✛

HARALD CALLED A full gathering the next morning. He stood on top of a dune, where the shape of the sand forced his men to stand in a semicircle below him.

"My friends and followers," he said, "there is much to discuss. King Erik is bringing his ships here from the Skanian camp, so we can make plans for the future. There is more to be done to root out these rebels and keep Norway safe, with King Erik's aid. But before he arrives—"

"Justice for my son," called out Aldi. "You promised me swift justice if I brought my ships to Skane."

"They are my ships," said Ragnvald. "You will have your justice, but you cannot demand that the king of all Norway bow to your whims." That seemed good to Hilda. At least Ragnvald was doing something.

"This crime is an unhealed wound," said Aldi. "I will have my justice."

"I did promise," said Harald. "And I keep my promises."

Something flickered across Ragnvald's face at Harald's words.

"Good," said Aldi. "You are a fair and just king. I will tell you what has happened, and this whelp will tell his story, and you will see what is just. My family line descends from the same as King Ragnvald's. At his request, I have been guarding Sogn for him for these past fourteen years, while he rules Maer from Tafjord. Some time ago, he sent his niece, Freydis, to me, and she was among those that we were taking with us to Vestfold. Again, at King Ragnvald's command. I have done nothing without his command for fourteen years, even though he set in motion the events that led to my father's death. He pit King Hakon against my father, and they both killed one another. Hakon's son Oddi and I both refrained from taking revenge, but how long can I ignore the cries of my father's blood?"

The crowd of warriors murmured to one another.

"Silence," said Harald. "Do you ask for justice for the duel your father and King Hakon fought, or do you ask for justice for your son?"

"My son," said Aldi, bitterly. "It is too late for justice for my father."

Aldi continued his tale then, the one that Hilda had heard from his own lips and Rolli's too now. He did not know whose blade had ended his son's life, but Rolli's other crimes, and his complicity, demanded a great punishment.

As Rolli stepped forward to tell his version of the story, Hilda rushed forward to stop him. "My son must have someone to speak for him," she said, ignoring the murmurs even louder than at Aldi's interruption. She saw the dark shape of Ragnvald standing within her field of vision but kept her eyes only on Harald—his opinion mattered right now, and

Ragnvald's did not. "His is not yet of the age of majority, and may have someone speak on his behalf."

Harald looked surprised. Hilda drew herself up to her full height. The habit of dressing in dark colors, making herself smaller, held her strongly, but she had dressed to be noticed today, in her richest and most vibrant dress. She had polished the turtle-shaped brooches that held up her overdress so they gleamed.

"He can waive that right," said Harald mildly, "if my memory serves."

"It does," said Hilda. "My father was law-speaker of Sogn for forty years. Before he died, he taught me everything he knew. I have memorized the laws as well as any man. I will speak for my son."

"Women may not testify," Aldi called out. "Or may, only if no man can be found to testify."

Einar stepped forward. "Let her speak," he said. "She is versed in the law. We studied it together, and she remembers far more than I do." Hilda flushed and nodded her thanks at Einar.

Harald shifted from one foot to the other. "Let Einar Ragnvaldsson speak for his brother then. But Rolli must tell his own tale first."

Einar looked at Hilda helplessly. "Einar has two half-brothers mixed up in this," she protested. "How can it be fair for him to argue for Rolli?"

"Enough of this," said Harald. "No speakers, then. I will decide."

Einar gave Hilda an apologetic glance and fell back into the crowd. Hilda twisted her fingers together as Rolli stepped forward into the open space below Harald.

He told a story that did not contradict Aldi's in the least. "I do not know if it was me, or Hallbjorn, or another of our crew who caused the death of Aldi's son. I will accept my punishment," he said, "as long as it is not my own death. But I ask that you weigh some of my other deeds against this one. I have rescued your beloved wife, my aunt Svanhild Eysteinsdatter, and I bring news from the Orkney Islands. Your own son Halfdan has allied with the king of Skane, and Ketil Flatnose of the Outer Hebrides, and together they plan to make war against you."

Rolli looked around, as though he still expected cheers, and his shoulders sagged when only murmuring greeted his announcement.

"That would have been useful to know if you had arrived earlier," said Harald. "But I'm afraid this cannot change your sentence. The lady Svanhild was already safe through our negotiations when she escaped.

King Erik has allied with me against his former friends. My son is recon-
ciled to my side. We have agreed to sail together to the Orkneys to root
out these raiders."

He looked down at the assembled crowd. "I am known for my swift
justice," he said, "so I pronounce this: in compensation for his loss, Aldi's
line will inherit the district of Sogn, and he and his sons will be called
jarls."

Ragnvald stepped forward. "My king, you cannot do this. You swore
an oath that Sogn should be mine."

"My uncle, my first and most trusted adviser, has counseled me to do
this," said Harald.

"He should have more care for your honor," said Ragnvald, angrily.
"You and I discussed the gifts that you would owe for this alliance with
Erik, and among them was not stripping my family of its ancestral land."

Hilda had never heard Ragnvald speak to Harald that way, and from
the expressions she saw around her, none of them had either.

"I have been assured that this is the best way to keep peace in Norway," said Harald. He frowned at Ragnvald sternly, but his voice sounded
uncertain. "I know that you are loyal to me, but some have questioned
it. If you accept this, that will prove it. I cannot make your son a favorite,
or make you a favorite by allowing your sons to inherit two of Norway's
districts, while Aldi has a just claim."

"What you do here will be remembered," said Ragnvald. "If you deal
unfairly with me, no other king in Norway will expect better. Think
on it."

Hilda felt sick at what she had set in motion. As though the power of
a seeress touched her, she saw the future in Ragnvald's words: war, with
every district of Norway against the others, as they had been in Hilda's
youth, when even a king might lose everything he possessed to a rapa-
cious neighbor or raiders from the seas. It need not come to pass, but it
would, if Ragnvald made it so.

"It is but one choice," said Harald reluctantly. "The other is for young
Rolli to accept seven years' outlawry, and Aldi to accept the generous
wergild payment that your wife offered. This is my gift to you, in compensation for the divorce of your sister."

Hilda turned to look at Svanhild. Her face blanched white, but she
met the eyes of each person who dared to stare at her until they looked

away first. She and Ragnvald shared a glance, one that Hilda could not read. Had Svanhild known? No wonder Ragnvald had spoken so harshly to Harald. He must be closer to breaking with his king than he had ever been before. A part of her leaped with hope. If Ragnvald defected from Harald, then his justice could not touch their son.

Harald held up a hand to still the chatter. "Do you accept this?"

"No wergild," said Ragnvald tightly. "Then I will accept."

"What of a wergild and no outlawry?" Hilda cried. She wished to speak the words she had said to Einar the night before, but anger stirred her differently. "Why do you think, in your anger, to send my son away like a mad wolf?"

She pitched her voice lower, so she could make it loud without sounding shrill. She commanded Tafjord's army of servants, and was obeyed without question. When they chattered and fought, it was her voice that sent them back to their tasks. For a moment she understood how Svanhild commanded the men of her ship, how Harald had risen to become king of all Norway—reins of power sometimes lay ready to be claimed by one bold enough to do so.

"You banish my father's namesake from me," she said. "Your cruelty to a mother who might die before seeing her best beloved son again heaps cruelty upon cruelty for our family." She glanced at Svanhild, to include the injustice against her in her complaint.

Murmuring from the crowd made Hilda feel a wash of fear. She had their attention, she who had never before sought it, and she must do something worthy with it. "You have been as wolflike as my son, and no punishment for it. Now you make my son a deer, to be hunted by every wolf that wants a man-pelt."

Some of Rolli's warriors applauded, and Ragnvald's too. A rift was opening, Hilda felt. Skalds made songs about such women.

"Well spoken," Harald said finally. "Your father could not have argued better. You are a fierce mother to a fierce brood of sons, sons who should make you feel proud, even if they must face punishment as well. I wish that I could do what you ask, but I cannot. My kingdom's peace is balanced on decisions like these. Seven years will pass quickly and your son will return, still a very young man, fully forgiven."

"This is not justice," said Aldi.

"I will marry your living son to one of my daughters and your daughter to one of my sons," said Harald. "You may be the grandfather of kings. Be satisfied with this."

Aldi bowed his head, but Hilda, still feeling the heightened awareness she had when speaking to Harald, thought that he had not bowed quickly enough, and that the expression on his face still promised revenge.

22

SVANHILD MET THE EYES OF HARALD'S FOLLOWERS WITHOUT truly seeing them, nor could she hear the words that Harald said following his announcement of their divorce. She had never before known anger like this, a heavy bowl sitting on her chest, keeping her motionless, for any movement would spill it. Even turning to meet the eyes of those who wished to enjoy her discomfort seemed dangerous. She met Ragnvald's last and saw helplessness in them.

She stood still, rooted to the ground while Harald finished Rolli's trial. Hilda wept, Rolli hung his head. Ragnvald looked angry and Harald empty. A wolf-king, hunting man-pelts, Hilda had called him. Svanhild saw a weak king, no match for the strength of her anger. The crowd flowed around her as she stood like a rock in a stream until Ragnvald came over to her.

He touched her shoulder hesitantly. "So much is happening at once—I did not want you to find out like that. Harald is divorcing all his wives, to pay for the lives of his sons." He tried again to get her to look at him. "And mine."

Svanhild did not move. The bowl of water on her chest felt heavier still. If she let herself speak, she would scream like an evil spirit, and Ragnvald would deserve her curses, but a small part of her, the part not wild with anger, nor pressed down by it, knew that she held some power here, even now, and would have only one chance to use it.

"We spent the last fourteen years building Harald's Norway," she said, holding her voice as steady as she could. "Our Norway. That was what you said when Harald stopped treating me as his wife. When he stopped being king. You told me it didn't matter because we were building a kingdom. We were its rulers." Her voice choked, which made her angrier still. "Svanhild Sea Queen." Angry tears spilled over her cheeks. "That's how you convinced me to remain married to him—you said we were ruling for him."

"And we can continue," said Ragnvald. "Very little will change."

"Everything will change," Svanhild cried. "I tied my life to this, to him, and my reward is humiliation heaped on humiliation."

Ragnvald squeezed her shoulder. How many times in the past had he comforted her when her husband would not? She accepted his touch for a moment and then shook him off.

He spread his hands helplessly. "Svanhild, he will take you back, don't you see? Just as soon as he has made an heir with Erik's daughter."

"Back to what? Ignored and humiliated—his wife when it suits him and only when it suits him. Were he not the king I would have grounds to divorce him ten times over, but now he has done it for me." She laughed, and the sound did not seem like her own. "You should have broken with him over this, as everyone thought you would. If you took Harald's place, everyone would follow you. Or if you prefer not to rule yourself, make Halfdan into your ruler for you."

Ragnvald clenched his jaw. "Not you too," he said. "Even if I had no honor, this thing you propose is foolishness. If I supported Halfdan against his father, who do you think he would kill as soon as he became king? He would find some pretext."

"Wouldn't he be grateful for your help?" Svanhild asked wildly.

"The help of a man who was loyal to his father for twenty years and then compassed his death? No, he would find a reason to have me killed as soon as possible." Ragnvald rubbed his forehead. "Why won't any of you understand that I am loyal to Harald? I do not want to be king in his place, I want *him* to be king."

"Even as he divorces your sister." Ragnvald had never chosen her over Harald, not once.

"I do not like that, but . . . Svanhild, I am the one who negotiated it. To save us all, to save our sons. He will divorce all of his wives and marry Erik's daughter. Once she has borne him a son, he will remarry all of you. There will be no harm, no loss to your status. Your sons will be cared for. Harald will make great gifts to pay for what he has done."

Svanhild swallowed. Ragnvald had been the one to do this to her as much as Harald. Suddenly her anger seemed to strengthen and lift her, fill her with a violent sort of happiness. She had not felt any emotion this intensely since the loss of her son, fifteen years ago.

"If there is no loss of status, then why the gifts?" she asked.

"Some may think it is, of course," Ragnvald said. "Svanhild, you were missing—that is why we came."

"So this is my fault?" she asked. "I escaped on my own. I did not need your help."

"They had Harald's sons and my own," said Ragnvald, his voice pleading. "This price is high, but it is a storm that will blow over. We can weather it."

"You can weather it, brother. You will weather anything for your Harald. See your son outlawed, your sister divorced, but I will not." This buoyant anger gave her the certainty that she had been lacking all this time. He had kept his beloved Sogn in Rolli's trial—he had been willing to give her up, but not his land.

"What will you do?" Ragnvald asked.

He had asked her that, or something like it, after his first battle for Harald, while she waited at Vestfold to be traded to Solvi for some prisoners. She had made her choice then, and Ragnvald let her go.

"I have not yet decided," she said quietly. "You have never held me back before, brother. Do not do it now."

She walked away from him down the beach. She felt his gaze on her back, watching her go, as he had many times before. At her feet, the water washing the pebbles on the shoreline made them shine. If she took one out, it would dry dull and plain.

She heard footsteps overtaking her and then saw a long shadow, with the broad shoulders and wild hair of her husband. Her former husband. A stranger to her for many years, and never more than now.

"Svanhild," Harald said, catching her wrist. "I did not mean for you to find out that way—it was only—it was the words I needed to speak to make your brother understand in that moment."

"You have done what was needed," she said. Still, her voice did not sound like her own but that of a wild stranger, wiser and more fearless than she.

His grip on her became gentler, and he stroked her skin with his thumb. "You understand," he said. "I knew you would. Your brother promised me that I could depend on him, and I always do. He is my best and most precious friend. Do not fear that will change, or your sons be any less dear to me. Little will change, I promise you."

"Ah," she said with a laugh, "so you will be as much a husband to me as you have been these last ten years. No husband at all."

Harald's face twisted. "Most of my wives are happy to be freed to return to their families after they have borne me a son or two."

"Am I much like your other wives?" Svanhild asked.

"You did not seem to mind."

"Did you ask me?" She shook her head.

"I have paid your brother, to keep his loyalty. What must I pay you?" Harald asked. "I am taking this force to the Orkneys to root out the seeds of this rebellion, and after that, you shall have whatever you de- sire. A larger ship perhaps?" She must have shown something in her face, for his eyes lit up. "Silk sails, the finest ship for the finest sailor in Nor- way. I will do it for you gladly."

Svanhild pictured the vessel she would request. She would involve herself in every aspect of its construction, and it would be a mighty dragon ship, but suited to a woman captain, with a steering oar she could turn even with her lesser strength. Silk sails would be lighter to raise than even the finest wool, and stronger.

"What will you do in Orkney?" she asked.

"I will root out the raiders that have made common cause against me, and put the Scottish isles under my control. And I do not trust Erik's hold over Melbrid Tooth. No doubt Solvi is the cause of it, again. You should not have let him go after the battle of Hafrsfjord."

Solvi had kept his oath, Svanhild was sure of it.

"I should have made an end to him years ago," said Harald, "and now I will do it."

The rising breeze made Svanhild shiver. No, she would not take Harald's offered ship and allow him to buy his way out of this insult. He did not even consider that he had harmed her honor as much as Ragnvald's.

"When do you leave?" she asked.

"Erik wants the marriage done first, and I will have to gather my allies, so not until next summer, I think." He hesitated a moment. "I cannot understand you at all, Svanhild, my love. Will you accept my gift, and come back to me once I have paid off the terms by which I bought my sons' lives? I would do no less for our sons."

Her sons, raised by Guthorm and Vigdis more than herself. Charming boys who had never known a day's hardship. They were better off in the care of others than in hers. She had brought Olaf Sigurdsson into danger, and condemned her first son to death through her wandering. "Will you swear it, before the gods? That you will do right by my sons, give them land and followers, no matter what happens?" she asked.

"I do swear it," said Harald. "Who is to know the future? One of them might still be king after me."

"Then I will take your gift," said Svanhild. He would not make her swear—he did not believe the oath of a woman was binding. He would not know until it was too late, then, that he had left her free to lie.

✦ ✦ ✦

SVANHILD LET HARALD walk with her back to the camp. He gave her a kiss, which she accepted on a cheek that felt numb. As she walked toward her men's hearth, Falki came running up to her.

"My lady," he said. It was such a mild day, with a light breeze and blue skies overhead. On any other day she would be enjoying the gentle touch of the air, for these days came so rarely to Norse shores.

"Svanhild," he said. He rarely spoke her name, preferring to call her "my lady" or even "queen" when he was particularly impressed by her. He was more of her husband than Harald had ever been, for all that they rarely touched. Svanhild had never trusted herself to keep casual touches from turning into lingering ones, ending in coupling and a moment's pleasure that would violate her oath to Ragnvald and Harald. Oaths that they had now broken for her. She should let him take her here and now, with the birds and all of Harald's men to see.

"What?" Svanhild asked.

"Are you—what do you mean to do?" he asked. Ordinarily he would wait for her to tell him, and never question her.

"You are a fine sailor," she said with a bitter laugh. "I am certain that

King Harald will give you a ship and let you ferry him around Norway again."

"My lady," he said helplessly.

"My brother says that Harald will remarry his wives after a few years. So I should wait. I have taken so many humiliations from him. You know—" She cut herself off. Falki did not know, none of them could know, except perhaps from rumors, that Harald had not shared her bed in years. The wound that this divorce had dealt her slashed at one far older, long-festering.

Falki looked at her expectantly.

"No," she said. "I will not swallow another humiliation. If my brother and my husband have no care for my honor then I must care for it myself. I will—" She looked at Falki, trying to read his intentions. "I will leave Norway," she said. "I will go alone if I must—"

"No!" said Falki. "This is an insult to all of us. You need not go alone. I will go with you, and I'm sure I will not be the only one."

"Perhaps not," said Svanhild. "Say nothing yet."

He gave his promise, and Svanhild walked over to where Rolli was packing up his ship to leave. She had taught him how to sail, and he had been a good student, though only years would give him the experience he needed to be a truly great sailor.

"The king has given me until tomorrow to depart," said Rolli in a choked voice. "What should I do, Aunt Svanhild?"

"Go raiding," said Svanhild. "Never come back." She had no time for his problems right now.

"I wish I could go to Solvi. He will know where Hallbjorn is, and then at least I will have one friend, if I am to be the deer to Harald's wolves," Rolli said plaintively.

"Where is he? Solvi—is he truly in Iceland?" Svanhild asked.

"That is what Thorstein said, and he had no reason to lie."

"You should go to Iceland, then. Tell Solvi that I sent you. Help my daughter—you owe her that much."

"Maybe I shouldn't. King Harald goes to fight him. My father will never forgive me if I fight against him. Perhaps I should go to Orkney and help instead. Then I might be forgiven sooner."

"For seven years your help will not be desired. Anyone may kill you on sight, without punishment," Svanhild reminded him.

"My father would avenge me," said Rolli.

"But you'll still be dead."

Rolli looked down at his feet. If he had been her son, she would have trained him out of that. "I do not know how to sail to Iceland or even the Orkneys," he said. "We followed a merchant last time. It was your daughter's idea."

If she needed one last push, here it was. Her daughter needed her in Iceland, and now her nephew needed her as well. In the tales she had loved as a child, women framed their entire lives around revenge, and chose husbands who would right their wrongs. She did not need to find a new husband who would right hers—she had left one behind, a man capable of the cruelty she needed. A man whom Harald and her brother would sail to kill next summer. A man whom she had never stopped missing, no matter how much she enjoyed being Harald's envoy, Svanhild Sea Queen.

"I will take you," she said. "We will convoy across the sea."

"You know how to go to Iceland?" Rolli asked.

Yes, her spirit would guide her there if the stars and the currents failed her. She remembered Solvi as she had seen him last, on his ship, bereft of everything but the three men she had left him, his oldest friends and his apprentice, who now ruled the Orkney Islands. She had demanded an oath from him that she had never heard of him breaking. And he had asked her to promise that if Harald mistreated her, she would come to him.

"I know how to sail to Iceland," she said. "I will not be deprived of my ship or my freedom for a feckless king or my disloyal brother."

Rolli looked shocked to hear her speak of Ragnvald so. He swallowed. "I would follow you," he said.

"Then let us leave on the next tide," she replied. She looked toward the west and saw three ships approaching—King Erik's ships.

Svanhild and Rolli went to join her men, who quieted, as if they had been speaking of her. She had chosen them for many reasons but chief among these was their sailing ability and their loyalty to her. Some were sons of farmers, others fishermen. Falki was the first of Harald's captains to recognize her skills as a sailor, and others had followed. All were smaller than the usual mold of Norsemen, and would never be mighty swordsmen, but small men meant a fleet ship.

Svanhild sat down near the cook-fire in the center of their ring of tents. "Men," she said. "I am leaving Norway, never to return. I would not take any of you with me against your will. If you join me, I will find land for you in Iceland, or a place in a viking ship where you can win gold. Whatever you wish. If you come with me, and change your mind, I will find a way for you to return, though I can make no guarantees about your reception if you do. Or you may stay here. Take service with my nephew Einar, if you like—of all Harald's followers, he is the most likely to see your value."

"I will come with you," said Falki.

"As will I," said Aban. "I wish to see more of your northern lands than Norway alone."

Other voices joined theirs, while some few, men who did have homes and wives to return to, came to her regretfully. Audbjorn, who had followed her as long as Falki, inclined his head sadly. "I shall tell tales of our voyages to my daughter and sons," he said.

"We will leave as soon as Erik's ships arrive," said Svanhild. "There will be too many ships for them to notice us." She heard some grumbling at the swiftness this would require but ignored it. And, as if to bless her decision, the breeze shifted, drawing tendrils of hair from under her scarf to brush over her forehead. "Let's catch this wind."

23

THORIR SIGHTED ERIK'S THREE SHIPS COMING AROUND THE
tip of Skane, relayed that news to Ragnvald, and suddenly the whole
camp seemed like an anthill under attack, full of scurrying warriors and
servants. Ragnvald and Harald stood onshore and greeted Erik after he
descended from the biggest vessel. Erik and Harald clasped forearms,
awkwardly, since Harald was more than a head taller than him.

"Greetings, giant," said Erik. "I hope that even if you look like a wild
mountain man, you will be gentle with my daughter."

"I will wed your daughter and have my hair cut on the same day,"
Harald said. "And I cannot do that until I have slain these Scottish rebels.
I will bring Orkney and all of Scotland under Norse control if that's what
it takes to prevent these uprisings."

"What of the rebellion in your own family?" Erik asked. "Your son
Halfdan came to me for help killing you."

Harald let go of Erik's arms. "In the woods you tried to convince me
that Ragnvald the Mighty was in rebellion. If I'm to wed your daughter,
you must stop trying to sow discontent in my kingdom."

"If?" Erik asked, his hand going toward his sword. "You swore that
you would."

"I have never broken an oath," said Harald. "And I will not start,
even over a girl whose father had to take hostages to secure a husband
for her."

Erik now pulled his sword half out of his scabbard, and the great
crowd of his men gathered in around him, pinning Harald and Ragnvald

against the rocking wall of Erik's ship. Between the heads of two of Erik's men, Ragnvald saw Einar, trying to press his way through.

"Stop this," Ragnvald yelled.

Erik shoved his sword back in and his men retreated. "You are becoming difficult to trust," he said. "I will not accept delay. You must come to Jutland and wed my daughter, or you will be an oath-breaker and I will have no trouble gathering every northern king and jarl to do battle against you."

Harald clenched his jaw, and Ragnvald stepped in between them. "You promised your aid," he said to Erik. "After Harald weds your daughter, you will send men to help us do battle in the Orkneys next summer."

Einar had elbowed his way to the front of Erik's men, and now stood just behind King Erik's shoulder. "My lords," he said. "King Harald, your wife Svanhild has left with her ship. Rolli follows in his."

King Erik smirked. "You have many problems to attend to, I see, but at least one fewer wife. We will discuss the wedding later." He bowed and walked up onto the shore, his men following behind.

"When did she leave?" Ragnvald asked Einar as soon as Erik was out of earshot. "How long ago was this?"

Einar gestured at the sea, where two ships were growing small in the distance.

Harald looked out at the ships. "I did not send her anywhere," he said. "I was not certain where she should go next."

"She did not leave on an errand for you, I do not think," said Ragnvald. He did not want to make this better for Harald. Harald was too like Ivar, never believing that anything could go against him.

"So you think she has betrayed me?" Harald asked. "I cannot—she promised . . . she made me swear to care for our sons . . . And I was going to build her a ship. She betrayed me." He whirled to face Ragnvald. "What do you know about this?"

"I think she would say that you betrayed her first," Ragnvald replied.

"Would you agree?" Harald asked, his voice growing dangerous. "She has betrayed you as well."

Ragnvald only nodded. Harald had caused this by ignoring Svanhild and his duties for so long.

"Where has she gone then?" Harald asked.

"I can venture a guess," said Ragnvald.

Harald looked at him sharply, and Ragnvald felt Einar's questioning look as well. "Why?" Harald asked. "You said my other wives would be content—"

"She is not like your other wives," said Ragnvald, "and you must still look to their contentment before you lose them as well. Svanhild is the boldest, but not the only one with spirit."

"You are full of anger this morning," said Harald. "You are my adviser, not my father or my uncle, to speak to me like this."

It was not anger Ragnvald felt for Harald now, but contempt. Harald had never valued his allies well enough, and had always counted on Ragnvald to smooth over the troubles he made. Not today. Not when Harald had ripped them to shreds.

"Do not take me for granted," said Ragnvald. "I would not betray you over my feckless sister's decisions." He swallowed. He had mourned Svanhild once, and knew how to do so again. A part of him had always expected this day. "Do not imagine that I would. We have much work ahead of us. You must wed Ranka Eriksdatter, and still keep peace among the districts. My sister is gone, true, but all you have lost there is one wife and one small ship."

"I have lost more than that," said Harald. "She is the stone that may start the avalanche. I need to hold on to my other allies, and show them what they will lose if they betray me."

The heat of Ragnvald's anger cooled to fear. In the distance, Svanhild's and Rolli's ships had all but disappeared. "What will they lose?" he asked.

"You asked for Sogn as compensation for my divorce of your sister. But she has left, so that compensation is not deserved."

"Is that how you see this?" Ragnvald asked. "You still divorced her. You promised Sogn to me long ago, before you had ever looked upon my sister, and now you would break your oath?"

"My oath was to get it for you, not to never pass it to someone else," said Harald.

"You argue like a law-speaker who knows he is in the wrong," said Ragnvald. "My line has ruled Sogn since the beginning of time."

"So has Aldi's," said Harald, his voice soft but implacable. "You are the richest man in Norway, taking the taxes of two districts. Would you let your greed rip Norway apart?"

"Give me Sogn, and take Maer," Ragnvald said, hating the begging tone in his voice. He should not have to ask for this—it was his by right and acclamation. "Maer is not my family's land."

"I need you in Maer," said Harald. "I have never understood this stubbornness of yours. Maer is bigger and as rich as Sogn."

"It has never been about riches," said Ragnvald. "You surround yourself with greedy men and forget what a true king looks like."

"And that is you? You are the true king? I have been hearing this from my sons and King Erik. I have discounted it, but now I hear it from your lips? What am I to think?"

"If I don't give up Sogn, will you say I am in rebellion?" Ragnvald asked.

"Are you not? You asked for Sogn as payment for making Svanhild accept the divorce. She did not."

"Are you a king, or a merchant in the marketplace?" Ragnvald asked. "A ring-breaker cannot take back the rings he has broken for his followers, and make them whole."

"You may fight me if you wish," said Harald, his voice still soft. "If you best me here, now, you will be king in truth. They will follow you—I am sure of it. Is that what you want?"

Was this his time? Would he die now on Harald's sword? And what would become of his sons if he did? "I am loyal," said Ragnvald, through clenched teeth. "No matter how often you test me, I am loyal."

Harald stared at him until Ragnvald had no choice but to meet his eyes. Harald was tanned from weeks outside, and looked as strong as ever, Ragnvald's golden wolf. "Prove it, then," Harald said. "Say you accept this. Surely you are wise enough to see it will help my cause with the other districts."

"Yes," said Ragnvald, his voice shaking with anger.

"You will not leave me?" Harald asked. "Even though your sister has?"

"Are you trying to push me into it?" Ragnvald asked. He sighed heavily. "As you said, she left me too."

"I should not doubt you," Harald replied, relief in his voice. "You are my best and wisest friend."

"And yet you punish me," said Ragnvald bitterly. "I will follow you, but I will never be happy about this. Will you at least forgive Rolli now?" If Harald forgave Rolli, then Hilda might forgive him. Though he would no longer have Rolli as a weapon against Halfdan.

"Yes, I suppose so," said Harald. "Aldi said he would accept that."

At least Ragnvald would have some good news to give Hilda. He would send a messenger inviting Rolli to meet their forces in the Orkneys next summer. And he would wait for the opportunity to get his land back. Perhaps Aldi would take Maer as a trade. Or marry their children and join the two districts, as he had always intended.

"You will come with me to root out these pirates," Harald continued, "and all of my other allies must send a son, or come themselves."

"Hostages?" Ragnvald asked, with a hint of humor, though he felt like a warrior who had been badly wounded and feared to look at the damage. Sogn had been cut off from him, his ancestors cut off from him. He would have rather lost a limb.

Harald grinned. "Allies."

"Father, let me go after her," said Einar. He had been hanging back this while—perhaps listening to what passed between Ragnvald and Harald. Well enough—he should know what it cost to be a king's friend. "While you collect these allies, Ivar and I can overtake her and Rolli."

"You think so?" Ragnvald asked. "She is blessed by all the gods of wind and sea. You will not catch her."

Harald turned his gaze back toward the horizon. "I want no more songs sung of Svanhild Eysteinsdatter," he said. "I will tell the skalds. They must all be forgotten."

✣ ✣ ✣

AS RAGNVALD WALKED back toward his camp, he saw Ivar with Harald's sons Halfdan and Gudrod, playing as though they had not toppled all that Ragnvald had worked for. Ivar noticed Ragnvald, said something to Halfdan and Gudrod, who laughed, and then he trotted over to join Ragnvald.

"I do not want to speak with you," said Ragnvald. "You are better off with your new friends. One of them will probably be king of Sogn one day, so you should make sure to ingratiate yourself with them."

"Not Halfdan, surely!" said Ivar. "Harald must punish him for his rebellion. I was only trying to cheer him up."

Ragnvald shook his head. "I wonder that you can be so cheerful with all that you have cost me."

"Father, we were trying to help! You have done many bold and foolish things over the years, you cannot begrudge me this."

"Can I not?" Ragnvald asked. "You will find that men judge outcomes, not intentions. If you don't believe me, ask your brother Rolli."

"I did my best," Ivar insisted.

"Did you present your wrists to them? And when you were captured, you very cleverly diced with them?"

"What else was I to do, Father?" Ivar asked. His lightheartedness rasped at Ragnvald. "Should I have run away only to have them tie me up? Should I have forced them to torture me?" He glanced at Ragnvald's hands. Ragnvald's knuckles felt tight, on the edge of pain, as they always did, even on his best days, and he flexed them in answer.

"That was different," Ragnvald said. "I wanted Solvi to believe that he could still beat Harald. I was setting a trap."

"And I was setting a different kind of trap. Why should I make them hate and fear me if I could make friends among them? Halfdan trusts me now—is that not an advantage?"

"Have you learned anything useful from him?" Ragnvald asked.

Ivar looked down at the pebbles that made up the beach. Ragnvald began walking again. Ivar was as useless as he feared, Einar as untrustworthy. Thorir was a follower, not a leader, and Rolli foolish enough to get himself outlawed before he even reached the age of majority. The proverbs said that a man rich in sons was rich indeed, yet Ragnvald was still a pauper.

"He hates you," Ivar called out behind him. "Far more than his father. He blames you that he is not more elevated. He thinks you plot against King Harald."

Ragnvald whirled to face him. "And did you encourage him in this? Complain about your fathers as boys have done since time began?"

"You are more suspicious than ten men, Father," said Ivar. "You always expect the worst of people."

"And you will be killed, expecting the best," Ragnvald replied. "Well, you will face some punishment for this. Harald is giving Sogn to Aldi—you will not inherit the land of our ancestors."

"Does that mean that Rolli's outlawry is lifted?" Ivar asked brightly. Ragnvald wanted to hit him—perhaps violence would teach him where words had failed.

"Do you not hear me? Your inheritance is gone."

"What of Maer?" Ivar asked. "Harald would not take that from you too."

"He has left me Maer," said Ragnvald. "But that is a gift from him, not ours by right. And gifts can be taken away."

"I don't understand," said Ivar. "You said he took Sogn."

"I did," said Ragnvald. Ivar would not let himself understand—he had lived his whole life in Maer. Maybe it truly would make him happier than Sogn, and he would not mind ruling there at Harald's sufferance. "It will take all of my guile and craft to hold on to even Maer for you, when everyone around me wants to take it away."

"Everyone, Father? You sound mad."

"It is not madness when King Harald has taken Sogn from me again."

Ivar still looked at him blankly. Ragnvald saw Hilda crouched by the fire, arranging some sticks to hold a pot of stew over it. Her shoulders seemed rounded, defeated. "Go to your mother," said Ragnvald. "Harald will allow Rolli to come back to us, but your mother will still miss him terribly. She will want your comfort. Rolli left without even bidding her farewell."

Ivar looked happy to have a task as he walked away. He had revealed something useful, at least, though Ragnvald could have guessed Halfdan's hatred of him.

Halfdan was still talking with his brother Gudrod, now showing him a dagger covered with Irish metalwork when Ragnvald approached. Must he fear that Halfdan had made an alliance with the Irish Norse as well?

"Greetings," he said to Halfdan. "I have been talking with your father. What punishment do you think is fair for your rebellion?"

Halfdan looked shocked for a moment but covered it quickly. His eyes were a paler blue than Harald's, lacking his warmth. "My father does not believe me a rebel. I have told him I was only working on his behalf, as you were, these past years. Or so you claim."

"Without your allies, I suppose you are little danger," said Ragnvald. "Still, I will be watching."

"Good," said Halfdan. "And I will be watching you."

"He does not believe me a rebel either," said Ragnvald. Gudrod stood still, next to Halfdan, looking as though he hoped his stillness would keep him from notice. Perhaps Gudrod would be a witness Harald would trust.

"Maybe not," said Halfdan. "But he will. Your wife has spoken words that will be echoed by every rebel in the north. 'Wolflike,' making men into deer—your wife is more clever than I ever thought before."

She had found the worst time to exhibit that cleverness, but Ragnvald felt some grudging pride at Halfdan's words.

Halfdan's smile faded. "You have too much ambition to be trusted," he said.

"We are much alike then," Ragnvald replied.

"In this we are not," said Halfdan. "Even if I kill you, my father will forgive me. But if you kill me, my father will kill you in turn. Think on that."

"Is that what you want from me? To die on your sword?" Ragnvald asked.

"It would be more advantageous to have you as my ally than my enemy. You want your son Ivar to inherit Sogn, even with all of my brothers clamoring for land. Do not oppose me when I make my move, and I will make certain that he does."

Halfdan did not even know yet that Harald had taken Sogn from him, and he still knew what to offer. Ragnvald supposed that any other man would betray Harald after today, but he could not think that choice would lead to anything other than his ruin, no matter what Halfdan offered. Ragnvald had pledged his life to Harald, and he would give it. His only choice was whether to die with honor or not.

"And if I do oppose you?" Ragnvald asked. He should at least find out what alliances Halfdan had made. King Erik of Jutland would back Halfdan again if he saw an advantage in it—and Halfdan could have made cause with any number of overseas vikings and district kings.

"Battles are uncertain, and Ivar is young and untried." Halfdan shrugged. "I will protect him as well as you protect me."

24

SVANHILD HARDLY SLEPT ON THE CROSSING TO ICELAND. SHE felt alive as she had not since the battle of Hafrsfjord. Now, leaving Norway behind, her blood sang with the breeze. Solvi would be old, she knew that. He might hate her. They would fight, she knew, cry and rage. She would call him a fool and a lout and throw things at him, and then kiss him and make love to him. She had been missing him for so long.

The last time she had made this crossing, she had been sick with worry for her dying son, angry at Solvi for making him leave Iceland. The time before that, they had been fleeing King Hakon's forces in the Faroe Islands. She had not been as good a sailor then but was still able to outrun his ships, with her hand on the steering oar, her voice commanding her sailors. She remembered Solvi's eyes shining with pride when her ship caught up with his. Every time she had made a difficult crossing since then, she imagined his approval, his advice. It would be strange and wonderful to sail with him again.

Now Rolli followed her in his ship as they skipped up the Norse coast, camping on islands, using pieces of treasure to buy food for her men and Rolli's crew of youngsters. A strong wind carried them out of view of the last of Norway's barrier islands, so strong that Svanhild had to order the sail reefed down to only a third, and it still made the lines hum and the mast groan. Falki stood next to her, saying nothing, but he seemed full of the same energy that drove Svanhild. When the wind slackened enough that Svanhild no longer worried it would tear the mast from the deck, she said to him, "I am glad you are with me, my friend."

"You could not have doubted it," he replied.

"King Harald dishonored me," she said. "I had to leave."

"Of course."

"I wonder that I waited so long," she said with a laugh.

"I do too," he replied. "We go to your husband now—Solvi?"

"Yes," she said. Falki spoke carefully, but she still felt his longing. He would have happily shared her bed anytime in these past years, and had she not promised Ragnvald that in exchange for her freedom and this ship, she would take no lovers, she would have done it. Now her body thrummed with the promise of sailing to her true husband. If she did not go to him, she would have gladly lain down with Falki. She would have a lover soon, she promised herself. Whatever she found of Solvi.

"You will be rewarded well," she said to Falki. "I have heard there are not many women in Iceland, but I will find you a wife if you want—I want you to be happy."

"Should I turn viking or turn farmer, do you think?" Falki asked.

"Turn what you like," she said joyfully. "You will never lack for a roof or food, not as long as I am living."

They stopped on the tip of the southernmost Faroe island for a night's rest. A waterfall plummeted over the cliff that sheltered them from a lake high above, a silver-gray ribbon coming out of the clouds to join the sea.

Rolli seemed to stand straighter away from his father, though Svanhild could not bring herself to think too much of Ragnvald. She had not even said good-bye, as she had the first time she left him for Solvi. At least she could do something for his son.

"You must let Falki captain your ship for the crossing," she said to Rolli as he took off his boots so he could climb the cliff with some of the other young men.

"I did cross before," Rolli reminded her.

"You followed a merchant, you told me. And you feared to cross without me. One in three ships that attempts this crossing does not succeed," Svanhild replied. "This is a good time of year for it, but I want every advantage."

"It's my ship," said Rolli. "You always said that on a ship, the captain must make all the decisions and bear responsibility for them."

"Yes," said Svanhild, "and I want you to allow a more experienced sailor, who knows and can follow my commands immediately, to pilot you to Iceland. This decision may save the lives of your followers."

He agreed without much more argument. He was not a boy who feared to take direction from a woman like many young men did. No wonder Hilda valued him so.

He and some of Svanhild's other sailors killed a brace of small shore-birds for dinner and helped Svanhild skewer them to cook over the fire. "Do you think I can find a way to make it right with my father? Before my time is up?" he asked.

Svanhild thought Rolli's outlawry was just—whether it was a mistake or not, her daughter had suffered for it, and might be suffering still. "I don't know that it is your father you must convince," she said slowly.

"He is Harald's friend," said Rolli. "If he forgives me, Harald will have to as well."

"In seven years, all will have forgiven you," Svanhild countered. Seven years looked like an eternity to a boy his age. And she had been gone from Solvi twice that long.

"What am I going to do?" Rolli asked. "I wanted to be a sea king, but not . . ."

"Not so soon?" Svanhild asked.

"Yes," Rolli agreed. He drew squiggles in the sand with a stick of firewood. "And not without . . ." He sighed. "Not without my father's blessing."

"I am sorry," said Svanhild. He had always been Svanhild's favorite nephew, so big and earnest, with a stubbornness that reminded her of herself.

"Why wouldn't he help me?" Rolli asked. "I am not his favorite, but I am still his son. What is the use in being the most powerful man in Norway if you can't help your own son?"

"Or your sister," said Svanhild quietly. She thought that Ragnvald could have found another way to save Ivar and Harald's sons. He had made so many other clever bargains over the years. She looked at Rolli, at his cheeks, still full with a boy's plumpness, and rosy from the chill here under the cliffs. "I do not know what I will find in Iceland, but I will help you. I will teach you everything I can of real sailing—not just following fjords and coastlines—and if Solvi will not teach Ragnvald's son to be a sea king, he will know who can. There is still room in the world for adventurers, if not in Norway."

✢ ✢ ✢

THEY CAST OFF the next day with Falki in command of Rolli's ship. Once Svanhild could no longer see land in the distance behind them, she had to remember the tricks of navigation that she had only used a few times in Harald's service: steering by sun and stars, and half-remembered lore about the currents in this part of the sea. Every question Rolli asked her reminded her that she had always followed Solvi or ridden in his ship when they crossed open sea. On a cloudy day she pulled out her sunstone, which she had rarely needed when sailing Norway's coast, and used its magic to find east again.

One day a great collection of whales, each many times the size of her ship, bubbled up from the depths. A few gently bumped the vessel with their huge foreheads. Svanhild watched them, her heart in her throat, and recited every prayer she knew. Such vast creatures could easily spell their doom.

Rolli watched too, wonder and fear making his eyes wide. The whales kept pace with the ships for a whole day, during which the crew spoke only in whispers, before the great creatures disappeared in the evening. Svanhild nearly collapsed with relief. Some Norsemen hunted small whales, and all harvested the bounty from when they beached, but these seemed another order entirely, gods of the deep.

"Aunt Svanhild, what were those?" Rolli asked, his voice high.

"Some of Solvi's men told me whales are the ghosts of drowned ships, and they hate those who can still sail on the surface and bear their passengers to dry land," she replied, still feeling the strange weight of their presence, far below.

"I did not know whales could grow so large," he said, confusion crinkling his smooth forehead.

"There is so much out beyond Norway's shores," she said. "Many things bigger than us, bigger than Harald."

"Bigger than my father?" Rolli asked with a hesitant smile.

"Perhaps," said Svanhild, smiling in return. "I used to find it so, and I will again."

✛ ✛ ✛

FINALLY, THREE WEEKS after leaving the coast of Norway behind, Svanhild saw the dark stripe on the horizon that could only be Iceland. As they drew nearer, the bright days gave way to clouds. She remembered this: the gray skies that often covered Iceland, making the black of the soil and the beaches all the more forbidding. One of the mountains belched smoke. She was closer to Solvi than she had been in so long. She felt as though the tether attached somewhere in her chest, that had always stretched back to Iceland, and the land she had claimed here, grew shorter again, its pull relaxed, giving her spirit a comfort that she had missed all this time.

They made landfall that night on a wide black beach that did not have a single speck of green upon it. A milky river flowed through the sand and tasted of the silt it carried down from the mountains. She gave thanks to the gods for the ease of their crossing. A few weeks' sailing, and after fourteen years apart, she could again stand before her husband.

"This is Iceland?" Rolli asked. "It looks very different from the Orkneys."

"Yes," said Svanhild.

"It looks dead," Rolli added.

"It does," said Svanhild. "But there is green and fertile land, I promise."

Another day of sailing brought them to the Reykjavik settlement, through its fog-choked bay. Mist swirled around the ship, though the sun shone overhead. Svanhild's men rowed slowly to avoid crashing into rocks hidden by the fog. The voices of settlers carried to them across the water well before the mists dispelled. Svanhild could not see any buildings until her ship's keel scraped over the stones at the shore.

She breathed the air, and tears sprang to her eyes. She could smell a hint of the sulfur blast that had brought on the illness that killed her and Solvi's son. Rolli looked around at the settlement, eager as a puppy to greet new friends. At least Svanhild had brought a stronger boy to Iceland this time.

An old fisherman was mending his net near where Svanhild directed the ships to be beached. Behind him, a town to rival Nidaros had sprung up, composed of buildings of many shapes and sizes—a few of wood, and more of stone and stacked turf. The arrival of her ships had drawn a few onlookers, but gone were the days when every new arrival to Reyk-javik called forth a greeting from the settlement's leading men.

"You there," said Svanhild to the fisherman. "Does Solvi Hunthiofs-son live here?"

"Never knew Solvi to have so many visitors," said the fisherman with a cackle. He pointed toward the rocky border at the edge of the settle-ment, near the land Svanhild had claimed. She still remembered every footstep she had taken when she walked its borders, though she had never planted there, never grazed an animal of her own on the fields she claimed, never even slept one night on its ground.

Had Solvi lived on the land she claimed for all this time, waiting for her to return? That was not what she had meant for him when she sent him away from the battle at Hafrsfjord, after forcing him to swear never to try to reclaim his land in Norway. Whenever Svanhild left Norse wa-ters, she wondered if every sail on the horizon was his, or if she would find him as a guest in a court she visited. She had imagined him con-tinuing to raid and trade, to explore new lands, to sail off the edge of the earth perhaps, or be devoured by the Midgard serpent whose coils wrapped through all of the depths of the ocean. She had never suspected that he had bound himself to her land, and the farming he had despised.

She bid Falki and Rolli accompany her, and the others remain at the shore. The footsteps of many years had broadened the path. Even the iron rock of Iceland must yield to time.

The clouds hung low over Unna's hill. Should she go to see Unna first? No, Svanhild could not wait. She still wore the britches that were her costume on board her ship. Perhaps she should have stopped and changed into women's garb—she had a collection of rich dresses, shifts, and overdresses in colors that Solvi would like, but they were presents from Harald. He might prefer her like this; the woman with whom he had traveled the world wore britches far more often than gowns.

She touched her hair. She wore a narrow scarf, little more than a headband to keep loose strands from her braid out of her face in the wind. Her hair was crusted with salt, and oily from a long trip without bathing. But she would not go back and change now. Solvi would know her no matter what she wore.

The land—her land—was striped with lines of plantings and divided into fields. A weathered wooden hall, little more than a house, stood on the high corner. Not where Svanhild would have placed it, since it added more distance to the walk to the settlement. Still, having wood at all in Iceland showed that Solvi was rich enough to import it.

A fine rain began to fall, and field-workers walked toward the buildings to wait out the weather. And that was where she found Solvi sitting under the eaves of his house. A woman sat next to him on the narrow bench, laughing with him. Svanhild had pictured many things about their first meeting, but never this: to see him with another woman.

Jealousy made her flush. She should not have brought Falki and Rolli with her to see this—but she was unaccustomed to going anywhere without guards. And why should Solvi not have a woman? Svanhild had been gone for a long time. Still, her voice was strangled so she could not make herself heard when she tried to speak. She only looked at him mutely until he finally raised his head and saw her.

He had many more lines around his eyes, and the brilliant, red-gold hair he had given their daughter was mostly silver now. There was still something vital about him, though, laughing with this woman. Then he looked at her; shock, surprise, and anger replaced his smile. There he was, her Loki, changeable as fire.

When he stood she saw he had grown round at his middle. It made him look like a gnome, and for a moment she felt she did not know him. He had become an old man. This journey had been a mistake. She should have swallowed her pride, as all Harald's other wives would surely do, and waited until he could be her husband again.

Solvi remained where he was until the woman handed him a stick that Svanhild did not realize was a cane until Solvi began limping toward her. He grimaced, and she knew he felt ashamed, as always, of his injury, feeling it made him less than a man. That wound went deeper than any of his scars, a wound that she had made worse by leaving him. Her moment of regret faded. He was the end of all her paths, and she had come to him to rekindle what lay between them or see if it had truly burned to ash.

She closed the distance between them so she would not have to see what age and his old injury had done to him. He even smelled different from what she remembered, no longer like the sea, leather armor, and rope. She had taken on that scent, while his made her think of Iceland's loam, thistles, and green things. Under it, though, the warmth of his body near hers was the same. They could never change so much they would not recognize each other.

"Svanhild," he said, simply. She could not say anything at all. She could no longer see the woman who had sat with him—beautiful, homely, she did not matter. Seeing him now was worth everything she had left behind.

"Solvi," she said finally, smiling ruefully. They were fools together, and always had been. He reached out toward her and touched her fingertips. They were the exact same height, eye to eye, though she could not meet his for long. She looked at his firm mouth instead, framed by the beard he kept close cropped, as though he still captained a ship. No shaggy old man's beard for him.

"Did you come for your daughter?" he asked.

"I came for her and for you," she said. "She is *our* daughter—did you not believe that?"

"No, I believe that," he said quickly. "But if she had not been taken here, would you have come?" Of course, they must fight before they embraced. Best to get that over quickly, so it could burn bright and fast and be done.

"Harald divorced me," she said. "He divorced all of his wives to marry a new Danish queen. He said he will remarry the rest as soon as the girl gives him a son. That is what my brother negotiated, but I—"

"Your pride could not bear it," Solvi said.

Svanhild tossed her head. "I saw my escape and I took it. It was that, and not my pride."

"Ah, Svanhild," said Solvi. He brushed her hair from her face. His hands felt different touching her than any other's, full of care and love. "You are just the same."

"I suppose you don't mean my looks," she replied.

"You will always be beautiful to me," he said. "And now you have come back. To an old farmer waiting to die."

"Is that what you are? I think you are young still."

"You know I am not that," said Solvi. "Any pool of water shows me the white in my beard."

Silver with the barest hints of gold—she thought she could learn to like it. The spell holding them together, as though nothing else in the world existed, seemed to dissipate.

"I will take you to Freydis," he said.

"Our daughter," she said, wonderingly. She had tried not to think of Freydis that way, as a tie that bound her and Solvi together, though she looked too like Solvi for Svanhild to forget her parentage for long. She had not been much of a mother to any of her children, but with Harald's sons at least she had the excuse that they must be fostered to make alliances.

"Is she with Vigdis's son? Hallbjorn?" Svanhild asked. "Have you made sure they are married?"

"She did not want to marry him," said Solvi. "So I sent him away."

"Sent him away?" Svanhild asked.

"She was his captive," said Solvi, his voice strange and hollow. "Should I have made her marry him?"

Svanhild had once been Solvi's captive, and then married him. Still, Freydis was not her, and Hallbjorn was not Solvi but an untried young man, with no more to offer Freydis than the beauty he had inherited from his mother.

"How is it that both of our children are so different from us?" Svanhild asked. Solvi's gait with his cane had a rhythm to it, practiced and efficient as he could make it, though not quick. She had to keep her steps short so she did not run ahead of him.

"Is it already time to speak of that?" Solvi asked.

Svanhild frowned. "You are right," she said. "We have all the time left to us, to talk over things. To fight if we have to." She looked at him sidelong. "You will not drive me away again."

"You will leave sooner or later," he replied. "It is what you do."

"I?" Svanhild asked. "When we first met, you could not bear to stay in Tafjord longer than a few days at a time. I wonder that you have stayed so long in Iceland. How does the sea not draw you away?"

He did not answer her. Perhaps it would take the rest of their lives to learn how the long years apart had changed them. Solvi had scorned farmers, and now he had become one. Svanhild missed the part of herself that had claimed this land, that wanted to make a home, tend a husband, raise a daughter—raise a grandchild. If Hallbjorn had made Freydis pregnant, then Svanhild, who still felt like a girl sometimes, would be a grandmother. Perhaps a gray-haired husband would suit her.

25

FREYDIS LOOKED UP FROM HER WEAVING AND SAW THE VISI-
tors coming across the field: her father, walking like a three-legged dog,
dropping his left shoulder with each step, and a thin woman who walked
like a man, too far away for Freydis to see her face, but not someone she
could mistake. Her mother had come for her.

Freydis had felt calm these past few weeks, obeying Unna's instructions to eat more, even past fullness. The despair that had driven her to
Unna's mushrooms was still there if she reached for it, but every day that
passed, filled with moments of beauty, gave her another layer of armor
against it.

She spent time with pregnant cats and ewes, because Unna said that
their easy births would make hers easy as well. Alfrith would have said
the same, though those old charms did not always work. Freydis had
seen a woman die in childbirth with a cat next to her, and the infant
died as well before reaching its bloody doorway to the world.

She moved slowly to untie her small card-loom, first from her belt,
and then from the stump she had used to provide tension. Unna had
been called away to tend an old man who, she said, would probably be
getting around to dying in the next few days, but her herbs might help
him survive until the winter, if he wished it.

Freydis wondered how Unna could look at life and death so simply,
knowing life should be preserved when possible, but death and pain
were inevitable, and must be faced. Easier said than done, and easier
when it was someone else's pain. Childbirth would dwarf any pain she

had already experienced, and it might kill her. She could not help but rage against that.

Freydis brushed off her overdress and fixed her hair. When Solvi and Svanhild—her parents, how strange to think of them that way—came close, Svanhild left Solvi behind, running over the broken ground toward Freydis. Svanhild opened her arms to embrace her, but Freydis sidestepped her, and crossed her arms over her chest.

Svanhild cupped Freydis's face instead, holding her until Freydis had to meet her eyes. Her mother was shorter than her now, she realized. "Daughter, you can't know how glad I am to find you well," said Svanhild. "You are well, aren't you?"

With her mother's eyes and hands upon her, Freydis felt no choice but to nod, and at least that motion freed her from Svanhild's grasp. Solvi arrived then, puffing from his exertion. "Your mother's king has divorced her," he said, with an odd mix of sarcasm and affection. "So now she comes here to us."

Freydis liked how he did that, put himself with her, against Svanhild. Growing up, she had heard nothing of him except how much he loved her mother—the first to fall under her spell, Harald's fiercest enemy who quit his claim to Maer because of his oath to her.

"I plan to stay," said Svanhild. "Even if both of you reject me as he did." She paused. "It is my land."

Solvi laughed. "To be sure it is. I will have some compensation for tending it for you, though, as will Unna."

"Where is she?" Svanhild asked. Freydis told her. "And you are staying here?" She reached toward Freydis again but dropped her hand before Freydis had to decide whether to avoid it.

"Yes," said Freydis. Unna's quiet household had deepened her habit of answering no more than was asked, and barely that.

"Unna would let me stay with her if I asked," said Svanhild with a certainty that irritated Freydis. The irritation was a gift, far better than crying, showing the need that Svanhild had always seemed to despise.

"Where do you wish your mother to stay?" Solvi asked her. He had done it again, asked her what she wanted. He sounded curious, not as though he wanted to push her toward one choice or another.

If Svanhild stayed with Unna, she would crush Freydis's brand-new sense of freedom, but if she stayed with Solvi, it would bind them back together. Solvi would not resist her. Even now, he darted a glance at her that softened his stern features.

"Not with me," said Freydis.

"Unna is my friend," Svanhild protested.

"You do not wish to stay with your husband? Former husband, I should say?" Freydis asked. She did not like this cruel person she was discovering in herself, but she did enjoy the feeling of power her mother's hurt gave her.

Svanhild turned toward Solvi, and Freydis felt suddenly excluded. Her own fault. She had not gone to see her father since she had come to Unna's farm. She had been too wrapped up in her own pain, and fear that Hallbjorn would return from wherever Solvi had sent him.

"I want to stay long enough to greet my friend," said Svanhild. "Will you forbid me that?"

"No," said Freydis, feeling as though she was losing something. "Do as you wish."

Svanhild smiled a little ruefully. Solvi looked weary, leaning on his cane. "I will get you a seat and something to drink," Freydis said to him. She went into the house to get some stools and found that Snorri had arrived, so she returned for another seat and some cups of ale. Snorri accepted her welcome and drank from the side of his tattered mouth. Freydis found him easier to look upon when she concentrated on his eyes, which were a kind, even gray.

"You are well now?" Solvi asked her.

"Well enough," she said. "The child is well rooted. I—nothing has changed that." She found her hand going to her womb and stopped the motion. She had accepted this child, but she was not yet ready to love it.

"I am not displeased to learn that," said Solvi. "I had never thought to be a grandfather, or to know my grandchildren."

"I might die," Freydis reminded him.

"Don't say that," said Svanhild.

"I am over-young for a child," said Freydis. "Any healer would tell you that. Mothers my age often die—that is why the law says I am too young for marriage."

"You talk like a law-speaker," said Svanhild. "I had not thought you spent that much time with Hilda." Freydis remembered hearing Einar and Hilda talk over the law and former trials, arguing to pass the long winter nights, nights when Svanhild had been on other shores. Einar chose his words quickly and easily, but Hilda had a long memory of other cases, and won their friendly disputes as often as he did.

Svanhild put her arm around Freydis's waist too quickly for Freydis to avoid it, though she quickly pulled away. "Why do you hate me, Freydis?" she asked, her voice breaking a little.

Freydis gestured at her abdomen. "Because I am here, like this," she said, her voice rising.

"And you blame me for that?" Svanhild asked. "When I have come to find you? Do you know another woman who would cross the sea, alone, for her daughter?"

Anger felt better than despair, though it still came with tears. "I blame Hallbjorn and my foolish cousin Rolli," she said. "And Hilda for sending me to Sogn, and you for letting it happen, and me for not preventing this somehow!" She ran into Unna's house and began pulling her clothes out of the chest at the foot of her bed and shoving them into a bag. Wherever her mother went, she would go elsewhere.

Svanhild followed her. She sat down next to Freydis on her pallet, and went to put her arm around her again as Freydis edged away. Her mother's touch seemed as abhorrent to her as Hallbjorn's did, a touch of ownership that would smother Freydis's spirit.

"You do hate me," said Svanhild.

"Why do you care?" Freydis asked. "You don't care what happens to me, except it gave you a reason to come to Solvi when your king divorced you. You did not even ask how I am."

"You look well enough, though you're throwing a tantrum like a child," said Svanhild.

"I don't need you," said Freydis. "Solvi has offered to care for me, and Unna . . . though she said she was doing it for you. So I suppose you can tell her to send me away. Then I will have to stay with Solvi—do you truly mean to stay here in Iceland?"

"Yes," said Svanhild. "I have nowhere else to go."

Freydis did not want to see her mother's vulnerability. "You have some other plan," she said. "You always do."

"I don't know what I'm doing to do," said Svanhild. "Can you not help me discover it?"

Freydis dried her face instead of answering.

"Do you think your father is happy here?" Svanhild asked. "I have only just arrived, but it seems strange to me that he has stayed here."

"He stayed here to care for your farm," said Freydis. She would not tell her mother of the fear she had seen in Solvi's eyes.

"He tells me he wishes to stay, and I know you will not want to spend your days wandering. So I suppose I must learn the desire to stay here. I had it once. Perhaps I can again."

"Perhaps," said Freydis.

They sat in silence for a time. Freydis felt oddly sorry for her mother. Freydis could not count herself happy, nor did she know what she wanted her life to bring, but she thought she could be well satisfied with a farm and a husband, as long as he was not cruel to her. Some animals and children to care for, a garden full of vegetables and herbs—a household. Her mother was cursed if she could not be satisfied with that.

"Why did you claim your farm, if you did not want it?" Freydis asked.

"It was for"—she took a deep breath—"my son. Your brother. Eystein." Her voice sounded remote. She had never spoken of Eystein to Freydis before. Freydis had learned of him from women's gossip in Tafjord. They said that Svanhild's desire to act like a man had killed her son. "He would have been happy to inherit a farm," Svanhild continued. "I wanted it for him. He needed me more than anyone has ever needed me, and I would have done anything for him. You do not need me. Solvi does not need me. Ragnvald does not need me. And Harald does not want me. Rolli is . . ."

"What about Rolli?" Freydis asked.

"He has been outlawed from Harald's Norway, so I brought him with me. Perhaps he needs me. I promised I would help him. He seems cast adrift. Do you want to marry him?"

Freydis shook her head vehemently. Rolli felt like her brother in a way that her older cousins—like Einar—did not. She could not imagine having him in her bed with anything other than disgust.

"So nothing is settled or can be settled. I am sorry," said Svanhild. "I would make what amends I can."

Freydis heard Unna arriving, greeting Solvi and Snorri. She rose, and pressed her hands to her eyes again to cool them.

"You should go and see her," said Freydis. "I have chores to do."

Freydis did some tidying by the light that came in the open door, then gathered her pails for the afternoon's milking. Sheep and goats ambled toward her, desiring the relief that her hands would bring. She kept some sheep's milk separate for feeding her little lamb, Torfa, who grew bigger every day.

She could see Solvi and Snorri speaking with Donall, while Unna and Svanhild embraced, and then walked away together. Unna pointed out things in her garden and lands, likely what had changed since Svanhild had left. Pregnant with her, Freydis realized. Fifteen years ago, her mother had been as she was now. A little older, though not much. Solvi had forced her to leave Iceland then, and she had returned to an uncertain welcome now.

When her pails were full she walked back toward the house. She followed the path around the south side of the house to avoid passing anyone. As she took the milk into the dairy shed, she heard Unna and Svanhild speaking.

"She wants me to know that she could die in childbirth," Svanhild said, with a little laugh that did not sound happy.

"And so she could," said Unna.

"Oh, do not tell me that," Svanhild replied. "I will not see another of my children die here. And Solvi would never forgive me."

"He would blame you?"

"Of course. She does."

"She's a child," said Unna.

"A child who will bear another child," said Svanhild. "When I was not much older than she is, I had already run away from my family."

Freydis's throat felt tight, and she grew angry with herself that she might cry in front of her mother yet again. No, she could not measure up to Svanhild Sea Queen. Svanhild would have fled from Hallbjorn, not given in to him.

"Not all children are the same," said Unna. "And you had astonishingly good fortune when you did that."

"Good fortune—I came here and my son died. Why must I have such weak children?" Svanhild asked.

"I do not think she is weak," said Unna. "I think . . ."

"You know she is," said Svanhild. "She is strange and superstitious, and she always has been. She relies on prayers when she should rely on herself."

"I think we do not yet know what she will be. But she found her way here to me—that is something."

"That boy brought her here," said Svanhild dismissively.

Freydis could bear no more and emerged from the dairy not far from where they stood talking. "If I am so weak, I will trouble neither of you further," she said. "Mother, stay with Unna, and I will see if your weak daughter can find a place with her weak father."

"Freydis . . . ," Svanhild called after her, but Freydis did not turn.

As she walked away she heard Unna say, "She still needs mothering."

"She will not take it from me," Svanhild replied.

"Not when you think she is weak for wanting it," said Unna, her tone sharp enough that Freydis would have flinched if that had been directed at her. Unna raised her voice and continued: "You were a good mother to Eystein, but you have spent too long among men. You cannot bully your way through every problem."

Freydis snorted as she went into the house to gather the bag she had packed. No matter how loudly Unna spoke, her mother would not hear it.

Outside, Solvi and Snorri still sat with Donall. "Father, I would like to stay with you," Freydis said. Solvi looked so glad at her words that she felt guilty. "But only if she is not. I cannot stay with her. She hates me."

"She came here for you," Solvi reminded her.

"She thinks me weak." Freydis's voice broke again.

"And she knows no worse insult," said Solvi, half to himself.

"I cannot live with her, not and keep free of . . ." She could not speak it, her fear that her mother would make her desire death again, but Solvi nodded as though he understood.

"I don't know if I can either," said Solvi. "It is her land, but—"

"Would she expel you? Do you think she would be so cruel?" Freydis asked.

"I don't know," said Solvi. "We will learn together."

26

SOLVI'S LEGS FELT LIKE SODDEN LOGS AS HE WALKED BACK TO his farm with Freydis and Snorri. Unna had agreed to the trade, mother for daughter. She gave Solvi a significant look before they left, which Solvi understood as a command to keep his daughter safe, from herself, or anyone else. That might be easier at his farm, which did not have Unna's dangerous stock of herbs.

Svanhild had been angry at the trade, though she had not given full vent to it. "I will come visit you," she promised Solvi and Freydis, making it sound almost like a threat. Solvi wanted to laugh—at her, at himself—but Freydis seemed too brittle to risk it. This all seemed comical. Svanhild would quickly find she did not want a fearful old man, lame and useless to her.

As they walked back, Freydis kept a slow pace that Solvi could manage, though he still needed to rest a few times. When they reached Solvi's garden, Svanhild's captain, Falki, and Rolli Ragnvaldsson were laughing with Tova over the antics of one of the baby goats.

Tova ran over to Solvi and helped him down onto a rough seat. Sitting down took away the pain in his feet so swiftly it felt like pleasure. Tova brought him a cup of light ale, and it combined with his hunger to make his head float. She massaged his legs with hard, painful strokes that he knew would make them feel better tomorrow, as he leaned his head back against his chair and let her drive out the aches.

The talk quieted, and Solvi opened his eyes again. He waved Tova away. This was too intimate a service to be performed outside, with guests present. "Rolli Ragnvaldsson," he said. "You seem to be a trou-blemaking sort. Tell me why you are here. I know Svanhild did not need an escort."

Rolli's high-colored face split in a rueful grin. "I'm the one who needed help getting here," he said. "I've been outlawed for seven years."

Freydis crossed her arms over her chest. "That seems just," she said. She gestured at her still-flat stomach. "You could have prevented this. But you let him." How could Svanhild think their daughter weak? She sounded just like her mother now, hard as flint.

Rolli looked guilty. "Where is Hallbjorn?" he asked.

"I sent him away," said Solvi. "He is with the Scottish sea kings now."

"What should I do?" Rolli asked. "Aunt Svanhild said she would teach me of sailing, and that you could teach me how to be a sea king. But now she has left me here."

"That is what she does," Freydis muttered.

Solvi looked up at him. "Do you like farming?" he asked.

"No, no farming for me." Rolli puffed his chest out. "I will be a great raider."

"You will frighten everyone with your size, at least," said Solvi.

"Yes," said Rolli. "I was born for nothing else."

"You owe my daughter a dowry to compensate for her maidenhead," Solvi replied. "If you gain riches raiding, that can be the first debt you discharge."

"I—" Rolli began.

"You should have been her protector," said Solvi. "She is right about that. If you meant to marry her to Hallbjorn, it should have been done correctly, with a dowry, bride price, and ceremony. If you want to act like a man, you must do it all the way."

Rolli bowed his head. "Yes. I will bring my cousin a dowry enough to buy her a king. But how should I do it? I have not had much luck in picking my targets."

Solvi found he liked the boy in spite of his being Ragnvald's son. He saw almost nothing of Ragnvald in him. Rolli's mother must have been the one to give him his height and plainspoken charm.

Falki sat close by Tova, talking quietly with her. When Falki had arrived with Svanhild, he watched her with an intensity that Solvi rec-ognized. Svanhild Sea Queen still had one subject. Now Tova wore a happy pink on her cheeks, rather than disdaining Falki, as she had other Iceland men who had come courting over the years. Solvi felt a pang of jealousy.

Falki raised his head from Tova's and said, "Harald is coming to make war on Orkney next summer. Svanhild wanted to warn the Icelanders and the Scottish vikings to be ready for him. Rolli, will you come with us?"

So Svanhild would be leaving again, and soon. Solvi should not have expected anything different, but a foolish part of him had already begun to hope otherwise.

Rolli shook his head. "I will do nothing against Harald," he said. "When the term of my outlawry is over—"

"I thought you wanted to be a sea king," said Solvi. "If that is so, there will never be a place for you in Norway."

"My mother is there," said Rolli.

"Turn farmer, then," said Solvi. "I need help here, and then you and your followers may avoid offending Harald in that time."

"Yes," said Freydis. "Stay here. I do not want a dowry, I want protection if Hallbjorn should return."

Rolli looked uncomfortable but shrugged. Solvi judged he would not keep the boy for long. Still, he would accept a strong back during harvest, and a new face to enliven the long winter.

✣ ✣ ✣

SOLVI HAD TROUBLE falling asleep, with his legs aching from his walk. When he woke he felt oddly restless, and then he remembered the events of the day before. Svanhild had come, stirring up feelings he had thought long dead. Even when he heard tales of her over the years, he had learned to ignore them. Icelanders did not celebrate Harald, since he had driven so many of them from their homes, but they all liked a bold woman, and sang of how Svanhild helped win the battle of Hafrsfjord, which made Harald king of Norway in truth.

Solvi heard Svanhild's voice from outside. So she had already come to visit. Rolli's was a low rumble that still occasionally rose to a boyish tenor when he grew excited.

When Solvi joined them in the garden, Svanhild's eyes went to his cane before darting away. He hardly remembered picking it up—it was a part of him now. He forgot to feel ashamed of it unless someone looked at him like that.

Svanhild turned back toward the men at the rough outdoor table, her followers and Rolli's who had camped on Solvi's land without even asking his permission. "Falki, will you take my ship and let the Scottish vikings know of Harald's plans?" she asked.

"Of course, my lady," Falki was saying. "You do not want to come with us?"

"No," she said. "If you can, come back before the end of the summer, and you can winter here." She gave Solvi a sardonic smile. "After all, this is my land."

Svanhild had been the one to claim it, and had done it without Solvi's help or approval, making it hers by law, now that they were divorced. Falki departed, and Svanhild asked Snorri and Tova to show her the farm that Solvi had built. He had poured years of work and treasure into it. He could no longer drive a plow, but he could plant seed, milk the animals if they were brought to him, and with his powerful arms he had become adept at shearing. The wiry wool that Icelandic sheep produced was in great demand all over Europe for its warmth and weather-resistance.

Svanhild returned ahead of the afternoon rain. Solvi had learned the weather of Iceland as well as he had once known every eddy and current of Geiranger Fjord. Under the big sky he watched the storms chase one another across the fields before they reached him, as he had once watched the weather on the open sea. Svanhild's years at sea had whittled away all the roundness of her youth. She did not look like a girl, but she did not look old either—she looked how he imagined a goddess, timeless, made of something stronger than flesh.

He sat down across from Svanhild at the table. It was so strange to have her here, looking over his life like a tax collector. That had been one of her roles for Harald, he recalled: tax collector and assessor, visiting kingdoms, taking what she wanted, and leaving again.

"You have made a farm here," she said grudgingly.

"I have," he said. "With much help."

"You once scorned farmers."

"I still do," he said. "Farmers work too hard."

"But here you are. Where is my sea king? How did you come to this?"

He spooned some porridge into his mouth from a bowl that Tova offered, chewed, and swallowed it. She had sweetened it with honey and mixed in butter to please him, but it still tasted like ash.

"Are you not glad to see me caring for your land?" Solvi asked.

"If I thought"—Svanhild's face contorted in some pain Solvi did not understand—"I did not imagine that you would become a farmer. I thought you would live as we once did, raiding, trading, sailing from court to court. No home but our ship."

"I was obeying my oath," said Solvi.

"You are more than a farmer," said Svanhild, "even if you've forgotten it. Your name is legend. They still blame raids upon you. You could still rally Harald's enemies, and landless vikings."

"You made me swear I would not," Solvi said, far too loud. He would rather speak privately, but his legs ached too much from yesterday's exertion for him to walk with her out of earshot of his household and Svanhild's and Rolli's followers.

"And now I am here," said Svanhild. "Your old allies are gathering to fight Harald. He will be far from home, fighting battles from a ship, which is not where his skill lies. Plus," she added scornfully, "he has spent the last three years in bed with a Finnish sorceress, neither ruling nor fighting. He is weak. I thought you would want this—a chance to be victorious, finally. It will never come again."

Solvi's face felt hot. So, the gods would not let him die without a final humiliation.

"Svanhild," he said, "that time is past. I am lame. I tried for a time, but I could fight less and less as each year went by." He felt the eyes of all of Svanhild's men upon him. "The sea made me ache, and some mornings I could hardly rise from my bed. I lost . . ." Solvi could not say more, not without his fear shaking him apart. "Tryggulf died . . . and Snorri . . . Snorri had to save me. Do not ask me more."

"But you were strong enough to make this farm," Svanhild protested. Her face showed no scorn, but no comprehension either. He had flayed himself for her, and she had not listened. "I cannot believe that the great Solvi Hunthiofsson would flinch from this battle."

How much would he have to abase himself to make her see that he was not the man he once was? She had watched him struggle to walk to Unna's farm yesterday—how could she imagine he would fare better on a ship?

"I will not fight again," he said. "And certainly not to punish a man who has hurt your pride."

"The man I married before would have done it in a heartbeat," said Svanhild.

"Then go marry someone who will do this for you," said Solvi. "I will not."

"Do you want me to leave with Falki?" she asked.

"No," he admitted. "But you will leave Iceland sooner or later, and I am foolish for wishing it later."

"I want to stay," she said. "This is my land."

"Can you not leave me this, Svanhild? What do you want with this land, now?" he asked. He did not want to beg, but he would—for Freydis's sake, at least.

"I do not want to leave you at all," she cried. "You and Freydis decided I should stay with Unna instead. She hates me. My own daughter." Svanhild laughed brokenly. "You have more reason than she. How have I raised such weak children? At least my—"

"At least your sons with Harald do not have the taint of my seed?" Solvi asked, half choking on the words. "Go then. Leave your weak daughter and your weak husband—who is no longer your husband. Your men—if they followed you here, where won't they follow you? Make yourselves rich raiding Scottish monasteries."

Svanhild buried her face in her hands. "Never a day went by when I did not think of returning to you," she said. The sky was lightening, and a ray of sun touched her hair, showing its golden highlights, blurring the lines around her eyes so he had a glimpse of the fiery girl who had once been his wife. "Do not send me away, please."

"Svanhild," he said. He did not know what he could say to her. Their way toward each other seemed as strewn with rocks as Iceland's broken crust. "I will not send you away. Will you take my land from me?"

"No," she said. "I swear it."

"Our son was weak," he said slowly. "I do not think Freydis is weak. I heard from Tova that when Hallbjorn and Rolli wanted to sell their slaves south, she convinced them to come here. It was her idea to follow a merchant across the open sea."

"What? How?" Svanhild cried.

"She drank your milk and heard your tales," said Solvi. "How could she not?"

He felt the glow of pride from her. "She did not tell me," said Svanhild.

"And why should she? I will not try to drive you away, but . . ."

"What?"

"I *am* weak," said Solvi. Words a true warrior would never say—but when had he been a true warrior? Never, not since the fire that burned his legs when he was a boy. "Your daughter is not as weak as you fear, but there are none of us who do not have moments of weakness, even you. Hate that and you will hate her, hate me, and even yourself when you are as broken as I am. I would rather you leave than live with your contempt."

"I won't leave," said Svanhild. "Or, I will only go where you send me. Back to Unna's house for now, I suppose."

"Until Freydis is willing to welcome you," said Solvi.

Svanhild tossed her hair. "Is that how I will win you back again? By winning her?"

"If you like," said Solvi. He could not help but smile at her refusal to let him drive her away.

"Then I will," Svanhild promised.

⚜   ⚜   ⚜

SVANHILD SET OUT for Solvi's farm again a week later, after Falki left. She carried a loaf of bread and quarter round of cheese from Unna. Freydis stood at the door, watching her approach, her eyes hard. Svanhild tried to remember something about her daughter that might help them talk. She had been a quiet, superstitious child, more fascinated with Alfrith's spells and charms than anything Svanhild could share with her. Occasionally she looked so like Solvi, or her dead brother, Eystein, that Svanhild had to turn away.

Now she did not know who she saw standing in that doorway. A woman, not a child, a woman already a little taller than she was. She held herself with a wary grace that Svanhild had never seen in her before. Had she learned that from Alfrith in Tafjord? Or had that come later? Pregnancy made most women awkward, though she was hardly far enough along for it to show.

"As you desired, daughter, I have been dwelling with Unna," said Svanhild, feeling oddly formal.

"You are here again, though," Freydis replied sullenly.

Tova was passing with a basket of dried dung for the fire, and touched Freydis's shoulder with her own. "Freydis, be polite to your mother. She is our guest."

Freydis bowed. "Would you like some refreshment?" she asked.

"Yes," said Svanhild. She followed Freydis into Solvi's house, lit only by smoldering coals in the fireplace, a dimmer and dirtier place than Unna's dwelling. The ale Freydis served her was cold and herbal, Iceland's sere beauty made into a drink.

"Tova is an excellent brewer," said Svanhild.

"She's teaching me," said Freydis.

Svanhild nodded. "It is a good skill to have. One I do not possess." She could still milk a cow and oversee a dairy, but she had run away from her mother before learning the secrets of brewing, which were entrusted only to women of proven fertility.

"Is there anything I can do for you?" Svanhild asked. "I am sorry for what you heard me say." She took a deep breath. "I am sorry I left you in Tafjord for this—I am sorry for everything."

"I may give you a granddaughter," said Freydis stonily. "Are you sorry for that?"

"Not if—"

"Not if she turns out stronger than me?" Freydis asked.

"No!" Svanhild cried. "I hope she is weaker, if it means she does not kill you."

Freydis gave her a small smile. "That is how I feel too," she said. "And no."

"No, what?"

"I do not need you to do anything for me."

She did not say it in an unfriendly way, but Svanhild's chest still hurt. No, Freydis did not need her. Svanhild had been absent when she did, and now Freydis had grown beyond her.

"I need you, then," said Svanhild.

"For what?" Freydis asked, sounding suspicious.

"To come with me to Reykjavik and help me buy your father a pony," said Svanhild. "He has been trapped here too long."

✛ ✛ ✛

PONIES WERE FEW and expensive in Iceland and it took a few trips to various farms before they found a gentle, dappled gray gelding, whose owner was willing to part with it for a handful of Svanhild's hack-silver.

Freydis went with her each time, and each time their conversations became a bit easier. Freydis took her mother's request very seriously and made sure that the pony they chose had a smooth gait and was not too bony for Solvi's pained legs to grip.

He was carving a new handle for one of the scythes to make it ready for the harvest when Freydis led Svanhild, sitting atop the pony, into his yard. He looked up from his pile of shavings at Svanhild and said, "She suits you. What will you call her?"

Freydis had chosen well; the gelding had an easy gait—which was good, since Svanhild was not a practiced rider. Her inner thighs already ached from the short ride up from the settlement.

"He's for you," she said. "You can name him."

Solvi gave her a look that mixed affection with amused tolerance. "If I wanted a pony, don't you think I would have gotten one by now?"

"Yes, but men are often foolish," said Svanhild. "Why don't you want our gift?"

Solvi raised an eyebrow at Freydis, who laughed, a sound that surprised Svanhild, for she had rarely heard it.

"Don't be stubborn, Father," she said. She leaned over and kissed him on the cheek before going into the house.

"A dwarf on a pony?" said Solvi. "I court laughter enough already."

"Come riding with me," said Svanhild. "You can sit in front if you've forgotten how."

He gave her a skeptical look but used his cane to clamber onto a stump, and with a grip on her forearm, mounted behind her. Svanhild smiled when he leaned forward against her back. They had sat this way at the Sogn *ting* where they had first met, though then Solvi had held the reins, and Svanhild did not know who he was except a handsome warrior with a sharp smile who gave her an escape from her feuding family.

Iceland had ice fields like the one they had ridden up to on that day, but too far away for an afternoon's ride. Tomorrow the harvest would start on these upper farms, and roll like a tide down to the lower and warmer farms by the water's edge. Every farm helped its neighbors, weeks of backbreaking labor before the winter storms.

Today, though, Solvi wrapped his arms around her for the first time since she had returned to him. She guided the pony up toward the upper edge of the property, where hummocks of grass gave way to a broken slope that only the half-wild goats could navigate.

"Is this not better than walking?" Svanhild asked quietly when they slowed to a gentle amble.

"When you are not with me, I will still be a little man on a little horse," said Solvi, though he did not pull away from her.

"You never used to worry about things like that."

"Then I was a warrior. Now I am a farmer. And barely that."

"Why don't we rest here for a while, my love," Svanhild offered. Solvi tensed against her when she said "my love," and she flushed, glad she sat in front where he could not see it. She nudged the pony forward so they stood next to a mound of rock that would make dismounting easier for both of them. She jumped down and then helped Solvi off.

Storm clouds built to the east, waiting to sweep rain and wind across the plain. The sheep nearby had already sheltered in the hollows, the tufts of their white wool looking like the snow that would linger in those hollows in the spring. The wind brought with it the smell of sulfur from the mountains.

She settled on the ground against a soft grass-covered hummock and beckoned Solvi to do the same. She pulled him half against her, as though they were back on the horse again, with him in front.

Even with the smell, Iceland's beauty made Svanhild feel at home, though the vast scale of the landscape made her feel small in a way that Norway's narrow fjords and sheltered valleys never did. Before she ever set foot on Iceland, she had imagined coming here as a girl, to escape.

"The oath I asked of you was not to trap you here," she said. "I promise you that. Now please, tell me why you stayed. How you could bear it."

"I told you already," said Solvi.

"You told me very little," Svanhild insisted. "I promise, I will not . . . judge. I only want to know."

"This was the only place I could go after my defeat at Hafrsfjord," said Solvi. He seemed to find it easier to speak when they need not face one another. "A man thrice defeated by Harald Tanglehair, and this time with no one to blame but himself—I would not be welcome at all of those courts you remember so fondly."

He might have suffered that defeat with or without her, but Svanhild had captured many of his followers and condemned them to death at the hands of Harald and her brother. Solvi did not seem to blame her as much as himself—Svanhild had never seen many similarities between Solvi and Ragnvald, but in this they had some kinship. Harald never thought himself at fault for anything that went wrong.

"First," he continued, "I thought to make certain that Unna still held the land that you claimed, and she did. She had farmed it and grazed it, hired slaves to root up the scrub trees that grew upon it, and planted the beginnings of a windbreak. She had done her duty and more.

"I could have left then, but instead I hired men to build a small house, and stayed until the seasons turned. The next spring young Thorstein invited me to come raiding with him—there is so much trade with Dublin that a dozen ships can tax those merchants and hardly leave them poorer. So I went with him."

He fell silent, playing with the end of Svanhild's braid that he had pulled down over his shoulder. She remembered when she had spread her hair over both of them as part of their lovemaking, how Solvi said he enjoyed feeling the silken strands slip across his skin.

"What happened?" Svanhild asked.

"I can't. I couldn't." His voice changed, seeming to come out of him from somewhere far away. Svanhild felt a quiver in his muscles, like the shaking of a small, frightened animal.

"You don't have to tell me," she said sadly. She had glimpsed fear like this before, in men and women both—a loss of nerve that could never be regained. She had thought it cowardice and thanked the gods that she was made of stronger stuff. Perhaps, though, this fear was a curse from the gods, for Solvi, who had survived the terrors of his early childhood, could never be called a coward.

He took a shuddering breath. "We attacked a ship, and instead of being first into the fray, I held back. I was afraid—I have never been afraid in battle before, but I was. And then, when I overcame that fear, my legs failed me." He squeezed his eyes shut. "Tryggulf died defending me, and Snorri had to carry me out." His voice fell to a whisper, thick with pain. "A man who cannot go into battle is no man. He may as well be a farmer."

"You are more than your sword arm, more than your legs," said Svanhild. "You are still clever—those spikes at Hafrsfjord that ripped up the hulls of Harald's ships . . . You would have succeeded if your allies had been more effective."

"So I came back here. I knew you would not be using the land." Solvi continued as though he had not heard her. "I could not bring myself to go to another king's court, to be pleasant and clever, to charm nobles and inspire warriors. Better to retire and let the skalds sing songs of my old victories."

Svanhild took his hand from around her braid and intertwined his fingers with hers. The rainstorm would reach them soon. Already a few fat drops painted the copper-colored rocks a darker brown.

"I told you I had changed," said Solvi. "I know you will leave, having found me as I am. It is too late in the year to sail away, but don't worry, spring will come soon—though likely not soon enough for you."

Svanhild gripped his hand tighter and laid her cheek against the side of his head, the silver hair almost as fine and soft as his red-gold had once been. "When we parted, you asked me to come to you if Harald mistreated me. He was my husband in nothing but name for many years. I would have come long ago, but I wanted to keep my promises. And my brother was there. Now that he has betrayed me and I am free, I have come to you."

"You wanted me to make revenge on Harald," Solvi reminded her.

"When I first came here, I did," she admitted. "But when I sent Falki off, it was only to warn the Scottish vikings—your friends—that Harald would bring his forces. I will not try to draw you into it."

"Promise me that," said Solvi. "Promise you will not try to draw me into it."

"I swear it," said Svanhild. The rain was coming down in earnest now. Harvest would have to wait another day while the fields dried out. They must return to the farm soon, or become soaked. Before Solvi could get up, Svanhild moved into his lap and looked down at him. He avoided her eyes for a moment but met them when she would not let him turn away.

"I'm here," she said. She kissed him and he responded, wrapping his arms around her. "Now marry me, after harvest is done. Let me keep your house. Tova will still have a place, but I have never had a house of my own."

"You bought me a pony," said Solvi, lightly jesting. "How can I not? But all I can bring you is this farm, which is already yours."

"I wanted it for our son," she said, her voice hitching. "How can you live here without regretting that, regretting him?"

"I can no longer flee my regrets," said Solvi heavily. "And they would follow me anywhere. But Svanhild . . . our son was too weak to live."

"He was not weak," Svanhild protested. Unna had too recently scolded her for calling Freydis weak.

"His body was weak," said Solvi. "Weak from birth. You know this."

"He needed a different life than we could give him," said Svanhild.

"He would have died wherever we went," Solvi insisted.

"You have to believe that, or you would have to believe that you caused his death," she cried.

"It was both of us," said Solvi. "And the gods who gave us a sickly son. But we have a daughter now." He moved to cover her hand with his. "Tell me, how did you choose the name Freydis for her?"

Svanhild wiped her eyes with her other hand. "I thought our . . . I thought Eystein would have made a good priest of Frey. Remember when he chose that boar's head amulet? I had—Harald built a priesthood on the bank of Trondheim Fjord where his—where we left him. But even before then, when I gave birth to her, I thought to honor our son in her name."

Wordlessly, Solvi pulled a pebble from the pouch he wore at his waist and handed it to her. Svanhild held it gently between her fingers. In his pyre, Eystein's amulet must have melted over a stone. Over years of handling it, Solvi had rubbed away most of what remained of the design, but it still had the shape of a boar's head.

"I carry him with me everywhere," said Solvi.

Svanhild put the stone back in his hand and wrapped his fingers around it. "So do I," she said.

27

FOR THE LAST MONTHS OF HER PREGNANCY, FREYDIS FELT AS though she had no existence beyond her body, its needs, its pains. The child sat hard on her pubic bone, giving her an ache that could only be relieved by lying on her side, but that gave her different aches in her shoulder and hip, which were poorly padded, since she had only grown thinner through the winter. She could see it in her fingers, the residual plumpness of childhood sloughed off, the shape of the bones coming through.

After the harvest was over, her parents had wed, and Freydis traded places with her mother. Svanhild had asked Freydis to stay with her, Solvi, Rolli, Tova, Snorri, a few servants, and one of Rolli's friends, a thin, quiet young man who sometimes looked at Freydis with shy interest, but Freydis refused. Unna was easier company; she wanted nothing from Freydis but whatever work she had the strength to perform.

Unna pressed food on her, but it seemed like no amount of eating could fill the pit of hunger within her, nor restore her lost flesh. At times she did not even feel like a warm-blooded animal but a snail, her hard belly its shell, the rest of her soft and slow, dragging her, unthinking, to eat things both strange and ordinary. She craved seaweed often, which Unna thought was normal, but it was never something Freydis would have thought of at home. At the end of winter the wind sometimes carried a marine scent from the harbor that made her mouth water. Other times she craved fresh greens, so much she almost cried. Through the long winter, dried nettles came the closest to satisfying that desire. She drank down the teas Unna made her; even when the bitterness rasped against her tongue, she needed it.

At times, she craved her mother. When Svanhild visited, Freydis felt calm if they spoke of minor farm business: lambs that had died during the winter, too weak to survive on their mothers' thinning milk; Svanhild's plans for the following summer; how to use Solvi's farmland more efficiently. They argued, though, whenever Svanhild tried to press Freydis about her future.

Earlier in the winter, Freydis was called to Solvi's farm to nurse Snorri through a bout of pneumonia. Unna had been away at another sickbed, so Freydis followed Rolli out into the blinding brightness of a winter midday.

"He has trouble eating sometimes," Solvi told Freydis bleakly. "This has happened before."

"I have heard of this," said Freydis. "At least he will not spread the disease." If he had a piece of food in his lung, it would cause coughing and trouble breathing, even collapse of that lung. The only cure was waiting and treating the fever and breathing problems. "Is he strong otherwise?" she asked.

"Strong enough for a man near sixty winters," said Solvi. "Can you help him? He is the only companion of my boyhood left to me."

Though Snorri's powers of speech were even less than usual, Freydis was able to confirm Solvi's report that he had aspirated a piece of food, and now it was souring his lung. His chest hurt on one side, and when Freydis listened to his breathing, it had a thick sound. Freydis tapped on his ribs with her fingers and found that one side sounded dull while the other was still resonant.

A fever could be helpful, but not if it was too high. Freydis checked him through the afternoon for signs of delirium, and felt his forehead from time to time. When it became too hot she dosed him with willow-bark tea. She saw her mother watching her work and felt self-conscious.

Over the next few days Snorri began to improve. His fever fell and rose again, but never very high, and he was able to drink broth and slowly eat bread that had been well soaked in it. When Freydis was not tending him she joined Tova to help spin her endless piles of wool. Solvi told stories that Freydis had never heard, about growing up young and scarred, and how Snorri had been the first young warrior to care for Solvi, and to follow him rather than his father.

The weather turned brilliant, cold and clear. After three days Freydis decided that Tova could give Snorri all the nursing he needed, and resolved to leave the next morning. As she laced up her snowshoes she found her mother sitting next to her doing the same.

"I will go with you to visit Unna," said Svanhild. "I have been indoors too long." Boredom was winter's dullest weapon, but it could still injure. Still, Freydis thought it more likely that her mother wanted to be away from Snorri's sickbed, which she found discomfiting, as she did any sign of weakness.

Svanhild had skis, on which she moved faster than Freydis, unpracticed, in borrowed snowshoes. She stopped on the crest of a hill and waited for Freydis to catch up, shivering in the sharp wind.

"Has the child quickened?" Svanhild asked, starting to ski again.

Freydis nodded, though Svanhild could not see her, already pulling ahead.

Svanhild stopped again. "Well?" she said. This time she could see Freydis's nod. "Good. Have you given thought to what you will do when it is born?" She began to ski at a pace Freydis could match more easily. "If you want a marriage, I'm sure one can be found for you."

"But I don't have to marry?" Freydis asked.

"No, though what else are you going to do?"

Freydis heard the scorn in her voice. "I don't know," she said, getting louder on each word. She had thought of being a priestess of Freya, but she did not feel as though she could say that to her mother, who did not care much for the gods. And revealing that much of her desires felt too threatening. If her mother mocked her, or dismissed her, or said anything at all, Freydis did not think she could bear it.

"At least Unna—" said Freydis.

"At least Unna what?" Svanhild asked.

"At least Unna doesn't always look at me as though there is something wrong with me," said Freydis.

"I don't—" Svanhild began.

"You do," said Freydis. "You want me to be exactly like you, but if I were, I would have fled Snorri's side, rather than help him. Next time you think me weak, remember that."

Svanhild looked so angry, staring back at Freydis, that Freydis thought she might slap her, but after a moment Svanhild's shoulders sagged. "You are not weak," she said. "I was frightened of Snorri's illness, but you knew exactly what to do. I admire that." Against Freydis's will, her mother's praise warmed her. "You are my daughter," Svanhild continued, "and I should have done better by you. I would raise your child as my own if you wish to be a child yourself again."

She had offered that before, but Freydis did not think Svanhild had changed as much as she thought. She would leave her granddaughter as easily as she had her own daughter. "I thank you," said Freydis. "But I do not."

Svanhild stayed overnight with Unna and left the next morning, giving Freydis a hug good-bye. A series of blizzards gripped the settlement as the days grew longer, and Freydis swelled and hungered more every day for the fruits of a land across the sea.

✢   ✢   ✢

FREYDIS FELL INTO labor at the end of winter, during a foggy, dripping thaw that made the floor of Unna's house too muddy even for the stacked rushes to absorb. Suddenly she became aware of her body, its every process and need, as never before. Little existed for her save her sensations, pain and a feeling beyond pain, a doorway opening for her, if she could make it through the crushing tunnel that led there.

"I am worried," she heard Unna say to Donall. "Her hips are still narrow. She is over-young for this. Fetch Svanhild and Solvi."

She thought she had heard wrong, and did not believe Unna would have invited a man, her father, to this birth, until the wave passed and she saw him sitting on a chair, looking diffidently at his hands.

"How long will it be?" Solvi asked.

"It is a first child, and she is narrow," said Unna. "By morning we will know."

Freydis wanted to be angry that they spoke of her as though she could not hear them, but when the pain took her, she did not have the energy to spare. Svanhild walked with her, her voice low and soothing, the tones that Freydis wanted at that moment. She spoke of the birth of her firstborn, Eystein, this brother that Freydis had never met, and

rarely heard mentioned. Svanhild and Solvi had been in Spain, fleeing
the first of Solvi's defeats at Harald and Ragnvald's hands.

"I was surrounded by these dark-haired, dark-eyed beauties, and none
of them spoke Norse. I was terrified and I wanted my mother, as useless
as she would have been," Svanhild said. "Even more useless than I am
now."

"Glad you're here," Freydis said between harsh breaths.

"Solvi refused to be with me," she said. "He said it was women's magic,
but I wanted him there."

Freydis heard him make a noise behind her. "This is women's magic,"
he said gruffly. "But Unna said I should be here. I don't know why."

"You were born too," said Unna. "It is not only women's magic. This
is where you should be."

In case she died, Freydis realized. Unna wanted Solvi to be able to
say good-bye. Then the house grew dimmer, and Freydis was in the sea
again, riding swells of pain that filled her body and then ebbed. At times
the pain contracted, falling like the droplets of water that came down
from the ceiling, and then it swelled, filling, until it dripped down again.
Her father was there, scowling at the floor. She walked until she could
not anymore, and Unna and Svanhild helped her to her bed, frowning.

She was the ground where the forces of sleep and pain battled, and
wanted to follow the armies of sleep, to rest in their strong arms, until
she felt a blow on her cheek, and opened her eyes to see Unna standing
over her with an open palm. "Freydis, you must stay awake or you will
die," she said, her voice harsh.

"Your child will die," said Svanhild. Was she crying? Freydis struggled to sit up, and as she changed position, she felt the desire to push that
had been missing all this time.

"No," said Freydis, gritting her teeth, the effort of forming words
almost as difficult as her body's labor. "She is coming." She had made
this, made her child out of her body, giving it the flesh of her girlhood.
This child was hers. Hands were on her, all around her, steadying her,
lowering her onto Unna's birthing stool.

The moments of birth came with pain far worse than anything before, that she felt she could not endure except she had no choice, the
child would come out, and that—Alfrith was saying, cool and calm,

speaking to another birthing mother years and an ocean away—was far better than the alternative, no matter the pain.

Freydis felt the head and the shoulders come, the oddly empty feeling of the feet sliding through, and then the wrenching need to hold the child as quickly as possible, the eternity between the moment when it slipped forth and the little creature was placed, clammy and screaming, on her breast.

"A girl," Unna was saying. She was still feeling between Freydis's legs—for the afterbirth, Freydis thought dimly. She wanted so badly to sleep, and never think again about anything below her waist.

"Greet her," said Svanhild. "Greet your daughter, as I could not."

The child filled her vision, bald and crying, pawing furiously at the damp, unwelcome air. Freydis touched her tiny nose with a cold finger, and then slumped back into a dreamless sleep.

⁜ ⁜ ⁜

BY TRADITION A child remained nameless for the first seven days of her life. If Freydis had identified a father, it would be his duty to acknowledge the baby, and give her a name. Without him, the task fell to Solvi to claim the girl as a part of his lineage. A girl child would not pass on her name, though, so Freydis suspected if she wished to name the girl herself, she could.

The child also had to survive those first seven days. She showed every sign of doing so, drinking lustily at Freydis's milk, which flowed well enough from her small breasts, even after her exhausting birth.

After the baby's first feeding, Svanhild persuaded Freydis to let go of her little daughter so she could be more thoroughly washed and swaddled. She examined the girl while Freydis looked on hungrily, her whole body a soft well of need to have her daughter back in her arms.

"She will have bright red hair," Svanhild pronounced, handing the tightly wrapped bundle back to Freydis. "And either very good luck or very ill. No matter what, she will be as strong as her mother and grandmother, if not stronger."

Freydis's body ached all over, and she still had a sharp pain between her legs. Unna told her she had ripped, and had put in stitches to put her back together again. She had also bled more than Unna liked to see with the afterbirth, and Unna wanted her to drink beef broth to help her recover. Her daughter slept on her, eyes shut tight, mouth a little open. She moved sometimes in sleep, swatting at things she imagined with her tiny fists. Freydis kept dozing off, then startling awake so she could look at her again.

"I remember feeling like that with Eystein," said Svanhild. She sat by Freydis's bed and stroked her hair.

"Did you feel that way with me?" Freydis asked drowsily.

Svanhild was silent for a moment, and then sighed. "Your birth was very hard. It was not for many days that I could hold you, and by then you had been given to a wet nurse. I did nurse you, and you grew to like it, but it took longer for our bond to grow."

"And then you left with Harald," said Freydis. She stroked her daughter's cheek.

"Yes," said Svanhild. "Should I apologize for that? If I list the things I could have done differently, there would be no ending to them. You did not seem to need me as Eystein did, and I craved the adventure."

Freydis could not imagine leaving her daughter for anything, but she would not be here, with this miraculous scrap of a person, had her mother made different choices.

The coming of Freydis's daughter seemed to have started the tide of spring. The snow began melting even faster, and soon patches of brown showed on the fields. A thick, cold fog sat over the farm but carried in it a promise of warmer days ahead that lifted Freydis's heart.

By the time her daughter was to be named, Freydis could stand and walk around with only mild pain. Unna checked the stitches from her tearing every day and said she was healing well.

She had thought of many names for her daughter, and kept returning to Svanhild's words: a red-haired girl, stronger than her mother and grandmother. She had thought of a spring name for her—Freydis was a spring name—but tradition dictated she could not give her daughter her own name, so she settled instead on Thordis—Thor's priestess, or the goddess version of Thor's self. There could be none stronger than the blustery farmer's god. Freydis wanted a farmer's life for her daughter, tied to land and growing things, for her to feel the joy of her own daughter in her arms as Freydis did now—though hopefully a few years older than Freydis was. But if she was as strong-willed in life as she had been in the womb, she would do what she wished.

Unna cooked all of Freydis's favorite foods for the naming feast, and even slaughtered a cow. She invited all of the settlement to come, and they visited in waves, tramping mud into Unna's house, congratulating Freydis, asking if she would name a father, or choose a husband, and congratulating Svanhild and Solvi as well.

Whenever Freydis grew overwhelmed by the attention, she had only to look down at her daughter, enchanted by the bustle and new faces, her blue eyes wide, to feel at peace again.

Solvi pulled himself to his feet and used a voice she had seldom heard to quiet the crowd: "I am glad you are all here to welcome my first grandchild, Thordis, to our community." The pride in his voice made tears spring to Freydis's eyes.

The crowd cheered, and raised glasses, some demanding refills so they could toast properly. Unna sent her servants around with skins of ale for refills.

"It is customary for a woman to hold a sword in trust for her son, but my womenfolk do nothing customary," said Solvi. "For my daughter, and my granddaughter, a gift of daggers. Freydis, this one is for you, and this is for you to hold in trust for our Thordis. My wife, Svanhild, can teach both of you how to wield it, for good and ill."

Plenty of Icelanders still remembered when Svanhild had threatened Princess Geirny with a knife, and the trouble that had caused, and laughed, while Svanhild smiled tolerantly.

A latecomer pushed through the crowd to the front, and Freydis stood up to see Svanhild's man Falki. He had not returned before winter fell, and Freydis had watched Tova grow grave with worry for him as the winter nights passed.

Several grizzled old vikings came with him, including one whose smashed nose identified him as Ketil Flatnose, once a companion of her father's. Some of the earlier visitors spilled back outside; many Icelanders did not want much to do with the raiders who threatened the peace. Iceland was allowed its independence because it stayed out of the wars between the Scandinavian kingdoms.

Svanhild moved among all these fierce men as though she should be counted their queen, and they parted to admit her to their circle, and Solvi too, while Freydis fed Thordis. She had not seen Hallbjorn among them and that was all she needed to know.

Unna spoke loudly over the noise of the interlopers. "If you have not come to give young Thordis a blessing, you must go outside," she told them.

The men did come, one at a time, to make gestures of blessing with gnarled fingers. Ketil's fearsome face broke into a wide grin. "Solvi, you've made a good family here. Now you should marry her off to the father and get some grandsons as well."

Freydis felt a chill. Solvi looked down at her. "My Freydis can do better than him," he said. "But thank you, my friend."

By midnight the raiders had mostly gone, and Freydis fell asleep with Thordis nestled beside her.

Unna had many more visitors over the next week. Now that spring had arrived, those who had been putting off treatment during foul weather came for herbs and advice.

Freydis was napping in the afternoon, following a night during which Thordis had woken her three times for feeding, when Unna's yell from outside woke her. "She does not want to see him," Unna said, her voice harsh with anger.

Men's voices said something indistinct, followed by Unna again, "You need to leave now." Freydis heard sounds of a struggle, and then a grunt of pain. She remembered that Unna had sent Donall into the settlement to trade with the merchants who had arrived with the spring weather.

"She will see me," a voice said, a resonant voice Freydis knew too well. Her stomach clenched. "She will see me or you can use your doctoring to fix a broken arm." Freydis took a deep breath, picked up Thordis, and threw a shawl over her shoulders.

She stepped out into the sunlight and saw Hallbjorn holding Unna with her arm wrenched back, anger twisting his handsome features. He had men with him this time, warriors in leather armor, some of whom she recognized from Thordis's naming. Too many.

"Let her be," Freydis cried, running toward Hallbjorn before she could let her fear root her to the ground. "I would not be alive without her. My daughter would not be alive without her. Would you incur the gods' wrath by hurting her?"

"A daughter," said Hallbjorn scornfully, though he let go of Unna.

"A daughter," said Freydis. The gods did not want Hallbjorn to have a son. "No use to you, even if you were the father."

Hallbjorn sneered. "So you persist in that? Have you named a father? Or do you claim to be such a whore you do not know?"

Thordis began to whimper and Freydis bounced on her toes until she quieted, hoping her daughter could not feel her trembling. "Did Rolli tell you that King Harald has divorced my mother? I am not worth what I once was as a wife."

"You are still the mother of my daughter. *My* daughter." Hallbjorn nodded at one of his companions, a finely dressed man, who rushed forward and grabbed Unna again. Unna grimaced in pain. "See, now it will not be me who kills her," said Hallbjorn.

"What can you want with me?" Freydis cried.

"You are mine," said Hallbjorn. "You cannot change that, except with your death or mine. Come with me, and you will not cause the death of this woman."

"Let me leave my daughter with Unna," said Freydis, around the tightness in her throat. "She is only a girl. You can have no use for her."

"She is mine too," said Hallbjorn. "And you should know, even if you are too stupid to know anything else, that I will keep what is mine."

"You will risk her to a sea voyage?" Freydis cried. "She is only a few weeks old. The lives of babes are precarious. My brother died at six after too much sea travel."

"It is in the hands of the fates," said Hallbjorn. "Plus, if she dies you will be fertile that much sooner."

"If she does, then I have no more reason to live," said Freydis. Her own life was the only leverage she had left. She felt the same strange certainty that had filled her when she prompted Hallbjorn and Rolli to find Solvi in Iceland.

"Then I will tie you up so you cannot do yourself harm," said Hallbjorn.

"You can try, but you will need to watch me all the time and I only need one moment to escape." She met his eyes, waiting for him to falter, and he did.

"What do you want, Freydis?" he asked, in the seductive voice she remembered.

"I will come with you, if you spare my friends here: Unna and her household, Solvi and his household. I will swear not to escape you, either into death or divorce, if you let me nurse my daughter, Thordis, until she is two years old. Babes born in too quick succession are not healthy either."

Hallbjorn narrowed his eyes. That meant he could not try to impregnate her in that time. He could find other ways to take his pleasure with her, but not force her to risk another pregnancy so soon. And she had no intention of keeping her promises. A daughter of Solvi Sea King would always trade honor for freedom.

"Swear it," she said. "Do you want a slave wife, dead already in spirit, or do you want to wed Freydis Solvisdatter?"

"I swear it," he said. "Of course I want you alive, my Freydis. And now your father will have no choice but to be my ally." He nodded at two of his men who came forward and took hold of Freydis's arms. "My men will help you pack."

28

EINAR WATCHED THE SNOW-COVERED HILLS OF THE NORSE coast slip by as he traveled south from Yrjar with Ivar, Oddi, and two other ships full of Halogaland warriors. They had departed as soon as the sea lanes thawed enough for sailing, in order to meet up with his father, Harald, and all of the allies they could gather in Nidaros. They planned to leave for the Orkney Islands a month before midsummer and surprise the rebels gathered there.

After spending autumn helping Ragnvald and Guthorm convince Harald's less-willing allies to support their king in his Orkney adventure, Einar and Ivar had passed the winter in Halogaland with instructions to ensure King Heming remained loyal to Harald. Harald had paid his first wife, Heming's sister, handsomely to compensate her and her kin for the insult of divorcing her. She had better reason than most to accept whatever Harald would give her, since he had granted their son Halfdan mercy after his rebellion. Halfdan had been in Halogaland for some of the winter, proclaiming himself Harald's heir and successor.

Einar and Ivar left just after a wet blizzard that turned the ships' wood sodden. Oddi, who had spent the last ten years in Halogaland, said that he could smell spring in the air. Farther south, the snowdrifts were soft, and no higher than Einar's knee at their nightly campsites.

Bakur, who was sitting on a bench toward the prow, smiled at him, and Einar realized that he had been staring, though his vision was not on anything another could see. Einar had shared a few moments' pleasure with him earlier in the winter. After lying with Gyda, it had been harder for him to refuse the touch of someone who wanted him, but Einar had not allowed it to continue for fear his father would learn of it. A man might have a boy slave and not be thought less for it, but now that he was grown, he could not share another man's bed without being shamed.

By the time the ships turned east into the great Trondheim Fjord, Einar could see some patches of bare ground on the passing shoreline. Gyda would still be snowed in to her fort among the high plains and foothills of the Keel. She must be near to bearing her and Harald's child—or was it his? He tried to imagine her flat stomach distended by pregnancy, and could not.

He went to stand with Ivar at the prow of the ship.

"I think Nidaros is around the next bend," said Ivar.

He had been saying that for days, but Einar did see more farmland between the wooded hills here, and after they passed a field with snow caught in last year's furrows, the many roofs of Nidaros appeared over the next headland. Einar clapped Ivar on the shoulder.

"You're finally right," he said.

"It had to happen sometime," said Ivar with a grin.

Nidaros had not been kept up well in recent years and looked drab, choked with mud and dirty snow, especially next to Harald's flagship, with its vivid silk sail of scarlet and blue. Harald's other ships were interspersed with vessels that Einar recognized as his father's. No other allies had arrived yet.

Ragnvald met them, clad in his dark winter clothes, a peaked hat pulled down over his ears. "I see a force from Halogaland accompanies you," he said. "Is there anything to fear here?"

Einar shook his head. "No more than usual, Father," he said. "They are allies." His father looked worried anyway.

Oddi caught up to them. "Greetings, King Ragnvald," he said cheerfully. "I have been trying to fatten up your sons for the hard summer you have planned for us, but you see they are as lean as always."

"Lean men move faster," Einar countered. Oddi lunged at him, and Einar landed a mock blow in Oddi's midsection. He pretended to drive Einar off with an elbow to his stomach, and Einar was about to complete the dumb show by falling to the ground, clutching his waist, but stopped his play when he saw his father's grim expression.

"Your mother is here," said Ragnvald carefully to Ivar. "My lady

Hilda. She would like to see both of you." He looked at Einar. "The lady Vigdis is also here, with Guthorm, if you would like to greet her."

"I will," said Einar, "but Ivar, you should greet your mother first."

Ivar smiled, seeming not to hear the tension in his father's voice, and trotted off toward the hall where the women usually congregated.

Einar shivered from the stiff breeze and pulled on his own hat. Ragnvald began walking along the shore, toward Harald's largest ship.

"How is the lady Hilda?" Einar asked. "Her words 'wolf-king,' making her son into a deer 'hunted by every wolf that wants a man-pelt'—I have heard them repeated in Yrjar. I have heard Halfdan say them. I think he still means rebellion."

Ragnvald frowned. "Harald will not believe it, and Halfdan turns the accusation on me whenever I bring it up."

"You wanted my brother Rolli to . . . take care of him," Einar reminded him. "But after we meet Rolli in Orkney, he will come home with us. Do you think I should . . . ?" If he was outlawed for killing Halfdan, at least he would not need to worry about the witch's prophecy coming true.

"Do not mention it," said Ragnvald. "Do not even think it. There is something you said to me of Halfdan, when you were a boy, do you remember?"

"No," said Einar. He remembered Halfdan had been a bully, always bigger than him, and willing to use his size against Ragnvald's sons. He had prompted Einar to become skilled with a sword younger than most.

"You said 'There are some people you cannot hurt. They can only hurt you.'" Ragnvald met Einar's eyes briefly.

"What are you saying, Father? That we should just accept Halfdan's rebellion?" Einar asked.

"I don't know," said Ragnvald. "Only, we must all be careful." He cleared his throat. "How was Ivar this winter?" he asked.

"His captivity has done him no lasting harm," said Einar dryly, glad to be in more familiar territory. His father gave him an exasperated look. "Very helpful," Einar amended. "He will be a good king."

Ragnvald pressed his lips together. "How? Tell me."

"Heming likes him, he has made friends with all of the warriors, and bested them on the practice ground and at many winter contests. I know he displeased you earlier, but I do think he will be a good king. A king like Harald." Ragnvald did not look placated. "But less likely to forget his responsibilities," Einar added. "Because he had you to raise him and will have me for an adviser."

Ragnvald nodded, and gave Einar one of his rare, swift smiles.

"I am well content to be his companion," Einar said. "Do not fear for my ambition."

"I am pleased to hear you say that," said Ragnvald. "When we return from the Orkneys, Ivar must take on more of my responsibilities."

"What?" That took Einar by surprise—one day his father would no longer be king, but that day must be far off.

"I would have him set in the people's mind as king of Maer, before anyone can take that from him," said Ragnvald. "We must hold on to what we have."

✢ ✢ ✢

HARALD'S HALL, BUILT to feast hundreds of warriors, seemed empty with so few in Nidaros. Einar saw Hilda talking with some women at the other end of the hall.

"My lady, you look well," he said to her. She did. Something of the blazing anger that had given her the courage to speak on Rolli's behalf still clung to her.

"I will never be well until my son Rolli is back at my side," she said. "But I have been healthy. Have you heard anything of Rolli in Halogaland?"

Einar shook his head. "News does not cross the North Sea in the winter," he said. "But I am sure he is strong and able, blessed by the gods, and fated for greatness."

Hilda pressed her hand to her heart. "It does me good to hear that, though it is hard to make myself believe. Now, I think your mother wants you."

"Since when have you wanted to give her what she wants?" Einar asked.

Hilda gave him a wry smile. "We have a little more in common than I have always thought."

Einar fled to greet Vigdis rather than hear Hilda say that what they shared was their antipathy for his father. Vigdis sat with Guthorm and some other older warriors. In that circle also sat Halfdan, who had left Halogaland a few days earlier than Einar.

Einar embraced Vigdis, inhaling the sweet and expensive scent of her amber perfume.

"Do they not feed you well in Yrjar?" Vigdis asked. "The winter is for fattening."

"Asa Hakonsdatter is an excellent housekeeper," said Einar. One day, at Ivar's side, he would be important enough that none would comment on his skinniness. "Her table is always full."

"Are you ready to fight for Harald, my boy?" Guthorm asked.

"Always," said Einar. "Is the rest of Norway?"

"Yes," said Halfdan grimly. "My father is mighty, and all will fight for him."

Einar could not keep a small smile from his face. "I am glad to hear it."

"I am to be given Orkney after we succeed," Halfdan announced.

"That is excellent," said Einar. "You have sailed so much, you will be a good island king."

Halfdan's eyes narrowed at that, and Einar shrugged. He had meant no insult. Einar saw his father's hand in this—a bribe for Halfdan's loyalty, and responsibility far from home. This must be why his father did not want him to try to kill Halfdan. With him in Orkney, there should be no need.

✢ ✢ ✢

MORE THAN TWENTY ships set out for the Orkney Islands a few weeks later, sailing past the barrier islands, now clear of snow, and into the trackless sea. Each carried at least fifty men, Harald's followers and his allies—such a force that even Einar, steeped in his father's pessimism, could not easily imagine them being defeated.

Ivar whistled a melody that Einar found himself humming. The wind made the lines sing a tuneless counterpoint. The weather on this journey had been blessed, even five days away from land. Doubly blessed for so early in the warring season, when storms came up quickly, and a fleet of this size could not easily avoid them.

"Is this day not fine?" Ivar asked. "Look how many we are! No force can stand us."

"Likely not," said Einar.

"Not at all," Ivar insisted. "Do not tempt the fates by conjuring a tale of defeat."

"So long as you do not tempt the fates by declaring our victory already," Einar countered.

"All right," Ivar agreed. "I will trust to my sword arm, not the fates." He began whistling again, and Einar humming. The weather was fine. This was an adventure, a cap on a year of adventure, his first year of majority, a year that would guarantee peace on Norway's shores.

Until Harald's sons began fighting again, a small voice reminded him—his father's voice. No one was safe except in the grave—and not even then, since *draugrs* sometimes walked out of their burial mounds to eat human flesh. Let Ivar be cheery, and Einar would do the work of guiding him. The last year had tamped down Einar's ambitions to rule on his own. With the fates' favor, he might be able to take a wife and raise a son of his own one day, perhaps a son who could protect and advise Ivar's sons, as he did for Ivar. He wished he had been able, during the winter, to ask someone about the witch's prophecy, and how to avoid it, but Ronhild or Alfrith would probably tell his father, and Einar had regained his good opinion over the winter and could not bear to lose it again.

Ivar's whistling reached the song's chorus. Einar sang a few of the words out loud, and then stopped himself. The tune had carried many tales over the years, but the most famous was of his aunt Svanhild's courtship with Solvi Hunthiofsson. Solvi had come upon her near Geiranger Fjord, intending to kidnap her, and Svanhild had used no more than the power of her words and her beauty to turn Solvi's swords from the necks of the merchants with whom she had been traveling. Later she had tricked all of Harald's forces by putting on trousers and pretending to be Solvi at the helm of his ship. Ivar whistled on, oblivious.

"Good thing Harald isn't here," Einar said. "He would not like your song." His father thought that Svanhild would bring Solvi to lead the force against Harald in the Orkneys.

Ivar laughed. "She is no less a heroine because Harald divorced her," he said. "I will sing what I want."

Einar grinned—yes, Ragnvald's sons would sing of their aunt if they wanted to. This ship only contained men loyal to Ragnvald: warriors from Maer and Sogn, as well as Oddi and Sigurd. Ragnvald even seemed as happy as he ever allowed himself to be, taking a turn at the steering oar, telling tales of his first raiding trip with Solvi Hunthiofs-son, long ago.

The weather stayed fair until the Orkney Islands came into view, black blots on the horizon wrapped in a shroud of mist that seemed to approach the ships faster than the ships approached the islands.

Harald's captain had visited the Orkney Islands many times, so the convoy followed the blue and crimson sail of Harald's largest ship between the islands and into the bay at Grimbister. Einar kept his eyes on the cliffs above and his shield in his hand. They could not approach without being seen, and even a middling archer could land his arrows on one of the ships below with so many targets to choose from.

Thorstein's hall was halfway up the slope that rose from the water. The harbor contained only two ships, and a few small fishing boats. Harald's convoy sailed as close to one another as they could manage with the gusty winds and swift-flowing currents between the islands, planning to beach at the same time and be ready to mount the slope and attack the hall in force.

Einar thought it suspicious that no one came to the beach to greet them. A few curious children peered out from small turf huts as Harald's force, save a hundred men to guard the ships, marched up the hill, holding their shields at the ready.

A curl of smoke rose up from the kitchen end of the hall, and disappeared quickly against the relentless gray of the sky. It was not entirely untenanted.

"He will have gone into hiding," said Harald. "He must have scouts to mark our approach, and taken most of his ships to one of those little islands."

"Perhaps," said Ragnvald. He had told Einar that with Melbrid Tooth and Svanhild both fled across the sea, all would know Harald planned to attack here.

No one stopped them as they approached the hall. Harald went to bang on the great doors that stood at the southern end, positioned to let the hall catch the sunlight in the summer. He only had to knock once before the door opened and Harald almost stumbled in. A tall, strongly built man with a bright red beard stood in the doorway, unarmed. This must be Thorstein the Red.

"Welcome, King Harald of Norway," he said. "Welcome, King Ragnvald of Maer. I can only offer you simple fare, but my hospitality is yours as long as the food holds out."

Harald looked surprised and peered about, searching for an ambush.

"You look at me very fierce, King Ragnvald," said Thorstein. "I hope you have not come to do me harm." Einar glanced at Ivar, and they both jostled forward, hands on their swords. Thorstein had been the one who captured their father, and brought him to Solvi to be tortured.

"I will do you no harm if you give us hospitality," said Ragnvald.

"I cannot put all of your warriors in my hall," Thorstein said. "But perhaps you can choose a hundred to shelter here tonight, and let the others camp where they find flat ground."

"Let us have a welcome cup first," said Ragnvald.

Einar relaxed his grip on his sword. If Thorstein was willing to seal his offer of hospitality by sharing a drink dedicated to the gods, then he likely did not mean them harm.

"I will not dissemble," Ragnvald continued. "You have been named to us as an enemy who means to rebel against Harald. You have been a follower of Solvi Hunthiofsson. Now we have reason to think that Solvi is massing a force in the Orkneys to kill Harald and take back his land. What do you say to that?"

"That old song," said Thorstein. "I wonder if you will go on believing it when Solvi is dead."

"Is he?" Ragnvald asked hopefully. "Dead?"

Einar exchanged another look with Ivar. If Solvi was dead, would Aunt Svanhild return to Harald?

"No," said Thorstein. "But he might as well be. I promise you, he is not leading any forces here. He was once a mighty sea king, but now he is an old cripple. He has not fought a sea battle in more than a decade. You have nothing to fear from him."

"Or you?" Ragnvald asked.

"No," said Thorstein. "Some of your enemies may come here, but you should not count me among them."

"Do you style yourself jarl of this place?" Harald asked him.

"You seek to trap me. I am nothing more than a raider. I know that Halogaland kings have long claimed the Orkney Islands."

"Once," said Harald, "but not anymore. Now I claim them. Will you swear fealty to me, to pay my taxes and fight on my behalf?"

"No," said Thorstein. "I long ago swore never to have a king, to live a free man until my death." He smiled thinly. "To let no wolf-king make of me a man-pelt. But I will fight at your side while you are here. Today, I do not find it useful to quarrel with the king of Norway. Let that be enough for you."

29

THE BIRTH OF FREYDIS'S DAUGHTER HAD BEEN IN THE EARLI-
est days of spring, during a warm spell that ended with a freezing gale
and locked all of Svanhild's visitors inside Solvi's house for a few days.

Falki looked underfed after his winter travels, so Tova cooked up the
rations she had been saving in case of a late planting. Svanhild wanted a
chance to hear all the news, but she could not bring herself to interfere
with Tova and Falki's reunion, though at night when she heard them together in Tova's bed, she wished she had. Solvi had been willing to accept
her advances, but listening to Tova and Falki's whispers and sounds of
pleasure reminded her that she and Solvi were no longer in the flush of
first love, and might never recover that intensity.

Tova had told Svanhild earlier, one day in winter when she had found
Svanhild crying in the byre, that the same fear that had gripped him in
battle also found him sometimes in a woman's embrace. No wonder he
was so passive. Svanhild loved him still, but she wished sometimes for a
good reason to leave, now that Freydis was safe and had survived childbirth. Perhaps she could find a way to spend only the winters here.

One day, she and Falki braved the freezing rain and went outside
to check on the sheep that had just been released to their pastures for
forage.

"Tell me, my captain, what did you find in Scotland?" Svanhild asked.
Falki had only spoken a little of his travels, the rude halls where he had
spent his winter, full of bad food and ugly, unkempt men, but kept the
real news to himself.

He grinned at her, looking happier than Svanhild had ever seen him. "I like it better here. You said you would find me some farmland," he said. "I don't need your help to find a wife!"

Svanhild smiled back, wishing she did not feel Falki's happiness as a loss. His return should have made her into Svanhild Sea Queen again, but he did not want that from her anymore, no more than Solvi did. "Of course," she said. "I am very happy for you."

"She is with child, so we'll wed at the *alting* meeting," he said, his voice full of pride.

"Wonderful," said Svanhild. "You have my blessing. Now, what did you find in Scotland?"

"Many raiders, who sail to Orkney because of your message. Ketil Flatnose you saw at your granddaughter's naming—he came here to see if Solvi would return to battle with him. Melbrid Tooth is already on his way. Thorstein the Red, Geirbjorn Hakonsson, and many without famous names will join as well," he said.

"Then I suppose we will see Ketil again when the weather clears," said Svanhild.

✣   ✣   ✣

THE DAY AFTER the rain stopped, Rolli turned over the garden beds with a shovel, while Svanhild and Tova decided what to plant. Tova kept one eye on Falki the whole time, and Svanhild watched the path that led up from the settlement. Now that Svanhild knew Tova was pregnant, she could see the signs easily, in her morning queasiness and evening appetite. She supposed she had not paid attention before because Tova's beauty made her nervous, even though she had never shown jealousy toward Svanhild.

Tova liked spring onions enough that foraging for them would not give them enough, so she and Svanhild agreed to plant a full row of them. Better to keep them out of the pastures so they would not flavor the sheep's milk.

"If you are living on another farm when they bloom, I will bring some to you," said Svanhild to Tova, who smiled gratefully. Svanhild had done ill to think of this beautiful woman as another Vigdis.

She looked up and saw Unna riding along the path on a small horse. When she drew closer, Svanhild thought she looked ten years older than when Svanhild had seen her a week ago at Thordis's naming, and Svanhild realized she had never seen Unna discomposed before, not truly. Her hair was messy, and with every breath she seemed to be grasping for threads of self-control.

"Hallbjorn has come and taken Freydis," said Unna. "Perhaps there is time to catch him." She blinked a few times, and swayed on her feet. Svanhild rushed to catch her arm, and help her onto a bench.

Solvi hobbled over and leaned on his spade. "What happened?" he asked.

Unna told them of Hallbjorn's arrival, her voice quavering at times, and Svanhild had to look away from her to avoid the lump in her throat turning into tears.

"I will go," Svanhild said. A fine drizzle had begun, the droplets made stinging by the wind. It might make Hallbjorn's sail too sodden to leave the bay. "The tides favor their leaving immediately."

"How will you stop him?" Solvi asked.

"We have allies—Ketil and his men are staying in Ingolfur's hall," Svanhild called over her shoulder.

She had never felt the farm's distance from the settlement more than as she rode Solvi's pony over the broken ground toward the shore. The creature was agile but could not be pushed too fast, not without risking a broken leg. Svanhild welcomed the discomfort from the cold rain—it seemed just punishment for her hope that something would take her away from Iceland.

She glimpsed the shore just in time to see a ship pushing off, a narrow dragon ship, and knew she was too late. Still, she rode to the water's edge to make sure. Warriors milled about on the wet rocks, talking, and occasionally shoving one another. Ketil Flatnose was giving his men orders about how to load sacks and barrels of provisions into his ship.

"Did you know of this?" Svanhild asked him. "Did you know that Hallbjorn would take my daughter? Do you know where he's going?"

"The Orkneys," said Ketil. "Where you urged all of Harald's enemies to go."

"And what is your part in this?" Svanhild asked.

"Nothing. But why should I stop him—if Solvi Hunthiofsson no longer wants to fight, perhaps he will at least follow his daughter," said Ketil.

"After you came to her naming and gave your blessing?" Svanhild cried. Ketil had sailed at Solvi and Svanhild's side, a companion during their years of fighting Harald. He had more reason to hate Harald than most Scottish raiders, his father having been one of the Rogaland kings whom Harald defeated early in his conquest.

"He is the child's father," Ketil replied. "It will be better for both of them. What will you do, Svanhild Sea Queen? I have been hearing of your sailing for years. Come to Orkney, and make your men rich. You can help us take the revenge on King Harald that Solvi will not."

"What of my daughter?" Svanhild asked. "She is not two weeks from childbirth."

"You can help make her husband rich as well," said Ketil.

Svanhild stared at him, anger making her mute. In his mind, Freydis and her daughter were Hallbjorn's property, nothing more.

"I want to defeat Harald," he continued. "We need to be in place when Harald's forces arrive, with a plan of attack. The Orkney currents favor strong sailors. Come with us. Fill your ship—there are warriors enough here who would like to see Harald brought low. Bring that giant of yours and Solvi too. You can deal with Hallbjorn later. He needs some lessoning, but he has done Solvi a good turn here."

Solvi could not walk without pain, or face battle without fear. She had seen the depths of his weakness over the winter. Still, no one was more clever in a sea battle than he—even she and Ragnvald had only ever beaten him with luck and numbers, never with guile. Perhaps Ketil was right, and this would pry him out of Iceland.

In the distance, Hallbjorn's ship, moving swiftly under the power of both oars and wind, exited the Reykjavik harbor and disappeared behind a point of land. Hallbjorn must know he would be pursued. His was a well-built ship, perhaps not quite as fast as hers, but slim, and with a good-size sail. If he had, or was, a competent pilot and had good weather, she would be hard-pressed to catch him on the next tide. And even if she did, what would she do? She could not fill her smaller ship with enough warriors to best his, and only a fool would engage in ship-to-ship battle out of sight of land. No, he and Ketil had played this round well, and Svanhild and Solvi would have to pursue him.

✛   ✛   ✛

THE DRIZZLE HAD turned into a hard rain by the time Svanhild returned to the farm, but Solvi was still outside, kneeling in the garden
dirt and stabbing his spade into the ground. Rolli stood next to him,
dripping wet and shifting from one foot to the other.

"He won't let me help," Rolli said to Svanhild, giving her a hand as
she climbed down from the pony.

"I have talked with my men at the settlement," she said to Solvi. "We
can depart for Orkney on the morning tide."

"I wish you well on your journey," said Solvi.

Svanhild glanced at Rolli, who shrugged. She searched Solvi's face for
some hint of anger, a glimpse of his former self. He had liked, once, to
be so unpredictable that any raid might be blamed on him. Now he only
frowned at Svanhild and went back to his work. His eyebrows caught
the rain, and when it dripped into his eyes he wiped the water away
with the back of his hand. Gray eyebrows, not golden, with the long
hairs threaded among them that only old men grew.

"You will not come with me?" she said. "Not even for your own daughter? Your granddaughter?"

"What good can I do you?" Solvi asked.

"Hallbjorn wants to draw you into this fight. Ketil wishes you to be
there. Perhaps you would be as a figurehead for them, or perhaps you
have not forgotten all you knew about sea battles, all that you have taught
me. Perhaps you should not send your wife alone into battle."

"You don't have to go—let this battle finish and see what happens,"
said Solvi. "Do you truly think this force can defeat Harald? Can any?"

"I don't care. I want Freydis safe. She will be in the middle of it all,"
said Svanhild.

"Do you? Truly?" Solvi asked. "Or do you like the excuse to rush into
battle again?"

Solvi's words filled her with fury, and not only because they contained a grain of truth. "If Harald wins, he will come for you next," she
said desperately. "He has often threatened to go after you. He blames
you for this whole rebellion—you are the only one of his enemies who
has ever escaped him."

"I see he has grown no less foolish with age," said Solvi, standing up
and stretching his back. "If he blames me so much, why has he never
come to attack me?"

"I distracted him. My brother distracted him. He had better things to do in Norway."

Solvi's lip curled. "Yes, even in Iceland we have heard about these better things. Is that why you ran away? Was it jealousy over his other women?"

"Haven't we covered this ground enough?" Svanhild asked. "I could have stayed, but I came here. To you. To our daughter."

"Never enough," said Solvi. "You came to Iceland for your pride, and now you leave for the same reason."

"For ten years my brother and I ruled Norway in Harald's name," Svanhild said, trying to keep her voice even. "I suppose I would have been content for that to continue. I keep my oaths. Now our daughter is in danger. Have you become such a coward not even that will move you?" She could not even tell whether her words touched him. "Harald will be far from everything he knows," she said. "We have allies in all of the Scottish islands. If Harald falls in the Orkneys, my brother will be king of Norway, and I . . . I will make him promise that you can return."

Solvi smiled as she spoke, a sharp-bladed smile that she had both loved and hated, long ago, and had not yet seen in their new life together. "I taught you better than that," he said. "If Harald falls, Norway will break into warring kingdoms again, and your brother will be their first target. Come, Svanhild, you made me swear an oath never to attempt to claim my land again, and I have kept it."

"I release you from your oath. If you will not do it for your daughter, will you do it for the revenge you always wanted?" Svanhild asked.

"I told you I will not put myself in battle again."

"Not even for your daughter? Not even for me?"

"When I can no longer wield a sword? Do you want me dead all the sooner?"

The Solvi she had known before would have died before saying these things. "I have never been able to wield a sword, but it has always seemed to me that skill is the least a leader needs," said Svanhild. Her voice shook.

"You think me less than a woman?" said Solvi.

"Not unless you let me go without you."

"So you are leaving again, as I knew you would."

"I am going to our daughter," said Svanhild. "If you will not come with me, for her, then the man I loved has truly died. He would have sailed to her, even if he couldn't fight."

Solvi met her gaze for a moment, but then looked away. "Hallbjorn will bring her back to Harald and your brother. She'll be safe."

Svanhild wanted to scream. No one was as certain of a woman's fate as a man. "Do you know what it will cost her, what it has likely already cost her to be in his power again?" she asked. Harald and Ragnvald might decide that marrying Freydis to Hallbjorn was the best option, but Freydis would not agree.

"I know she is probably already dead at her own hand," said Solvi quietly. "Should I follow her into death? That is what you are asking of me."

Svanhild bit back a reply that he should, it was all he was good for. She did not believe it; she wanted him by her side if he could do nothing more than warm her in his arms on the cold crossing. "What about your promise that Freydis could choose her own fate?" Svanhild asked.

"That was foolish of me," said Solvi. "No one can choose their own fate. Not even you."

"No, but I can rise to meet it," Svanhild replied, "with or without you."

Svanhild went into Solvi's house to pack and found Tova staring into the fire, while Falki stood next to her, his arms around her. "I will come back to you," he was saying.

She did not answer, and Svanhild gathered this argument had been going on for some time, likely since Unna came with her news. Svanhild felt a small pang for Tova, but she was glad that Falki was coming with her. "I will bring him back to you," she said to Tova.

"You cannot promise that," Tova replied.

"I can promise this," said Svanhild. "Before the gods, and with Rolli Ragnvaldsson as a witness, I give you this farmland. It no longer belongs to Solvi Hunthiofsson or his heirs."

"I do not—" Tova began.

"Do what you want with Solvi Sea Coward, I will not be returning to him." Svanhild turned toward Rolli, who stood in the doorway, shaking water out of his hair. "You have heard what your one-time friend Hallbjorn did," she said. "Will you come with me to get her back?"

Rolli shook his head. "That will only make my outlawry last for life," he replied. "My father will surely be there, and I cannot fight him."

"I do not go to fight Harald," said Svanhild. "I go to get my daughter back, whatever it takes. I will ally again with Harald if I must—I will do anything for her. Will you not come with me for that?"

Rolli and Solvi wore such similar expressions of helplessness that Svanhild wished she could draw a sword on them for their cowardice, as a man would surely do. "Rolli, you have a ship, a ship I built for you. When my husband's shame becomes too great to let him stay here, carry him to me in the Orkneys," she said. "If you do not come to me, do not look for me again this side of Valhalla. Or perhaps not there either. The hall of mighty warriors will be no place for either of you."

30

THE WEIGHT OF THORDIS ON FREYDIS'S BACK MADE IT HARD
to climb the ladder into Hallbjorn's ship, but she refused let go of her
even for a moment. As they sailed away, she watched the settlement become smaller behind her. The ships that lined the shoreline remained
stubbornly in place, though each time they rocked in the surf, Freydis
hoped it was the motion of one of them pushing off, coming to take her
back to Iceland.

She had bargained for the lives of Unna, Solvi, and her mother, as her
mother had once done with Solvi. She did not trust that Hallbjorn would
keep his promise—he wanted a son, and he would not be content to wait
two years until Thordis was weaned. But at least he was not likely to
rape her on board the ship. She promised herself she would scream if he
did and make sure his men knew that she did not go to him willingly,
not this time.

Thordis, at least, was as strong as her name and drank from Freydis
lustily as Iceland disappeared in the distance. She wanted feeding five
or six times a day, whether midnight or noon, and Freydis, in a haze of
regret and exhaustion, did her bidding.

She found one friend on board, though. Her cat, Torfa, still lived on
this ship, and was now followed by a kitten bearing the same markings
of black and dun. One of the youngest sailors said that she had a litter earlier in the spring, and now most of the ships in Ketil's convoy carried one
of them. She curled up under Freydis's legs wherever she sat, alternately
purring and mewing to her half-grown kitten.

On the second day of sailing, Thordis screamed all morning, drowning out the calls of the gulls overhead, and refused to be quieted, even by Freydis's breast. Eventually she tired herself out and fell into a doze against Freydis's breast, yawning and lazily mouthing at her nipple. Hallbjorn sat down next to Freydis.

"Our daughter is strong, at least," he said, the first words anyone had spoken to her since he forced her onto the ship. "Let me hold her."

"Not until she's done sleeping, or she will cry again," said Freydis. Hallbjorn sat next to her in silence, the warmth from his body helping to keep Freydis warm even with her breast exposed. Finally Thordis fell into a deeper sleep and Freydis pulled her tunic back down.

"Let me hold her," said Hallbjorn, watching her awkward motions.

Freydis hesitated, narrowing her eyes.

"You learned to trust me once. You will learn again."

"I did not," said Freydis. "I succumbed rather than waiting for you to force me, after I learned that no one would help me." Her shy, old self, quailed with fear—she had spoken meaning to anger him, and she was in his power.

"You may tell yourself that," said Hallbjorn. "But I know that you desired me. You had pleasure with me. You cried out."

Freydis bent over Thordis's soft head to hide her shame. She secured Thordis in a sling across her chest where she could feel Freydis's heartbeat, and smell her milk. Her body had responded to his, a betrayal worse than Rolli's, worse than the betrayal of the empty sea behind them, the silence of those who should have protected her.

She picked up her mending and stabbed at the fabric with her needle. Hallbjorn took her hand, and she batted him away. "Stop it, you'll make me drop my iron needle. It was expensive."

He held her hand more tightly as she gripped the needle between her thumb and forefinger. "You said you would be my wife," said Hallbjorn. "Not a dead woman, waiting to escape into death. Now you won't even let me hold my daughter."

"She's sleeping," she said between clenched teeth. "And a wife would tell you not to interfere with her chores. A wife is not a slave."

He let her hand go. "I will let you rebel this time," he said, his tone somewhere between mournful and threatening, "but you will learn to respect me as a wife should."

✛ ✛ ✛

THEY REACHED THE Faroe Islands a few days later, in the early morning. She stayed close to the ship while Hallbjorn's crew foraged for wild bird eggs, and tried to hunt, though the birds were canny about both hiding their eggs and staying out of reach of clumsy warriors. Some of the men climbed high up the cliffs to where they could only hang on with their fingers. Freydis worried that one of them would fall and she would have to set his broken bones, though she half hoped for it as well. Perhaps the man would be lamed, and then she would have one fewer captor. But all of the men kept their balance, though some broke the eggs that they had put in their waist pouches, giving Freydis more washing to do.

"Are we leaving soon?" Freydis asked Hallbjorn after their midday meal.

Hallbjorn frowned. "Ketil Flatnose and Geirbjorn Hakonsson said they would meet us here by the full moon," he said. Freydis had heard of Geirbjorn Hakonsson—the outlawed son of the old king Hakon. He would never be allowed to return to Norway, having betrayed King Harald along with his father. He had also helped his brother Herlaug wreak a bloody vengeance upon a woman, disfiguring her in a way that had given Freydis nightmares when she first heard of it.

Hallbjorn ignored her until evening, when he bid her go to wait for him in his sleeping sack. She did not think she would sleep, but days of wakefulness on board the ship and Thordis's needs had kept her awake so long that she could not keep her eyes open. She fell asleep with Thordis sheltered by the circle of her arm, and did not wake until Hallbjorn came to join her.

She moved Thordis to a small cradle she had taken with her from Unna's house. "You swore you would let my daughter nurse for a full two years," she said reproachfully. "You cannot get me pregnant until then."

"You should stop telling me what I can and can't do," said Hallbjorn.

Freydis laughed, high and strained. "What is it that you think wives do, O wise one? Why do you think there are so many tales of grumbling husbands and nagging wives? If you don't like it, put me aside and trouble me no more. I did not ask for you to come and take me and my newborn daughter from my family. Don't tell me what wives are supposed to be."

He slapped her across the face, hard enough to drive the breath from her. Her cheek went cold and then hot, and Thordis began to cry. Freydis tensed to protect her daughter if she had to. He would have to kill her before she allowed him to harm Thordis.

But he only lay next to her for a few long breaths while Thordis wailed. "She will wake all of my men," said Hallbjorn. "Are you going to quiet her?"

"May I, my lord?" Freydis asked. "May I comfort my daughter?"

"Yes, of course," said Hallbjorn, and then more quietly, "you are right. I do not know how to be a husband."

Freydis crawled out of the sleeping sack and pulled Thordis to her breast. She rocked the girl back and forth until she fell back to sleep.

"Why did you want me in your tent tonight?" Freydis asked. "You swore not to make me pregnant, so it cannot be that. Tell me."

"You can still"—he seemed somewhat diffident now—"you can still give me pleasure, like I showed you before."

She could bear that, she thought, touching him with her hands. She did as he asked, following his directions, until he spilled his seed. He took her in his arms and nuzzled the back of her neck. He began to fumble at her clothes, but she was wearing two layers of skirts, narrow columns of fabric that resisted him.

"Time enough, my love," she said, trying to make her voice light and tender. "Even husbands who do not wait two years give their wives a few months respite after childbirth." Men hated to hear about women's magic, so she had some power there as well. "I am still sore and torn. You would not want to make it worse."

He rewarded her by rolling away from her, and soon enough, the sound of his low, even breathing allowed her to relax. She fell asleep as well, only to be woken well before dawn by Thordis's crying for milk.

"Does she always wake so often?" Hallbjorn asked sleepily.

"Yes, she is a newborn," said Freydis, speaking gently to keep Thordis from becoming upset and losing her latch. "This is one reason why husbands stay far from their wives' beds after childbirth. If they do not, their sleep suffers. Why not come when you wish my touch, but sleep elsewhere?"

He yawned widely. "I think you're right. Not now, though. She will sleep after being at your breast. I know I would."

✛ ✛ ✛

HALLBJORN WAS FAR kinder to Freydis during the following day in the Faroes, and Freydis snapped at him less as well. She spent the day washing Thordis's soiled clouts and preparing food for Hallbjorn and his followers. Hallbjorn had begun to trust her. In time, he would not watch her every minute, and she could sneak away. Back to her uncle Ragnvald, perhaps? Back to Iceland—that thought brought a stab of anger. They should have taken better care of her.

The next day another ship arrived, this one captained by Geirbjorn Hakonsson. He and Hallbjorn greeted one another heartily. Freydis looked at him, trying to see the monster of the tales, the one who had flayed a woman's face as vengeance against her son, but he looked like any other man. A bit colder in the eyes, perhaps. At first glance, Snorri had been far harder to look upon, with his smashed mouth.

The moon waxed to full, and they departed just after high tide the next morning for the Shetland and Orkney islands. The wind was not strong, but after two days, Freydis saw gulls in the distance, and more ships joined them, with sails of every color, and some of plain homespun. She wished she had paid more attention to such things in Tafjord, where ships visited often. Her mother would know whom all of these vessels belonged to, and what it meant for the coming war. To Freydis, they only meant that she kept her vital supplies near her, in case her opportunity to escape should come.

As the wind strengthened, Hallbjorn took command from his pilot and directed his sailors in a strong voice. He had improved as a leader and a sailor over the winter that he had been away. His beard had grown fuller, and his shoulders broader. For a moment Freydis wondered if it would be so terrible to be his wife. He had given her pleasure before and could be convinced to treat her well.

But when she turned her head, she felt the lingering ache in her shoulder from when he had dislocated it last year. She felt the bruises on her hand where he had gripped it earlier, and the swelling in her cheek. With him, she must always walk carefully to prevent him from using his strength against her.

✛   ✛   ✛

HALLBJORN APPROACHED THE Orkney Islands from a different direction than he had the year before and sailed toward the southernmost
island, marked by a huge, freestanding stone pillar and a deep, curved
valley cutting through its center. The islands collected clouds, even
thicker than those that surrounded the Faroes, so the pillar seemed to
peek out at her before disappearing into the mist again. Some of the
ships milling about followed them, while others seemed to be pursuing,
but then fell back. It was not yet time for war. The leaders on both sides
wanted to retreat so they could plan first.

The ships that beached on this island, Hoy, had plain sails, much
patched. Freydis heard names she recognized from among the men.
Melbrid Tooth, short, but thick with muscle, showing his famous tooth
whenever he smiled. Ketil Flatnose, with his nose smashed flat in a
long-ago battle. He had been at Thordis's naming, Freydis recalled, and
nodded to her when he saw her with her child. Here was Ogmund Gud-
brandsson, long an ally of Solvi's and enemy of Harald's. Others came
from Sweden and the Danish kingdoms, from Frisia and the Baltic ter-
ritories. Some had accents she could not understand. A few had women
with them, some as rough and fierce as the men themselves, others
cowed and beaten.

As more gathered, they crowded the small turf hall, making it stink
of earth, sweat, and wet wool. Some had to camp outside in the wet
weather of early spring. At least Hallbjorn had arrived here early enough
to secure a place for her inside. He shared her bed at night, and always
wished for her touch. She begged off accepting his advances in return,
but each time, she worried that he would not accept her excuses, and
indeed, the soreness faded every day; she feared that soon she would let
him, to keep the peace.

A few days after they arrived, some of the men killed a cow, and set
the women to roasting it for a feast. Freydis worked all day and was
covered with grease by the evening. She served with the other women,
wearing Thordis on her back when she was wakeful, and setting her to
sleep in a warm corner of the kitchen when she could.

After the men had eaten their fill and toasted one another's past glo-
ries, Ketil stood and said, "I am pleased to see so many of you, but we

must still be cautious. Harald has brought many ships here, and while they are likely not captained by sailors as skilled as we, they still match or even better our numbers. And worse, Thorstein has betrayed us. We must accept that he has shared the secrets of Orkney's currents and hidden bays, and so we cannot use those against him."

"What do you propose?" asked Ogmund Gudbrandsson. "We did not come here to slink away. Harald and that loathsome snake Ragnvald Half-Drowned compassed the deaths of my father, and brother, and took our land. We have all come here for revenge."

Other voices warred with one another until Ketil held up a hand for silence. "We are, all of us, here for the same reason," he said. His voice was loud, but nasal, forced through his smashed nose. "Harald Halfdansson, Ragnvald Eysteinsson, Oddi Hakonsson, these men have all done us wrong, but now they have done us a good turn: coming here to die."

Freydis glanced at Geirbjorn Hakonsson, to see if he would object to his brother being named among his enemies. His eyes were still flat and unreadable.

"But Harald will not be defeated on land," Ketil continued. "We must lure them out on their ships, and pick them off that way. It will take time, but it is the only way to win."

The men talked deep into the night about how best to carry out Ketil's suggestions, until they all grew so drunk they fell asleep on the benches or lying in dirty rushes on the floor.

The next morning, most of the men departed in their ships. Freydis asked the kitchen women if there was a bathhouse she could use, and when she went out to start a fire, she saw a hunched figure in black coming toward her. As the old crone drew closer Freydis was only mildly surprised to see the face of Runa, the old woman who had offered her escape before.

"Freydis Solvisdatter," said Runa, "you have returned."

"Yes," said Freydis, crossing her arms. "What does it matter?"

"The islands do not like so many warriors upon them, eating up their bounty, burning turf they have not cut. They will rebel," she said.

"Is that a warning?" Freydis asked.

"No," said Runa. She stepped in close so Freydis could smell her sour scent of age and sweat, peat and herbs. "It is a promise, daughter. Do not lose hope."

She walked by Freydis and had performed her disappearing trick by the time Freydis turned to look for her. Freydis continued walking to the bathhouse, feeling the hope Runa had promised mixed with exasperation. No wonder her mother had no patience for prophecy and superstition. Still, Alfrith would tell her not to discount this. She must continue to look for an opportunity to escape.

The warriors did not return until Freydis was ready to go to bed. They trooped in, loud, smelly, and hungry, and she and the other women had to serve them a late dinner. The next day they went out again and again returned late, so Freydis tried to nap during the following day at the same time as Thordis, so she would not feel quite so drained.

After a few days of this, the raiders began to grow irritable. None of Harald's ships could be lured into battle. They stuck close to the settlement at Grimbister, where the Orkney currents could not trouble them.

Hallbjorn crawled in next to Freydis at night and wrapped his arms around her, pressing the length of his body against her side. Freydis sighed and moved to satisfy him, but he touched her cheek instead, and then kissed her searchingly.

"Have you heard?" Hallbjorn asked. "This is pointless."

"Yes, I heard," said Freydis, resisting the urge to wipe Hallbjorn's kisses from her mouth. Sometimes she thought she could stand this, pretending to be his wife, and other times his touch was abhorrent to her.

"What do you think?" he asked. "You are the daughter of Svanhild Sea Queen and Solvi Hunthiofsson. Do you think that we will win this way?"

"I am no seer," said Freydis. But she had heard the stories of Harald's battles, told every winter in Tafjord to pass the long, dark days. Ketil had been right—Harald did fight better on land. Most of his successes had been in shield-wall battles. King Ragnvald had helped him win his sea battles, and even then, they had lured men onto land when they could.

"But . . . what do you fear?" she asked.

"I fear they will stay in Thorstein's hall and refuse to chase our ships, and another summer will pass before I get my revenge," said Hallbjorn. "King Ragnvald killed my father and dishonored my mother, and I have had to smile in his face for far too long."

She had never heard him sound so venomous. He must have prompted

Rolli to attack Aldi's ships for his revenge. Freydis felt a chill, even with the warm length of Hallbjorn's body pressed up against her. Runa had told her that the islands did not want him here, and Freydis could help them.

"You are right," she said evenly. "You must find a way to bring the attack to them. Do not hesitate to fight on land." That strange coldness prompted her further. "King Ragnvald's hands have never been the same since Solvi had them broken. If you fight a land battle and face him, you will surely win. Do not hesitate. He fears to be thought a coward, and so will be in the hottest part of the fighting, though he is too old for it. Find him there and kill him."

Hallbjorn looked at her wonderingly. "You sound as though you hate him as much as I," he said.

"He betrayed my mother," said Freydis. "He is her brother, and she is soft-hearted about him, but I see that he is a tyrant, as much as Harald is."

"Oh, wife," said Hallbjorn. "I do wish I could take you now."

"So do I," Freydis whispered. This new coldness let her lie without shame. She was talking to a dead man. "But I am still torn from Thordis's birth. Come back from this battle successful, and I will find new ways to please you." She touched him, wondering if he would feel the chill in her fingertips, but he still moaned with pleasure against her, and kissed her without hesitation. She did not sleep that night, instead staring up all night at the dirt of the ceiling, and feeling a foreign, dangerous energy, as though she moved the threads of the fates with her words.

The next morning, Freydis kissed Hallbjorn good-bye before he left in his ship, a deep kiss that she joined as passionately as he, for she knew in her bones that it was the last warmth he would ever have from her.

3I

HARALD'S FORCES PASSED A LONG, RAINY WEEK IN GRIMBISTER, trying to find the enemy. Thorstein's hall could only sleep a hundred of Harald's warriors and seemed able to feed even fewer. They ran through the food they brought quickly, and Ragnvald saw some of the men looking longingly at cows that should not be slaughtered out of season.

Some scouting missions had encountered enemy ships, but Harald's men feared to follow them far enough to find their hiding place, and for good reason. Thorstein was no help—he said that the Orkney Islands contained so many hidden bays and beaches that the enemy forces could be hiding anywhere.

After five inconclusive days, Harald called a meeting with Ragnvald and his captains to share his frustration. "If we can't pry them out, we should take war to Scotland," he said. "I am told that is where many of our enemies make their homes."

"We will have to raid their mainland to keep Thorstein from starving over the winter anyway," said Ragnvald.

Harald waved that off. "I've paid him."

"He cannot eat silver," Ragnvald replied. He stretched and turned himself so the fire heated his other side. The dampness in his clothes turned into steam that made his skin clammy. "Our enemies may have heard that Thorstein has abandoned them," he added. "If they don't come in force, we may never root them out. Who has enough knowledge of the Scottish islands for us to attack there?"

"Thorstein, of course," said Harald.

"He will help us here, a little, but will he take battle to his former allies?" Ragnvald asked.

"If he will not, then he can be killed," said Harald.

Ragnvald blinked—in the past few years of diplomacy and deal-making on Harald's behalf, but not at his side, he had forgotten Harald's impatience with anything but immediate capitulation. He did not like to hear this talk while they warmed themselves under Thorstein's roof. The laws of the gods required that they leave first, thus ending Thorstein's hospitality, if they wanted to kill him.

Thorstein had been out taxing fishermen, and he returned to report that his scouts had sighted more ships coming from the Scottish mainland. With the tides and currents, they could land by the afternoon.

Harald, Ragnvald, Thorstein, and their sons and captains gathered to discuss their plans. "They are a divided force," said Thorstein of the enemy. "Too many captains, no leader."

"What of Solvi Hunthiofsson?" Ragnvald asked.

Thorstein shrugged. "He is not the man he once was. Forget him. Your enemy is here, and it is not him."

Ragnvald looked at him suspiciously—Thorstein might be concealing the location of his old mentor. "We should hide all the ships out of the harbor to trick them into thinking we have left. Sail some elsewhere and pull others up onshore to hide," he suggested. "Harald has always had better luck on land."

"I have good luck everywhere," said Harald.

"Ragnvald is right," said Thorstein. "Luck favors those who do not risk the currents here. I have been raiding from Orkney for fifteen years and only last year lost a ship upon these rocks."

Harald's forces did as Ragnvald said. Harald himself used his massive strength to help drag some of the ships up and behind hillocks that hid them. Ragnvald helped as well, and spent the following day with his hands so weak and painful he could hardly hold his dagger for eating.

He passed a fretful day while enemy ships sailed around Grimbister like crows circling a dying animal. Harald deployed scouts to all corners of the island to keep watch, and each time they reported back to say that the ships had not beached nor put off any warriors in boats. They must know their advantage lay in navigating Orkney's currents rather than in coming ashore.

Word came the next morning that over the night, attackers had burned some of Harald's ships left in other harbors and killed their guards. The mood at breakfast was sour. Only Halfdan ate with much enjoyment. Ivar attempted halfhearted jokes with some of Harald's sons, while Einar ate his porridge methodically. The rain had departed, taking with it the pain in Ragnvald's hands, but the wind blew so hard that even within Thorstein's hall, the rushing noise nearly drowned out the voices of Harald's warriors.

Harald pushed his porridge away only partially eaten, and sighed. "I am ready to go home and have you finally cut my hair, but not without at least one battle." He turned toward Ragnvald. "What is your new plan to draw them out?" he asked. "You used to have so many—you were never without a trick for how to defeat our enemies. Now you are silent."

True, he had nothing to offer here in this island kingdom. The tactics that might work for a fjord battle, with predictable winds and currents, and only two directions to sail, could not be used in the chaotic stretches of water between the islands. Ships captained by men who knew this place could hide, while Harald's forces would be as disadvantaged as a blind man fighting a sighted one. And, as he watched Harald stretch out his long limbs, unconcerned as a cat, Ragnvald realized he did not want Harald to be too successful here. Harald had conquered Norway and taken Sogn from Ragnvald, from his sons, from his sons' sons. He had given Harald enough.

He raised his head and saw Einar watching him, and then looking away after he met Ragnvald's eyes. "What do you think, Einar?" he called out. "You look as though you have something in mind."

"Nothing sure," said Einar. His frown made lines between his brows. For a moment, Ragnvald saw his son in old age, with a longer beard, one eye shadowed like Odin Alfather. He shook his head to dispel the vision.

"Join us," said Ragnvald. "My sons," he added, nodding to Ivar.

"And mine," said Harald. "This needs many heads."

The gaggle of young men joined them near the fire, with Einar at their vanguard. "What was your thought?" Ragnvald asked Einar.

"I was remembering the battle of Solskel, in Geiranger Fjord," said Einar. "What the skalds sing of it, and what you've told me of it. Stavanger too. You used a few ships to draw other ships into a trap. Thorstein, is there a bay we could use as a trap?"

"What is wrong with this bay?" Thorstein asked.

"We can hardly get them to chase us where we are best armed," said Einar. "If that was going to work it would have already."

"This settlement is on a narrow neck," said Thorstein. "On the other side is the Bay of Scapa—it is better protected than this one, but tricky sailing to get there. It might serve." He looked intrigued despite himself.

"That sounds good," said Einar. "Then we could send some ships out, under cover of darkness, to be ready at dawn to let themselves be chased into the Bay of Scapa. They can beach and lead their attackers up to our waiting forces."

Harald laughed. "Your son is as wise as you once were," he said to Ragnvald. "I am surprised you did not think of it."

"There are a hundred reasons why it may not work," said Ragnvald. He flexed his hands, which were still stiff even though the weather aches had passed. Seeing Einar's disappointment, Ragnvald added, "And a hundred reasons why my plan might not have worked at Solskel. But it did, and we do not have a better idea. If we do nothing, these raiders will continue attacking by stealth, picking off our ships and scouts while we wait. What do you think, my king?"

"I like it," said Harald. "Who will be in those ships?"

"Only the bravest and most foolish, as usual," said Ragnvald.

"It was my idea," said Einar. "I should go."

"Einar goes nowhere without me," said Ivar. "We swore an oath, and I will not violate it a second time."

Ragnvald swallowed. He did not want Ivar there. The bait ships would face the most peril. Einar should captain one, since it was his idea—Ragnvald had always faced the most peril in his riskiest plans—but he would not separate his sons again, or gainsay Ivar in front of everyone.

Harald's sons all clamored to be in the ships, putting forth the reasons they should be chosen.

"Halfdan, I do not hear you volunteering for this," said Harald. "Do you think it is a good plan?"

"It is good enough," said Halfdan. "It may draw in some ships or it may not. But I have seen that not all of these ships are fighting in concert. That is to their advantage in this terrain, where we are not fighting big battles and communication is difficult. We may draw some, but not others."

"What would you suggest instead?" Harald asked.

Halfdan looked uncomfortable. "As I said, Einar's plan is good enough—and as he has said, this sort of thing has worked for you before."

"Then you should not object to captaining one of the ships," said Harald, with a challenging smile. "You are as able a pilot as any of my sons, and better than many of them."

"Of course, if you wish me to," said Halfdan grudgingly.

The meeting broke soon after, as men went to prepare for battle, sharpening swords, making sure that their armor was in good repair, trading with one another for bits they lacked.

Ragnvald went to check the status of his own arms, a habit he had developed to keep himself from growing too nervous. Halfdan followed him to the pallet where he had been sleeping and storing his gear.

"You have to keep me from the bait ships," said Halfdan in a low whisper.

"Why should I do that?" Ragnvald asked, continuing to pull out his supplies. "Do you think this battle may turn against Harald? Are your allies here?"

"Just keep me out of those ships," said Halfdan.

"That is where your father wants you," said Ragnvald. "I will not gainsay him."

"You can survive my becoming king, or perish even before my father," said Halfdan. "It is your choice."

"I follow my king," said Ragnvald. "As I have always told you." Halfdan shoved his shoulder, but Ragnvald refused to react. Halfdan wanted an opportunity to duel with him and kill him. Ragnvald feared for his sons sailing with Halfdan, but if Halfdan did not want to be in the bait ships, that was probably the safest place for him to be. Better there than at Harald's side in battle, where he could kill his father in the chaos.

✛ ✛ ✛

ALL OF HARALD'S forces feasted well that night, devouring the last of Thorstein's stores, as well as a few old heifers that Thorstein claimed no longer gave good milk. The meat was tough but welcome after too long eating only salt fish and hard rye bread.

Ivar and Einar stood on the dim beach with the rest of their small crew, both already armored for the long night and day ahead. Ragnvald wanted to talk with Ivar alone, so he sent Einar off to find out how many would be crewing the other ships.

"My son, this is a needless risk," Ragnvald said.

Ivar gave him a confused look. "What kind of king do you want me to be?" he said. "You would have me let Einar go and face danger without me while I cling to your skirts?"

Ragnvald tensed at the insult—Ivar should not imply that any man was really a woman, not unless he wanted to die in a duel. He opened his mouth to scold him but instead simply said, "You are my heir, and my first true-born son. You must survive."

"Then you should go in my stead," said Ivar. When Ragnvald did not reply, he added, "Why won't you? Halfdan says it is because you value your life too highly. Now that skalds sing songs saying you have risked your life for Harald and his dream, you no longer need to."

Ragnvald grew hot with anger, but clenched his fists and willed it aside. It was not cowardice that kept him from the bait ships; he needed to survive to secure Ivar's inheritance. He drew breath to speak, but before he could, Ivar said, more quietly, "They sing no songs of me, Father."

"Fight well on land, and they will," Ragnvald replied. "You have a long life to have songs made about you. This is too dangerous."

Ivar tucked in a strap on his flank. "You made me fight without my brother once and I was captured. I will not break my oath again, and neither will he."

"Then he should have asked you before volunteering for this," said Ragnvald.

"His plan is good, and he is brave," said Ivar. "Why do you not love Einar as you should a son? He would not tell me what he has done to anger you, only that he deserved your anger. But he is your son too, and you should forgive him."

"I have," said Ragnvald. He was surprised that Ivar did not know of the affair between Einar and Gyda. Surely Einar, who shared everything with his brother, would have told him that. But no, he had kept his promise and that secret. He took a deep breath. "Before you were born I swore to your mother, Hilda, that I would never put another woman's sons ahead of you, and I have not. I never break an oath."

"But you made Einar and I break ours when you separated us, Father," said Ivar. "I am going with my brother, who has always protected me and never tried to hold me back, and when we have our victory, I will demand a gift from Harald: to elevate Einar so he and I are equal. North Maer and South Maer were once separate districts, and can be again. We will rule side by side, and it will not be your doing, and Mother cannot blame you."

Ragnvald's chest felt tight. Ivar could inspire men to follow him, but he was not wise enough to rule without Einar by his side—his behavior in Skane had shown that. Ragnvald had always wished to have as close a companion as Einar and Ivar were to one another, but he had lost Oddi through his ambition, and Harald's kingship had always stood between them. "Your love for your brother does you credit," he said thickly. "We will discuss this when you return. Please take care to keep yourself safe."

"I will take care of my brother," said Ivar, "and he will take care of me."

✣ ✣ ✣

RAGNVALD CROUCHED DOWN in the high grass of the plain that led down to the Bay of Scapa. Sigurd was somewhere to his left, and Harald to his right. Nearly three hundred of Harald's other warriors hid in the grass around him. Ragnvald worried that the absence of the birds that usually fed on the wild grains here would give them away.

He had slept poorly the night before, imagining all the ways that a battle could go wrong, and now, waiting in the grass, he could not stop running through his conversation with Ivar. He was still angry that Ivar had questioned his bravery for not wanting to crew one of the bait ships himself. Ragnvald had a kingdom that depended on him, and could not risk himself like that. Ivar should not either.

As to this idea that Ragnvald should divide Maer between Ivar and Einar, it was pure foolishness. Hilda was already angry with him for allowing Rolli's brief outlawry, and would be even more angry if Rolli did not come to Orkney. He would not compound it by setting up Ivar and Einar as brother kings.

Somewhere below, three ships—Einar and Ivar's, Halfdan's, and another crewed by a captain from Halogaland—were leading the attackers on a chase. They planned to sail as though they were trying to escape the Orkney Islands toward the Scottish mainland, then allow themselves to be blocked, and flee to the Bay of Scapa. No matter what the enemy suspected, they should give chase.

The knees of Ragnvald's trousers were wet through from kneeling on the ground, and he would be stiff when he stood. How long had it been since he had fought in a true battle? Long enough that he feared his damaged hands and aging muscles would not be a match for a young opponent.

Mist clung to the field where Ragnvald hid. Dawn turned into day with a slow brightening of the sky and air. Finally, after Ragnvald had begun to worry that the trap had failed, the scouts whistled their signals, and he readied himself to charge with the first wave of warriors.

Between stalks of grass, he saw that Halfdan's ship had beached, along with six other ships belonging to their enemies, crowding the small landing. Halfdan's stature made him easy to pick out as he raced up the hill, leading a crowd of warriors behind him: some his own, identifiable by their clean new armor, and others—the enemy, in salt-stained armor that showed years of wear.

Ragnvald, Harald, and Sigurd led their forces down to meet the attackers. They could not form a shield wall without crushing Halfdan and his followers between the two groups, so the battle quickly turned into a melee. Ragnvald advanced toward the most expensively armored of the enemy fighters—the leaders of the battle. Kill them and the rest might lay down their weapons.

He fought through a few lesser warriors armed only with small axes, whose armor did not protect them from his Frankish sword, before reaching the center of the fighting, where the tallest and ablest warriors crashed against one another.

For a moment Ragnvald thought he saw Einar among the enemy. A strange vision, and it could not be true. If Einar was here, it was only because he and his ship had landed and drew more of their enemy behind them.

Another young man attacked Ragnvald with a ferocity that made it hard for him to hold his shield. Each blow made Ragnvald's hands tingle, and he dreaded a return of the weakness that had plagued them since Solvi's torture.

Ragnvald was growing short of breath, with his grip slipping on his sword, when something wet thudded against the side of his opponent's helmet, splattering blood over his sparse beard. Ragnvald took advantage of the distraction and smashed the boy under the chin with the splintered edge of his shield. As he reeled back, Ragnvald lunged forward and slashed his throat open.

Then he saw Einar again, with his golden hair and beard, his angular face, dealing a blow to Harald's son Dagfinn. Had Dagfinn joined Halfdan's rebellion, midbattle, or had Einar changed sides?

Ragnvald fought his way toward the two of them, but when he drew closer he saw something alien in the movements of Dagfinn's opponent. His face was a little longer than Einar's, and fuller as well. This was Ragnvald's stepbrother Hallbjorn, the son of Vigdis and Ragnvald's stepfather, Olaf, whom Ragnvald had killed more than twenty years ago. And he was getting the better of Dagfinn, who was bleeding from two gashes on his forearms that had laid the flesh open to the bone.

Ragnvald maneuvered in beside Dagfinn, who fell back, letting Ragnvald advance on Hallbjorn.

"I always knew we would face one another, stepbrother," said Hallbjorn. "My mother will be glad when I kill you. She has been trying to get me to do it since I was a boy."

Ragnvald was too out of breath to reply. He tasted blood in his throat from his exertion.

Hallbjorn lunged at him. Ragnvald could not raise his shield in time so he had to block the blow with his sword; the force of Hallbjorn's strike made his fingers spasm in pain. His sword fell from his hand. All he had to defend himself now was his rapidly fraying shield.

Suddenly Sigurd appeared, fighting Hallbjorn back. Hallbjorn looked suddenly frightened. "Brother!" he said to Sigurd. "Do not kill me."

Ragnvald picked up his sword as Sigurd glanced back at him. In that moment, Hallbjorn lunged again, ripping a long slash through Sigurd's forearm. Sigurd yelled in pain. "Will you kill your brother?" he asked Hallbjorn.

Hallbjorn did not answer, only attacked again. As Sigurd fell back,

Ragnvald scrambled forward and blocked Hallbjorn's blow with his shield. Hallbjorn's sword snagged in the last of the wood still attached to the shield boss, while Ragnvald hurled it toward the ground so the momentum carried Hallbjorn down onto one knee.

Hallbjorn tried to push himself up to standing again, but before he could, Ragnvald brought his sword down on the back of Hallbjorn's neck. A lucky blow—Ragnvald's sword sliced between the neck bones, parting Hallbjorn's head from his body. It rolled onto the ground and stared up at him, looking sickeningly like Einar's again, an omen that was too frightening to dwell upon. Ragnvald looked down the slope toward the bay where ships now crowded the harbor. He could not see the other bait ships, and Einar and Ivar had not appeared in the battle.

"Brother," said Sigurd. Ragnvald looked up at him—he had now killed Sigurd's half-brother, as well as his father many years ago. "I think he would have killed me, and I couldn't move."

"I'm sorry for it," said Ragnvald. "I always thought better of him."

"Me too," said Sigurd.

Ragnvald glanced down at the head again. Its face, now blue and bloodless, still looked like Einar's. Hallbjorn had been Ragnvald's step-brother, and at least deserved a warrior's burial.

The battle had begun to subside, with Harald's forces victorious. Some pairs and trios still fought, but many of the attackers were retreating back toward their ships. Harald and some of his warriors gave chase. Ragnvald was glad to let them go. He had never been in a battle more taxing. Only fate had kept Odin Alfather from marking Ragnvald for death this time.

Some healers had already begun to drag the wounded off the field. Ragnvald made his way toward them. That task would suit him. He still had the slow, plodding strength of an old man, but he hoped he would never have to face a true battle again. If he and Oddi were still friends, Oddi would laugh at him for his grim thoughts after a battle where he had been successful. But Oddi had left him long ago, and Ragnvald had seen a vision of his own son dead on his blade. And he had, in truth, killed Vigdis's son. Even if Sigurd forgave him, Vigdis would find a way to revenge herself for that, Ragnvald feared.

32

THE SKY WAS THE DARK BLUE OF A LATE SPRING MIDNIGHT, and down at the bay, shadowed by the high cliffs, men's faces took on the same hue. Einar tightened one of the straps on Ivar's wrist-guards, and checked the other. Halfdan's men started to push his ship off the beach. Einar and Ivar would go next, followed by the third, crewed by some Halogaland men Einar knew less well.

Ivar touched his wrists, checking the fit. "I told Father I would ask Harald to make you king of South Maer, and me king of North Maer," he said.

Einar's eyes burned with sudden tears. He did not deserve a brother like Ivar, who hated any honor they could not share. "And what did he say?" he asked in a low voice.

"I don't remember," said Ivar.

"He could not have been pleased."

"I don't care," said Ivar. "You deserve this."

Einar only smiled, and then it was time to depart. He steered their ship to follow Halfdan's out into the bay. As he had hoped, as soon as the sun rose after midnight, the raiders sighted them and gave chase. None of the bait ships carried enough men to work the oars, which Einar hoped would not give away the game. At least their lightness meant they moved quickly when the sun climbed higher and the day's breezes strengthened.

It was just before breakfast time, or so Einar's growling stomach told him, when a rainstorm swept across the water, alternating mist and squalls. Halfdan's ship fled onto the beach at the Bay of Scapa, and six of

the enemy ships followed. The warriors who disembarked quickly fell
to fighting with Harald's forces, who charged down from the grassy hill.

Another of the ships descended on the Halogaland ship and used
lines to draw the two together into a fighting platform. The attackers
were more heavily crewed, and Einar feared they would slaughter all of
the Halogaland men. Then a gust of wind knocked the attacking ship
around, spinning it out into a channel where another gust smashed the
two ships against a cliff.

They rebounded from it, but as the current pushed them out between
the two islands the attacking ship's starboard side dipped under the surface and then the Halogaland ship began going down by the stern.

"We should help them," Ivar called out from the prow.

"We have to finish this," Einar replied. They still had to draw their
pursuers onto shore. The winds were tricky here between the islands,
and Einar needed all of his attention on the steering oar, and all of the
men on the lines, to keep the ship from crashing into the cliffs.

He made a few runs at the shore, only to be turned away by gusts and
downdrafts. His pursuers had better luck, and landed, so Einar decided
to try to rescue some of their fellows after all. Landing against this current would require a far better sailor than he was—the fates must want
him to go to their aid. He ordered the men on the lines to swing the sail
around to help take them closer to the foundering ships.

The attacking forces had managed to loose their ship from the Halogaland ship, and were bailing and rowing at the same time. They made
the narrow shore below the cliff just as their efforts began to fail. As
soon as the men jumped out onto the strip of pebbles, they engaged with
more of Harald's warriors. Good, that would make the rescue go more
smoothly.

Ivar ordered his men to pull survivors from the sinking ship on
board. Einar could spare an arm to help a few times, but mostly he held
the steering oar to keep the ship from being dashed on the rocks or flung
against the other ship in this narrow strait.

His attention was so concentrated on those tasks that he did not see
another ship approaching until a rock hit his shoulder, hard enough to
make his hand slip from the steering oar for a moment. His teeth banged
together and he had to shake his head to clear it.

He glanced behind him to see the ship upon them, its prow close enough that within a moment they would collide and the steering oar would be crushed between them. Einar hauled up the giant board with an effort that felt as though it would tear his shoulders out of their sockets. Raised to lie alongside the ship, it might not be torn loose in the fighting. But now he could not control the ship at all.

The warriors from the attacking ship flung hooks across—the captain was willing to risk it, even in these treacherous currents. Einar ripped his ax from where it was strapped on his back and began hacking at the lines as they landed. But too soon a tide of men poured after them and Einar could not stop them.

He transferred his ax to his left hand and drew his sword with his right. A man with a battered leather helmet attacked him. Einar had the longer reach, and was able to land a killing blow on his neck before he could strike. Einar pushed the body toward the boarding sailors so they would have to deal with that dead weight for a moment while he caught his breath.

A shadow crossed the ship as it drew under the looming cliffs. Einar braced for impact, but the current caught the linked ships as it had the two before and began carrying them out into the broader, deeper waters of the bay.

Einar had no time to notice anything else for, in a moment, more men were upon him. He fought back wildly. Someone cut his arm and he did not notice it until his hand grew cool and itchy from blood drying upon it. He did not know if he killed his attackers or if they only fell away from the ferocity of his attack.

During a moment of respite, he saw Ivar fighting at the prow. Ivar looked desperate, beset by three men, hardly able to move. A tide of red flooded Einar's vision, Odin's battle madness, which made men invulnerable when it touched them.

He cut through the warriors surrounding him, swinging with ax and sword, with a strength that felt like it did not belong to him. He swung his ax so hard it became stuck in the head of one of his opponents, so he left it there and drew his dagger instead. Warriors parted before him, fear in their eyes, until Einar reached the prow where Ivar still fought.

Now Einar recognized one of Ivar's attackers—he looked very like King Heming of Halogaland, so this must be his brother, the outlaw Geirbjorn Hakonsson. Ivar fought hard against him, better than Einar had ever seen, but his attention wavered when he saw Einar approaching, and in that moment Geirbjorn struck, a wild blow that nearly severed Ivar's neck. His eyes went wide and he collapsed backward into the water.

A part of Einar felt the blow as though it had been aimed against him, choking him on steel, killing him and Ivar in the same moment, but Odin's red tide still moved his limbs. He rushed toward Geirbjorn and slashed him across the throat, not caring that Geirbjorn's sword could reach him too. Let Geirbjorn kill him, as long as Ivar could be avenged. He did not see the blow Geirbjorn landed as he died, only felt a searing pain rip through his cheek and eye. He lashed out unseeing. His sword encountered nothing but air, and he too fell.

✝   ✝   ✝

AS SVANHILD APPROACHED the Orkney Islands, a fine soaking rain began to fall, so she was nearly under one of the cliffs before she could see anything of them besides vast dark shapes in the mist. She heard the sounds of battle, but the hiss of the rain distorted it, and when she sailed toward the noises, she only found another cliff that must have been reflecting the sound from some other place.

She was exhausted from the sea crossing, the days of sleeplessness, and had hoped for some rest before having to decide whether to join a battle. Hers and Ketil's ships had separated during the journey— Svanhild could not tell if they were ahead or behind, but based on the battle that had already started, they must have gotten ahead somehow, hidden by the banks of cloud and fog that had dogged her journey.

When she did find a ship, it seemed nearly unmanned, drifting. She thought it looked familiar, and the colors were Ragnvald's, but raiders used whatever sail they could find. She called out the order to fling a line across. There was no resistance as her men pulled and brought the two ships together. The wind abated as the rain intensified, so she only had to worry about the currents. She wanted to go closer and see what had happened on the ship, but she needed to keep a hand on the steering oar to feel how the current pulled on her and steer away from the cliffs and sharp rocks of this headland.

"It's ours," Falki called out from the other ship. "I mean, it's your brother's," he amended. "Your nephew is here. Wounded, maybe dead."

Svanhild's heart leaped to her throat. No matter which of her nephews it was, she had to help him. She handed off the steering oar to Aban and climbed between the ships.

There in the stern lay Einar, almost unrecognizable with half of his face bloody, the ruin of his right eye lying upon his cheek. Still, a man did not die from losing an eye, and she saw no other wound upon him. Unless the blow that had disfigured him had shaken his brain too much for him to live, he must only be insensible.

She bent over him and felt at his neck, where a pulse beat, strong and steady. "Bring him over to our ship," Svanhild commanded.

As Falki put an arm under his shoulder to help him up, Einar's head lolled and he shuddered and woke. He pushed Falki off and scrabbled back, feeling at his belt for his sword. "Where is he? Where is he?" Einar cried.

"Hush," said Svanhild. "It's me, your aunt Svanhild. You are alive."

"Where is he? Where is Ivar? I can't see."

"You lost an eye," Svanhild told him. "But your other one should still work." She had heard that a man who had lost one eye could lose sight in the other one, but that should not happen immediately.

Einar looked around wildly, blinked his remaining eye, and finally seemed to see her. "Ivar—he—Geirbjorn Hakonsson. Cut his—" Einar broke off, choking on the words.

Svanhild knelt down by him and stroked his hand, hard and sword-callused for one so young. "What happened?" she asked.

"Geirbjorn, he—he can't have—he—it looked like he killed him. Svanhild, Aunt, tell me it is not so. Tell me it's not true." He began to weep, tears pouring from his unwounded eye. He put his hand to the other one, and flinched when he touched the mess of his eye still on his cheek.

"He is not here," said Svanhild.

Einar looked hopeful for a moment, then sagged. "He fell," he said. The tears started again. "He fell and I could not save him." He slumped down and closed his eye, and Svanhild and Falki had to drag him over to their ship.

"Hostage for us?" asked Bjorn, one of Ketil's men who had traveled with her.

"For me," said Svanhild. "I am the captain."

Bjorn gave her a scornful look. "You're a woman."

Falki advanced on him, hand at his sword. Svanhild saw Ketil's men about to square off against hers, and shouted, "A hostage for me, a ship for you."

Bjorn gave her a greedy smile. It was a well-made ship, worth more than a small farm, especially to a raider. "I accept," he said. He beckoned to Ketil's other men, and they left Svanhild's small ship for the larger one.

Einar paid no attention to any of this, still lying on a rowing bench, his lips blue with cold. If Ragnvald decided she was an enemy, then Einar would be her hostage, but she need not tell him that now. She would only use him that way if she had to, and even then, if Ivar, Einar's beloved brother and Ragnvald's favorite son, was truly dead, then Svanhild did not know if she had the stomach to bring them more pain.

Bjorn had sailed it off in the direction of the battle sounds, which still continued, and Svanhild had decided to follow, when she saw a body washing in the surf of a nearby pebble beach. She could not be sure, but it looked like Ivar, with his dark hair, fine armor, and helmet that might be the one that Harald had given Ragnvald as a young man.

Svanhild did not want to make Einar look, so she directed her ship to sail toward the beach. When she drew closer she saw Ivar's handsome features, and the mess of torn flesh at his throat, gone blue from washing in the waves. She could not let him lie there; Ragnvald would want his son's body back for a proper burial.

The damage looked worse the closer they came. Svanhild cringed to see the ruin of such a fine young man. At least her son Eystein had died without violence. Though Solvi had done his body violence after death, insisting on burning him on a pyre, on the shore of Trondheim Fjord. Ragnvald would be able to choose what happened to his son.

Falki and Aban brought Ivar's body on board. Svanhild knelt down next to Einar. "We've found Ivar's body," she said, wanting to be sure she did not give him false hope. Einar sat up and stumbled over the benches to lie down next to Ivar, curled around him.

A pair of hostages, one living, one dead. If they had not been her own blood, and her brother's most precious sons, she might have been pleased by this turn of events. She could not join this battle on Ketil's side, though—Einar and Ivar, lying next to one another, made the costs too clear. Let Harald have his divorce, let Solvi retreat back into his frightened little life in Iceland, as long as Svanhild could find her daughter again.

She sailed after Bjorn and the ship captured from Einar, trying to peer through the rain to see a place to land. Einar needed a healer and she needed to feed her crew. As the rain lifted, though, she saw another ship in pursuit of hers. A larger ship, with all of its oars out—it caught her in a moment, its stern slipping past her prow, so she could see the big, red-bearded man who captained it.

"Thorstein the Red, it is I, Svanhild Sea Queen," Svanhild declared. She made a quick calculation. "I have come with Ketil Flatnose to lend my forces to you."

"If you came with Ketil, you are my enemy," said Thorstein. "I have promised aid to Harald."

Svanhild tensed. She had only stopped steering Harald's alliances a few months ago, and already she could not read the currents. Thorstein's larger ship carried enough men to outnumber hers three to one, so Svanhild surrendered to him. Saving Einar and retrieving Ivar's body should be enough to buy her favor with Ragnvald. At least he could not make her go back to Harald, not after Harald had divorced her. And Solvi did not want her enough to sail to war with her. As long as she found Freydis, she would willingly return with Ragnvald to Maer. He would need her comfort after the death of his son.

She did not notice at first, lost in her thoughts, that Thorstein carried her not to the Grimbister settlement but to a small island beyond that the local folk called Hoy. She recognized it by the huge rock pillar that flanked it, hewn by wind and time and the whims of the gods until it wore the face of a man. She had navigated by it in fine weather when sailing to the Orkney Islands.

Hoy was tenanted by sheep farmers, who mostly dwelt in the deep valley that bisected the island. The shape funneled the wind through it, but the valley's high walls sheltered it from the worst of the winter storms that blew across the North Sea.

Thorstein pulled up his ship on a small, steep beach almost at the base of the tall pillar of stone on Hoy's coast. He bound her hands and had his men take all of her crew captive. They let Einar remain unbound but took his weapons. Four of Thorstein's men carried Ivar's body into the valley to a hall of piled turf.

"Why did you bring me here?" Svanhild asked before they entered the hall. "Why should you attack me at all? I am Solvi's sea queen, once, and now forever. And why would you side with Harald? What has he ever done for you but kill your friends?"

Thorstein looked at her. "Are you done?"

"No," said Svanhild. "I sailed with Ketil, but I have not fought Harald, not since I've been married to him and then divorced. There is not a side in this battle that would not be happy for you to deliver me to them."

"Exactly," said Thorstein. "Now I can get the terms I want. Which of your men is the best sailor?"

"Why should I tell you that?" Svanhild asked.

"Because if you do not want to grow into an old woman herding goats on Hoy, I must send him to get a ransom for you. And that half-dead boy in there." Einar had allowed himself to be shoved into Thorstein's hall on Hoy, enduring slaps and prods from Thorstein's men without complaint as long as he remained in view of Ivar's body.

"Ransom from whom?" Svanhild asked as Thorstein grabbed her shoulder and prodded her toward the hall. Inside was dim, and the door looked like a great black mouth yawning open.

"From King Harald, of course," said Thorstein.

The wind whipped her hair into her eyes. "I thought you were his ally," she said.

"I said I wouldn't fight against him. But now I have something he wants, and if I give it to him, he will give me these islands to rule."

"Ha," said Svanhild. "You should know better than to trust him. You sailed with Solvi—"

"Where is Solvi? You throw his name around as easily as the Norse kings who blame him for every raid upon their shores. But he is not here, is he? And he has not been worth worrying about for years."

"He is not here," Svanhild admitted.

"Who is your best sailor?" Thorstein asked.

Svanhild sighed. "That is Falki. If you let him go, he will carry your message to Harald." She ducked under the beam of the hall's open door, and went inside.

33

SOLVI WOKE TO A KNOCKING ON HIS DOOR AND GROANED. HE
had been sleeping long hours since Freydis was taken and Svanhild
left. When he was awake, his weakness taunted him; when he slept, he
dreamed of losing battles, but at least in those battles, he could still walk
and fight.

Tova answered the door. She had been quiet again with Falki gone,
and this time it seemed like a reproach. She let in Unna, who carried a
basket that smelled of new-baked bread, a scent that made Solvi's mouth
water. Unna put the basket down on his bed, in the space where legs
longer than his would be, and pulled out a wedge of cheese, and a pot
of honey. These she spread on a crust of bread and gave it to him, along
with a cup of light morning ale.

She ate and drank her own portion without speaking. Solvi wondered
if she noticed that he had not welcomed her.

"How long have we been friends, Solvi Hunthiofsson?" she asked.

Solvi frowned. Her Scottish accent seemed very strong this morning;
perhaps she had chosen the wrong word. "No time," he said. "We have
never been friends."

"Is that true?" Unna asked. "We have shared farm labor, and cared for
one another's sick animals. I housed your daughter and—"

"For Svanhild," Solvi said.

Unna continued as though he had not spoken: "—and helped her bear
her child. If that is not the work of a friend, I do not know what to call it."

Solvi had not thought he could feel any more guilty, not after Freydis's capture and Svanhild's departure, and he too useless to help, but Unna's words still made him hot with shame. "For Svanhild," Solvi insisted, drawing his knees up. "You did it for her."

"At first," said Unna. "But it is you who have been my neighbor these last ten years, while she was gone. It is you who welcomed and protected your daughter when her mother failed to."

"What do you want?" Solvi asked.

Unna pressed her lips together, looking as though his words had caused her pain. Did she truly bear him some affection?

"I suppose we are friends by your definition," he allowed. "A king's son does not have many friends. Neither does a lame, ill-tempered farmer. If you are my friend, I am blessed by it."

The sharp cheese tasted familiar, and he remembered her sending a servant to give him a wheel of it last winter. Tova made a small amount of cheese, but they did not have enough servants for a full dairy, nor did Tova have the knowledge to make more than soft cheese and whey. And that had not been the first time Unna had shared something with him. He had taken it for granted, or seen it as a veiled insult, a sign that she had surplus at her farm, enough to be charitable to Svanhild's lame former husband, even though she did not like him.

"Good," said Unna brusquely. "I do consider you a sort of friend, the kind that can only be made by long acquaintance and suffering through Iceland's seasons together. You are my nearest neighbor. Keep that in mind when I tell you this: you must go after Svanhild. I do not know how you bear the shame of staying here."

"You think I can't bear shame?" Solvi replied angrily. "I have eaten that along with your neighbor gifts these past ten years."

"Do you value your life more than your daughter's?" Unna asked. "Or Svanhild's? Or is it that you will see old comrades and enemies and they will know your shame?"

"You just want my farm," Solvi grumbled. "Well, you can't have it. Svanhild already gave it to Tova and Falki."

Unna gave him a fond and exasperated look. "That is not why I have come. I am old. Older than you, and all of my children are dead. What use would I have for your farm?" She shook her head. "Know this, Solvi Hunthiofsson: if I could do something and make my children live again, I would do it, even if it meant my shame and death."

"I would go if I thought I could do anything for her, but I would be a burden, another hostage," Solvi said, clenching his fists in his blankets.

"How do you know you cannot help her?" said Unna. "You gave her the words she needed to make her live when she wanted to die. You held her hand when she delivered her child. You will do far less harm if you go than if you stay, and you may do some good. Young Rolli Ragnvalds-son is waiting outside—he will tell you that you must as well."

"You think I would rather listen to that boy than to you?" Solvi asked. "At least let me get dressed first."

"Very well," said Unna. "But then invite us in, and give us the welcome that guests are due."

Solvi splashed water on his face, pulled on his trousers, wrapped his legs to keep out the cold, and then invited in his guests. He spoke the ritual words of welcome as Tova handed them glasses of ale. The wind must be strong today—Rolli's cheeks were pink from it.

"Uncle," he said eagerly, "some spring merchants bring a message from my father telling me to come to Orkney, that my outlawry is ended. My ship is yours to steer if you will go after my cousin and my aunt."

"I cannot," said Solvi. "I would be useless."

"I need you," said Rolli. "I did not go before because I knew what it would look like if I arrived with Ketil Flatnose and Harald's enemies."

"It will look equally bad if you arrive in my company," said Solvi.

"Perhaps," said Rolli, glancing at Unna. "But now I have been invited, and I . . . I don't know if I can make the crossing on my own. Aunt Svan-hild led me here. Before"—he spread his hands—"all this, I had hardly sailed farther than the length of Geiranger Fjord. She taught me some, but she said you could teach me more, and now . . ."

That tugged at Solvi unexpectedly. He and Rolli had little in common, but they were both exiled sons of Tafjord, and left behind by Svan-hild Sea Queen.

"So I can help you sail across the open sea to Orkney," said Solvi.

Rolli nodded. "Yes, and we will rescue my cousin and my aunt to-gether."

Solvi got to his feet and limped across the floor. He did not try to exag-gerate his limp but neither did he try to hide it. Without his cane, his walk had a lurch that almost overbalanced him, so he had to slow to a shuffle.

"What use am I to her if I cannot fight?" he asked.

"You know sea battles," said Rolli.

"It has been so long. What do I still know?" Solvi asked.

"Do you truly think you have forgotten?" Unna's voice was quiet, softer than the wind that rustled the turf of the roof overhead.

Solvi closed his eyes. In his early years here, even after he sold his ship, he had taken a boat out sometimes so he could feel the breeze in his hair, feel free of his shame and fear. He could never forget the balance of wind and his own touch on the steering oar. But he had put it aside when it grew too hard for him to make his way down to the shore and when he knew he would never again cross a great sea, never again see another new land.

"Even if you could do nothing else other than go to her—go to them," said Unna, her voice as gentle as Solvi had ever heard, as gentle and firm as when she talked Freydis through her childbirth, "you must do it. For what else did the fates send you to Iceland than to be here when your daughter arrived? She needs you, and your wife needs you too."

"Even if I die doing it," said Solvi, and though he spoke the words as a protest, he knew they were a promise. "You old carrion crow," he added, with a grin that he had never before turned upon her. The corner of her mouth twitched up, the first sign of humor he had ever seen on her stony face. He wanted, suddenly, to live, to return to Iceland with Svanhild and Freydis, to be husband and father again, and to know Unna as the friend she truly was, but he must face his fear, his shame, and even his death if need be.

"Rolli, you will take me?" Solvi asked.

"As long as you don't plan to fight Harald," said Rolli. "Or my father."

"I cannot fight," said Solvi. "I am only going to try to get my family back. Will that suit you?"

"Of course," said Rolli.

A gust of wind made the candles waver. This kind of spring storm would blow through quickly, and tomorrow would be clear. Solvi still knew the weather and tides like his own heartbeat. "We will leave on tomorrow's noon tide," he said. "Be ready."

✤   ✤   ✤

SOLVI FELT A careful joy, even during the sleepless nights of the long sea crossing to the Orkneys. He had missed sailing even more than he missed his ability to walk without pain—and even the pain in his legs seemed lessened with the give of the ship underneath them.

Rolli asked him many questions about his time as a raider, and Solvi answered them, describing its hardships and delights honestly. He taught Rolli what he could of navigating by sun, stars, and currents, though time itself would be the best teacher. Rolli understood quickly and had a good feel for the steering oar.

The weather too favored them so well Solvi felt suspicious. On a day of strong wind and blinding sun they covered so much distance that Solvi did not trust his reading of the stars the following night, and was only relieved of his worry when he saw the distinctive silhouettes of the Faroe Islands growing before him. They spent a day and a night replenishing their fresh water from one of the many waterfalls that cascaded down the cliffs and then continued to the Orkneys.

He tested his fear, thinking about facing all of his old enemies, Svanhild's anger, swords that he could not defend against, and felt the old tightness in his chest. But it lifted when he looked out at the waves, and felt the deck move under him. Svanhild had been right; he had been wrong to leave this behind. Even if he could not walk at all, he could still sail.

When they reached the Orkney Islands, Solvi sailed cautiously, keeping well away from established settlements, and other ships. Rolli's small ship would be easy prey for either side. Finally, he saw a tiny sailboat such as a fisherman might use, fighting a squall that was trying to push it against a cliff. Perhaps its owner would have helpful information.

He drew Rolli's ship very close to the sailboat, and saw a man slumped over the steering oar, though he shook himself when Rolli threw a rope down to him.

"Falki!" said Rolli after they pulled him up and tied off the boat to Rolli's ship.

"It is good you are here," he said, clasping arms with Rolli and then Solvi. He told them some of what had passed during the battle, that Svanhild, as well as Ragnvald's sons Einar and Ivar, were captive of Thorstein, who was playing both sides against one another, and had sent him to bring a ransom request to Harald. "But I had not slept in a week after our crossing, and this is hard sailing. Now you can take me to Harald at Grimbister."

"I will do no such thing," said Solvi. "Why should I put myself in Harald's hands?"

A shadow blocked out the sun, and Solvi looked up to see Rolli towering over him, with his hand on his sword. "You will," said Rolli. "My father has asked me to come, and he is sure to forgive me if I help him rescue his favorite son." He set his jaw.

Solvi touched the dagger at his belt, little good though it would do him against Rolli. "He may, but I will not forgive you if you draw a sword on me," he said. "You will only be carrying a message that Falki could have carried himself. How will that help you?"

"We don't have enough men to go up against Thorstein," Rolli protested. "Uncle Solvi, you know this is true. You who were once a great sea king must know poor odds when you see them."

"If you put me in your father and Harald's power, they will kill me," said Solvi. "We must find another way."

✦ ✦ ✦

RAGNVALD PACED BACK and forth on the highest point above Grimbister, watching the sea below, straining for a glimpse of the ship that Einar and Ivar had taken out as a lure. Harald was happy with the outcome of the battle against Ketil's forces, with Ketil taken prisoner and most of his men killed. His men grumbled that there were too few opponents, which meant too few spoils of weapons or armor from the corpses of fallen enemies, not enough to compensate them for the effort of having sailed so far. And they were hungry.

Ragnvald had deployed other scouts to other lookout points to watch for his sons or other attackers. It had not been a decisive battle, but perhaps if no other attacks took place, they could call themselves the victors and leave. Halfdan could stay to rule Orkney and deal with any other raiders, and Ragnvald could return to Maer, and begin his old age in earnest.

He walked back down to the hall, the damp grass soaking his boots through. His scouts would tell him if they saw anyone; their young vision was better than his.

"Do not fear," Harald was telling his captains when Ragnvald entered. "Melbrid Tooth, who is also my enemy, has fled for Scotland.

Who knows how much more treasure we may find in his caches when we find him. And Ketil may yet have followers who will ransom him."

Rolli and Svanhild's captain interrupted this celebration, both looking as though they had not slept in a week. Ragnvald rushed forward to greet Rolli, relieved from one worry, at least. Rolli was, if anything, even bigger than when Ragnvald had seen him last. He had surpassed Harald's height, and grown as big as him in the shoulders. Someone must have been feeding him well.

Aldi and a few of his men pressed forward with hands at their swords, but Harald stopped them by handing Rolli a cup of ale.

"My king," said Rolli. "I thank you for lifting my outlawry. I bring vital news."

"What is it?" Ragnvald asked.

"When I came from Iceland, I found Svanhild's captain, Falki, and he told me where Svanhild and my brothers Einar and Ivar are," said Rolli. "They are in danger, unless we go to their aid."

"Tell me," said Ragnvald.

"Terms first," said Rolli. "Solvi Hunthiofsson has come with me to make sure that Svanhild comes to no harm. Now I need you to promise no harm to him either. It is not he who sends raiders to Orkney or the Norse coast. He has sheltered me this past winter, and I have promised him my protection."

"Solvi Hunthiofsson has never needed protection," Ragnvald scoffed.

"He is old and lame now, and he does," said Rolli. "Promise me."

"You would risk your brothers' lives for Solvi's?" Ragnvald asked angrily. "What kind of son are you?"

"One who had been outlawed and had to learn who my true friends are," said Rolli implacably, though worry made him look a boy again. "If you refuse, I will try to rescue my family myself, but it would go better with aid."

Ragnvald looked to Harald, who nodded. "As long as Solvi takes himself back to Iceland," Harald said, "and it is true that he has had no hand in this rebellion, then I will do him no harm. Now where is my wife?"

"I am Falki," said Svanhild's captain. "Thorstein the Red has taken Svanhild Sea Queen and Ragnvald's sons Ivar and Einar captive. His ransom is no less than rulership of the Orkney Islands."

Many voices sounded at once, with Halfdan's loudest, and continued until Harald raised his hand for quiet. Ragnvald hardly heard them. His sons lived.

"Thorstein is an oath breaker, then," said Harald. "He should know how I deal with oath breakers."

"He did not swear an oath," said Harald's son Dagfinn, always the first to correct a mistake. "He refused to."

"No matter," said Harald. "He said he would help defend the islands, and this is not that."

It was, though, Ragnvald thought—he defended them for himself. "Let Thorstein have them," he suggested.

"No," Halfdan yelled. "They are mine. You are always taking what is mine."

"You traded away far more than some remote islands to redeem your sons," said Ragnvald to Harald. "Make this trade and let me have mine."

Aldi had pushed toward the front and was eyeing Rolli, but now he turned his eyes on Ragnvald. "You did not want to trade Sogn for this murderous son of yours, but you will trade away another man's land? You pretend to so much fairness and virtue, but it is all a sham."

Ragnvald put his hand on his sword. "Is it?" he asked. "When you are fighting with swords purchased by taxes from land that should be mine? I paid a fair price for your son, and then some."

"Silence, silence," said Rolli, his voice booming out of his huge chest. Ragnvald felt old and irrelevant next to this huge young man. "Solvi Hunthiofsson has a plan to lure out Thorstein. He will save my brothers' lives and the Orkney Islands for King Harald. He will not come ashore, though—he fears for his life in this company. He will speak with King Ragnvald, no one else."

"How will this be safe?" Harald asked, his voice cutting through all the chatter after Rolli's words.

Much talk followed, and eventually Ragnvald agreed to the terms. He would negotiate with any man to win his sons' lives. Sigurd volunteered to accompany Ragnvald as well.

They were all allowed to keep their weapons, and they rowed against the wind in Falki's little boat, until a small ship appeared as if from behind a curve in the coastline, and one of the crew threw a ladder down. Rolli and Falki climbed up first, followed by Ragnvald, who was glad for Rolli's help over the gunwale. Solvi stood, watching him board, leaning on a cane, his hair gone all to silver. Ragnvald flexed his fingers. He had never felt the passing of the years as much as he did now, looking at Solvi, shrunk and gnarled into an old man. Then Solvi smiled, and Ragnvald's knuckles seemed to ache all the deeper. He had won every time he and Solvi faced one another, but Solvi always left his mark.

"Solvi Hunthiofsson," said Ragnvald. "I am not pleased to put myself in your power again."

Solvi grinned more widely. "I will treat you better this time, I promise. Tell me, how goes battle against Harald's enemies?"

"We have captured Ketil Flatnose and—" Sigurd began, but Ragnvald cut him off.

"Well enough that you would not be living had you landed," he said. "Now what is your plan to save my sons?"

"My wife as well," said Solvi. "I will not let you forget her."

"As she has forgotten me?" Ragnvald asked.

"And my daughter," Solvi continued. "She was taken off by one of Ketil's followers. She must be found. You will swear to it and to this: to let myself, my wife, and my daughter go where we will when battle is done."

"Let me hear your plan," said Ragnvald, "and if I like it, I will swear. You already have me in your power."

34

FREYDIS WAITED CALMLY THROUGH THE DAY OF BATTLE, HELP-ing in the kitchen, tending to some minor ailments. When dinnertime came and went and the men had not returned, she comforted the women who feared for their men's lives, and felt a light touch of regret. She had no doubt that Hallbjorn had perished, along with many of the warriors who had gone with him. They had been growing frustrated with sailing away every morning only to return having spilled no blood. They would be receptive to her advice, voiced by Hallbjorn, to take the fight onto solid ground.

Late in the evening, a few ships straggled back, bringing news of defeat. Melbrid Tooth had escaped with ten of his men. Ogmund Gud-brandsson was calling one of the other men a coward, and Melbrid had to force an apology from him to avoid a duel. The remaining raiders collected their women, supplied their ships, and sailed off again the next morning, planning to return to their halls in Scotland.

Freydis had little time to decide what she would do, for another band of warriors came at noon the next day, bearing one wounded man with a bandage on his face, and another dead with a shroud over his head. They laid them both on pallets near the kitchen.

"These men need healing," a warrior said to the kitchen women. Freydis looked around for the crone Runa, whom she had not seen since her first day on Hoy, and found she was still absent. Freydis stepped for-ward, and motioned for the men to drag the pallets into the light from the cook-fire.

The wounded man was half insensible, keening and whimpering, and kept reaching out toward the dead man. He did not stop his fretting until he was able to link their hands together. Freydis spoke a prayer of peace over the dead man and then pulled the rough bandage from the wounded one. It was Hallbjorn, red-gold hair stained with blood, and his beard close cropped against his sharp jawline.

Freydis drew back. She had done wrong to meddle with the threads of fate if it meant she must now care for an injured Hallbjorn. She should let him die of the fever that would surely come from such a wound.

The man's hand, crusted with blood and dirt, squeezed the gray fingers of his dead companion. Freydis frowned; she had not known that Hallbjorn loved any man enough to reach for him in extremity.

She peeled back the shroud over the dead man's head, and stumbled when she saw a face she recognized. Her cousin Ivar, still handsome, even in death. She could not quite believe it, even though his skin was bluish gray, so she bent close to him, hoping to feel his breath on her cheek. Of all the men she had ever known, Ivar seemed the most firmly tied to life.

Hallbjorn would never cling to Ivar, but his half-brother Einar, wearing nearly the same face, would. Freydis looked again at Einar, the mess of his missing eye, the ragged slash laying open his cheek, and then at the other side, leaner than Hallbjorn's heavier cheek. When she lived at Tafjord she had sighed over his handsome face, and imagined that she loved him. How cruel of the fates, to allow him to survive Ivar's death. Was this the cost of her sending Hallbjorn to his doom?

She could not restore what he had lost, but she could sew up his wound, keep the fever away, and bring him what healing was possible when his sworn brother lay dead next to him. She had brought a small satchel of healing supplies with her from Iceland, including a bone needle and silk thread. She washed Einar's wound with wine and dabbed it gently with fresh cloths. His cheek was hot; she feared infection had already set in.

She tried to give him some spirits to make him insensible to her needle, but he pushed the cup away. She sighed and began, speaking soothing, meaningless words as she brought together the flesh of his forehead and made the small stitches that Alfrith had taught her.

She heard others come in, even heard someone say her name, but she did not turn away from her work. "I will greet you when I am done," she said, and the voices went away again.

Around his eye she could do little—his eyelid had been cut in half, the eye beneath it gone. She began her stitching again as close to his lower lashes as she could, wincing when he flinched with each stab of the needle. She remembered Alfrith telling her how King Ragnvald had hated her for a year after she reset his broken fingers, because he could not look at her without thinking of the pain. If Einar hated her after this, she would deserve it for her part in sending Hallbjorn against him.

She sang a lullaby under her breath and, after a moment, heard Einar's low, broken humming as he tried to match the song. When she finished sewing him up, she made a poultice of honey and cobwebs and applied it to the wound with pine pitch, thanking the goddess Freya that the warriors had not eaten all of it before they went off to die. Sweets would do them little good in Hel's dim kingdom.

Finally, she applied a new bandage over the poultice, and tied it on, cradling his head as she lifted it up to bring the bandage around the back. This time, when she touched Einar's lips with a cup, he parted them and let her give him some spirits to make him sleep. Even when his breathing turned slow and deep, he still clung to Ivar's hand.

Freydis went into the kitchen to find some water to wash Einar's blood off her hands, feeling the dislocation that always gripped her after a difficult task, and there she saw her mother sitting on a stool, eating a hunk of bread and cheese as though she had not been fed in a week. Her hands were bound before her.

"Freydis, I am here," she said. She stood and brushed the crumbs off her skirt as best she could with bound hands. "I bless Thorstein for bringing me here, even if he means me harm."

The tears Freydis had been keeping at bay since Hallbjorn had taken her from Iceland came spilling out in deep sobs. She hastily untied her mother's hands and then clung to her. Svanhild's back shook as though she was crying too.

"Freydis, Freydis, my beloved daughter," she said, stroking Freydis's hair. "I have come for you. I will always come for you."

✦ ✦ ✦

AFTER HEARING SOLVI'S plan, Ragnvald returned to Harald, leaving Sigurd behind as a surety for his return. He outlined Solvi's suggestion: a great charade of ships, performed to draw Thorstein out of Hoy. While Harald sent out his vessels, Falki went back to Thorstein to bait the trap by telling him that Harald's forces were massing against him, but that Melbrid had returned to fight, and if Thorstein joined the battle now, he could defeat Harald and claim Orkney as his own. Harald's ships acted their part, and some captured vessels, crewed by more of Harald's men, pretended to be Melbrid's. As soon as the fleet made it look like the battle was turning against Harald, Thorstein's ship left Hoy, and Solvi guided Rolli's onto the small landing. They all disembarked and began climbing the slope of wet and broken rocks. Scouts might see them, but Thorstein could not have left enough of a force behind to be a real threat.

Ragnvald climbed quickly, and had to stop several times to wait for Solvi to catch up. "You move too slowly," he said to Solvi. Rolli was far ahead, his young legs working faster than either of his elders'. "You should have stayed on the ship."

Ragnvald scrabbled up the slope using his hands, while Solvi had to lean on his cane with every step. He waited again for Solvi to pass him. From behind, Solvi was nothing more than a short, lame, old man. Could Svanhild still want him, rather than Harald? Ragnvald certainly could not fear him any longer, at least not when Solvi faced away from him.

"I could carry you," Rolli suggested to Solvi when he caught up to them again.

Solvi chuckled, a strange sound in this place. "I suppose since I ride that foolish pony, I've no more need for dignity," he said. "Very well, young Rolli, you may be my steed."

Ragnvald watched incredulously as Rolli helped Solvi up onto a rock, then knelt down so he could hoist Solvi onto his back. Sigurd laughed, and the small group of warriors with them joined in. Ragnvald wished he felt easy enough about their mission to enjoy the image his son and his old enemy made together, but instead something about the gentleness of Rolli's movements as he lifted Solvi made Ragnvald's throat tighten. So would Rolli carry his own children one day.

They moved more quickly now, up the broken slope to a well-trod path that led toward a small turf hall. A few goats nosed at the refuse heap near the kitchen side.

"There will be guards," said Ragnvald to Solvi, "and you can't fight."

"I know," said Solvi, clenching his jaw. Ragnvald was glad to hear some frustration in his voice; Solvi was lame and past his usefulness. No man, not even one as lawless as Solvi, could fail to feel shame at that. Ragnvald's hands were still tired from yesterday's battle, but at least they felt like they would obey him today.

"Leave me behind that rock," Solvi suggested, with a sigh, "and Rolli, you come get me when it's safe."

"You should have stayed behind," said Ragnvald again, and again Solvi ignored him.

Solvi hid as the rest of Ragnvald's men advanced toward Thorstein's little turf hall. Rolli loomed behind Ragnvald's right shoulder, and Ragnvald kept wanting to turn, to make sure he gave Ragnvald enough space to move, that he did not run off and do something foolish. Rolli might be big and strong, but he was also young and untried, and his first attempt at battle had been full of mistakes.

They encountered scant resistance until they entered the hall, and then only from a few dagger-wielding men, whom Ragnvald disarmed, causing little more than bruises. A woman came screaming from behind a curtain, swinging a cauldron around her head, and knocked out one of the younger warriors. She went on swinging and screaming until Rolli caught her arms and shook them to make her let go of the pot. It all happened so quickly that Ragnvald's eyes had not yet adjusted to the dimness inside the hall before he saw Falki coming toward him, his hands bound in front of him. Rolli quickly cut his bonds, and went to retrieve Solvi.

"Come this way, my lord," Falki said to Ragnvald. "Your sister and son—sons are here. But beware—greet your sister first, I beg you."

The fear in his voice gave Ragnvald pause, briefly. Svanhild emerged out of the darkness. He had missed her over the winter months—the one woman who had ambition to match his, who had been his right hand for so many years.

But the way she looked wildly around—for Solvi, Ragnvald assumed—saddened him. "He—Solvi—is here," he said. "He rode my son's back to get here." He laughed a little. "Not a sight I had ever thought to see."

"Brother, thank you for coming." She put her arms around him, and hugged him tightly. He accepted her embrace for a moment, then extracted himself.

"Where are my sons?" he asked.

Svanhild glanced at Falki. "They are here," she said. "But first, you must know: Ivar is dead, and Einar is fevered and near death—though he may yet live. I will take you to them."

Ragnvald laughed again. He could not have heard the words correctly.

"Dead?" Sigurd asked.

Now Ragnvald felt as though a frigid rain fell on his skin, numbing where it touched. "Ivar—what? Dead? No. No."

"He is, brother," said Svanhild.

"Dead—how?" Ragnvald asked. "Did Thorstein kill him?"

"In battle," said Svanhild. "He was already gone when I found him."

"But Falki . . . ," said Ragnvald. Only a small part of him was here, in this dim turf hall with the roots of grass furring the ceiling just above his head. The rest had fled from her words, inward to a cold and barren place.

"Let me take you to them," Svanhild was saying from somewhere far away. "My daughter, Freydis, has been tending Einar. She is an excellent healer."

"Can she heal the dead?" Ragnvald asked dully. He pushed past Svanhild, toward a shadowed chamber in this barrow of a hall. He could make out only forms until Svanhild joined him with a lantern, and then he saw Einar, lying motionless, one side of his face covered in a bandage, and the other blank. His eye was open and staring at the ceiling, as though he were already a corpse, like the form that lay shrouded on the pallet next to his. Ragnvald smelled the sweet, terrible scent of death.

"I want to see him," he said. His voice sounded far away to his own ears, as though it came from out of the land of the dead.

Svanhild walked over to the body, and pulled back the shroud covering its face. It was Ivar, his face ashen in death, shades of blue and gray above the black of the wound on his neck. By his side Einar, even with his bandage and illness, looked obscenely alive, a mockery of the still, dead young man next to him.

Svanhild covered Ivar's face again, and Ragnvald stumbled forward, and tripped, falling to his knees. He touched the stiff, clay body of his son. Svanhild stood next to him, cradling his head against her waist. Her hard hip bone dug into his arm. She had none of the softness that a woman should, denying him the comfort he needed to sob out his grief like a child, even if it could cross the vast, wintry emptiness that lay within him.

"Father . . . ," he heard Einar say. His eye opened and closed, and he looked around. "Father, I am sorry."

"Did you do this?" Ragnvald asked. He came back to his feet and looked down at Einar, at the sweating, stinking bandages. What was underneath that? Would he be turned into a creature of death, a horror to look upon?

"You told me to protect him," said Einar, staring up at the ceiling again. "I would have gone with him if I could."

Ragnvald's chill threatened to consume him. "You should have," he said hollowly. He pushed past Svanhild and back out into the main body of the hall. There Falki was drinking a cup of ale by the fire with Sigurd, Solvi, and Rolli.

"You," said Ragnvald to Falki, putting his hand to his sword. "You told me my sons were here."

"And so they were," said Falki, rising.

Ragnvald drew his sword and lunged at Falki. Something caught his arms, a god's own strength holding him in place.

"What are you doing, Father?" he heard Rolli ask.

"He lied to me," said Ragnvald, struggling against Rolli's grip. Falki's eyes were wide with terror and he pressed himself back against the turf wall by the fireplace. "He told me my sons were here. But I have no sons here. There is a dead body and a young man who has betrayed me for the last time."

Falki looked wildly at Svanhild. "I thought King Ragnvald might not come for you and his elder son," he said. "I let him think . . ."

Ragnvald tried again to free himself from Rolli's grip. "You lied," he cried. "My sons are dead." He tried to look at Rolli. "And they betray me. I am surrounded by traitors."

"Brother, you are not yourself," said Svanhild coolly. "Lay down your sword."

Rolli's hand tightened on Ragnvald's wrist, making his hand grow so numb he had no choice but to let his sword clatter to the ground.

Svanhild put her arms around him. The cold inside Ragnvald seemed to have a crack, the same one that the anger at Falki had come through, and now a flood would pour out if Ragnvald let it. Should he give vent to his grief and anger in tears instead of violence? He felt something at his wrists, and Rolli again holding him still. Before he could resist, Solvi had bound his hands behind him and Rolli pushed him to the ground.

"What are you doing?" Ragnvald asked, looking up at Svanhild.

"I will let you do no more harm until you have come to yourself again," she said.

"I think he is better now," said Rolli uncomfortably while Ragnvald struggled against his bonds.

"I do not," said Svanhild. "I lost a son too once. So did my husband. And neither of us attempted murder because of it. Leave him bound."

35

RAGNVALD DID NOT RESIST AS ROLLI WALKED HIM OUT TO THE ship. He wondered what would happen if he lay down and refused to move like a recalcitrant toddler—would Rolli carry him, as he had Solvi? Svanhild was the one who helped Solvi down the steep slope this time. Then Ragnvald waited in the ship with Solvi while Svanhild, Rolli, and some of their crew went to move Einar and finally Ivar's body.

"Do you want to be near him?" Svanhild asked Ragnvald, tenderness and anger warring in her voice. Rolli carried the body of his brother in his arms, as a man might carry a woman he loved, or an injured child.

Ragnvald nodded. He did not trust himself to speak. Rolli placed Ivar, wrapped in a thin, homespun shroud, on the bench next to him. Einar lay on another bench, staring up at the sky. Ragnvald could not bear to look at Ivar's covered form, and when his gaze landed on Einar it gave him almost as much pain. Einar had not come back from that battle any more than Ivar had. Some half-dead creature, like the *draugr* Ragnvald had once faced, lay there in his son's stead.

As soon as they landed at Grimbister, Harald's warriors surrounded the small ship and pulled its passengers onto the beach. Someone cut Ragnvald free from his bonds, while warriors surrounded Solvi and Svanhild, and separated them.

Up in Thorstein's hall, Harald was already fuming when Ragnvald's party arrived. "Thorstein escaped us—south to Scotland with Melbrid Tooth. His turn will come," he said.

His anger seemed strange to Ragnvald, a hot anger, compared with the coldness Ragnvald felt. "Your men told me what happened," Harald said. "Your son and your own sister took you prisoner. They will pay for this."

Ragnvald only looked at him, wishing he could feel what Harald wished him to.

"Your son Rolli is outlawed again for the full term of seven years," Harald added. "I never should have rescinded that. He has no loyalty and no honor."

Rolli threw off the men who held him with a shrug. "I wanted to save my father's honor," said Rolli. "Father, would you have rather murdered an innocent man?"

Ragnvald stared at him mutely. He saw Ivar's dead features on Rolli's face.

Harald stalked forward. "And my former wife—Solvi promised that he came in peace, but now I find his oath broken. Your sister, Svanhild, is a traitor and she should die with him," he continued. "You have put up with enough from her."

"You speak of oaths?" Svanhild asked Harald contemptuously. "You break oath after oath and now you would kill the mother of your children?"

Ragnvald watched as if at a dumb show. Harald hated to be called oath breaker, and this brought him up short. "True, I have never yet killed any of my sons' mothers," he said, "no matter how much they tempted me, but perhaps I should start."

Ragnvald shrugged. What did it matter if Harald killed Svanhild? Ivar was dead. But the habit of defending her was too strong, and Harald was already backing down in the face of Svanhild's anger.

"You divorced her," he said dully. "If you were not king of Norway, her kin would have punished you for that insult."

"You said it was the only way," said Harald. "You said you would convince her."

"I was wrong," said Ragnvald, still in the same empty voice. "You may be above the laws of Norway, but you are not above the laws of shame and honor."

Harald put his hand to his sword. "You agree with her?" he yelled. "With this traitorous woman? I will not allow any man to speak to me this way."

"If you mean to kill her, then do it," said Ragnvald. He sat down on a bench, and turned his head away. The knowledge of Ivar's death was a pit inside his chest, a void as great as the emptiness before creation. "And kill me too. Your mother said I would sacrifice greatly for you, and I am ready."

"You are my dearest friend," said Harald, sounding shaken. "You speak in pain and anger. I will not kill you. I swear it."

"I have sworn to let Svanhild and her Solvi go," he said. "They have nothing to do with this battle, except to save their daughter from it."

Harald clenched his jaw. "If she swears never to return to Norway, she may live. Outlawed, she may live."

"I swear it," said Svanhild. "And though you may not trust the oath of a woman, any man in Norway can tell you that mine is good."

Harald made a dismissive gesture. "You are outlawed from Norway for the rest of your life. You have lived as a man and you will die as a man if you set foot on Norway's shores again."

Harald's men parted from around Solvi, and Svanhild walked over to him. He took her arm and limped with her toward the door. Svanhild looked back at Ragnvald, her eyes haunted.

The hall grew loud as men argued over Harald's decision, but Harald did not mind doubt from others as he did from Ragnvald. Some tried to speak with Ragnvald. He ignored the fingers clutching at his sleeves, the faces he hardly recognized that appeared before his own, and when they gave up and went away, he shuffled out into the drizzly wet of an Orkney afternoon.

He did not know where they intended to put Ivar now that he was dead. Into the water, to let the sea goddess Ran have him, as she should have had Ragnvald all those years ago? Ran was a greedy goddess, and she would take them both in time. If Ragnvald had given himself to her when she asked before, he would have been spared all of this.

He walked down to the harbor, where the waves rocked the pebbles back and forth, scraping them against one another. He wanted to claw at his own throat to let out the pain that built there. Where had Einar been when his brother fell? Not defending him, or he would be dead too. Never before had Einar let his brother go anywhere ahead of him.

He did not know how long he sat there. Sometime later he heard footsteps behind him and looked up to see Rolli helping Solvi slowly down the steep slope. Oddi, wide of belly and shoulder, climbed down after him.

"Brother," said Svanhild, "Oddi spoke for me to Harald. I have been allowed to stay for the funeral of my nephew."

Oddi met Ragnvald's eyes. "Harald will not lift Rolli's outlawry unless you speak with him," he said.

"Father," said Rolli. "I am saddened by Ivar's death as well."

His open face showed the marks of grief: red eyes, and tears upon his pink and boyish cheeks. An easy grief that Ragnvald envied. "You do not know how I feel," he said. "You were against me. You were all against me."

Rolli looked as though he might begin crying in earnest. "You will let him do it then? You will let Harald outlaw me again?"

Ragnvald shrugged. He did not care.

Rolli squared his shoulders. "Without me, you could not have saved Svanhild or Einar. Even now my cousin Freydis tends to Einar and says that he will live. Surely that is worth something."

"No," said Ragnvald. "It is worth nothing."

"I will take Svanhild and Solvi away then, and stay away forever," said Rolli. "If my mother hates you for what you've done, then send her to me, and I will care for her."

"Ragnvald. Brother," said Oddi. "Reconsider this."

"You told me long ago that you were no longer my brother," said Ragnvald. "Do not claim it now."

"Your son Einar lives, though he is wounded," said Oddi. "Come and see him."

"He should not," said Ragnvald. "He should have gone with Ivar, as he swore. I am surrounded by oath breakers."

And Ivar would lie here, in this water, or buried on this rock. He would never rule Maer now; that would go to Thorir. Ragnvald had only lesser sons remaining.

"Do you mean to follow Ivar into death?" Oddi asked.

For a moment it seemed like a perfect solution, but no. He still had Maer. Thorir must inherit. He had revenge to take. If not on Falki, who had only been trying to serve Svanhild, then on someone else, on everyone who had a hand in this. Others must feel what he felt now.

"Will you go to see Einar?" Svanhild asked. "The women of Orkney will care for Ivar. It is their duty. He will find the best of heavens."

Something in Ragnvald broke open on the word *heavens*, and he cried out.

"You must see Einar," Oddi said. "You still have sons who need you."

"How bad is Einar's wound?" Ragnvald asked.

"My daughter is a skilled healer," Svanhild said. "He lost his eye, but if he avoids infection, he will live."

Einar living, and Ivar dead. Einar's face forever marred, Ivar's to decay. The fates were too cruel. Ragnvald allowed Oddi to help him stand and followed Svanhild back up the hill.

Einar lay on a pallet in Thorstein's hall with the other wounded. Young Freydis sat by his side, singing to him gently. His bandage had been changed, Ragnvald noted, and he was propped up on some pillows.

Freydis rose when she saw him, and cast her eyes down. A deferential girl, so different from her mother. "King Ragnvald," she said. "Your son's fever is breaking."

Einar did look somewhat better. The side of his face that Ragnvald could see was still lean and handsome. And living. Wrongly, horribly living, when his brother was dead. Ragnvald's grief threatened to overwhelm him again.

"You were supposed to protect your brother," he said in a choked voice.

Freydis moved sharply toward Einar as if to protect him, but Einar laid his hand on her arm, and she pulled away, so Ragnvald could come closer.

"I'm sorry, Father," said Einar. He looked over at Ragnvald then back at the ceiling. He raised his hand to the missing eye and opened his mouth, soundlessly, an expression of pain that tore at Ragnvald's insides.

"You swore," Ragnvald said. "You swore to protect him. Why did you fail?"

"Ragnvald, my friend, he took this wound trying to protect Ivar," said Oddi.

"Get out," said Ragnvald. "I will not hear you defend him. Why do you live? Why?" A part of him wanted to cradle Einar as though he were still a child who might accept such a thing.

"I am so sorry, Father. We were surrounded—Geirbjorn's warriors all over the ship. I killed so many I don't remember, and Ivar was fighting three at once—I was trying to help him when Geirbjorn dealt him the wound that killed him. And then I killed him, but his blow . . . I fell. I was too late to protect him. Ivar . . ."

"You had only one purpose, and that was to protect him," said Ragnvald. "You swore. You swore."

"We swore," said Einar. "We swore that we would never go into battle without one another. I swore to protect him."

"With your dying breath, you said. And yet you live."

"Should I die, Father? Would you kill me now? I do not want to live without him either." His voice held too much bitterness for such a young man, even a young man who had bedded a queen and killed many men. "Kill me or forgive me, Father. I would rather have died than him."

"Do not call me 'Father.' You have failed in your duties as a son, and so you are no longer mine," said Ragnvald, and now he was crying too. "You swore. You swore."

"You separated us first," said Einar, half to himself.

"What did you say?" Ragnvald asked, almost grateful—Einar's words had brought back the cold emptiness that could freeze these tears.

"You left me in Vestfold without him. You caused me to break my oath first."

"You blame me for this?"

"No, I blame myself," said Einar. "And I blame Ivar for letting himself get killed. I blame Geirbjorn Hakonsson. I blame King Harald for attacking here—what is Orkney to him? I blame Aunt Svanhild for leaving him and pricking his pride, and I blame you for not talking him out of it."

"So you do blame me," said Ragnvald.

"What good does blame do, Father? Or what shall I call you now? King Ragnvald? Go away and let me heal or die. If you are not my father, then I am not your son, and I will no longer do your bidding."

He rolled over and turned away, his back shaking like a boy's. Ragnvald stumbled out of the hall. It was a gray day, clouds moving swiftly overhead, gray on gray on gray, with moisture in the air, cooling his hot cheeks. No matter what Oddi said, Einar should have died with his brother. It was the fates who had done wrong in saving him.

⁜　⁜　⁜

WHEN RAGNVALD LEFT, Freydis's child erupted into great, desperate screams, so loud and angry that Einar felt jealous. He would scream like that if he could, at his father, at the fates, at Geirbjorn Hakonsson, who had, Einar supposed, finally exacted his vengeance for the death of his own father from Ragnvald's scheming.

Einar heard people milling around, but missing one eye and with a great bandage over his face, half the room was blank to him. Svanhild walked around to his seeing side and took his hand.

"Einar," she said gently, "your brother will be buried tomorrow, and then I will leave. Do you want to come with me to Iceland? I will always have room for my family there."

Einar ignored her.

She squeezed his hand, and then let it go. "I cannot stay past the funeral. But remember my offer. There is a place for you in Iceland."

She departed with Rolli, leaving only Oddi, and Freydis, who sat down in her chair by his side.

"He didn't mean it," said Oddi. "Your father. He loves you."

Einar did not answer him either.

"He's in pain. He didn't mean it," Oddi continued.

"He did," said Einar. "He says nothing he does not mean, nothing that is not true."

"No," said Oddi. "He is not such a paragon as that. And this is not true. This is not your fault. Are you a god, who should prevent every death?"

"My task was to protect Ivar, and I did not. I should have died protecting him, and I did not. Can you deny that?" Einar asked.

"Yes, I can," said Oddi. "You cannot control fate. And you are not a slave to die for your brother on his pyre, so do not think of it."

"He will not be burned," said Einar.

"Then to die with him. That is not your fate, to be buried next to him."

"I broke my oath," Einar insisted.

"You were both fighting off your enemies when he died. You should think of avenging him now," said Oddi.

Einar opened and closed his sword hand. What vengeance could he take when he had already killed Geirbjorn Hakonsson?

Oddi sat with him for a while longer, and then left when his stomach began to growl, leaving Einar alone with Freydis. She stayed by him, as she had since Hoy, sometimes singing to her daughter, sometimes giving him broth by the spoonful. Once he caught the names "Diarmuid" and

"Grainne" in her song, and tears had come that burned his missing eye, causing salty blood to leak from the wound. He thought of Gyda, also red-gold and pale, like Freydis. She would never call him beautiful now.

Freydis lay in a pallet next to Einar's as he tried to sleep, waking to give him watered ale when he coughed. He had not felt the peace of sleep since his wound, only fevered unconsciousness and painful waking, but he must have fallen asleep this night, for when he woke, Freydis and her daughter were gone.

Einar sat up. His head spun, and his wound throbbed from the unaccustomed movement, but that subsided after he sat still for a moment. He found his shoes and tied them on. Standing brought the same rush, and he stumbled over to the door, where he could lean on the lintel until the dizziness passed.

Outside, it looked to be past midnight. Low clouds made the island's hills seem draped in shrouds. Near the top of the slope, light shone from a small hovel. Einar climbed toward it, though he had to stop and catch his breath every few steps. He had lain too long abed.

The door to the hovel was open, and when Einar drew close he saw that within, on a wooden table, lay a body—Ivar. An old woman sat on a stool, spinning out gray wool into a fine thread that would make the winding cloth for the next visitor to this hut. Einar stepped closer. Ivar wore the breastplate of the leather armor that would be buried with him. Freydis was there, combing back his hair and braiding it into a warrior's braids, neater than a man would ever manage himself. Einar watched the movement of her hands, transfixed.

When she was done braiding, she picked up one of his wrist-guards, the same that Einar had tightened onto Ivar when he was living, and raised Ivar's forearm to put it around his wrist. The tenderness of her touch brought tears to his eyes. He wished that this was a man's task, so he could do this last service for his brother, but no, this was women's magic, and he intruded even by watching.

Freydis raised her head, and Einar shrank away, back into the night's dimness. Tears blinded him even in his good eye. He scrambled upward until he came to the crest of the hill, then rested for a moment, blinked to clear his vision, and walked down to the cliff's edge. He stood above the very water where he had failed to protect Ivar.

The clouds had lifted enough that the other islands were visible in the distance, dark gray in the predawn light, against the soft, pure blue of the sky. The air smelled of sod and wildflowers. The breeze had a light touch as well, teasing Einar with pleasure when all he wished to feel was pain. The rocks at the cliff's foot beckoned. If he found his death upon them, he could lie next to Ivar. Though perhaps his father would not even allow him that.

Einar heard the noises that Freydis's daughter made when she was happy and well fed, a familiar and comforting sound. He turned to see Freydis standing a few paces behind him, with her daughter strapped to her chest.

"Einar," she said quietly. "I am glad you are well enough to walk about."

The calm beauty of her face made him want to cry again. "Why did you come?" he whispered. "I meant to join him, here where he died. I will—I am going to."

"Why?" Freydis asked.

"What have I left to do?" Einar asked. "I have no father, no brother, no land, nothing."

"I am sorry," said Freydis. "You have lost too much, and you did not deserve your father's cruelty on top of that."

"But I did," said Einar. He turned away from her again and looked out over the water. He tensed, ready to jump, but Freydis moved quickly, to close the distance between them and put her hand lightly on his arm. She did not use enough force to hold him if he did decide to fly, but her touch still stopped him for a moment.

"I sought death too, very recently," she said, speaking hardly above a whisper. "I was pregnant and alone in Iceland, far from everything I knew, with a man who wanted to use me, and a father who did not know me. Spoiled for marriage with all but the man who had taken me. Fearing death in childbirth."

"My brother Hallbjorn did that," said Einar bitterly. "My blood is tainted, as my father always said."

Freydis shook her head. "I tried to rid myself of the pregnancy and failed, and it seemed like I had no hope left," she said. "So I tried to die."

Did she mean that it was womanish to think of ending his life? Not so—warriors sometimes killed themselves when they could no longer fight, seeking a more courageous death than one from old age and infirmity.

"Men, women, we are all weak sometimes," Freydis said more harshly. "Your father is weak, letting grief and anger rule him."

Did she now call him weak? Perhaps she was right.

"Then I found in Iceland that I was not as alone as I feared," Freydis continued, "and the people who reminded me of that are the ones who saved me." She gripped his arm more tightly. "You are not alone. You still have brothers who would value you by their side. You have friends. And you have me. I would stay by your side for the rest of my life if you would have me."

"I?" Einar laughed hollowly. This gentle, beautiful girl wanted him? Now that he was ugly, scarred, disowned, no woman should want him. "I, who am too much of a coward to jump?"

"You," said Freydis. "Who are strong enough to live, to stand by those who still need you." She sighed. "And to take your revenge, if you must. Come back with me. Do not add to everyone's grief by dying. Instead, stay to comfort us."

Einar gave one last look at the water, and then turned to put it to his back. He could still feel the cliff behind him, the escape it promised, but it would still be there tomorrow, and then he need not force Freydis to witness his death.

"Little Freydis—who are you to say these things to me?" he whispered.

"I am Freydis Solvisdatter, now with a daughter of my own. The woman whose stitches are still in your face. I have known you a long time, and I know you are more than Ragnvald's son, and more than merely a handsome face. I worked hard to save you," she said. "Do not throw it away."

"Svanhild Sea Queen's daughter," said Einar, with a slight smile that pulled at those stitches. "You are not much like her."

Freydis bent her head down over her daughter, Thordis, who was now sleeping. "I am like her enough," she replied.

36

THE NEXT DAY, THE DAY OF IVAR'S FUNERAL, WAS AS BEAUTI-
ful a day as Einar had ever seen in the Orkney Islands, marred by only
a few high, puffy clouds in the distance. Ivar would have loved this
weather; he would have wanted to ride their horses to the one broad
field near Tafjord where they could go for a good gallop, forgetting that
Einar's horse was barely capable of that gait. Now he lay wrapped in a
shroud next to the pile of earth that Einar had helped make.

Oddi had come to wake Einar not long after he returned from the
cliff with Freydis, and he went out with his godfather to help make Ivar's
mound, on this hill. Many of Ragnvald's warriors came to help, for Ivar
had been much loved.

A man had handed him the long tool that Orkneymen used for cutting
turf, so Einar could be the one to chisel the first square. He lifted it out,
a whole mat of grass, bound together by its roots. He later dug with the
spade that Oddi put in his grip, and then with his hands when someone
took it away from him. Finally, his wound began to weep from the exertion, and Oddi led him away and bade him sit down and drink some ale.

By the time the mound was ready, and Ivar's body brought, Einar
felt light-headed. The ale sloshed around unpleasantly in his stomach, as
though his body rejected anything of the living world. He had tried to
eat some of the bland porridge from the bowl that Oddi thrust into his
hands, but every swallow tugged at his injured face. The texture of the
wet cereal made him think of the jelly inside a man's eye, and his stomach rebelled. He thrust his bowl away, into the hands of a serving girl.

With a helmet pulled down over the fine braids Freydis had made, Ivar looked no different from any other fallen warrior. Broader in the shoulder, perhaps, with good proportions. Einar had already been tricked by another man in the corner of his eye who, for an instant, moved like Ivar had, and the leap of joy in his chest was more punishment than anything else he had yet endured.

His father had arrived when the digging was half done. He would not look at Einar, who tried to avoid glancing at him as well, in case their eyes should meet and his father look away, rejecting him again. Einar had decided to live, or at least not die today, but he did not know what he would do tomorrow.

Last night Freydis had offered to stay with him—was she expecting marriage? Perhaps he owed that to her for her care, and to settle the debt that his half-brother Hallbjorn had incurred by making her pregnant. Save for a few weeks in Vestfold, he had lived his life entirely with Ivar. What would his life look like alone? All he knew was that he would never be welcome in Maer again, not after his father's words.

His father led funeral prayers, his voice cracking, and tears upon his cheeks. Rolli cried too, his nose and eyes red like a boy's. Tears burned fiercely from Einar's missing eye.

Harald's skald spoke a short verse about how Ivar had bravely attacked a ship full of his enemies, and would surely be among Odin Alfather's most valued warriors in Valhalla.

Einar, half unthinking, stepped forward next. He recited, diffidently, his voice thick:

> *My brother lies here dead,*
> *The son of Half-Drowned gone.*
> *The ravens will starve with*
> *His sword forever stilled.*
> *The steeds of the bright sea*
> *Will carry him no more.*
> *His sword, forever dulled,*
> *Must rust in treeless ground.*
> *Son of mighty Half-Drowned,*
> *Tell Odin of your deeds,*
> *Of those who now half-live,*
> *And wait to feast with thee.*

Men nodded their appreciation when Einar finished, touching his shoulders as he returned to his place among the mourners. It was not good poetry, and his father would surely hate it. Einar dared a look at him, and saw him staring fixedly at the mound of dirt that now enclosed his son.

Harald led a procession of men, each of whom laid a block of turf back over the top of the mound, filling in the places between with packed dirt. In a season, it would be covered entirely by grass, and no longer have fissures running through it. Time heals, Einar supposed he should think. But time would not bring back his brother, or his eye.

"We will drink and toast our fallen comrades tonight," said Harald. "And tomorrow we will take the fight to Scotland to root out more of these raiders. None of them will threaten Norway again."

The cheer that greeted his words surprised Einar. He did not desire any more revenge for Ivar's death. The only death he desired was his own. Freydis had stopped him last night, but an arrow could still find him, a sword cut, shipwreck. He could not believe the gods would keep him separated from Ivar for long.

At the funeral feast Einar, without thinking, took his accustomed place among Harald's sons—his first feast without Ivar. How many other feasts, how many other firsts, must follow this?

He raised his glass for toasts when they were called, ate little of what was put on his trencher, and hardly spoke even when spoken to. Harald's chief skald recited a tale of a warrior that one of Odin's Valkyries had loved too much and carried up from battle to be her groom. A compliment to Ivar—unheeded by Ragnvald, who sat picking at his food next to Harald.

Harald rose after the skald's tale and raised his cup. "Ragnvald Eysteinsson—he has been called Wise, and Mighty, and he is both. My truest friend who, it has been prophesied, will sacrifice much for me. But I will not let his sacrifices go unrewarded. Ragnvald of Maer, you may now call yourself Ragnvald of the Orkney Islands. These lands and all of their incomes are yours, my friend."

Halfdan let out an indignant shout and lowered his glass. "Father, you promised Orkney to me," he said. "What has King Ragnvald done to deserve it except question your wisdom?"

"As you are doing now?" Harald replied. "When you have sacrificed as much for me as my friend Ragnvald has, then you may question me as he does."

"My king does me too much honor," said Ragnvald. His voice did not have its usual strength, but its quiet made the rest of the hall grow still. "I fear you have given me too many responsibilities."

Halfdan looked hopeful for a moment. Then Ragnvald looked directly at him, and said, "I will give this land to Sigurd Olafsson, my stepbrother who has been as loyal as any brother could be. Rule this place, Sigurd, and let your sons inherit when you are gone."

The murmur among the warriors sounded displeased. Ragnvald had refused an honor from his king, and had not returned the islands to Halfdan. Father and son both wore identical, offended expressions.

Harald recovered more quickly. "Of course," he said. "Sigurd has been an able captain. This elevation suits him." He raised a toast that his sons echoed halfheartedly.

Even Sigurd did not look happy. He must know that Ragnvald had made enemies for him this night.

✣   ✣   ✣

EINAR LEFT THE feast early and went to sleep on his usual pallet long before the drinking was done. He woke in the morning and saw that the pallet where Freydis slept was empty.

He would have liked to see her this morning, her sharp, wary face softened by looking down at her child. Had she looked that way when she had offered to stay with him? He had been too wrapped up in his pain even to turn and face her. What could he offer a woman, any woman? He might not even be able to fight without his right eye.

He stood up and turned in a circle to make sure she was not hiding on his blind side, but the chamber was empty. He heard the sounds of women moving in the kitchen, and the voices of a few men flirting with them, talking to one another about the coming battle. His stomach growled. He tried not to think of Ivar and of the ruin of his own face, which he had still not seen—mirrors and still water were scarce on these remote islands—but his hunger refused to obey him. His body wanted to live, even if his spirit rebelled.

He begged a slice of bread with cheese and honey from the kitchen, and went outside. The last of Harald's warriors were emerging from their tents. Their eyes seemed to slide off him when they looked in his direction. No one wanted to be too close to the son that Ragnvald the Mighty had rejected.

Just around the curve of the building Einar heard his father, Sigurd, and King Harald arguing.

"You gave these islands to me," said Ragnvald. "Now they are mine to do with what I wish."

"I gave them to you," said Harald. "And you threw the gift in my face."

"Giving their rulership and income to my loyal brother is throwing them away?" Ragnvald asked. He sounded reckless in a way Einar had never heard before, not even on the beach in Skane when Svanhild left, and Harald took Sogn from him. He did not seem to care what damage he did to himself or others.

"No," said Harald, after a long pause. "I did give these islands to you, to do with what you wish."

"Good," said Ragnvald, a sneer in his voice. "You are a just king, who would never take back a gift."

Einar remembered his mother's words, heard them almost as if she had spoken them again in his ear. "Your father's fate is coming for him," she had said. "I will not need to compass his death." Ragnvald would not live long beyond the death of his friendship with Harald. If he could not see that, then he had never deserved the byname "Wise."

Harald's captains called him away, wanting to plan their attack on Scotland. Some of their prisoners had given up the locations of Melbrid's favorite camps in return for their lives.

Einar turned to leave when Harald did. He did not want to see his father. But Sigurd caught up to him on his blind side and startled him, saying, "Einar, nephew, I wanted to see you."

"And I to see you," said Einar dryly. He hated how unbalanced his altered field of vision made him feel. "Or the half of you I can still see."

Sigurd laughed at the joke. "What do you mean to do?" he asked.

"You mean now that my father has disowned me?" Einar asked. "I am a man with no family and only half my sight. I do not know if I will be able to fight, and without that, I have no use."

"Your father did not mean—" Sigurd began.

"Oh, but he did," said Einar.

"I wanted to ask you to stay here, in Orkney, with me," said Sigurd.

Something loosened in Einar's chest that had felt constricted since Ivar's death. "Did my father tell you to do this?" he asked.

For a moment, Sigurd looked as though he wanted to be able to answer his hope, but then bit his lip and shook his head. "No, it was Oddi's idea, and I thought it wise. I am a simple man, and I need someone clever by my side. You are as wise as my brother—wiser now, perhaps, than he is being. You will see trouble before it comes."

"Even with only one eye?" Einar asked.

Sigurd gave him a pleading, hesitant smile. "Stay," he said. "You will have a place here."

The Hordaland witch had been wrong predicting that Einar's prospects would grow with Ivar's death. Before Ivar's death he had been best friend and adviser to the next king of Sogn. Now he would be nephew and adviser to the Orkney jarl. But he would have a place, a place better than a farm in Iceland, better than he deserved for breaking his oath to Ivar.

"What will my father think?" Einar asked, his voice breaking.

"I do not think Ragnvald is thinking or planning anything right now," said Sigurd. "I am not sure if he knows what he does. Perhaps I should give the islands back to Halfdan—he was promised them. But then I think that would anger him more."

So a slave might speak of a capricious master—was that what they were, slaves to his father's moods and whims? Einar had never thought of his father as a tyrant before, only a just ruler and father, hard but fair.

"Will you do it?" Sigurd asked. "Will you stay here?"

He could travel with Harald's army to Scotland and see if he could find a way to die on a Scottish viking's sword. He could make his way back to Vestfold—his mother would surely push Guthorm to give him a place among his warriors. But Sigurd needed him. And perhaps here he could make a home for himself and Freydis.

"I will think on it," said Einar. It did feel good to be asked, just as Freydis's declaration had felt good. He had been used to admiration and feared that the knife that cut open his face had sliced away everything praiseworthy about him.

Einar was still thinking of Freydis as he walked down toward the water. On the shore below, figures were loading a small ship. One had bright bleached hair and was larger than the others—Rolli. Freydis stood next to her father, who was as short as the legends said, but with a keen intelligence in his face that drew the eye.

Freydis had her daughter tied across her chest, the weight tilting her hips forward. She was watching sailors pack the ship, her own bag sitting next to her on a rock. Einar willed her to turn her gaze to him, and she did, meeting his eye for a moment, until her pale skin became tinged with pink, and she bowed her head down toward her daughter instead.

Einar descended to the beach, where Svanhild greeted him. "How much longer must you wear that bandage?" she asked.

Einar looked at Freydis for an answer.

"It is healing well," she said. "I think the poultice of honey and herbs is keeping it from becoming infected. A few more days at most."

"Solvi and I cannot remain here much longer," said Svanhild. "We will leave on the next tide."

Einar turned to Freydis. "Are you going with them?" he asked.

Freydis nodded.

"Was it a lie then, the other night?" he asked crossly. "To keep me from the cliff?"

"What if it was?" Freydis replied. Her face went red, but she held Einar's gaze. "It would have been a good lie, since it worked."

"I should have known," said Einar. "What could you want with a man with no future?"

"You did not answer me," she cried.

Her hurt made him feel protective. "I did not," said Einar, more gently. Her words had kept him from a shameful death. "I can offer you little, but . . ."

"Are you offering marriage to my daughter?" Solvi asked, looking stern.

"Yes," he said, before he could think of all the reasons not to. "She has been kind to me, and I want to be the father to my half-brother's daughter, since he cannot. There is no one to ask for her hand but me—my father will not do it, nor will he care."

Solvi gave Einar a challenging smile, though it turned fond when his gaze touched Freydis. "I am a simple farmer now," he said. "I can do nothing for your prospects."

"Sigurd Olafsson, jarl of Orkney, has offered me a place here," said

Einar. "I will not be wealthy, but a wife of mine will not starve. I am told it is not hard to cut turf and make a house here."

Solvi nodded. "I have sworn that Freydis shall follow the path she wishes," he said. "Daughter, do you want to stay with this man? To follow him into battle when his lord requires it, or to live in turf with him here?"

"Yes," said Freydis. She gave Einar a look that made him feel shy and afraid. She cared for him, more than he deserved, and while he liked her comfort and valued her healing, he feared that she would find ashes where she wanted affection. Still, he did not want to watch her sail away, never to see her again or feel the touch of her cool fingers on his heated skin.

"We must still leave on the next tide," said Svanhild.

"They can marry now," said Solvi. "I know the words, and we can spare some ale to make the toasts. Rolli may be a little thirsty on the voyage, but he will live."

Rolli glanced up the hill. "If you wish, I will go and bring Father," he said.

Einar met his eyes with some difficulty. "Who I marry is no longer his concern."

So they were married there on the shore. Svanhild held Thordis while Solvi made the blessings. Freydis was taller than her parents, and though not as beautiful as Gyda, she had similar coloring, and a similar sharpness to her features. And she seemed to desire him as a husband, perhaps even love him, which Gyda never had.

"I don't know what is to come," said Einar after Svanhild's sailors toasted them. "But you will not starve. I promise that I will starve before you do."

"No one knows what is to come," said Freydis. "We are in the hands of the fates."

✛   ✛   ✛

SVANHILD STOOD NEXT to Solvi as they watched Einar and Freydis climb back up toward the Grimbister hall. Einar climbed slowly, still weak from his wound, and Freydis turned toward him every few steps. Svanhild feared for her daughter, still so young, and wed to a man who had been so wounded inside and out. But Freydis was stronger and wiser than Svanhild had any right to expect.

Solvi put his arm around her waist. "Where do we go, then?" he asked. "You have given away our land."

"I was angry," said Svanhild. "As well I might have been. You should have come. If you blame me for leaving you, when I went after our daughter . . ."

"Of course not," he said. "I do not. I blame myself for not going with you. It took Unna and young Rolli to force my hand. Even now I am ashamed that my pride kept me away."

Rolli shifted from one foot to the other. "It is well he waited," he said. "If he hadn't, I could not have come. But then . . ."

Svanhild held out her hand to Rolli. "Your father has many faults—" she began.

"Harald is the one who outlawed me again," said Rolli. "But my father . . . he is not who I thought."

Svanhild gave Rolli a sympathetic look. Ragnvald had not disowned Rolli, but he had abandoned him almost as cruelly.

"You are better away from Norway," Solvi said.

"We were going to Iceland for Freydis's sake," Svanhild said slowly to Solvi. "I will not leave you again. If it is your wish that we return to Iceland, and farm there, then I will follow you and stay by your side. Tova and Falki will probably let us stay. But . . ."

Solvi smiled. "Rolli has much to learn before he can call himself a sea king," he said.

"I would value your guidance," said Rolli. "Yours and my aunt Svanhild's."

"There are still courts that would be glad of our visit," said Solvi, "and seas that I long to sail again. I cannot fight, but I can sail better than I can walk."

"And I can fight," said Rolli. He grinned. "And carry you, when you need it."

"And I have lived too long on a ship to be happy anywhere else," said Svanhild.

She glanced up the hill, to where Ivar's mound lay, tears gathering in her eyes. She had lost her son, not far from here, on a voyage many years ago. Now her brother stood in danger of losing three sons when he need only lose one.

"Husband," she said. "I must—I need to speak with him again. My brother. I cannot leave him again, forever, without saying something."

"Harald still means you ill," said Solvi.

Svanhild glanced at Falki, but it was Rolli who stepped forward. "I will guard you," he said. "My father will not harm me further, and I too would bid him farewell." Falki looked relieved.

Svanhild climbed back up toward the hall, with Rolli following. She found Ragnvald sitting on a damp stone near Ivar's mound. The slanting sunlight picked out every line on his face, every streak of gray in his hair. So might he look when he was laid out for his own burial.

Rolli hung back as Svanhild approached. Ragnvald's eyes flickered at her, but otherwise he did not respond to her arrival, even when she sat down next to him.

"Your Einar has wed my daughter, Freydis. Cousins marrying . . ." She trailed off with a little laugh. "But I think they will be good for one another."

"Without my permission," said Ragnvald.

"You cannot have it both ways, brother," said Svanhild, more harshly. "Either you disowned him, and he may make his own choices, or he is still your son. He would rather still be your son. So would Rolli, though I will give him a place if you do not."

"It's better if you do." Ragnvald's voice was hardly above a whisper. "Look what I do to my sons." He made a sound, a sob cut in half. "Look what Harald does to them."

"I"—she swallowed—"want to offer you the chance to come with me again," she said. She picked up his hand and held it between hers. "How foolish is that?"

"Very foolish, Svanhild," he said. "You cannot stand between me and my fate. Though this is not . . . not what I would have chosen."

"If you must die for Harald, at least forgive Einar before you do," said Svanhild. "He deserves better from you."

"I cannot." Ragnvald pulled his hand away.

"Will you not bid good-bye to Rolli, at least?" Svanhild asked.

Ragnvald nodded tightly, and Svanhild beckoned Rolli over. She gave them a moment alone, and when Rolli came back to her, he was wiping tears from his cheeks. "I will not see him again," he said.

Svanhild returned to Ragnvald's side, and he stood and embraced her. "Go now," he said. "And farewell."

Svanhild stood on her toes to kiss him on his cheek, which was cold from the wind. "Farewell, King Ragnvald," she said. "I will see you in the halls of the gods."

37

EACH DAY THAT RAGNVALD REMAINED IN ORKNEY, HE CLIMBED
up to sit by Ivar's mound. He told Ivar that Einar had married Freydis,
and grew angry again that Ivar would never wed, never father children.
Ivar had wanted to be a father soon—he had told Ragnvald that last winter, when Ragnvald called him away from playing with some of the hall's
younger children. Ivar had hardly grown beyond childhood himself, and
Ragnvald had always thought that a part of him never would. He had
been able to protect Ivar as he and Svanhild had not been protected, and
had enlisted Einar in protecting him after Ragnvald could not. But now
he would never grow older, and must lie in a burial mound, far from
Sogn. Perhaps he had died because Ragnvald could not hold on to his
birthright for him.

Harald found him there on the day before his forces were to leave for
Scotland. "Ragnvald, my friend, tell me what I may do for you. You are
not yourself," he said.

Ragnvald had joined every council, and given his advice when re-
quested, while his spirit remained here, next to the mound of cracked
turf that covered Ivar's body. "How would you know?" he asked. "It has
been many years since we warred together. I have changed."

"Not like this," said Harald. "It was not meant to be like this."

"Did your mother make a prediction?" Ragnvald asked.

"No," said Harald. "No new predictions, but she has always promised
success for me."

"You did have success," said Ragnvald. He thought of Hilda when she grew angry, how she lay in bed for days with her face turned to the wall. He would do that now if he could.

"With such losses as you have suffered, how could I count it a success?" Harald had tears in his eyes that Ragnvald both hated and envied.

"I am sorry, my king," said Ragnvald. "All your sons are living. You cannot know."

"I would give anything to bring your son back," said Harald. Ragnvald did believe him, but no god would come out of the dark ocean to offer to take that bargain, to take Harald's crown, or one of his sons, to redeem Ivar from death.

"Sons," said Ragnvald. "I have lost more than one son."

"Is that what you want? Rolli restored? I would give that to you."

Ragnvald had told Rolli to stay far away from him and from Norway—that he was a curse to his sons. Better for Rolli to be a son of the sea, a son of Svanhild and Solvi.

"I don't care," he said to Harald. "Do as you like."

From near the hall below, Oddi waved to Ragnvald. He would be leaving soon. Ragnvald bowed to Harald and went to say good-bye to Oddi.

Oddi embraced him as he had not since they had ended their friendship many years earlier. "Ragnvald, how are you faring?" he asked.

"I am dying," said Ragnvald. It did not feel like an exaggeration—dying must be like this, just one more step away into the fog that now separated him from the living.

"You are not," said Oddi. "You are grieving."

"I have grieved before," said Ragnvald. "I lost my father, my mother. My sister, more than once. I grieved the loss of you as a friend." That admission made his voice catch, but he pressed it away, back into the fog. "I know what grieving feels like, and this is not that."

"It is, though," said Oddi. He raised an eyebrow. "And maybe some guilt for how terribly you treated your son."

"Rolli?" Ragnvald asked. "Harald has offered to lift his outlawry. But he will be better off away from Norway, where Harald and his sons are wolves, biting off pieces of my land."

Oddi stared at him incredulously. "No, not Rolli. Einar," he said.

"He is no longer my son," said Ragnvald.

Oddi shook his head. "And I had thought we might be friends again."

The fog seemed to lift slightly. When he and Oddi had fought side by side, he never needed to fear that his black thoughts would consume him. "Had thought?" Ragnvald asked.

"I cannot forgive your cruelty to Einar," said Oddi. "I fear for him."

"You think he will kill himself?" Ragnvald asked.

"He has already come close, I think," said Oddi.

No, he had not wanted that. "Did he?" Ragnvald asked.

"Yes," said Oddi implacably. "Do you truly blame him for his brother's death? You know what battle can be."

"He should have died with Ivar," said Ragnvald. "Then I would not have to see his face. Then my Ivar would not be alone."

"The living matter more than the dead," said Oddi. He sighed. "He has taken a good, kind wife, and perhaps he will be better off here, away from you."

That hurt too. "Come back with me, my friend," Ragnvald offered. "Live in Tafjord, by my side again. You have a son in Yrjar, I have heard—bring him to Tafjord. He will grow up as brother to my younger sons, and have every advantage."

"I cannot do that," said Oddi. "You and I are no longer friends, and I would not put my son . . . it is better we stay apart."

Did he fear Ragnvald's fate, or Ragnvald himself? "I understand," he said. "All are better off away from me." He felt less hazy as he spoke, and the knife of his grief cut more keenly. "Are you going back to Halogaland then? Or coming to Scotland?"

"Halogaland," said Oddi. "I will take my men tomorrow."

"And we go to Scotland tomorrow. I go where Harald wishes, no matter how much I want to rebel," said Ragnvald.

He had been looking at Oddi's feet and had not seen Halfdan and his brother Gudrod approach followed by Aldi and a few of his men. "I have witnesses now," said Halfdan. "You all heard it. It is as I said—he wants to rebel."

Ragnvald had his hand at his sword, and so did Oddi, but they could not stand against so many, and Ragnvald did not want to. If they meant to kill him, let them do it.

"You will answer to my father," said Halfdan, holding his blade at Ragnvald's throat. He looked like Harald, though Harald's eyes had never held such madness.

"I hope to," Ragnvald replied calmly. "Where is he?"

"You should be bound, and given to him as a common traitor," said Halfdan. "I knew you were planning some treachery—I have heard nothing in the past three years except how you would be a better king than my father."

"Did you hear that from the men with whom you planned your own rebellion?" Ragnvald asked.

Halfdan lunged at him, and Ragnvald stepped away so Halfdan had to bring himself up short to avoid cutting Aldi.

"Sheath your sword," said Ragnvald. "Take me to Harald. You can tell him what you suspect, and look a fool. Oddi—Oddjborn Hakonsson will witness that I only spoke to him of my grief and weariness."

"Oddi, the baseborn son of a traitor?" Gudrod asked with a sneer. "What kind of witness is he?"

Still, Ragnvald's captors sheathed their swords, crowded around him and Oddi, and walked them down to the shore where Harald had gone to decide who and what supplies would travel in each ship on the journey to Scotland. It was a short voyage, but the currents and wind were tricky enough they could still get separated.

Ragnvald found it difficult to walk down the steep slope with Halfdan's followers giving him no space, and was half tripping by the time he reached the bottom. Gudrod shoved him to his knees on the rocks in front of Harald.

"What is this?" Harald asked.

Halfdan drew himself up to his full height, nearly as tall as Harald, dwarfing all the other men. "I will not fight in Scotland with this man by my side," Halfdan said. "He wants to rebel against you."

Harald looked unimpressed. "My memory is good enough to recall some credible rumors that it was you who tried to betray me last summer. I have forgiven you, but my forgiveness is not unlimited, not if you make baseless accusations against my friend Ragnvald."

"I did not rebel—you were gone, and Ragnvald was taking over," Halfdan insisted. "I needed allies to push back against his usurpation. I have told you this. You are blind to the wolf who walks by your side. I heard him say he wanted to rebel."

Harald turned to Ragnvald. "Did you?" he asked, though he still seemed unworried.

"I used those words to describe my weariness," said Ragnvald. "My heart is weary of war and wants to rebel against it, though I will go where you ask. I have no desire for your throne. I will swear by any gods you wish."

Halfdan paced around the narrow space between the ships. "Father, he is pitting his own sons against yours—if you do not fear for your throne, what about ours?"

Ragnvald felt a slight, distant worry—he had hoped that Rolli would kill Halfdan—but fate had provided him with far too good a defense. "I have lost any sons who might rival you," he said.

"Then come with me to Scotland," Harald replied. He put his hand on Ragnvald's shoulder. "You will feel better about the loss of your son when we can take some vengeance against Melbrid Tooth."

Halfdan backed away, toward the water. "Then I will not go," he said. "I will not fight by his side. Perhaps I should stay here and take back the islands my father promised me. Sigurd cannot be so hard to kill."

"You tread on dangerous ground, my son," said Harald. "If you kill any of my followers without cause, I must outlaw you. I cannot be more lenient with you than with Ragnvald's son."

"Send me back to Tafjord, my king," said Ragnvald. "Then I will not trouble Halfdan, and I will be able to take comfort with my wife and my remaining sons. Send for me when you are finally ready to cut your hair."

"See?" Halfdan cried. "Everything he says is a reproach to you, Father." Harald ignored him. "Is that what you want?" he asked Ragnvald.

"It is," said Ragnvald, bowing his head.

"Then, my friend, return to Tafjord, but on your way, I want you to bring back the treasure we have won here as presents to all of my former wives. Remind them that I will marry them again."

The rebellious part of Ragnvald wanted to ask if he should take some to Svanhild as well, but he did not want to make Halfdan's words sound any more true. "Thank you, my king," he said. He gave Halfdan a hard look. "Keep my brother Sigurd safe in Scotland."

✠ ✠ ✠

EINAR STOOD WITH Freydis on the hill to watch Svanhild's and Rolli's ships leave the harbor.

"I don't know what Sigurd wants of me," Einar said again. "I don't know what our lives will be like."

"Of course not. Only the fates do," said Freydis, touching her cheek to his shoulder.

There should be a feast to celebrate their marriage, at least, but Einar did not want to draw attention to himself, so they sat together at dinner that night, unnoticed, speaking little. His isolation felt all the worse now that he had brought another person into it, and he grew more and more fretful. Should he take Freydis to bed tonight? She still wore Thordis with her everywhere.

If he was Sigurd's man, he should at least tell him of his marriage. Perhaps he should have gotten Sigurd's permission first. He told Freydis what he meant to do, and she gave him a small smile, so he caught Sigurd's eye and motioned for them to talk.

Einar held her hand when he told Sigurd, and his face, always a bit sullen in repose, broke into a friendly, happy smile. "There has been so little good news, we must toast this!"

He began to raise his cup, but Einar stopped him. "There will be time enough to celebrate after my—after King Ragnvald has left," he said.

Sigurd looked troubled, though it passed quickly. "I wish you were the one ruling here," he said. "I am a better fighter than a ruler. Will you stay while I go with Harald's force to Scotland? Or do you want your revenge?"

Wedding Freydis had pushed aside thoughts of killing or revenge, and with her hand still in his, it had little appeal. "I have already killed Geirbjorn Hakonsson," he said. "My brother's shade must be content with that."

Sigurd gave him a relieved smile. "Then you can stay here and guard Orkney while I am in Scotland." He turned grave again. "Ragnvald told me that Orkney will starve this winter without grain and livestock to replace what Harald's warriors have taken. I will not return without provisions."

"I will do my best for you," said Einar. Of course his father would find a way to rule Orkney through Sigurd even from afar.

"Will you bless our marriage, then?" Freydis asked. "You are jarl here."

Sigurd spoke the words of blessing with more than a few mistakes, though he wore an expression of reverence that made up for it. After he went back into the drinking hall, Einar led Freydis toward the private chamber that they had shared for many nights already. If he was no longer the son of Ragnvald the Mighty, he no longer merited a quiet place to heal, but no one seemed to want to take it from him. That would require noticing him.

"I wish they were all gone," said Freydis quietly. "I think I will like these islands without . . ."

"I thought I would hate to stay so near where my brother . . ." He swallowed. "But I am glad not to have to leave him."

When they reached his chamber, Einar put his hand up to his bandage. It felt loosely attached now, like a scab ready to come off.

"I do not know what kind of husband you will have to look at," he said.

"A very handsome one," she said. "I know your wound, as well as you do yourself, and it will not take that away."

Einar made a noise of disbelief.

"Is my father not handsome, even old, even short and lame?" Freydis asked.

"I suppose he is," said Einar. He was used to thinking of young, dark-haired men as handsome, but Solvi did have even features and a winning grin. "I am no Solvi Hunthiofsson, though."

"No, you are taller," Freydis replied, with a burst of hectic laughter. Einar took her hand. She was nervous too.

"Do you . . . should you wait until your daughter is weaned? To have a wedding night?" Einar asked, trying to master his embarrassment.

She touched his chin. "I want your bandage off first," she said. "But that can be now." She gave him a look that surprised him with its heat. "I would wait a few years to give you a son, if you are willing to spill your seed on the ground. I was over-young for my first child."

Einar had not been sure he could feel hunger for a woman again, not after breaking with Gyda, and Ivar's death, but he did, imagining the same cool hands that had tended him touching him again, this time to give him pleasure. "I think . . . ," he said. "I think I want more than simply a child from you."

"Oh," she replied. She kissed his jaw on the whole side of his face, and his lips, very gently. Then she touched the edge of his bandage. "May I?"

"If it is time," Einar said, his lust draining away like water. He tensed as she slid her cool fingers under the edges of the bandage, pulling at the pitch that affixed it to his face.

"This will stick to your skin for a while," she said. "It will come off eventually, and you will look more handsome then."

The pitch did tug on his hair as Freydis's careful, patient work freed the bandage. Then she washed the wound with a clean flaxen cloth, and dried it with another. She touched its edges with her fingertips. "Some heat still, from the healing," she said. "I will take out the stitches tomorrow, and then I will show you."

The cool air on the hot skin of his face made him shiver, and he realized she was still half on top of him, still looking down at him with love.

She kissed him, and then guided them together, slowly, with tantalizing gentleness, until he could stand it no more and rolled her over under him. He remembered just in time to spill his seed into his hand instead of her, and then lay down next to her. He did want to make a son with her one day, and it felt like pure luxury to experience a longing that he knew could be fulfilled, after a lifetime of desires he had forced himself to deny. He slept lightly, woken time and again by the smell of Freydis's skin, woman and mother smells mixed.

When he slept, though, he dreamed of Ivar, standing in the prow of a ship, beckoning Einar to join him. It seemed that Einar could not see his face, though he knew Ivar was smiling, his head tossed back, headed for adventure. He woke happy, eager to see his brother and tell him about his lovely, kind wife, how lucky he was to have found her, after overlooking her growing up in his own household, and then he realized again that Ivar was gone.

Freydis slept on, insensible to his grief and pain. Ivar had left him. Einar had failed him. He disentangled himself from Freydis without waking her, and went out into the gray before dawn. A few dark-clad watchmen walked slowly back and forth to keep awake through their shifts. His stitches itched. When he grew tired of his own maudlin thoughts, he went into the kitchen to find some berries and porridge.

All babies looked the same to him, but the one sleeping in the corner of the kitchen, her mouth open and eyes tightly closed, was swaddled in the same homespun that he had seen Freydis wrap around Thordis. His bride had put her baby away for their first night together. As if his staring disturbed her, Thordis woke and began crying, until one of the women, a crone with a face like a dried apple, picked her up and began cooing to her.

"Yes, yes, we'll find your mother soon," she said in her thick Orkney dialect.

"I'll take her," said Einar. He checked his sleeves for anything sharp that could hurt the child, and, finding none, took her from the old woman. Thordis was a good solid weight in his arms, not as light as he expected. When he returned to his chamber, Freydis was just sitting up. She slept in the short tunic and long skirt she wore during the day, and she yawned and took Thordis from him, raising her tunic to expose a small round breast, white with a little, pink nipple. Einar had a quick and vivid fantasy of being the one to suckle there, and turned away as Freydis arranged her daughter to nurse. She stroked the child's cheek until Thordis began suckling with a will, then sighed contentedly.

"You seem to—don't women think this is a chore? Do you want a wet nurse?" said Einar.

"It can be," said Freydis. "But Thordis is such a good child. She hardly complained even when—" Freydis broke off and pressed her lips together. Thordis began to fret until Freydis stroked her cheek again.

"When?" Einar asked.

"When Hallbjorn brought me here," said Freydis flatly.

"Can you tell me about that? Without upsetting her?" Einar asked.

Freydis sighed and moved Thordis to her other breast. "Likely not," she said. "She feels my moods too well, and I . . . I will tell you, though perhaps you will not like to hear ill of your brother."

"Half-brother," Einar corrected. "And we were never close."

A moment later Thordis had fallen asleep on her mother's breast, making tiny snores. She was like a newborn lamb, a simple creature knowing nothing but her appetite for sleep and food.

"Well, if I could have chosen freely, I would not have gone to his bed." Freydis spoke now with a quiet fierceness that made Einar want to take up his sword for her. "When I had free choice, I refused to be his wife. And when he came to take me from my family in Iceland, I threatened to kill myself and her."

"But you are not—you love your daughter," said Einar, disturbed.

She must not leave him, not when she was the one who held him away from the cliff's edge. "You would not—?"

"No, and that was a lie," said Freydis with a sigh. "I would do anything to save her. I would not have freely chosen to bear her, but now that I have, I will cherish her. The fates spin our lives as they will, and it is only for us to live them."

"You are young to have many regrets," said Einar.

"So are you," she replied.

He touched the stitches on his face. "When can I see?" he asked. "I want to know."

"Now if you wish," said Freydis.

She rummaged under her pallet and pulled out a silver mirror. "Hall-bjorn gave this to me," she said apologetically. "I think he got it raiding in Scotland."

The small, cloudy surface and low light made it hard for Einar to understand what he saw at first. He had rarely looked at his own face except in pools of clear water. There was his hair, greasier than he thought—he should bathe. Below that a high forehead, and one eye, clear and blue, the other a mass of red scarring that he could only look at for a moment before averting his gaze. The wound that had split his eye and traced the outside of his cheek was a red fissure, crosshatched by sutures dyed dark red by his blood. He touched it and felt the pull of the stitches anchored in flesh.

Many men had scars—a powerful warrior could count his scars as trophies, evidence of a long, violent career. But Einar had the marks of age without its gifts.

"It is a horror," he said, putting down the mirror. "Why would you—you knew what this looked like. And it was your choice, not your father's—though how he could allow . . . I am not rich, and neither am I handsome. Why, Freydis?"

He did not notice, as he sat and tried to master himself, that Freydis had come around behind him, until she leaned over his shoulder, and he felt a strand of her hair on the temple next to his wound. The skin that had been covered by the bandage was sensitive now to the slightest touch. Einar had to clench his fists to keep from flinging her off.

"Look," she said. She held the mirror up before him, this time to his unwounded side. She ran a fingertip down the side of his face, his eye, which he noticed was very like his mother's, down over his jawline, sharp like his father's, covered by a short red-gold beard. She turned his chin so he saw his wound again. "This side is still swollen."

He turned his head back, to see the unblemished side, the one his parents had made, and the other, carved by the sword of a dead man, dead on Einar's sword.

"Like Hel," he said. Like the witch he had seen in the woods, the goddess of death had one lovely side, and one side livid and scarred with age. He could be a god of death. With both of his eyes he had been a skilled fighter, and could be again, though he must always guard that side more carefully.

"And Odin," said Freydis, "who traded his eye for wisdom."

"So I should at least have the wisdom to stop fretting about my looks?" Einar asked, with a hint of humor.

"Yes," said Freydis. "I have always liked your looks, and I like them still." She touched the knot of silk at the lower edge of his wound, just above his chin. "Now you wear some of my handiwork upon your face."

38

FREYDIS FELT THAT THE ISLANDS EXHALED WHEN HARALD and his forces departed, a few days after Ragnvald's ships. That day, she removed the stitches from Einar's face. He winced when she pulled out the threads, which left little weeping holes behind. Einar then met with the men who remained in Thorstein's hall—or Sigurd's now, she supposed—and the surrounding farms, to learn what their troubles were while Freydis took an inventory of supplies to see if the food they had could be stretched over the winter.

That night, Freydis's blood came with the new moon, and she could not sleep. It was the first time since Thordis's birth and she felt uncomfortably full, a pressure in her womb and between her legs that only time and the moon's passing would ease. She left Einar's side, drawn by the mild weather, rare even in summer. She put Thordis in the kitchen again, with the women who slept there, traced a charm on her forehead to keep her quiet, and then walked up the hill above the hall.

When she crested the hill, the moon, fat and orange, was sitting on the darkest horizon, lighting the sea in ribbons. Torches shone in a circle some ways off, and Freydis walked toward them. Near a ring of standing stones, she saw the old women who had helped her prepare Einar's body. And, with a feeling of inevitability, she saw the crone Runa among them.

"I told you she would come," said Runa. Freydis bowed. She had been drawn here by something, the same magic that had brought her to Alfrith's side during the women's ceremonies.

"She is not one of us," said another, Sigga.

"She will be," said Runa.

"No, she is Norse, not Pictish. Golden-haired giants have no place among us."

Freydis waited. She did not mind this rejection; it seemed part of the ritual. She reached her hands toward the women. "I have guided life and death with these hands. I have studied healing with the guidance of two great sorceresses." Unna did not call her work magic, but even she sometimes recited certain charms to help her medicines work. "I have borne a living daughter," she added. Priestesses of Freya sometimes required women to pledge their daughters to gain access. Freydis could pledge that she would teach her daughter what she knew, and let her daughter decide how to use it.

"You will leave here as soon as your people have finished their plunder," said Sigga. "Indeed, we meet tonight because we do not know how we will survive the winter. We must pray for the best harvest the gods have ever given us, especially after your people's battle trampled our island's most fertile field."

Freydis bowed her head. "My husband will choose how long we stay," she said. "But while I am here, I will honor your gods, and do what I can to make the fields fertile."

"No," said Runa. "That is not enough. You must make him stay. Your husband will be jarl in this place."

"My uncle Sigurd is jarl here," said Freydis.

"He will die," said Runa. "Will you doubt my prophecies again?"

"If he dies his young son, Olaf, will be jarl," Freydis replied uneasily. Runa had been the one who told Freydis that she would return to the Orkney Islands, before she sailed away with Hallbjorn.

Runa shook her head. "No, your Einar will be jarl here, and his sons after him, if you make it so."

"I will have nothing to do with the death of my uncle and cousin."

"No, you will not," said Runa. "But you can make your man ready. I wish he was of our people, but I see more and more of your Norse coming here, and it will go better for us if he is jarl than one of this Harald's sons."

"If this is a place that Einar Ragnvaldsson can stand and rule, then I want that for him," said Freydis. "But how will we survive the winter?"

"Not now," said Runa. "Now you must dance with us."

Freydis joined in the dance that whirled around and between the stones. The torches painted streaks through the darkness, complicated patterns like those found on the finest Dublin jewelry, like the warp and weft of her weaving. She forgot her cramps, forgot anything but the movement, following, then leading, then mourning when the moon set, and finally resting, unthinking, at the base of one of the stones, her hand still clasped with that of a woman she did not know.

Eventually Sigga and Runa rose, and Freydis followed them, with the other women, back up over the hill.

"Your man will be tested soon," said Runa to Freydis as they parted. "Be ready."

✛   ✛   ✛

FREYDIS WATCHED EINAR's boat from outside the hall as his rowers fought the wind and the current until the bay's walls sheltered them enough to let the sail do the rest of the work. He greeted her quickly, then he and his men fell upon the meal she had prepared, devouring it with little speech. Afterward, he went directly to their bed, flopping down on the mattress with a carelessness that made Freydis smile. He did not hold himself as warily as he had as a boy, knowing that all eyes were upon him. Freydis had once envied that boy's perfect self-possession, how untouchable he seemed, but she liked this man better.

"The outer islands are doing better," he said. "Closer in, Thorstein taxed them very hard, and Harald's men took the rest. I hope that Sigurd can bring us something from Scotland, but even if he can, it will not be enough without everyone sharing their harvests. I wish he were here—he is jarl. I cannot be the one to call a *ting* meeting."

"You do not know when he will return," said Freydis. "You should do whatever is needed."

"No one would come," Einar protested. "They would barely even come for Sigurd."

"They will come," said Freydis. "I will speak to the wise-women. Send your messengers."

Einar did so, and Freydis visited the crones. She brought a wheel of new cheese, fat and tender as a spring moon, as a gift, along with a basket of herbs she had picked. Sigga opened the door. She was shorter than Runa, and rounded, shaped like sea-washed stones stacked upon one another, wearing dark homespun.

Wordlessly, Freydis presented her gifts. Sigga passed the cheese to Runa, and sorted through the herbs Freydis has brought. She held up one, yellow-flowered rue sprig.

Freydis named it. "It will loose a child from a womb."

"Not without some danger," said Sigga.

Freydis held her gaze and nodded. "I have learned ways to lessen that danger, but yes."

"This is a worthy gift," she said. "And Runa will like the cheese."

Freydis then told her why she had come.

"This is not a thing that you can ask for and then walk away like a queen," said Runa. "We are not your servants. Your man will have to ask the men, and you will ask the women, and all will come." She gave Freydis a stone with a hole through it, and tied a braid of grasses around her wrist.

"Even the out-islands?" Freydis asked, touching the objects. They had some meaning that she could not know, and was not meant to know.

Sigga and Runa looked at one another for a moment, and then Runa said, "No, we will call them."

Freydis wanted to ask how they would do that, two limping old women, but if they wanted her to know, they would tell her.

She told Einar some of what she had learned, and what they had promised her. "They think you will rule one day," she said.

Einar frowned and told her a strange story, of a tongueless witch in Hordaland who still gave him a prophecy. "I do not trust these women," he said. "Their prophecies never mean what you think they should."

"Nonetheless, women can help convince the men to come to the ting," she said. "You should not scorn their help."

Over the next week, she and Einar visited every household on the mainland. At each one Freydis talked with the woman of the house, showing the stone and the braided cord. She began to recognize the different features of the original Scottish—Runa called them Pictish—and the Norse newcomers. Some Irish features shone through as well, and the languages and dialects were a mix of those languages. Freydis had only Norse, and a smattering of words that Donall had taught her, which she used haltingly. When she spoke them, she missed Donall's handsome face, his way with animals, and Unna's hard unchangeability, but she never thought that she had made the wrong decision by staying here with Einar.

✝ ✝ ✝

EINAR STOOD BEFORE the assembled men of Orkney—the *ting* meeting he had called. Some had come from the outer islands, sent to represent the communities that scraped out their living upon rock and scrub grass. Some from closer by brought their whole families, from small children who stuck fingers in their mouths and looked around at the gathering with wide eyes, to grandmothers with caved-in cheeks who leaned on sticks to walk.

Freydis rested her hand lightly on his arm. Einar was proud to stand next to her; she held herself as much like a queen as Gyda would have. He opened his mouth to speak, but found he could not begin, and closed it again. He had commanded attention easily before his wounding. But how could he see how an audience reacted to him with only one eye?

Freydis moved her hand to the middle of his back, which made him stand more upright, and then she pushed him slightly forward. He must speak.

"Men, women, people of Orkney," said Einar slowly, "winter will be here soon, and we must all face starvation, if we do not pull together for the harvest. My uncle Sigurd, who is jarl here, has gone to Scotland to raid and trade for grain, but if he does not return in time, or does not bring enough, we must all share our stores."

"Why should we?" called out one man whom Einar did not recognize. "We did not have these troubles when Thorstein ruled here. He left us alone, and took no more than we could replace."

Then he had not truly left them alone, Einar thought, but he had not done as much damage as Harald's thousand men had. All of the islands together did not support more than twice that. He felt the pressure from Freydis's hand on his back again, urging him to speak.

"The past cannot be undone," said Einar, "nor stores uneaten. But I am here now to make sure you can live through the winter, even after losing so much."

Another man stepped forward, this one from a farm near Thorstein's hall. His stores would have been hit very hard by Harald's depredations. "You mean *you* don't want to starve," he said. "You don't care about us."

"True, I do not want to starve," said Einar. "But I will promise to eat no more than the lowliest Orkneyman, and share all that I have, if all Orkneymen agree to do the same."

"Lies," said the first man. "You come from the Norse lands, and you will go back to them as soon as things get difficult for you here. You live in a hall of wood while the rest of us live in turf. You will never be one of us."

His father had also said he was not one of them, not one of his sons. Einar had never wished for more than that, not truly. Being one of Rag-nvald's sons seemed the highest honor.

He drew his dagger and held it high in the air. Freydis pulled away from him, and he sensed her fear, though she stood on his blind side. He waited for the crowd to quiet in anticipation, and then plunged the blade into the ground near his feet. He cut a long line through the thick root structure of the Orkney grass, and then another, parallel to that.

Tears burned his eye—he had last cut turf for Ivar's barrow. With blurred vision, he sliced a line at the bottom, then one at the top, and peeled back the layer of earth, as Orkneymen had done since the begin-ning of the world. He picked up the earthen mat and held it in the air. "I can cut turf as well as any of you, and live in turf too. I am an Orkney-man now. My brother's bones lie here, and one day, if the gods will it, mine will too. We will live together, or die separately."

He had their attention now, his arms shaking from holding the heavy earth. "Thorstein's hall—Jarl Sigurd's now—can still give ten sacks of rye," he continued, "and three of barley. We have twelve barrels of ale. We can afford to slaughter five young steers and one old heifer before the winter is over. There are yet uncounted cheeses. That is what we can give and still feed Sigurd's warriors when they return."

It was a large amount, possibly more than he could spare without hunger, but a lord must be generous. "Now, you"—Einar shook the rect-angle of turf at the man who had first questioned him—"what can you give to keep your neighbors from starving?"

The man stepped forward again, and looked around. "I have a sack of grain that I can share," he said grudgingly.

"My stud ram is old," said one middle-aged woman, who did not seem to have a man to speak for her. "He can be slaughtered, if my neighbor Markus can offer me the services of his ram next fall."

"Valka, you've always wanted his services," said another man. "Is it for your ewes, or are you missing your husband that badly?"

The woman, Valka, guffawed. "You've been trying to get your ewes pregnant yourself, so I think your ram is bored," she shot back. Many of the assembled crowd laughed, and after that, they made more and more offers to share. Einar listened carefully, memorizing them as he once had the law, and when everyone had said what they could give, he repeated it all back to the crowd.

Freydis gently detached herself from Einar's side, and went to speak with the knot of out-island visitors, as Einar spoke with those on the mainland, arranging how their goods would be shared over the winter, when they would return: once after the harvest, and then again on the first fair day after Yule, when they would decide a final visit later in the winter. Poor weather could still force them all into bad choices, like slaughtering so many livestock that they would need to do more raiding to replenish their stocks, but Einar was hopeful.

Most of the farms already had arrangements for sharing labor at harvesttime, and Einar added himself and his men to their number, sending a few off to the farthest islands, so they could make friendships and debts of gratitude, as well as report back to him. Until the crowds dispersed, he forgot his fear that his father was right, and that he did not belong here or anywhere.

Freydis would host some of the out-island visitors in the hall tonight, but many had friends on the mainland to visit. They had survived on these harsh islands for centuries before Harald's coming. If Sigurd remained here, his main task as jarl would be to prevent Harald from doing too much damage with taxes and other raiding missions. The Orkneymen could take care of themselves.

✢ ✢ ✢

THE HARVEST WAS easier than Einar was used to, which worried him. The fields were not as large as those around Tafjord, nor did they have the same yield. After the harvest was over, during the same dry days that favored mowing hay, the Orkneymen began to cut turf for the winter. Here turf served many of the purposes that wood did in Norway including housing and fuel. When burned it gave off a thick, choking smoke that made Einar cough and his eye water, but at least it made warmer walls than wood did, so they could burn less of it.

Einar harvested turf side by side with the men of the mainland. He was clumsy at first with the long sharp spade usually used for the task, but soon he grew better at it, turning his warrior's muscles to this homely task. At length the men began to call him Turf-Einar in grudging acceptance.

Still Sigurd did not return, and Einar made plans for dispensing grain, cheese, and meat for the winter if they received no additional supplies. The men elected at the *ting* to help distribute the grain all detested one another, and argued constantly, but that meant that everyone in the islands had someone they could trust dividing up the grain.

Einar gave up on seeing Sigurd until the spring. Perhaps he had decided to return to Norway with Harald. Or perhaps something worse had befallen him, and Einar was alone at the edge of the world with distrustful strangers, and Freydis, half girl, half goddess, loving, but so strange to him.

A fierce fall storm came up after all the envoys had returned to their islands. The sound of the wind called to Einar, and he could not force himself to remain within the thick walls of Thorstein's hall. He wrapped himself in his cloak and went out into the gale. Overhead, the sky was mottled gray, clouds passing over and behind one another. The wind blustered around him, first sweeping his hair back, and then smacking it into his face. The rain plastered him with fat drops that quickly soaked him even through several layers of wool, and then turned to a harsh needle spray that stung his face.

Every discomfort made him want to press farther on, to the edge of a cliff that overlooked the bay. The channel below surged, white and roiling. Waves slammed into the cliffs, reaching up with fingers of white foam before falling back into the sea. He thought of his father's tales of Ran, the cold and hungry sea goddess, who always desired more prey, and for the first time since Ivar's death, the thought of his father made him feel only a resigned sadness. They were equal, as all men were equal, before the might of the gods.

He saw a ship in the distance, rocking in the swells, well outside the angry water of the bay. He watched it for a time, but it could come no closer in this weather, and then a change in the wind drew a curtain of rain between him and the small black silhouette. He began to feel the cold, and pulled his sodden cloak around him before tramping back to the hall.

He was shivering mightily when he got there. Freydis met him and helped him strip off his clothes behind the curtain that hid their bed. She dried his hair when he bent down, and finding he was still shivering, stripped off her own clothes and pulled him next to her under the covers of their bed, until the warmth from her body reached the coldest parts of him. His body began to respond to hers. He kissed her neck, the swollen mounds of her breasts, hard with milk. His hair left wet trails across her skin, and she shivered.

It seemed to him, as they joined, her warm skin burning on his cold, that she was part of the islands now, that joining with her was the same as taking the name Turf-Einar. He woke the next morning feeling fierce and whole as he had not since his wounding.

When he went outside, he saw that the storm had blown away all the clouds, and a steady wind drew the ship closer to the bay. He recognized Sigurd's colors and called the whole household down to greet him.

Sigurd waved to Einar as the ship beached. He climbed down, holding a strange object in his right hand. As soon as his boots touched the shore, he held it up: a severed head, gray and rotting. In death, the upper lip had drawn up, revealing the protruding incisor of Melbrid Tooth, sticking straight forward like a walrus's tusk.

"We have been successful," Sigurd announced. Einar could not tell if the horrible smell coming from him was the head, or the gore caked onto his clothes, and the clothes of his men. His eyes were strangely bright, as were the eyes of some of his men. Einar remembered a tale that Alfrith had told one long winter night, about a company of undead sailors, trying to recruit more members for their grisly crew. It had given Einar nightmares for years.

Then Sigurd grinned, and he was once again Einar's friendly uncle, no matter how gruesome his trophy. "More than successful. I met up with an enemy that has done us much wrong, and made an end to him."

Sigurd's men began to cheer, and the shouts resolved themselves into a chant, "Sigurd the Mighty! Sigurd the Mighty!" Sigurd flushed, and grinned, holding the head up high, then swung it down by his leg again.

"Welcome," said Einar with real warmth. He wondered what his father would think to hear Sigurd given the same byname that he had. "The Mighty"—few men were called that in earnest. Sigurd must have fought a great battle.

"I brought this so you could see he is truly dead," said Sigurd. "Melbrid Tooth is one of the reasons your brother fell."

"Father," cried Sigurd's son, Olaf, "when are you going to burn that thing?" Olaf looked cleaner than the others, though his cheeks wore a hectic pink that troubled Einar.

Sigurd shook the trophy at his son, who waved his hands to ward it off. Pooled blood and decay had blackened the cut edges of its neck.

"After we feast," said Sigurd. "I have brought back more than just this head, glad as I am to have it. I also have many sacks of grain and big cheeses made by Scottish monks. No one here will starve this winter!" The Orkneymen who had assembled to greet Sigurd's ship cheered.

True to his word, the head sat next to Sigurd during his welcome feast, and Sigurd proposed a toast to their fallen enemy and fed him a sip from his cup. Sigurd told of the battle—not well, but thoroughly, and when he used the head as a prop for his tale, his men cheered. Einar still thought his eyes looked strange, a little glassy, even before he grew drunk on strong Orkney ale, but perhaps he was only tired from his journey.

As Sigurd turned to set down the head Freydis, who had been refilling his cup, pointed at his leg, and asked, "Did you take a wound in the fighting?"

Sigurd stood up and showed the rip in his trousers that Freydis had noticed. "It's only a small wound—I think this fellow's tooth gave it to me!" He held up Melbrid's head again, pulling up the mouth to show his famous tooth. "Perhaps he was trying to get revenge!"

✛ ✛ ✛

WHEN EINAR JOINED Freydis in bed the next night, she said to him, "I examined the wound on Sigurd's thigh today."

"That scratch?" Einar asked. "It is nothing."

"It is not nothing," she replied. "It will likely kill him."

"Did your crones tell you that?" Einar asked.

"No, the smell tells me that. He has an infection, and it is too high up on his leg to cut it off, even if he were willing to risk it. He will die, and soon."

Freydis washed the wound several times the next day with wine, but the following day his entire leg was red and swollen, the streaks of blood poisoning stretching up into his groin and over his belly. He cried out in agony whenever anyone touched him. One slender slash of red extended up to his navel. Were it not for the suppurating wound below, it would look like nothing more than a scratch. A love scratch, perhaps. But Sigurd would never love another woman.

"Einar, please kill me," he begged. "Do not let me die like this."

Einar promised to help him, though looking at the wound made him feel ill, and he left to talk to Freydis, who was grinding some herbs in the kitchen.

"Can you do nothing for him?" he asked Freydis. "Must he die like this, like a coward?"

"I can give him an easy death," said Freydis, gesturing at the powder in her mortar, "but only you can give him a warrior's death. You must ask him what he wants."

Freydis brought Olaf into the chamber to bid farewell to his father, and then led the boy out again, both of their faces wet with tears. Einar stood outside Sigurd's chamber, gripping his dagger.

"You can find another of his men to do this for him," she said. "He is well loved. Someone will be willing to send him to Valhalla other than you."

"No," said Einar. "I should do this. I can do this for him, even if I failed him."

"How did you fail him?" Freydis asked.

"I should have gone with him to Scotland."

"He asked you to stay." She shook her head. "This is the strangest of deaths, so strange that it must be ordained by the gods. You could not have prevented it if you were there."

He did not believe her, and he gripped his dagger.

"Put that down for a moment," she said. She pulled his hand to her neck, to the place that always made her shiver with pleasure when he kissed her there. "There is a great vein here. If you want to give him a kind death, do not cut his throat and watch him choke on it. Cut this vein, deeply, and he will bleed away in an instant."

"You have given this a great deal of thought," said Einar. "How do you know how to kill a man?"

"I have had teachers, for both good and ill. I saw Hallbjorn kill one of Aldi's men by cutting his throat, and this is quicker." She pressed his fingers against her neck and he felt the pulse there. "Now go speak with him," she said.

Einar had never wanted to do anything less. At least Freydis had given Sigurd herbs to take away the pain, to bring him closer to death. She could still give him a peaceful death, if he wished it.

"Your wife is skilled," said Sigurd. "I feel more clearheaded." He shifted in his bed, sending a waft of his wound's odor to Einar's nose.

"She wanted me to ask if you wanted to die from her herbs, or have a warrior's death," said Einar, trying not to flinch.

Sigurd's eyes washed with tears. "She is skilled but she cannot heal me," he said. "I thought not."

"No, she cannot," Einar said. He stood silently next to Sigurd. His face was gray and sweaty, and his blond hair looked like dried winter grass.

"I killed Melbrid Tooth," said Sigurd. "My men—they called me 'Mighty.' Tell your father."

"He disowned me," said Einar.

"He loves you," said Sigurd. "Tell him."

"I will," Einar promised. "He loves you too."

Sigurd smiled brokenly. "He never thought much of me," he said.

"He did," said Einar. "Enough to give you Orkney."

"And look what I've made of it," he replied. "At least I will die here." A crisis of pain gripped him, and he cursed, flexing his hands against the empty air, and then reached out and gripped Einar's hand. "Give me my sword, and then kill me. I want a chance at Odin's hall of warriors. Perhaps I will see Ivar there."

Now Einar began to weep—these islands would claim his uncle as they had his brother. Was there no end to the deaths he must witness before finding the peace of his own?

He put Sigurd's sword into his hand, though he could barely grasp it. "Tell me when you're ready," he said.

"My son, Olaf," said Sigurd. "Look after him until he is ready to be jarl."

"I will," Einar promised.

Sigurd sighed heavily. "What a foolish way to die," he said, half to himself. Einar feared to touch him anywhere that might give him more agony, but he did brush Sigurd's sodden hair off his forehead. Sigurd closed his eyes, and Einar hoped he would die then, without Einar's blow. But then he opened them and looked up at Einar. "Do it," he said. "I am ready."

39

RAGNVALD'S JOURNEY UP GEIRANGER FJORD TOOK A FULL FIVE
days, and on each day, Ivar's ghost seemed closer. He had sailed a small
boat with his sons past some of these waterfalls, and pointed out the warrior's visage in the cliff's face, where he had nearly drowned as a young
man, after Solvi slashed his face and threw him into the fjord. Ivar would
never grow beyond the age Ragnvald had been when he had seen his vision of Harald's victory as a golden wolf under these waters.

The household came out to meet Ragnvald when he reached Tafjord,
forming a crowd at the shore, cheering, though Ragnvald heard some
uncertainty. He saw Ivar everywhere, in the shoulders of the plain young
man who helped pull the boat up through the marsh at the fjord's end, in
Hilda's thick brown hair, the same shade that Ivar's had been, and in his
young sons by Alfrith, who both had dark eyes like Ivar's. Hilda did not
yet know what had happened, and Ragnvald could hardly meet her gaze.
At least he still had his skald with him, to tell the full story, but he owed
Hilda the words from his own lips.

"Thank you for this welcome," he said to those assembled. "I come
with both good tidings and ill. King Harald has been successful in Orkney, and claimed those islands for Norway. My stepbrother Sigurd now
rules there. Harald and his sons will return after they have routed the
rebels out of their strongholds in Scotland. They will surely have great
success and return to Norway, their ships swollen with treasure."

He should have started with the bad news and gone on to the good,
but he knew that once he told of Ivar's death, he would be able to say no

more. "Some good men have died brave deaths, though," he said. "My stepbrother Hallbjorn, and"—he took a deep breath, as his throat threatened to close off—"my own son Ivar."

A cry of dismay went up from many throats, for Ivar had been well loved, a handsome boy with a sunny disposition, who had grown into a happy young man. Ragnvald gestured to his skald, who said that he would tell the whole story that evening. Hilda opened her arms, welcoming and comforting Ragnvald as she had not since Rolli's outlawry. She looked as stunned as he felt when he first heard the news from Svanhild's lips, too frozen for tears.

At length he let Hilda go and she walked with him, taking his elbow so she could support him if he needed. They passed Alfrith, who looked at Ragnvald with her deep, black eyes that saw too much, before she bowed her head in welcome. She would forgive him anything, but she would force him to look at the shameful things he had done, if not immediately, then when they turned to dreams that needed her wisdom to understand.

Ragnvald's scouts along the fjord had warned the household of his coming, so Hilda had prepared a rich welcome feast. He made a toast to bless the bounty of his Tafjord household and the loyalty of the warriors who had remained behind, hardly hearing the words as he spoke them, and then drained his glass of ale in one gulp. He drank the next one slowly, but after the first few courses, as his skald began to tell the story of the battle, Ragnvald drank more heavily. His younger self would have scorned this old man, full of shame and fear, lacking all discipline. But that young man had never lost a son.

Ragnvald listened to the tale of the battle, of Ivar's bravery in manning one of the decoy ships, how the gods of the sea wanted him, but he would not let them take him, dying instead with his sword in his hand. He did not speak of Ragnvald's last argument with Einar. Ivar would hate that Ragnvald had left Einar behind. But he was not around to argue for his brother anymore.

The last time Ragnvald had seen Hilda, she had blazed with anger, looking younger than she had in years. Now, with the news of Ivar's death, she looked old again, the silver strands in her thick braid standing out more clearly, her face dull and tired. When his skald was done speaking, she sat down next to Ragnvald in his chair.

"Where is Einar?" she asked in a low voice. "He can be a comfort to me with Ivar gone." She and Einar had grown close during her father's final years, when he had taught them both the law that he had learned from his own father.

"He stayed in Orkney with Sigurd," said Ragnvald.

Hilda blinked. "He did not want to return with you? His father? Or come to me? I thought him a better son than that."

Ragnvald gritted his teeth. "He did not keep his brother from death, so he is not the son I thought he was."

"Was it his fault?" Hilda asked.

"He swore an oath to protect his brother, and he failed," said Ragnvald. "What more is there to say?"

He heard the tale of battle taken up again and, out of the corner of his eye, saw Hilda sit up straight when Rolli's name was mentioned. "You did not tell me Rolli was there," she said. Her voice sounded like a boulder dragged across rough ground, halting and scraping.

"He came with Solvi," said Ragnvald.

Hilda seemed not to hear him. "Surely, if one good thing can come from the Orkney battles, it is Rolli's return. Why did he not come with you?"

"He made cause with Harald's oldest enemy," said Ragnvald. "He cannot be allowed to return."

"So in this journey, you have lost three sons," she said in a low whisper, "two of them needlessly, through your own pride and folly."

She might be able to understand the true reason for his decision, that Rolli would be safer away from him, from the doom that his fate promised him, but he had no more words, so he only called for more ale and drank enough that he did not care what she thought any longer.

✢ ✢ ✢

IN THE DAYS after Ragnvald's homecoming, he often felt Thorir's eyes upon him, and heard Thorir's name in the chattering of servants, which always quieted when he came near. They had good reason to discuss him, since he would one day be their ruler.

Thorir spent his days sparring with Ragnvald's warriors. Once when Ragnvald asked where he was, his steward told him Thorir had taken a horse to ride out to the nearby farms to see how the summer growing season was treating them. Thorir had always been the most politic of Ragnvald's sons, best at adapting himself to the moment. This moment required grieving, so that was what Thorir did, even as he carried out the tasks of the likely heir.

He had grown less awkward in the year since their journey to Jutland, and his beard was coming in better now, a uniform fur of soft brown over his jawline, though it would be a few years until it did not seem a youth's self-conscious affectation. His expression was always sober when Ragnvald saw him, even when his fellows were laughing. Ragnvald mistrusted the perfection of his performance, but that skill would help him in the land of Harald's sons, all of whom loved flattery.

A month after Ragnvald's return, a horse trader traveled overland to Tafjord escorting a fine stallion and mare as gifts for Ragnvald, along with an invitation to join Harald in Nidaros at Yule. After the trader had been given ale and a place to rest, Ragnvald said to Thorir, who had been with him to receive their guest, "This stallion is yours if you like him. Let us ride."

They followed the path up and out of the bowl that the cliffs and hills made around Tafjord, up to the crest that overlooked Geiranger Fjord. They rode without speaking, accompanied only by the breathing of their horses, and the sigh of pine needles underfoot, which turned to the crunch of stone when they reached the crest of the cliff. From this vantage, the whole of the fjord stretched out below. One of Ragnvald's scouts had a lookout here, marked by a ring of stones and a blackened patch of earth.

"It is a blessing that you stayed here to care for your mother," said Ragnvald as they looked down at the sapphire water.

Thorir nodded, but said nothing. The sun was shining and the fields below striped with green and yellow. For a moment, their beauty made Ragnvald feel as though he could truly live after Ivar's death, though that thought itself brought pain and guilt.

"What is the use of all of this?" Ragnvald asked out loud, not thinking Thorir would have an answer either.

"It is fate, I suppose," said Thorir. "The thread of a man's life is measured, and the Norns know where they will put its end."

That trick of knowing Ragnvald's thought and answering it reminded him of Oddi for a moment. "So say seers and priests," he replied.

Some force shaped the moments in between, though. Ragnvald looked down at the bend in the fjord called Solskel, the site of one of his greatest gambles for Harald, and greatest triumphs.

"What did Einar do?" Thorir asked quietly. "So I may avoid his mistakes."

Ragnvald felt a wave of horror and shame so intense it stole his vision for a moment. Thorir deserved a better father than the broken man who had cut off one of his sons as cruelly as Harald's executioners had severed hands and feet after the battle of Solskel. Ragnvald had burned the charnel house where that sentence was carried out and caused the ashes to be raked away. Marsh grasses had reclaimed the ground, the site erased, though the deed and its effects never could be.

"He was never my heir," said Ragnvald, "not as Ivar was and you are now. Do not fear."

"But what did he do?" Thorir asked plaintively. "I have heard it was because he failed to protect Ivar, but Einar avenged him, and a man's life is measured. It was the end of Ivar's then. It must have been. I am grieved that Ivar is gone, but he was fated to die then—how could Einar have done any different?"

He prayed Thorir would never know the pain of losing his firstborn son, but if he did, he might one day understand how Ragnvald felt now. "I cannot tell you," he said. Einar's affair with Gyda had made him untrustworthy once, and Ivar's death a second time. Keeping Einar away meant he need not fear a third. "But for his safety and the safety of our family, he must remain in exile. Do not ask me again, and do not fear for yourself. You are my son and heir. You will rule in Maer when I am gone."

If it had been Einar here with him, he would have spoken of Halfdan next, of his fears that Halfdan meant to rebel against his father again, and kill Ragnvald and his sons in the process. But Thorir looked at him with awe and fear—he was not yet old enough to believe that his father had any doubts.

✦   ✦   ✦

TO RAGNVALD'S SURPRISE, Hilda had agreed to come with him to Harald's Yule celebration, and as she worked to pack the goods they would need on the journey, he had felt almost as he had during his good years with her. On an impulse, when he saw a lock of hair come loose from her head scarf, he tucked it back in for her and lifted her hand to kiss it.

"What was that for?" she asked.

"Thank you for coming with me," he said. "I know you do not like Harald much, or leaving home."

"I am not going for you," she replied, "but because I know you will not do enough to safeguard Rolli's future. So I will go, and do what I can for him. It will not be much. I do not know all the politics at court as you do."

Ragnvald swallowed down a pang of guilt. Perhaps he should have allowed Harald to forgive Rolli—then he would not need to fight this battle at home as well as with Harald's sons. But Rolli was not Thorir, to shape himself for success. He was better off gone.

When they reached Nidaros, Ragnvald had trouble finding a place for his ships among the vast numbers that beached along the shore. In the past few years, Nidaros had become dilapidated from Harald's long absence, but now Ragnvald saw the signs of repair on all of the artisans' houses and the great living and drinking halls that dominated the town.

His friends among the crowd came to greet him: Oddi, looking ever fatter, and Heming with his blond hair going more to gray with every passing year. Now, as a king, he dressed more simply than he had as the young man known as Heming Peacock. He greeted Ragnvald with affection.

Closer to the hall, two columns of women, wives and daughters and queens, formed outside the door, and cheered when Ragnvald arrived, happy to see him, more for what he represented than for himself. When he cut Harald's hair, Harald would give over conquest and rule Norway in peace. All longed for this day.

He passed by Asa, now looking younger than her brother Heming. He glimpsed Vigdis in the crowd, turning away from him with venom in her eyes. He saw Gyda near the hall's entrance, coming to speak with him. She held a golden-haired baby in her arms and wore a dress of cream and blue that made her pale skin look like a smith's hottest flame, and her hair like molten gold.

"King Ragnvald," she said. She accepted his embrace, though he held his cheek away from hers, fearing that if he touched her skin, he would find she burned with cold. "I am sorry for your loss," she added.

"Do not talk to me about my son," said Ragnvald.

"I had hoped you would tell me something about"—she swallowed—"your son Einar. I heard he was wounded in Orkney, and he has not returned."

"Did you hear anything else?"

"Some whispers," said Gyda. "I have heard that he would not return to Norway and displease you."

"And have you come to speak with me to plead his case?" Ragnvald asked.

"I wish him well, and thought he would be your heir now. But that is not to be. Still, you have a hold over me," she said. "I want to see if you mean to exercise it."

"You mean, I will see his features on your son's face when he grows older," Ragnvald said.

Gyda looked troubled and turned toward the child in her arms. "Do you not think it is better for him to be Harald's son?" she asked. "Even if I am divorced? But it is much like being married, or betrothed. I find no difference."

"If you betray Harald, you will still die for it," said Ragnvald. "But yes, it is better for him to be one of Harald's sons. Their luck is much better." He wanted to blame her for making the first fissure between himself and Einar, but he had done that, from Einar's birth. He had never given Einar the trust he did Ivar, for Einar had come from an untrustworthy place. "Now leave me be, woman."

"Very well," said Gyda, "but if you have need of me or any service I can do you, know that it is yours."

"Why?" Ragnvald asked roughly. "Your secret would do me as much damage as you, were it to be known."

"I don't think that's true," said Gyda. "Women always suffer more." The smoothness of her words angered him. Svanhild had fled, whole and unpunished, back to the arms of her first love, while Ivar died and Einar lived scarred for life. Gyda's only wounds were those of time; she had lain with Einar and would never be punished for it.

"It is true," said Ragnvald, and turned away.

"Do you mean to break with Harald?" Gyda asked suddenly. "Everyone wonders it."

Ragnvald whirled back to face her. "What?"

"They say that he has pushed you to your breaking point, insulted you by divorcing your sister, taking your ancestral land, and now he has heaped gifts upon you that you have refused. You travel here under duress."

"Halfdan has been spinning tales," said Ragnvald. "I have come here because I have nowhere else to be."

✧ ✧ ✧

NEW OATHS WERE traditionally made at Yule, while the days before Yule were spent in discharging the obligations for old ones. On the night of Yule, Harald held a feast, then led a procession to the sacrifice grove. There he announced what everyone already knew: Ragnvald would cut his hair, and Harald would declare his oath to conquer Norway fulfilled.

Ragnvald dressed in his finest clothes and bid Hilda do the same. After the sacrifices, Ragnvald sent Hilda along to the feast, and Halfdan peeled Ragnvald away from the procession.

"This is your last chance," Halfdan said in a low voice. "Cut my father's throat and declare me king. Or you will not long survive afterward."

"You know I will not," said Ragnvald, startled, despite himself, to hear Halfdan say it so baldly.

"I will kill you if you do not," said Halfdan.

"Your father will surely punish you if you do," said Ragnvald wearily.

"But you will still be dead."

"So we are at an impasse again," Ragnvald replied. "Perhaps we must learn to live in peace."

"No," said Halfdan. "My father will punish me, but he will forgive me. And you will be burned alive in your hall like a coward, along with all the poison you pour into his ear about me."

Ragnvald shivered. His stepfather, Olaf, had burned his father's hall; he himself had burned King Vemund of Naustdal, at Harald's request, and never ceased to have nightmares about it. He had always thought if he did not die in battle, he would drown, going finally to the goddess Ran, who long had a claim on him. Could she still find him if he burned?

"Should I come out of the chamber, holding Harald's head in my hands?" Ragnvald asked. "Should I break every oath I have ever sworn? Get out of my way, Halfdan Traitor. I do not stand between you and your ambition. Your own foolishness does that."

He pushed past Halfdan and into the hall. He hardly heard the words that Harald and his uncle Guthorm spoke in the shaky voice of an old man, retelling the campaigns and battles that had made Harald king— the battles of Vestfold, of Solskel, of Hafrsfjord, Harald's oath and Gyda's pride. He heard his own name mentioned from time to time, and rose to be cheered when called to, all the while, holding the hilt of his dagger, sharpened to a perfect edge.

Ronhild had said that if he followed Harald, he would give up everything he held dear, ending with his life. And now he knew how that would happen. Ronhild had prophesied that Harald would be as a tree whose branches spread out all over Norway and beyond, but one of those branches wished to kill him.

Finally, Harald, who had been sitting while his chief skald recited a new song about his victories, stood and said, "It is time. All of you may eat, but I will not eat until my most loyal friend and ally King Ragnvald of Maer, Ragnvald the Wise, Ragnvald the Mighty, cuts my hair."

The room immediately quieted. Ragnvald did not look at Halfdan, where he sat with Vigdis and Guthorm, but he could feel their eyes upon him.

"This is too great an honor for me," said Ragnvald. He had longed for this day and had been ready to set his dagger to Harald's long and tangled hair on a far happier day than this one.

Harald laughed. "Come, you have given me success in every battle we have ever joined together. The sacrifices you have made for me are too many to name, and too great ever to repay, though I will spend the rest of my life trying," he said. "For now, do this thing for me, as a sign of our unbreakable friendship, a mere droplet of honor in the giant horn that I must fill for you. When I return, you will see me clean-shaved, and I will give out golden gifts to all my loyal followers."

"Not your hair," someone called out.

"You will not be that lucky," Harald replied. He gestured for Ragnvald to follow him into a small anteroom.

"Congratulations, my king," said Ragnvald.

"I could not have done it without you," Harald replied.

"Perhaps not, but you would have found someone to fill my role, and I would not be who I am without you," Ragnvald answered. For good or ill, it was true.

They embraced, and then Harald sat on the stool that had been prepared for him. Ragnvald drew his dagger. "Before I do this, you should know your son Halfdan has not stopped conspiring against you. He wishes me to cut your throat now, and declare him king of Norway."

"He grieves me deeply," said Harald. "I do not know what to do about him."

"Nothing will make him stop, save outlawry," said Ragnvald. "You were willing to outlaw one of my sons. Twice. You can do no less to yours."

"Halfdan has not yet committed murder," said Harald. "Rolli did. With Halfdan it has only been words."

"So you will wait until he kills you?" Ragnvald asked. "Or me?"

"No," said Harald. "I will send him away—to clear the Danish vikings out of the Shetland Islands. That will keep him occupied."

But too close to Sigurd and Einar in the Orkney Islands for Ragnvald's comfort. Though perhaps Einar would find a way to kill Halfdan after all. "That is something," said Ragnvald. "Shall I cut your hair now?"

Harald still looked troubled. "My uncle and sons never cease to tell me that you are in rebellion, that you wish it was you who ruled Norway."

"Not this again," Ragnvald cried. "It is not true. I do not want to rule Norway. I wish it was you who ruled Norway!"

"What do you mean?" Harald looked taken aback.

"Do you think your kingdom would have survived if I spent a year in some Finnish woman's bed?" Ragnvald asked. "Do you care how close you came to losing Hordaland—your legendary queen in rebellion? Do you know what I've given for your kingdom? My hands, my sister, my son, and my land, while you pay no price, and fret about changing the wild hair of your youth?"

Harald rose, towering over him as Halfdan had in the hallway earlier. "You never stop complaining of your losses," he said, "but still, no man in Norway would not want to trade places with you."

"Then you have a kingdom of fools," said Ragnvald.

Harald sighed, and sat down heavily. "What do you want? Do you want me to give Sogn back to you?"

Halfdan would come for his death all the faster if Ragnvald said yes. He had been right in that, at least. Ragnvald had controlled too much land. And without Ivar—Ragnvald clenched his jaw to keep his tears at bay.

"My son Thorir—let him keep Maer, and divide it between his sons, not yours," said Ragnvald. "Spend a year as I have spent the last fifteen, making alliances, settling disputes, making peace among your warring kings. Make plans for your sons, not only Halfdan, challenges they can attempt and succeed at. Your kingdom needs more than me to balance it."

"And what will you do?" Harald asked.

"Teach Thorir, make him into a worthy king to replace me. Grow old, and one day soon put down my sword."

"And if I do all those things?"

"Then I will cut your hair."

"Then do it," said Harald. He smiled at Ragnvald, as pure and winning a smile as he had as a boy, dreaming of his conquest. "When I come out clean-shaven, and still living, all will know that you are loyal, and that I am still a worthy king, for I have kept your loyalty."

Harald spoke again as Ragnvald worked, of his dreams for his sons, his sadness at having to divorce his wives, the women who had been his support as their brothers and fathers had been his companions. Ragnvald was glad to have this simple task first, since his hands shook as he cut through the thick, ropelike locks with the shears that had been left in the room for that purpose. He had to cut close to Harald's scalp to get rid of all the tangles. Then he trimmed the remaining hair to one even length, which showed off the symmetrical beauty of Harald's head.

"Now your beard," said Ragnvald. This he cut with the shears first, but finally the moment came when he had to set his blade to Harald's neck. His hands shook again.

"I trust you," said Harald. He looked at Ragnvald so directly, his eyes blue and sunny.

"You have never had reason not to," said Ragnvald, and he began to shave.

Harald was scratching at his close-trimmed beard and shorn head when they returned to the hall. A cheer went up, begun by the skald Hornklofe and carried by Harald's son Dagfinn, then Oddi, Heming, and many others, the voices of men and women greeting their king: "Harald Fairhair! Harald Fairhair! King Harald, long may he reign!"

Ragnvald felt Halfdan's eyes burning into him, but he only watched his king, for whom he had given much, and for whom he must give still more.

FREYDIS HAD NOT REALIZED HOW MUCH OF HER TIME SHE HAD spent caring for Sigurd until his death. Then she emerged from the exhaustion of nursing him and found that half of the men he brought back with him from Scotland were sick with a high fever and chills. Some Orkney men and women became sick as well, but within a few weeks most recovered, while many of Sigurd's followers perished. His son, Olaf, weakened by grief, lay abed with a fever. His illness had not seemed as bad as the others' at first, but as time went by, and he did not improve, Freydis grew more and more worried for him.

Einar had come back from Sigurd's side with a thick splash of blood across his clothes and face, each droplet still perfectly formed. He sat down heavily on their bed. Freydis took one of her rags and washed his face. When he was clean, and Freydis had taken his shirt from him for laundering, he stood, and said, "I will bring his body to your crones for preparation. He was jarl of Orkney, no matter that it was a short time. His body will lie in a mound here."

"Did he say anything?" Freydis asked.

"He asked me to guard Olaf until he is full grown and can be jarl after him," said Einar. "And I will do that."

They buried Sigurd next to Ivar, with some of the gold he had won in his raiding trip, and the ashes of Melbrid's head, as evidence of his boldness.

Olaf Sigurdsson had fled when he saw Einar at the funeral, and refused to come near him, until sickness kept him on his pallet and he could no longer escape Einar's presence. He suffered deliriums and had no desire to eat for many days after the funeral. The same fever sent Einar to bed for a week, where he slept it out, and emerged, shaky and thinner.

The fall storms turned to winter gales, coming out of the dark and bringing driving snow with them, and waves that reached almost as high as the cliffs' edges. The wind felt like an icy knife whenever Freydis went outside. Olaf's friends among the Orkney boys came to his bed-side to tell him how they had proved their bravery by standing where the waves hit the cliffs and then running back just as they crashed over the edge.

Families visited between storms, a few at a time, to spend some days in the hall, and share provisions. Though the outer settlements had suf-fered less from Harald's depredations, Einar had supplied them well, and when Freydis saw the winter weather and the stormy seas that separated them, she was glad of it.

Freydis grew more and more worried for Olaf as others recovered and he did not. Some children had already died, along with a few of the elderly, though the crones Sigga and Runa seemed to grow stronger in the dark of winter. Thordis raged loudly for her milk through all of it and never seemed to suffer a moment's sickness. At nine months old she was starting to make sounds that reminded Freydis of words, and, if Freydis set her down, would wriggle around in the rushes no matter how dirty they were. She was a big, strong baby, and Freydis thought she might be an early walker and keep Freydis busy running after her.

Freydis tried every remedy she knew on Olaf and when they failed, she went to Sigga and Runa to ask if they could help. She found their hut filled with thick black smoke from burning poorly cured turf.

"It has been a long time since you visited us," said Sigga. "You have the islander loyalty you wanted for your man, and now you leave us alone?"

"I thought to see you at Yule," said Freydis. "At the sacrifices to bring back the light."

"I remember when we still sacrificed a man on that day," said Sigga. "Our priests did it, but then the Christians came, and the Norse. I would have thought you raiders would have the stomach for it, but I have never seen it."

Freydis made a face at her bloodthirstiness. Alfrith had taught her that men and women should only be sacrificed in times of greatest need. More often, the gods and goddesses took their own sacrifices—in battle, sickness, and childbirth.

"You will not need a man's sacrifice this time," said Runa, from where she stirred a pot over the fire, half obscured by the smoke. "That boy will die at Yule, and bring back the light."

Freydis wished she could be surprised by the words. She had always known that Olaf must die for Einar to become jarl, but she had hoped the cause would not be that she had failed as a healer.

＋　＋　＋

AS RUNA PREDICTED, Olaf died at Yule. The ground was not yet too frozen to bury him next to his father, so the Grimbister settlement gathered to lay another jarl to rest during the short and rainy day, before making Yule sacrifices of goat and lamb to bring back the light.

The sickness carried off a few more during the winter, mostly the very young and the very old. A young mother on the mainland died after a difficult birth and left her newborn son with a grieving father who appeared out of the freezing rain one night at Thorstein's hall, desperate for Freydis's help.

"They say you are a healer," he said. "I do not know what to do."

Freydis took the child from him, unwrapped sodden swaddling, and said, "You don't need a healer, you need a wet nurse. I will feed him now, and we will see who we can find."

Thordis was starting to eat some stewed cereal but still nursed as well, so Freydis had milk to feed this child. He was almost too weak to latch on, and Einar returned while Freydis still sat with the child's father, and her tunic pulled up to give the child her breast. He frowned at Freydis when she explained what she was doing.

"Should you bare your breast to every commoner with an infant?" he asked her later that night, when they lay in bed together. He had grown quiet and grim since the death of Sigurd, and Freydis feared what Olaf's death would mean to him.

"You cut turf, I nurse infants, and together we are welcomed here," she replied.

"It will not be for long," said Einar, his voice hard. "I must return to Norway and tell my father that Sigurd and his son have died. Then he will give Orkney to Halfdan, or Thorir, or someone else."

"Certainly, he must be told," said Freydis. "Can you not send a messenger?"

"No," said Einar. "Sigurd asked me to stay, first for him, and then for his son. I have no more reason to be here."

"The Orkneymen would vote you jarl, if you put it to them," said Freydis.

"This is my father's land. I will not betray him again by taking that place."

"Betray!" said Freydis, sitting up so she could look down at him. The shadows hid the scarred side of his face and the lamplight made his skin and hair both look as though they were shaped from molten gold. "You are prophesied to be jarl, and your father has betrayed you far more than you ever could him."

"If I am jarl, then my brother, Sigurd, and Olaf have all died to make me so. I cannot accept that," said Einar.

"It will be spring soon," she replied. "You could send a message with a merchant, and you would not have to go."

Einar clenched his jaw. "If I knew what my father wanted . . ." He looked away from her.

"What should I do while you go to Norway?" Freydis asked. "What should the islands do without you?"

"They have managed without me for many years," said Einar. "I do not know where I will be sent next. Can you face the open sea again? Will you come with me?"

Now Freydis had to avoid his eyes. She wanted to say yes, that she would go anywhere with him, anywhere he asked, but though Thordis was strong, Freydis did not want to risk her health with more sea travel. "It is time to take what you want," she said, trying to keep her voice calm. "Go to Harald, go to your father, and ask for Orkney. You are Turf-Einar. You belong here."

"And you?" Einar asked.

"I will stay and give you a reason to come back."

"Freydis . . . ," he said, reaching up to touch her face. He turned and now all she could see was his scar, the long puckered furrow, the missing eye. His father had been named Half-Drowned, and Einar too existed half in the land of the living, and half in twilight.

"Ask for Orkney—if not for yourself, then for me," Freydis asked. "Tell me you will. Promise me."

"I promise," said Einar.

✢   ✢   ✢

THE WEATHER FAVORED Einar on his journey to Tafjord. Only two weeks after kissing Freydis good-bye, his ship entered Geiranger Fjord, but it took another four days of sailing and rowing to reach Tafjord at the far end. It seemed that the skies became grayer as the ship drew closer, as the walls of the fjord reached up higher and higher overhead, and Einar became fearful about his welcome.

He saw many memories in the fjord, in the places where he and Ivar had learned to sail, hunt, fish, and ride. He dozed off on a rowing bench, only to wake with his throat sore from unvoiced protests at a father who rejected and blamed him. Still worse were the dreams where his father embraced him and they grieved together. Einar woke from these with tears on his face, knowing they would not come to pass.

Hilda, Alfrith, and some of Ragnvald's warriors assembled to greet Einar's ship when he drew up to Tafjord's marshy shore. Einar kissed Hilda's cheeks, and embraced Thorir, all the while looking for his father.

Only as they had started walking toward the hall did Ragnvald emerge. He seemed older and dimmed from when Einar had seen him last, full of rage and grief. Now it was as though he stood in shadow even when those around him stood in sun. His skin was very pale, and his dark hair dull and lank.

"I have not welcomed these guests," he said.

"I have come in peace to give you important tidings," said Einar. "Do you hate me so much you will deny me hospitality?"

Hilda turned toward her husband with fury on her face. Ragnvald bowed his head, as if preparing to move a heavy stone. "Hospitality is the duty we owe the gods," he said. "You shall have it. Now what is your news?"

"Can he at least come inside?" Hilda asked.

"I will tell you," said Einar. "Sigurd and his son are both dead." Einar

told his father of Sigurd's great battle and the death and sickness that
followed.

"When the gods see a good ruler, they keep his people from harm,"
said Ragnvald.

Was there no end to his father's ill will? Einar had said what he had
come to say—now he could leave. He would go to Harald, since his father wanted nothing more than to hurt him. Harald would likely give
Orkney to one of his sons, though, and he had promised Freydis he
would at least ask for it.

"Sigurd was jarl there," said Einar.

"You're the one who let him die," said Ragnvald.

"If you think I am so powerful I can prevent or cause the death of
anyone near me, you should let me rule Orkney." He had not meant to
ask it that way, and certainly not as soon as he arrived.

"I may as well," said Ragnvald. "There is no one I love left there for
you to kill."

"Come inside and rest," said Hilda desperately. "You can bathe and
eat, and then I am sure you men should discuss this further."

Einar felt a prickling between his shoulder blades, as though he
might find a knife between them if he let down his guard. He would, he
supposed, but it would be a knife of words that could only cut his spirit.

✛ ✛ ✛

HILDA SEATED EINAR far from his father at dinner. Maer farmers
filled the hall, all with the usual litany of complaints about one another,
rodents, bad weather, either too much sun or too much rain. Einar
watched his father listen to each of them, give advice when required,
settle minor disputes. He still seemed a natural king, with no self-doubt,
even as grief made his voice dull.

The next morning, Einar walked up to the waterfall above the hall,
where he knew his father liked to go, even when it was half-frozen, to
dip his hands in the cold water, and say a prayer to the spirits of this
place. He waited until the ritual was completed and Ragnvald had
turned to walk back to the hall before he stepped out from his hiding
place between two trees.

His father's face showed a moment of hope, before closing in on itself. Einar knew that feeling—he experienced it every morning when he

woke, having forgotten that Ivar was gone. He knew, as well, what his father had seen: the ghost of Ivar beside him.

"I see him everywhere too," Einar said quietly.

His father looked at him, and Einar's heart rose in his throat. "You must go," he said. "Halfdan is coming for me, and he will kill everyone he finds here."

"You should give Orkney to him, to buy him off," said Einar. Freydis would understand this.

"It will not help," said Ragnvald. "He will come for me. Or he will come for his father. My death is the only way Harald will see the danger he poses. Better I should give Orkney to you."

"So I can lose it avenging your death?" Einar asked.

"My death will buy Thorir a kingdom, and you those islands," said Ragnvald. "Do not throw that away."

"Father," said Einar, though he had promised himself he would never call him that again. "I would rather no kingdom, and for you to live."

Ragnvald looked back at him, shaking his head. He gave Einar a look that, for a moment, erased all of the enmity between them and took Einar back to the time when he thought he could read his father's mind, anticipate all his requests. He felt a fresh wave of longing to be his father's right hand, as he had once sworn to be Ivar's. He would even serve Thorir when he inherited, as long as he could stay here and feel useful again.

"Halfdan wants my kingdoms, and to be Harald's heir, or nothing," said Ragnvald.

"Does Harald have anything to say about that?" Einar asked.

"Not enough," said Ragnvald.

"So you will sit here, waiting for death? If you don't have a care for your life, what about your sons? What about Hilda and Alfrith?"

Ragnvald sighed. "I have faced many more worthy foes. I wish I had met my end on one of their swords instead. But this is my *wyrd*."

"Let me stay and protect you," said Einar softly. "I will not let this happen."

"You?" Ragnvald asked. Einar steeled himself for what his father would say next, accusations that Einar could protect no one who was put in his care, so he could never protect his father, but instead his father's shoulders sagged. "No. I can make room for one of my sons in this

Norway I have built, but no more. Go back to Orkney, rule there, my son. I do not want to see you on these shores again."

Einar wanted to say something more, to embrace his father, to grieve together as they ought to have done, but the look Ragnvald gave him was cold again. He followed him back to Tafjord's hall, and went to find Thorir. If his father would not see reason, perhaps his brother would.

Thorir was standing on the shore, looking down the fjord—looking for Halfdan's ships, perhaps.

"He has been like this since he cut Harald's hair," said Thorir.

"Since the death of our brother Ivar," said Einar. "He does not want to live."

"No," Thorir protested. "It is not like that." He touched his beard, looking very young.

"It is," said Einar. "Do not die with him. Come to me in Orkney, or go to Svanhild in Iceland. There will be a place for you. Do not let your mother or Alfrith die with him either."

Thorir only shook his head, and Einar was glad to see Alfrith and Hilda walking toward them, Hilda, big and solid, and Alfrith narrow and otherworldly. "Do you want me to stay?" Einar asked desperately. "Or to come with me?"

"Do not fear," said Alfrith. "It is fate."

"How can you all accept this?" Einar cried.

"It is fate," said Alfrith.

"Is there nothing I can do?" Einar asked. "I will die protecting you from Halfdan if I must."

"Then you will die," said Alfrith. "Go, and live to avenge him."

"My lady Hilda," said Einar, "you are wise too. What do you wish of me?"

"Take care of my son Rolli if you see him," said Hilda. She embraced him tightly. "I am glad for another chance to bid you good-bye. You have been as good a son to me as if you were born to me, and I bless you for it."

41

RAGNVALD COULD NOT BRING HIMSELF TO SAY GOOD-BYE TO
Einar, so he went to talk with his steward while Einar pushed off. He
emerged from the barn to watch the ship sail away down the fjord, until
the spring mist enveloped it before it passed the fjord's first turn.

In the following days the spring thaw came to Tafjord in earnest, further melting the waterfalls, sometimes by slow degrees, sometimes in
great crashes that woke Ragnvald in the middle of the night. Ragnvald
rolled over and saw that Hilda too was awake. "Go to your sisters in the
mountains," he said. "Take Alfrith with you."

"Should she not go to her sons?" Hilda asked.

"I don't care where she goes, but I want her safe," said Ragnvald.

"And I want you safe," said Hilda.

"I thought you hated me, for Rolli," said Ragnvald.

"I will never stop being angry with you for that," said Hilda. "I will
never stop mourning our sons and the family we had. But I don't want
you to die."

"Tell me how to escape Halfdan, then," said Ragnvald. He wanted to
sound angry, but he felt like a boy, begging his mother to tell him that
everything would be all right. "Escape him without throwing away everything that I have built?"

Hilda put her head against his shoulder. "If you cannot, your wise
Alfrith cannot . . . if your clever son cannot . . . then I cannot either."

"I am sorry I did not do more for Rolli," he said to her.

"He is safe from this," said Hilda, grudgingly. "I will have to be content with that."

"I should have been a better husband to you," he continued.

She kissed his cheek and then his forehead. "You have seen your death."

"Every day since I earned the name Half-Drowned," said Ragnvald.

"Then bid me farewell, as a wife deserves of her husband. I am past the age of childbearing."

That had not been between them for many years, but he had loved to be in her arms when they were young and still making sons together. Her big, strong body warmed his from shoulder to ankles, and her long thick hair spread over him. It seemed a shame that he had given this up for so long, though that had been her doing as well.

"Why will you not flee and hide?" Hilda asked afterward.

"When would it end?" Ragnvald asked. "I would spend my whole life fleeing and hiding, and lose my land. No, this is the only way to preserve Thorir's inheritance, and save Harald from his sons."

"And you do not want to live," said Hilda.

"The day of my death is already chosen," Ragnvald replied, "as it is for all men." As even Ivar's must have been. At least Ragnvald should soon see him again.

✛ ✛ ✛

EVEN WITH HIS death coming for him, Ragnvald enjoyed the spring, the budding of the trees, the mild breezes that touched his skin. He enjoyed Thorir, growing taller and more confident with every passing day, turning into a man worthy of his inheritance.

But it was selfish to keep him here much longer. A month before midsummer, he commanded Thorir to take Alfrith and Hilda away.

"Father," Thorir protested. "We must fight. Or flee. This is madness."

"I have made my decision," said Ragnvald.

Hilda shook her head. "I am not going. Take Alfrith."

Ragnvald gave Alfrith a pleading look. "Our sons will need their mother," he said. If Alfrith agreed to go, then Thorir would go, and his remaining sons would be safe.

Alfrith nodded. She stepped in close to Ragnvald and kissed him, a kiss that tasted of her tears, and then pulled away. "Farewell," she said. "We will meet in the valleys of the underworld, if nowhere else."

Hilda sent most of her servants back to their families. Without them, the hall was quiet and empty. She spent her mornings in the kitchen and went outside in the afternoon to weave in the sunshine, while Ragnvald weeded in the garden. He wondered if this was what their life would have been like if he had never followed Harald, never gone to war: their daily tasks only the simple ones of living and making a home.

When midsummer drew closer, Ragnvald began to wonder if Halfdan would come at all. Perhaps Harald had disciplined him as he deserved. Perhaps he had lost his stomach for rebellion.

He and Hilda celebrated the midsummer feast with a few nearby farmers. They drank strong-brewed ale, and spent the night sitting together silently under the sky's blanket of blue, so thick that only a few stars showed through, whirling above as Ragnvald's head spun with the ale.

The next day they lay long abed, both nursing sore heads, though Hilda rose at midmorning to bring Ragnvald light ale to soothe his stomach. He got up for his midday meal, but still only had the will to harvest some early vegetables in the afternoon.

The sun had fallen below the fjord's cliffs, and Ragnvald had gone inside for an evening meal, when he heard the knock on the hall's great oak doors, a hard banging that could only mean one thing. They must have come through the woods, rather than sailing up the fjord, and risk being seen by Ragnvald's scouts.

He felt both cold and hot, as he always did before a battle; his body wanted to fight, even if he knew he must die. But he would not go unarmored and unarmed. He dressed himself quickly and belted on his sword.

"Who is it?" he asked through the thick oak. Hilda stood nearby, in the hall's shadows.

"Halfdan Haraldsson, and a hundred of my followers," he said. "We have your hall surrounded with dry kindling, ready to be put to the torch. You have deserved death many times over, and now you will find it."

"What good will this do you?" Ragnvald asked. "Do you think your father will love you more?"

"He will have to treat me as a king when I have a kingdom," said Halfdan.

"I am ready to fight you," said Ragnvald. "Fight me like a man with honor, don't burn me like a coward. And let my wife, Hilda, go free."

"This is the death you deserve, Ragnvald Half-Drowned," said Halfdan. "You burned King Vemund alive in his hall—why should I show you more mercy than that?"

"It was your father's order," he said.

"This, still!" said Halfdan. "See, he is brazenly in rebellion against my father."

"I offered King Vemund mercy," Ragnvald continued. "I offered to save his women and children, and let him and his men die on our swords. Are you a lesser man than I?"

There was some low-voiced discussion outside the door.

"Send your women out," said Halfdan finally. "No harm will come to them."

"Swear it," said Ragnvald.

Halfdan spoke the words, and with his men as witness, Ragnvald had no choice but to believe him. He pulled Hilda to him and kissed her, then sent her out through the hall's big doors.

Halfdan was just outside, his helmet pulled low over his eyes. Next to him stood Gudrod, slim and gleaming in his polished armor. Both of them had been foster sons to Ragnvald, for a few years in their youth. For a moment, all of this seemed like a misunderstanding, a boy's game that had gone too far. Then they were men again, men who had come to kill him.

Ragnvald wanted to rush them, to die on Halfdan's sword, but he did not know if they would then hurt Hilda, so he waited until her tall form had disappeared into the shadowy night beyond Halfdan's warriors before speaking again.

"Do you remember your summers here?" Ragnvald asked quietly.

"The coward begs for his life now," Halfdan announced. "I remember always hearing how wise and mighty you were, how no man could ever measure up to you. That is what I remember from my boyhood."

"Fight me then," said Ragnvald. "Are you frightened of an old man, whose hands have never recovered from Solvi's torture?"

"You are trying to bait me," said Halfdan. "I do not fear you, but I do not want to spend eternity with you in Valhalla. You die by fire." He jerked his chin up and his men began to push the great doors shut.

Ragnvald stood and let them, not wanting to shame himself by trying to steal his death from Halfdan's sword. Halfdan had the hall surrounded. If he tried to leave through any of the other exits, they would push him back in, and carry away tales of his cowardice.

"You do me great honor to give me so vast a pyre," said Ragnvald through the door. "I will take many jewels and crates of gold with me to the next world."

He felt a little ashamed at that lie—he did not have much gold, but he hoped Halfdan and his men would burn their hands sorting through the hall's timbers looking for it.

He went to the kitchen, took his finest bottle of Frankish wine, made of precious glass, chased with silver and gems from Frankish jewelers. He sat at his long table, which had hosted farmers and kings, and drank from the bottle. The wine was light and fragrant, and tasted of the autumn that would follow on this summer, which Ragnvald would not live to see.

He had nearly finished the bottle by the time the kindling burned enough that he could see bright glints of fire through gaps in the hall's planks. It took longer still for those planks to catch, still sodden as they were with spring rains. Ragnvald's head spun from the wine before he began to cough from the thick smoke.

He drained the last drops from the bottle and inhaled deeply, trying not to cough, only to let smoke fill his lungs. He might die this way before the fire ever touched him. Drown on the smoke. Perhaps he would not be sensible when the flames took his body. He wished Hilda could know how easy this was. He felt no pain. Perhaps Alfrith would tell her.

Ragnvald lay down on the table. In the heat, it gave off the smells of feasts past, feasts presided over by his steadfast Hilda, flavored by the herbs from his wise Alfrith. Einar had recited his poems here, while Ivar applauded, and Rolli ran around the long fire, chasing after the dogs. Svanhild had been here too, smiling with a full heart, glad to be part of Ragnvald's family.

This hall in Maer had never seemed as much like home as Sogn, but now it seemed fitting his bones would lie here, with Thorir to carry on his line. His other sons' bones would lie across the sea, setting a claim on a wider swath of land than Ragnvald had ever hoped for.

His vision wavered. He was very hot now, sweating, the air searing his lungs.

Then the whole hall seemed to inhale, and suddenly he felt chilled. The wavering light made him think of Ran's cold hall again where he had seen his vision of Harald as the golden wolf, the golden wolf who would both burnish him, and then devour him in flames. He saw Harald, Halfdan, and his son Einar, crowned in golden hair, wolves all. And here it was, the burning, the burning that had always been waiting for him. Halfdan was only carrying out the will of the fates.

He would go to Ran's hall, even if he died under a wave of flame. Ran had claimed him when he was barely a man, and she would have her due. Alfrith would find him. And wherever he went, Ivar would be there, his beautiful son whom he had failed.

He hoped Einar would not try to avenge him.

He cried out, wishing he could see his family one last time, not simply Ran's cold, wavering hall, gold turned green by sluggish seawater, but this was his fate. Then, through the walls of Ran's hall, he saw Ivar, standing on the slope of a treeless hill. He smiled. At first, Ragnvald thought the smile was for him, but then Einar walked up to stand next to him, and they climbed arm in arm over the crest of the hill.

"Yes, wait for him," said Ragnvald. The heat stole his voice. Everything around him was fire. "And do not let him join you too soon."

<h1 style="text-align:center">42</h1>

EINAR WAS IN HALOGALAND, TRYING TO RALLY HEMING'S
warriors to defend his father, when a messenger came with the news of
Ragnvald's death. He immediately set sail for Nidaros, to demand punishment for Halfdan and Gudrod.

They were not in Nidaros, but many others were: Harald and his followers, his wife Ranka Eriksdatter, swelling with a child. Hilda, Thorir,
and Alfrith had all come as well, to find out what would become of Maer,
and of Ragnvald's murderers.

Einar found only a cool welcome in Nidaros from all except his kin.
Men often avoided grief as though the bad luck that had touched him
might infect them. Thorir too had few companions—no one wanted
to talk with those who might be planning to murder Harald's son, no
matter how justified they were. He had arrived just in time, for Harald
intended to make his decree that very afternoon, before the evening
meal.

"I am grieved more than I can say at the death of my finest friend,
King Ragnvald of Maer," Harald said to his court. "And I am further
grieved that it was two of my sons who did this: Halfdan and Gudrod.
This is a great crime." Harald did at least look sorrowful, his tan face and
golden hair looking as though covered with a layer of dust. "They and
all of their accomplices are hereby outlawed from Norway for a term of
three years."

Einar clenched his fists—this was less than Rolli's sentence for the
death of Aldi's son.

"More than that," Harald continued, "I will make restitution to King Ragnvald's son and kin. Thorir Ragnvaldsson," he said. Thorir stepped forward. "Your father asked that you receive the kingdom of Maer as your inheritance. This is your restitution."

Einar could stop neither his movement nor his voice. He rose to his feet and cried out, "No! A man's inheritance is not restitution, and three years' outlawry is not a just punishment for this murder. Halfdan and Gudrod have been in rebellion against you for years. If this is the sum of their punishment, you might as well ask every king in Norway to bare their throats for the teeth of your wolfish sons."

"Who is this who speaks to me so?" Harald asked.

Einar walked forward, his shoulders back, his head up. He hated that half the room was hidden to him by his missing eye, and that Harald's court would see weakness and ugliness in his maiming. "I am Einar, firstborn son of King Ragnvald of Sogn and of Maer. Son of Ragnvald the Wise, Ragnvald the Mighty. Ragnvald Half-Drowned, who your son Halfdan condemned to die by fire because he was too cowardly to face him with a sword."

Harald looked taken aback, but he still said quietly, "Ragnvald's firstborn, but not his heir. What does Ragnvald's heir have to say?" His low voice forced the chatter of the assembly to quiet as well.

Thorir stepped forward, holding his hands awkwardly. Einar could see that he wanted to put them to his chin, to smooth his sparse beard. "I am Thorir, King Ragnvald's heir," he said. "Maer is my inheritance, not my father's wergild."

"Well said," Harald replied, skilled as ever at reading the mood of his court. "Your father does deserve more than that. What is a kingdom if it cannot be defended? How many ships do you have?"

"Five now, and it will be ten if you return the ones that went to make war in Scotland," Thorir answered.

"Five and ten, that makes fifteen," said Harald, with a smile to show he knew he was getting the count wrong. "For King Ragnvald's wergild, I will bring it up to an even twenty, and fill them with armed men to defend Maer for you, not a man among them outfitted with less than a sword and a helmet."

Thorir swallowed a few times, and said, hardly above a whisper, "This I will accept."

"And you will swear that this makes restitution, that you will not seek revenge against my sons?" Harald asked.

"I swear it," said Thorir.

Einar shot him a venomous look. With the death of Ivar and his father, Thorir had come into an inheritance he could never have expected before. No wonder his silence was for sale.

"And what about you, Einar Ragnvaldsson?" Harald asked.

"My father's rest is not to be purchased so cheaply," Einar replied. "Let my brother hereafter be known as Thorir the Silent, since he did not protest."

"And you as Einar the Noisy?" Harald asked. "I remember your grandfather Eystein was called 'Noisy' for his boasting. And I hear boasting in your words as well. Still, you deserve something. Young Thorir has told me that your father gave you Orkney before he died. Since you were not to expect any inheritance at all, let that be your portion of your father's wergild. But if you will not swear to obey my justice, as your father always did, then I cannot have you in my kingdom. Go to Orkney, and if I hear that you have set foot on Norse soil, I will think it is for no good purpose, and act accordingly."

"And what if your son comes for me?" Einar asked. "He is not here to learn of your justice. Do you ask me to bare my throat for his blade, as you asked my father to do?"

Harald met Einar's eyes for a moment, and Einar felt then a touch of Harald's own grief. "I did not ask that of him," he said, looking away.

But you did, Einar wanted to cry out. He swallowed down the words. At least Harald had not forced him to swear off revenge. He sailed from Nidaros with his crew that very night.

✠   ✠   ✠

AS EINAR'S SHIP approached the bay at Grimbister, Aban, sharp-eyed, said, "Something is wrong here."

They drifted a few more boat lengths and Einar saw the same thing—too many ships in the harbor, and not merchant ships either. One looked like Halfdan's—the same one that had helped Einar set the trap to ensnare the Scottish raiders, when he had lost Ivar.

"Where can we land?" Einar asked, half to himself. Perhaps he could sail around to the Bay of Scapa, where he had crewed a bait ship, and Ivar had gone to his death. But Halfdan would know of that place.

Aban pointed at the tall pillar on the island to the south. "There is Hoy," he said.

Einar shivered. Hoy was where he had lain next to his brother's body, racked by fever, waiting to escape into death. He would rather go anywhere else. But it was close to Grimbister. He could attack from there.

He clenched his jaw. "Hoy, then," he said.

The only place to land was a steep, rocky slope, above which stood the rude hall where he had lain. He remembered its shape, glimpsed through his swollen eye, and its smell, of earth and death, smells he thought would be his last.

Freydis greeted him at the hall's doorway, and Einar ran to her, and collapsed to his knees, holding her waist.

"My father is dead," he cried. He could never shed tears without them burning his missing eye, and the pain felt like it would tear him apart.

"I know," said Freydis, stroking his hair. "Halfdan came here a few weeks ago. He slaughtered two of the best milk cows on the mainland for his feasting, and made us toast your father's defeat."

"How did you come here?" Einar asked, looking up at her.

Freydis smiled. "Halfdan does not believe that a woman would ever rebel against him. He did not guard me well."

Over the next few days, messengers came to Hoy, saying that Halfdan's men were eating up seed saved for the next year's planting, slaughtering an animal every day for their feasting, and taking Orkney daughters as concubines.

Freydis came and related Halfdan's latest abuses to Einar after he woke from a long night's sleep, deep and dreamless, as though he had visited the dim lands of death. The rage that Einar had swallowed for so long felt as though it would come through his skin. He had half-starved the winter before to make sure that Orkney did not, and now it was for nothing.

Freydis touched his arm. "I do not think Halfdan will cut turf with the Orkneymen," she said. "It is a wonder they have not already killed him."

"They are farmers," said Einar.

"Now that you are here, it is time to go to Grimbister and rally them," said Freydis.

"So they can all die?" Einar asked.

"So they can fight," said Freydis.

They sailed a small boat with Aban across the strait that separated Hoy from the mainland and around the western coast until they reached the Bay of Scapa. If Halfdan feared attack, he would set a guard here, but Einar saw no one.

"Go back and bring the rest of the men," said Freydis to Aban. "I think we will need them."

Aban looked to Einar, who nodded, and then he sailed off again. Einar and Freydis walked up the slope, Freydis leading the way, until they reached a small, rude hut, the same one in which Ivar's body had been prepared. The door was tightly closed now, and smoke worked its way out of tiny gaps in the turf.

Freydis knocked on the door, and the taller of the crones, the one called Runa, opened the door. She beckoned them in. Einar immediately started coughing from the smoke inside.

Runa laughed at him and handed him a cloth to cough into. "This house is snug, eh?" she said. "No cold gets through in the winter, I'll tell you that much."

"I'm sure not," Einar croaked.

The other crone, the shorter and fatter one, gave each of them a hunk of bread spread with butter that tasted of smoke and sea, as must everything in this house. "Good, you are here," she said. "In the morning, take your men and march on these invaders, and you will defeat them."

"That's it?" Einar asked. "March on the invaders?"

"Yes," said Runa. "We have been waiting for you. We have all been waiting for you. What have you to lose?"

"Will Freydis be safe, even if I fall?" Einar asked.

"Who is safe?" Runa asked in return. "No one. All will suffer and all will die at some time or another. No one escapes."

"Then what should I do?" Einar asked.

"Sleep here." Runa laughed at the face Einar made. "Outside if you prefer. And then you will see."

Einar could not leave the house quickly enough. He made up a sleeping roll on the deep grass of the hillside, while Freydis stayed inside with the crones.

By the time she emerged, more of Einar's men had come, a pitiful group, it seemed, no more than twenty. Freydis crawled under Einar's cloak next to him.

"The moon is right for you to make a son with me tonight," she said to him. "Orkney is yours, and you should pass it down to him."

All around them, Einar's men slept and snored, or waited, wakeful, for the morning. But Freydis was hot in his arms, pulling up her skirt, and he found a hunger in himself that had been missing at least since his father's death. Many men did like a woman on the eve before battle, to remind them that they yet lived, and had things to live for.

He heard one of his men laugh, and another joke, seeing their movements under the blankets. Let them laugh, Einar thought. They could laugh and tease his son when he was born, and if they were lucky, grow old enough to call Einar's son jarl.

When the sky lightened, Einar sat up and saw the sleeping forms of his men, lumps in the grass of the hill, too small and so few, against Halfdan's crowd of ships. This was foolishness.

He looked over at Freydis, who also began to stir and wake. She always opened her eyes like a kitten waking, and Einar felt a great wave of love for her. She was too precious to risk in a battle. They should escape to Iceland. They would not starve there.

Then Einar heard a quiet rhythm, no louder than his own heartbeat, but less regular, and then a low chatter, like a gull colony heard from far away. He made sure his trousers were tied and stood up.

On the hill below stood hundreds of men and boys, and even a few women, clutching axes and cruelly hooked turf cutters. The army of Orkney. One man, Thorkell, short and weathered before his time by Orkney weather, had appointed himself their leader. He came forward and said, "We would all cheer for Turf-Einar, but we don't want to wake the invaders."

"Invaders?" Einar asked.

"Yes," Thorkell said. "They have already killed many of our animals and levied a tax. They are invaders. We voted, and we would rather have you."

Einar turned toward Freydis, who was standing next to him, and gave her a kiss that made the men around him hoot softly.

"Freydis, my love, guard yourself until this is over," he said.

✛ ✛ ✛

EINAR WOULD NOT have thought that an army of short, tool-wielding Orkneymen could put so much fear into Halfdan's forces, but there were not as many of them as Einar had heard Halfdan brought to Tafjord to kill Ragnvald. Perhaps Halfdan's stronger warriors had soured on his rebellion.

Two hundred Orkney fishermen and farmers ran down the hill to slaughter Halfdan's men as they woke from a long night of feasting. Einar killed several unarmed men before he encountered armed opponents.

With Orkneymen to his right and left, Einar did not fear for his blind side, only drove forward until he had reached the thickest part of the fighting. The battle seemed slow around him, every stroke he made sure and easy, his muscles moving without tiring, until he saw Halfdan. Halfdan, still tall and golden, fought like a god, and Einar felt every sleepless night, every hard thrust he had already forced from his tired arms. He had not fought a true battle, nor sparred with a worthy opponent, since losing his eye. Halfdan always had the reach on him, and now he would have the skill and endurance as well.

"You should not have come," Einar said to Halfdan while he caught his breath. "You would have been safe if you didn't come here, but this is my land. I am the jarl of Orkney, I am Turf-Einar."

"Turf-Einar?" said Halfdan with a laugh. "Your face looks like torn-up turf—is that why they call you that?"

"Yes," said Einar.

He plunged toward Halfdan as his men drove Halfdan's back. Halfdan attacked Einar's blind side time and again, and each time Einar had to turn to see him, and turn again, until he had turned around entirely, and his back was to Halfdan's forces, and Halfdan's to his.

Halfdan lunged at him again, and Einar parried with leaden arms. If Halfdan did not get through his guard this time, he would with his next thrust, or the one after that. Halfdan was stronger than he was, even with Einar's anger and hatred, even though Einar had the right of revenge. He squeezed his eye shut, anticipating death.

But something checked Halfdan's swing, and when Einar looked, he saw the end of a turf cutter protruding through Halfdan's shoulder, pinning him in place. Einar took his chance and slashed Halfdan deeply across the neck. Strangely, he remained standing, holding his bloody throat. Behind him, a small man held the handle of the turf cutter, his muscles shaking as he tried to support Halfdan's giant body.

Einar ducked out of the way, and the man let Halfdan's face hit the earth.

"What is your name?" Einar asked.

"Arknell," said the man. "I'm just a farmer. I didn't know if—"

"My thanks, Arknell," said Einar. "I will name my first son for you, and your name will never be forgotten."

"I—didn't you want to kill him?" Arknell asked. "I heard he killed your father?"

"I think we both killed him," said Einar. "And I don't think you want the credit. His father is the king of Norway."

"No indeed," said Arknell. "I won't tell anyone, if it's all the same to you. But"—he grinned—"go ahead and name your son Arknell. It's a good name."

Einar grinned back. "To be sure I will."

✢ ✢ ✢

AFTER HALFDAN'S DEATH, his men quickly surrendered, beginning with Gudrod, Harald's son by Gyda's sister. Einar was glad of that—he did not think he had another fight in him. He would have to practice until it felt as easy as it had before. And though Gudrod had helped Halfdan kill his father, he was also Gyda's foster son and looked very like her.

Einar borrowed an ax from one of the Orkneymen and chopped off Halfdan's head, then picked it up by the hair. Blood from the severed neck dripped on the thick turf. Fear contorted Gudrod's beautiful face as Einar strode over to him, carrying his trophy. Two Orkneymen held his arms behind his back.

"I was only following my brother," Gudrod explained, desperately. "He told me it was the only way to get kingdoms for ourselves. It was he who ordered your father burned. I wanted us to kill him fairly, in a duel."

Einar shook his head, and his men pulled Gudrod's arms back farther.

"My father will kill you if you kill me," Gudrod gasped out.

Einar held up Halfdan's head. "I've already killed one of your brothers. Your father's wrath is assured. Why should I not kill you as well, and all of your men? Then at least I will delay my death for a time." He walked in close to Gudrod, so he could smell his fear-sweat and the blood spattered on him from the battle. "That is all any of us can do, delay death. But some are more cowardly about it than others."

Gudrod's face twisted in rage. "Coward? When you have me bound? Face me like a man."

"I already did," said Einar. "I faced you like a jarl, the jarl of Orkney, and you lost. Now tell me why I should let you live. How will you help me?"

Gudrod swallowed. "I will tell my father that you spared my life when you could have taken it. I will tell him that you only took your just revenge."

"Revenge he should have taken," said Einar.

"Revenge he should have taken," Gudrod repeated. "I will say all of that if you let me go."

"And your men?"

Gudrod nodded. "Yes, yes, them too."

Einar curled his lip. "Of course. Them too. Swear it, before me, your men, and the gods, and I will let you live, provision your ships, and send you back to your father. If you break your oath, I will know and the gods will know, and you will draw every breath in fear until you die on my sword."

"How will you know?" Gudrod asked, still fearful.

Einar saw Freydis out of the corner of his eye, bringing water to the wounded. "The gods that have taken my eye have given me sight to make up for it," he said, a lie, but one Gudrod would believe. His father had seen visions.

Gudrod shuddered and nodded. "I will swear," he said.

EPILOGUE

EINAR STOOD NEXT TO FREYDIS AND SVANHILD AS THEY watched Thordis and the warrior Thorgeir exchange their marriage vows. Thordis wore a deep green dress that looked well with her red-gold hair. She was beautiful, but the impression she gave was of strength even more than beauty. She had grown up taller than Freydis, nearly as tall as Einar, and all said she looked so much like him, she could have been his daughter. Indeed, she had known no other father.

Einar knew that Freydis wished her daughter were marrying a younger man, but Thorgeir had been fighting at Einar's side since Harald's final visit to Orkney, and Einar esteemed him well. And Thordis had chosen him herself.

Einar's sons Arknell, Thorkell, and Thorstein stood together, watching Thordis and Thorgeir share their wedding cup. Thorkell and Thorstein giggled and shushed each other, while Arknell tried to act as though he was above their foolishness. At fifteen, he considered himself a full-grown man.

"I wish Father could have seen this," said Freydis.

Einar glanced at Svanhild, whose hair had gone all to white now. She had sent out Solvi's body on a burning boat the previous year, and come to Orkney after Freydis sent a messenger to Iceland inviting her to see Thordis wed.

"I do too," said Svanhild. "He would have been pleased to see Thordis grown, to see your sons turning into men. But he was in so much pain last year that I am glad he was spared another winter."

The guests tramped up to the hall for a long afternoon and evening of feasting before putting the couple to bed. After Einar had toasted the couple, and so had Thorgeir's companions, Svanhild stood, raising her glass.

"I know it is unusual for a woman to give a toast," she said, giving a self-deprecating smile, "but I bring well-wishes for the couple from Rolli—Hrolf Ragnvaldsson, who now styles himself a Frankish duke. The Emperor Charles gives him more gold than he knows how to spend, so he has promised to send some to you."

A cheer went up, and Freydis raised a toast to Duke Hrolf. Svanhild had told them how she and Solvi taught Rolli everything they knew about making war and seafaring, and how he had gone on to surpass them. He never returned to Norway but gained followers wherever he went, and was known as Hrolf the Ganger, Hrolf the Walker, too big a man to ride even the largest horse. He attacked the Franks for years until their Emperor Charles bribed him with land, a title, and gold rather than face his continued raids.

Perhaps Rolli would send aid to his half-brother if Einar asked. Thorir sent ships sometimes, even though Einar's byname for him had stuck, and he would go to his grave known as Thorir the Silent for refusing to speak up for his father. Wedding Harald's daughter Alof had helped ensure his silence. Still, Einar did not scorn his help. The Danes threatened the islands as regularly as summer. Einar's new son-in-law had fought battles against them at Einar's side for many years before this day. Thorgeir had been wounded in the shoulder last summer and Freydis said he would not recover his fighting strength. Thordis had tended his wound all winter and, in the spring, decided to wed him, and bring him to take up her inheritance in Iceland—the farm of old Unna the Wise. Thorgeir was still strong enough to be a farmer, and weary of war.

Einar too was weary of war, but it was the price he paid for peace with Harald, and freedom from his revenge, and so he paid it willingly.

All throughout the hot summer that had followed Ragnvald's death, Einar looked for Harald's coming. Gudrod would deliver his message, Einar had been sure of that. He had shown enough fear that many of his fellow warriors looked at him with disgust. Some of them had asked Einar if they could stay in the Orkney Islands, since they would not be welcome in Norway again, not having been at Halfdan's side when he killed Ragnvald, and then having failed to prevent Halfdan's death, and so Einar let them stay, though not without misgivings.

That summer too Freydis's stomach had taken the curve that became Einar's first son, growing inside her. He had not thought that he could ever feel pure joy again, but touching the swelling of life within her made Einar feel as full and blessed as he ever had at Ivar's side, though never without a twinge of pain. Ivar would never meet Einar's sons, nor father his own.

But he brought his sons to Ivar's grave mound, high on the Orkney hillside, and told them of their uncle. Perhaps that was why the fates had moved to keep him in Orkney.

Harald did not come until the autumn, bringing ten ships, enough to kill all the men of Orkney if he chose. Einar called a meeting of the mainland farmers, and stood before them, with Freydis by his side.

"There is no chance of defeating Harald, as there was with Halfdan," he said to them. The men had brought their makeshift weapons, ready to fight for him again. "I will go and make the case for my life. If he kills me, it will be me alone."

"If he kills you, we will make sure your son is jarl of Orkney after you," said Arknell.

If Harald killed him, Einar hoped that Freydis would be able to make her way to Iceland, to her mother and father, and give her children a different inheritance, since he would leave her nothing. But he nodded his thanks to Arknell. He had not thought to find belonging here, at the edge of the world.

He walked down to the shore, unarmed, with his hair unbound, as if in mourning. He met Harald and his ships, standing still while men surged around him, tied his hands, and brought him into Harald's vessel.

"What is this?" Harald asked, gesturing up at the mainland's great hill.

Einar turned and saw the men of Orkney arrayed on the slope, watching. He bowed to Harald, and said, "My king, you are welcome to the Orkney Islands. Will you accept hospitality from their jarl?"

Harald looked very grave, and for the first time Einar saw what he would look like as an old man, with the furrow between his brows drawn even deeper. Ragnvald had wanted Harald to know what it was to lose a son, and now he did.

"You offer me hospitality when you stand on my ship?" Harald asked, his voice quiet and dangerous. "I have come to kill you for killing my son."

"I know," said Einar. "I did not think you would come to reward me, even for avenging your best adviser and closest friend."

Harald's jaw tightened.

"Before you kill me," said Einar, "please tell me—do you miss him? My father was not an easy man, but I know you valued him."

Harald sighed. "I did. Now . . . I am surrounded by men who are loyal and praise me often, but not a one will tell me the truth, no matter how much I need to hear it, and their advice has no more sense than the noise of the wind in the grasses. Your father was as crafty as Odin."

"In the end, not crafty enough," said Einar. "Not to find a way to keep your friendship and his life. He knew that he must choose, and he chose his death. When your son came to Orkney, I made a different choice." He gestured up at the Orkneymen. "We defended our lands."

"Your father told me you were a gifted poet," said Harald. "Tell me, did you give Hilda the words she said against me? I still hear them repeated whenever I displease someone. A wolf-king who makes his subjects into deer?"

Einar shook his head. "No, those were her words, the words of a sorrowing mother. And here are my words, the words of a sorrowing son, a sorrowing brother, with no more poetry: I wish there had been a way for my father and your son to both live, for myself and your son both to live. For my brother to live. But fate sets us on these paths. If you let me live, I will be your loyal jarl in Orkney, I will defend these lands and send you taxes. And I will avenge wrongs done against you." He looked at Harald until he had to meet Einar's gaze. "Wrongs like the murder of Ragnvald the Mighty."

Harald bowed his head. "I will not kill you, Einar Ragnvaldsson. But I will demand a wergild of you, and if you do not pay it, your lands and your life will be forfeit." He named a sum that even his father, at the height of his wealth, would have been hard-pressed to raise.

Einar nodded—perhaps it would be better if Harald killed him now, rather than forcing him to beggar Orkney to pay for his life. "When must I deliver this to you?" he asked.

Harald gave him a small smile, touched with sadness. "I had thought to lead an expedition against the Danish raiders who now occupy the Shetland Islands, so I would not make this journey only to kill one young man. But I find I am weary of war, and want to go home again. I can, however, leave you some warriors and ships. Send them back to me when you have put the Shetlands under your power, and send my wergild with them."

"Thank you, my king," said Einar. Ships and men—men to feed through the winter, but at least he could take the wergild from the Danish raiders.

He bowed to Harald and took his leave, but as he turned to go, Harald called after him. Einar looked back.

"Einar Ragnvaldsson," Harald said, putting a hand over his heart. "I miss him. I will never stop missing him."

Einar nodded, and returned the gesture. "Neither will I."

Einar had sent Harald the wergild he required, and rich taxes taken from Danish raiders every year since. Yet the Danes still threatened the islands, and one day Einar's sons would go into battle against them. Would his father have been pleased to see this day? To see Thordis wed, to see his family line continue and spread across the north? To see his grandsons growing into strong young men? Einar hoped he would have, and been glad, as well, to see his son acclaimed and praised as Turf-Einar Ragnvaldsson, jarl of the Orkney Islands.

AUTHOR'S NOTE

LIKE *THE HALF-DROWNED KING* AND *THE SEA QUEEN*, *THE GOLDEN WOLF* is a work of fiction that takes its inspiration from "The Saga of Harald Harfagr" in Snorri Sturluson's *Heimskringla, The Saga of the Kings of Norway*. It further incorporates some information from the Orkneyinga Saga, a thirteenth-century history of the earls of Orkney.

In *The Golden Wolf*, I have dramatized many of the semihistorical events from *Heimskringla*, but I have also combined some characters, and compressed some events for narrative effect, particularly those leading to Einar becoming jarl of Orkney. I have also invented some events and relationships, like the affair between Gyda and Einar. Sigurd's death from a scratch dealt him by a tooth on the head of a man he had decapitated is from *Heimskringla*, and it was too good a detail to leave out. Ragnvald's anger with his son is present in *Heimskringla*, and though he does not blame Einar for Ivar's death in the saga, it seemed natural to me that this is where his anger would have come from.

In writing *The Golden Wolf* and the other books in the trilogy, I have used the stories in the *Heimskringla* as a jumping-off point, and also asked myself what might have been the real events behind the stories that Snorri Sturluson and others passed on and recorded.

Ninth-century Norway exists on the boundary of myth and history, and the existing sources for the life of Harald and his contemporaries were written many centuries later. Much of what we know about the era comes from the archaeological record, not written records. Vikings did not have written language besides runes, the angular writing found on markers like the Danish Jelling stones, which were raised in memory of great deeds and departed family. Runes in Viking Age Norway were used for fortune-telling, as well as some religious and other monuments but not for historical record keeping.

In the thirteenth century the Icelander Snorri Sturluson, a historian, poet, and politician, would write down the *Heimskringla* and many other sagas. The *Heimskringla* was based on oral tradition and almost certainly has gaps and inaccuracies. Furthermore, many scholars believe that Snorri Sturluson used the saga to make certain implicit arguments about Iceland's political situation at the time, leading him to highlight some stories and leave out others.

Other historical records do attest that Einar Ragnvaldsson, later known as Torf-Einar, became jarl of Orkney and the progenitor of a line of Orkney rulers. Similarly, Hrolf Ragnvaldsson became Duke Rollo of Normandy and was the great-great-great-grandfather of William the Conqueror, who invaded England in 1066.

By the late ninth century, Arab explorers had begun to travel to Scandinavia and chronicle their travels, which also have given us some glimpses into viking culture, as in the writings of Ibn Fadlan. The minor, invented characters of Aban al-Rashid and Bakur are my small acknowledgment of that.

SOURCES

Here are a few, but not nearly all, of the books I have found valuable in researching Viking Age Norway and early medieval Europe. This includes works used for researching *The Half-Drowned King* and *The Sea Queen* as well. Christie Ward's Viking Answer Lady website, www.vikinganswerlady.com, is also a helpful resource.

Bagge, Sverre. *From Viking Stronghold to Christian Kingdom: State Formation in Norway, c. 900–1350.* Copenhagen: Museum Tusculanum Press, 2010.

Bauer, Susan Wise. *The History of the Medieval World: From the Conversion of Constantine to the First Crusade.* New York: W. W. Norton, 2010.

Davidson, Hilda Ellis. *Gods and Myths of Northern Europe.* New York: Penguin, 1990.

———. *The Roles of the Northern Goddess.* London: Routledge, 2002.

Fitzhugh, William W., and Elizabeth I. Ward, eds. *Vikings: The North Atlantic Saga,* Washington, DC: Smithsonian, 2000.

Foote, Peter G., and David M. Wilson. *The Viking Achievement: The Society and Culture of Early Medieval Scandinavia.* London: Book Club Associates, 1974.

Griffith, Paddy. *The Viking Art of War.* London: Greenhill, 1995.

Hjaltalin, Jon A., and Gilbert Goudie, trans. *The Orkneyinga Saga.* Edinburgh: Edmonston and Douglas, 1873.

Jesch, Judith. *Women in the Viking Age.* Woodbridge, England: Boydell, 1991.

Jochens, Jenny. *Women in Old Norse Society.* Ithaca, NY: Cornell University Press, 1995.

Jones, Gwyn. *A History of the Vikings.* Oxford, England: Oxford University Press, 1984.

Larrington, Carolyne, trans. *The Poetic Edda.* Oxford, England: Oxford University Press, 2014.

Lindow, John. *Norse Mythology: A Guide to Gods, Heroes, Rituals and Beliefs.* New York: Oxford University Press, 2002.

Short, William R. *Icelanders in the Viking Age: The People of the Sagas.* Jefferson, NC: McFarland and Company, 2010.

Sturluson, Snorri. *Heimskringla; or, The Lives of the Norse Kings.* Translated by Erling Monson. New York: Dover, 1990.

Thurston, Tina L. *Landscapes of Power, Landscapes of Conflict: State Formation in the South Scandinavian Iron Age.* New York: Kluwer Academic Publishers, 2002.

Wells, Peter S. *Barbarians to Angels: The Dark Ages Reconsidered.* New York: W. W. Norton, 2009.

ACKNOWLEDGMENTS

THE *GOLDEN WOLF* REPRESENTS THE COMPLETION OF A LONG process of research, travel, and writing. It owes much to the support of my husband and travel planner, Seth Miller. My early readers, Nicole Cunningham and Amber Oliver, provided invaluable feedback. Heather Drucker and Katherine Beitner have done amazing publicity for this trilogy, and Milan Bozic, Patrick Arrasmith, and Shelly Perron did beautiful work to turn the book into its final polished, physical form. And finally, my editors Terry Karten and Clare Smith shaped this book mightily, as did my agent, Julie Barer. I could not have done it without you.

ABOUT THE AUTHOR

LINNEA HARTSUYKER can trace her family lineage back to the first king of Norway, and this inspired her to write her trilogy about the Vikings. Linnea grew up in the woods outside Ithaca, New York, studied engineering at Cornell University, and later received an MFA in creative writing from New York University. She lives in New Hampshire with her husband.